IF THE SEAS
CATCH FIRE

L.A. WITT

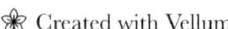

If The Seas Catch Fire

Sergei Andronikov was a child when the Mafia wiped out his family, leaving him with nothing but a hunger for revenge. Years later, through ruthless strategy and tireless patience, he's a contract killer working for the three families ruling Cape Swan... and he's nearly in position to bring them all down from the inside.

Domenico "Dom" Maisano is Mafia royalty, a made man... and a hitman. He's caught up in a violent life he can't escape, struggling to maintain an image he doesn't want, and suppressing desires he can't have.

A chance encounter throws the killers into each other's paths. Though Dom knows he's playing a dangerous game, he's intrigued and keeps coming back. Sergei can't resist him either—Dom is everything he set out to destroy, but he's also everything he's ever ached for in a man.

Then Sergei gets the contract he's been waiting for— the hit that promises to bring the town's Mafia to its knees.

But when a boss makes an unexpected move, Sergei must choose between dropping the hammer on the families he vowed to annihilate, and protecting the man he swore he wouldn't love.

And the wrong choice—or even the right one—will destroy them both.

Acknowledgments

Huge thank you to Erica, Allie, Suzanne, Chris, Danielle, & Jules!

"trust your heart if the seas catch fire,
live by love though the stars walk backward."
– e.e. cummings

Chapter 1

Sergei Andronikov hadn't been in the guy's lap thirty seconds, and there was already a hand on his ass.

Carefully schooling his expression—keeping the irritation well beneath the surface—Sergei batted the asshole's hand away. This was Sergei's fourth or fifth client of the night, and he was one of those middle-aged financial types. The kind who'd been behind a desk in a bank long enough to think he was God. Sergei hated those fucks.

But he was getting paid, so he writhed and undulated on the banker's lap, sharing it with a sizeable paunch. And after a few beats, the hand was back, this time coming up off the armrest to caress Sergei's hip. Before it could inch toward his ass—these fuckers were so goddamned predictable—Sergei again pushed it away, adding a playful, "No touching. That's the rule."

The banker grinned, revealing teeth that were flawless aside from the misfortune of being in this man's head. "I'm paying you good money." He placed a defiant hand firmly on Sergei's leather-clad hip. "I'd say the rules are negotiable."

1

"Actually." Sergei dropped the playfulness as he grabbed the man's wrist and shoved his hand away. "They're not."

Do it again, and you'll be swallowing those pretty teeth.

The guy snatched Sergei's arm, gripping it painfully. "Customer's always right. Now you'll—"

In a heartbeat, Sergei had him shoved back against the chair, fingers around the asshole's throat. Blood pounded beneath the skin, one squeeze away from being cut off, and Sergei dug his knee against the man's crotch.

"What the fuck?" the guy ground out.

"The rules are not negotiable, and this dance is over." Sergei dug his thumb just hard enough against the banker's jugular to make him nervous. "Now get the fuck out of here before I turn all three of the ex-Special Forces bouncers loose on your ass." He leaned in closer. "You know what kind of ex-Special Forces guy becomes a bouncer in a gay strip club in a shitty little town like this?"

Eyes widening even more, the asshole shook his head. "N-no…"

"The kind who are too fucked up in the head to do anything else." Sergei pushed himself up, using the stupid sap's throat and balls for leverage and nearly tipping the chair back in the process. "Get the fuck out of here."

The banker wisely got the fuck out of there. Probably the smartest thing he'd done all night. He'd have moved even faster if he'd known just whose ass he'd been trying to grope.

But he was gone, and Sergei still had a few hours left on his shift, so after he'd straightened his hair and clothes, he stepped out of the booth.

Roy, the burly black bouncer hovering near the entrance to the private dance booths, grinned at him.

"That guy left in a hurry. You feed him that ex-Special Forces line?"

"Maybe." Sergei batted his eyes. "You have to admit, it gets the point across."

Roy laughed. "Well, I think you scared him good."

"That's the idea." Sergei headed back out to the lounge, ignoring the creepy tingling where the asshole's hands had landed. He was used to a lot of things in this job, but the groping still made his skin crawl. Oh well. Occupational hazard.

As he stepped up to the bar for some water, Jesse, one of the other strippers, came running up to him.

"Hey, Sergei." Jesse grabbed his arm, eyes huge and face *white*. "We gotta call the cops."

"What? Why?"

He gestured shakily at the back door. "I was outside having a smoke, and some guys pulled up. Started fucking up some dude they pulled outta the trunk."

Oh, shit. Not here. Not this close to where I work.

"No cops." Sergei squeezed his shoulder and started toward the back. "I'll chase 'em off."

"What?" Hot on his heels, Jesse said, "Dude, they're big guys! They're—"

"I've got this. Relax."

Jesse exhaled sharply and muttered, "Your funeral."

"I mean it." Sergei spun around and stabbed a finger at him. "*No cops.*"

"Okay, okay!" Jesse showed his palms. "No cops."

"Good."

Sergei quickly went into the back, opened his locker, and pulled up the false bottom. Beneath it was a .22 pistol and an extra magazine. With those in hand, he replaced the false bottom and headed out to the back alley where the goons were apparently conducting business.

This was just not his night, was it? He'd already had to deal with the son of a bitch who couldn't keep his hands to himself. Now there were Italians in the back alley, one of them getting his ass handed to him, and Sergei wasn't having it. *Nobody* brought Mafia business this close to his club. Not unless they were there to discreetly contract him for their dirty work, and only a handful of people knew who he was or where to find him. Otherwise, the Italians were taking their lives in their own hands if they brought their kind—and potentially the cops—this close to his club.

Especially now. It had only been three days since Lorenzo Barcia's body washed up by the docks, and up until tonight, everybody in Cape Swan had been laying low, keeping their heads down while the cops hunted for anyone who might be connected. Shit like that happened here all the time—violence was unavoidable with three Cosa Nostra families vying for dominance—but when a murder was clearly set up to send a message, it got attention. After all, though the saltwater had fucked the asshole up good, it was a safe bet he hadn't died of natural causes. Not with his balls torn off and shoved into his fat mouth.

In the days since he'd been found, the town had been as quiet as the July heat had been oppressive. Tensions were running hot, someone was going to get blamed for that murder, and *nobody* wanted to be anywhere around when any bullets started flying.

Least of all the man who'd stuffed Barcia's balls in the guy's own screaming mouth before shoving him off the pier for the crabs to snack on.

But Sergei wasn't in charge of what went on in this twisted little world, and now, before the shit had even begun to die down, some fucknuts were beating up some wise guy in the *wrong* alley. Of all the times and places, they'd decided to rough up the asshole here, on the outer

4

edges of Cape Swan, just a few blocks down from the Pacific waterfront, behind the *wrong* fucking strip club.

Sergei shut the back door and barricaded it with the folding chair that his coworkers sat in whenever they smoked. This was the windowless club's only rear exit, and he didn't want anyone following him outside. At least the other businesses along the alley were closed this time of night. As long as a roving police officer didn't happen by, he was in the clear to shut this bullshit down.

As soon as he'd stepped outside, Sergei knew exactly where the assholes were, as if there'd been any doubt. Their Italian-accented shit-talking made his teeth grind —*way to be subtle, guys*. Two men had a third backed up and bloody against the bumper of a late model Cadillac, and they weren't done with him. A punch doubled the poor fucker over, and he grunted and wheezed as they hauled him upright again.

Gun in hand, Sergei strode across the gravel. He knew he hardly cut an imposing figure—he was half their size, for one thing, and his skintight red leather shorts and crop top weren't exactly the stuff of nightmares. Fine. They didn't need to be intimidated.

One turned and did a double take. He snapped his fingers and pointed toward the club, as if Sergei were a stray dog who'd come to investigate the noise. "You! Get the fuck outta here, fag."

Sergei continued his approach. "How about *you* idiots get the fuck out of here."

The second man muttered something as he lowered his fist, which he'd probably been about to shove into the third guy's gut. "You got a problem, fag?"

"Yeah, I do." Sergei stopped, keeping the gun at his side. "How about you assholes take this somewhere else?"

The first rolled his eyes. "Or what?"

Sergei nodded toward the unfortunate asshole pinned to the bumper. "Or you both get to bleed more than him."

Both men glanced at the pistol, but laughed.

"Get out of here, fag." The second turned and balled his fist, drawing back to punch the goon again.

"Don't say I didn't warn you." Sergei raised the .22 and put a bullet through the Italian's knee.

The first guy jumped back. "Holy shit!"

The second howled in agony and dropped to the ground.

The third, with no one to hold him up, crumpled to his knees. His head lolled a bit, and he blinked a few times, probably trying to stay conscious. He'd taken a hell of a beating. Sergei couldn't tell how much of the blood on his knuckles was his, but it looked like he'd given as good as he'd gotten. And he was alive. That said a lot.

The one with the bullet in his knee whined and writhed on the ground beside his own victim, blood seeping through his fingers. "*Pezzo di merda! Figlio di*—fuck!"

Sergei faced the man still standing. "Weapons?"

"I…"

"Don't fuck with me. Weapons on the ground, or bullet through the dick."

The uninjured Italian's eyes widened. Hands shaking, he withdrew a pistol from inside his jacket, and a set of brass knuckles.

The man he'd been beating saw the brass knuckles and gulped.

"Put them on the ground." Sergei gestured at the man he'd shot. "Out of his reach."

The Italian glanced at his wounded partner, then crouched and laid his weapons where the other guy couldn't reach them. Hands up, he stood again.

Sergei nodded sharply toward the car. "Open the trunk and get in."

"What?" The guy laughed, a borderline hysterical sound. "You crazy? I'm not—"

Sergei leveled the gun at the goon's face. "Get in the fucking trunk."

His eyes widened, and his tanned Italian complexion paled. Then he shoved his would-be victim aside, sending the man crumpling the rest of the way to the ground, groaning and clutching his chest. The goon eyed Sergei and the open trunk, and then he climbed inside.

With his foot, Sergei nudged the one he'd shot. "You too. Get in."

"What?" The Italian blinked up at him. He clutched his knee, blood soaking his pant leg and streaming from between his fingers. "I can't walk, you fuck!"

"Stop being a pussy." Sergei aimed the weapon at his other knee. "Or I'll make sure you can't crawl, either."

The man struggled to his feet, using the car bumper for support and whimpering whenever he moved his wounded leg. He started to climb into the trunk but couldn't bend his knee.

"Fuck. I can't…"

Sergei shoved him unceremoniously into the trunk, and despite their significant size difference, he knocked the sobbing Italian on top of his partner. Sergei didn't even flinch when the guy's head smacked against the trunk lid. By the time both men were completely inside the trunk, the wounded one was howling in pain, and from the smell, Sergei was pretty sure one or the other had pissed himself.

Whatever. Wasn't Sergei's fault they'd chosen this alley out of all the other options in this town. He grabbed a roll of duct tape from the trunk and put a piece over the screaming man's mouth, but it didn't muffle him all that much.

"Shut the fuck up," Sergei snarled. "Or your other kneecap is gone."

The man shut up. Tears were streaming down his face, and he was hyperventilating now, but he was more or less quiet.

Sergei bound the first guy's hands, and then put duct tape over his mouth too. Thank fucking God—another minute of his bullshit, and Sergei would've shot them both then and there. Even now he was tempted just to rid the world of two more Mafia scumbags like the ones who'd murdered his family.

But not here. Not this close to the club.

He slammed the trunk and turned to the other thorn in his side—the guy they'd been roughing up. Leaving him here wasn't an option. The cops were too jumpy to ignore a battered Italian, and they'd start prowling around in this part of town. A little too close to home for Sergei's taste.

He didn't care if the man lived or died as long as he didn't do it here, so Sergei crouched beside the wounded man and quietly asked, "Can you walk?"

"Don't know."

"Let's see if we can get you into the car." Sergei offered him an arm, keeping his pistol firmly in his other hand in case the wise guy decided to try something funny, and helped him to his feet.

He didn't try anything. The poor bastard probably had some busted ribs, maybe even some bleeding on the inside, judging by the way he doubled over and kept an arm around his middle. With Sergei's help and a pained sound, he lay back across the backseat.

Sergei shut the car door and scanned the dark alley. As

far as he could tell, no one was around. No one had seen a thing. He fully intended to keep it that way.

None of the men in the car were going anywhere without his help, so after he'd collected the weapons and kicked some gravel over the blood, obscuring it enough that it wouldn't draw attention, he headed back inside. He took the chair away from the door and strolled into the club.

He found his boss by the bar, and flagged him down. "Hey, Paco. I need to step out for a bit. Take care of something."

Paco raised his eyebrows. No doubt Jesse had told him about the shit going on in the alley. "You need a hand?"

"No, I've got this. Just need some time."

Paco didn't ask questions. People in Mafia-run towns usually didn't—the less they knew about shady shit, the better.

With his boss's blessing, Sergei left the club. In the car, he found a pair of leather gloves in the glove compartment and put them on so he didn't leave any more fingerprints in or on the vehicle. Then he drove the goons' car out of the alley and safely away from the row of clubs. He continued along the waterfront, past a deserted park and down to the marina, where he stopped.

As the engine idled, Sergei drummed the wheel and gazed in the rearview, debating how to handle the wise guy in the backseat and the two idiots in the trunk. If they hadn't killed the guy, they were either inept, or they'd only intended to send a message. Pity for them they'd chosen the wrong post office for that message.

And one way or another, they *were* inept. They were also competition. More importantly, their ineptness could get them caught, and once the cops got their hands on anybody in this fucked up underworld—especially with bodies washing up on the beach—everyone remotely attached to La Cosa Nostra were in danger, and that included independent contractors like Sergei. If these morons were stupid enough to rough someone up this brazenly with a police station six blocks away, then they were a liability to everyone.

They had to go.

Sergei got out of the car. He opened the trunk, and without any fanfare or hesitation, unloaded two bullets apiece into their foreheads. Then he slammed the lid again.

As he'd done in the alley, he smeared his footprints in the gravel. With a towel he'd found beside the two dead men, he wiped every surface to make sure he didn't leave any fingerprints on the inside or outside of the car. There could be no trace of him here; though the rounds were nearly impossible to trace and even the .22 would be in the ocean before sunrise, he took no chances.

And now he was left with the beaten up guy in the backseat. In theory, he could've offed him and walked away. One less Mafioso to pollute this town.

But Sergei didn't kill indiscriminately. Even when he was absolutely certain a man was Mafia—and thus fair game for a bullet—the fact remained that offing the wrong guy could mark him for death if anyone ever connected him. He was good at covering his tracks, but he refused to take unnecessary risks.

And besides, he only committed murder under three circumstances. One, when it was a paid hit, because even for an independent contractor, saying no to the Mafia was a death sentence. Two, when he was in actual immediate danger. Three, when the mark needed to be removed from the Mafia chessboard so Sergei could push them all one body closer to extinction.

The goons technically hadn't put him in immediate danger, but they posed a threat to Sergei and the handful of other hired guns in this town. They'd also seen his face. They'd brought Mafia business too close to where he conducted his business. They'd had to go.

That wasn't to say his life as a stripper and his life as a contract killer never crossed. Quite the contrary—he had a very select group of contacts who met him at the club, and through a series of coded comments, gave him work that paid a hell of a lot more than making horny bankers pant. He deliberately handled his transactions there, hiding in plain sight. No one but his contacts ever saw his face, and none of the macho Mafia assholes would ever suspect a sometimes flamboyant gay stripper of being the hitman equivalent of the boogey man. The assassin they told their children about when they wouldn't behave.

What they didn't know wouldn't hurt him.

And he wanted to get back to the club tonight, but he still had one more mess to clean up.

Sergei tilted the rearview down and studied the Italian's still form. What little he could make out in the darkness, anyway. There was no telling exactly who the semiconscious Italian was. Well-dressed—that was *not* an off-the-rack suit—so he probably wasn't just some random wise guy. Involved enough with La Cosa Nostra to take a ride in the trunk of a Cadillac and have his ass kicked in a back alley. But his name? His role? What he'd done to earn a beating like that? Anyone's guess.

Sergei's best bet was to let him go. Besides, the guy could be someone he actually wanted alive. Not that he wanted any Mafiosi alive, but some needed to keep breathing while Sergei continued pulling strings to move people into position within the families' hierarchies. Once the dominoes were in a row, they'd all fall in good time, but for now, some of them needed to stay alive until the pieces were in place.

He opened the car door. "Time to go."

The Italian groaned softly and struggled to sit up. Sergei helped him, and with some cursing and grunting, the wounded man made it out of the car.

Once he was on his feet, he leaned against the car, clutching his side. "Fuck..."

Sergei gave the man a quick down-up. This was the first chance he'd had to actually look at the guy, and surprisingly the Italian wasn't one of the greasy, weathered assholes he was used to seeing. Even with the blood and the bruises, he had a much prettier face than most of his kind. The streetlights picked out a few strands of silver in his otherwise jet black hair, but he couldn't have been older than forty. Mid-thirties, maybe.

And he probably had that lightly tanned olive skin like the other Mafia scumbags, but between his sickly pallor and the blood and sweat glinting beneath the milky light, it was impossible to tell.

Sergei shook himself. "You need a hospital."

The man spat blood on the pavement. "No fucking hospitals."

Stubborn idiot. Hospitals routinely called the cops when people came in with signs of assault and battery. When well-dressed Italians came in with signs of assault and battery? Nobody called nobody.

"You could be bleeding internally."

"I'll take my chances." He shifted, wincing. "But I'd rather not stay out here."

Sergei bit back some profanity in his native tongue. The less this guy knew about him, the better.

"Listen." The Italian groaned, holding his side protectively. "If you're gonna shoot me, just fucking get it over with."

"If I was going to shoot you, we wouldn't be having this conversation. What's your name?"

The Italian lifted his head enough to meet Sergei's gaze. "Who wants to know?"

Sergei rolled his eyes. "The guy who's going to decide whether you wake up tomorrow in a hospital, a jail cell, or a morgue."

He blinked. "Domenico Maisano."

Sergei's blood turned cold and he muttered, "You're shitting me."

Maisano laughed, but then grimaced, and managed to croak, "You've heard of me."

"Yeah. I have." Sergei knew that name well. This guy was the nephew—more like adopted son—of Corrado Maisano himself, the boss of the powerful Maisano clan. A contractor like Sergei, who worked with all three of the big families, had to tread carefully. He had no way of knowing if he'd just interrupted a sanctioned hit, albeit a sloppily executed one. If it wasn't sanctioned, and by some chance, someone figured out he'd been the one to finish the job, he'd bring the wrath of all three families down on his own head.

Son of a bitch. All he'd wanted to do was get all this crap away from the club so the cops wouldn't come knocking on doors. Now he had Domenico fucking Maisano on his hands.

"Can you walk or not?" he asked sharply.

The Italian groaned again. "I don't... I don't know." He tried to take a step, but stumbled, and when Sergei caught him, the man gasped. "Fuck. That hurts."

"You got a phone?"

Maisano gingerly patted his pockets, and then shook his head. "Not... not anymore."

"Of course you don't." Sergei looked around. They were pretty far from town, and no one would be wandering around here this late at night. "Don't move."

Maisano mumbled something about that not being a problem.

Still wearing the stolen gloves, Sergei made sure Maisano hadn't bled on the backseat—he didn't care if Maisano was connected to the assholes in the trunk, but on the off chance someone happened by before he'd relieved himself of the limping Italian, Sergei didn't want anyone connecting *him* to them.

Then he went to the trunk, opened it, relieved one of the dead guys of his phone, and slammed the lid. "Come on. We're going for a walk."

"Maybe you are," Maisano said through his teeth. "Look at me."

"Well, it's up to you. The paramedics can find you over there"—Sergei gestured with the phone toward a park a few blocks away—"or they can find you here." He tapped the trunk with his gloved knuckle.

Maisano's eyes widened.

"So." Sergei nodded toward the park. "Let's go."

Maisano cursed again. Then he carefully pushed himself off the car and took a few slow, painful steps. "Don't expect me to walk fast."

Sergei bit back his impatience. "Need a hand?"

Maisano eyed him suspiciously, but then nodded. "I could use one, yeah."

Sergei took his elbow, and together, they shuffled toward the park.

On the way, Sergei expected questions. Who the hell

was he? What the fuck was he doing interfering with Mob business?

But Maisano didn't ask. Maybe he was in too much pain to give a damn. Or he could've been silently thanking one of his Catholic saints for the leather clad angel who'd swooped in and saved his ass.

Good thing he kept his mouth shut. Sergei hated questions. And Maisano could thank all the saints he wanted— he didn't need to know he was walking with an angel of death.

Chapter 2

Every step Dom took was agony. Thank God this kid had intervened when he did. Left to their own devices, Floresta and Mandanici may or may not have killed him, but they sure would've done some more damage.

Clutching his side and holding his breath, Dom stole a glance at the slight blond enigma walking beside him. He didn't know what to make of this kid. Not a fucking clue. He had to be around twenty-five, give or take a year, and judging by his accent, he must've been a Russian immigrant. There were a lot of those in Cape Swan. The way he was dressed—tight red leather and not a lot of it—he was either a stripper or a hooker. Nobody in this town dressed like that unless they were selling orgasms.

He obviously wasn't a pussy. There was no telling what he'd done to Mandanici and Floresta. Dom had been on the verge of blacking out when the kid had shown up, and he'd only just been aware of the shot that had apparently hobbled Mandanici. Then Floresta had knocked Dom to the ground, and everything that happened after that was hazy at best. Next thing he remembered, he was being guided out of the car and onto his feet, and why the fuck were they down by the marina?

"Here." The kid gestured at a bench beside a bus stop. "Sit."

Dom didn't argue. With some help, he eased himself down onto the hard bench, groaning as blinding pain ripped through him. "Fuck…"

"You really need to see—"

"I'll be fine." Dom moistened his lips, pausing to gingerly tongue the sweet raw spot where a fist had apparently shoved the tender flesh against his tooth. It had stopped bleeding as near as he could tell. His mouth tasted metallic, so he couldn't tell spit from blood anymore, but the wound didn't seem too severe. And he hadn't lost or cracked any teeth, so… He'd call it a win.

He lifted his head and blinked a few times, trying to bring his eyes into focus. Whoa. If this kid was selling sex, he was in the right line of work. He was slim and ripped, the contours of his muscles standing out thanks to the harsh overhead light. The blanched light made his bottle blond hair almost white but didn't quite pick out the color of those intense eyes. Or maybe it was just because Dom couldn't focus his own enough to tell if they were blue, or black, or… whatever. Piercing, that was for sure, especially coupled with those sharp Slavic features.

Dom gingerly drew a breath. "You never told me your name."

"It doesn't matter."

"Who am I gonna tell? The cops?"

The kid glared down at him.

"You asked *my* name," Dom said.

"Yeah. I did. Anyway, you'll be good here till help shows up."

Dom glanced at the phone in the stripper's hand—those gloves didn't seem like part of his ensemble—then at him. "You calling, or am I?"

"You are." The stripper tossed him the phone. "I'm out of here."

Dom eyed him. "You're pretty tough for a hooker."

He bristled. "I'm not a hooker. I'm a stripper."

Dom didn't laugh—his ribs wouldn't allow it anyway, and he really didn't want to piss off this kid till he had a better idea what he was dealing with. "My mistake." He gestured at the piece tucked into the kid's waistband. "Strippers always pack heat like that?"

The stripper looked at the gun as if he'd forgotten he had it, and then shrugged. "This is a shit part of town. Everyone's armed."

Dom glanced around. His vision was a little fuzzy and doubling around the edges. He was up the road from the marina, that much he knew. This area was all too familiar.

How the hell had he gotten here tonight? In the trunk of one car and the backseat of another, that much he knew, but at the beginning of the evening, he'd been clear on the other side of Cape Swan. He'd been parked behind an upscale restaurant, palms sweating and stomach sick over a date he didn't want to be on, when the assholes got the drop on him. How long ago had that been? Shit. He had no idea what had happened, or when, or where…

All he knew was that he was fucked up and he needed to get out of here. He turned on the phone. It didn't require a passcode, fortunately, and thank God he'd committed a few key numbers to memory. "Do you need me to get you a cab or something?"

He lifted his head, but the stripper was gone.

He scanned the deserted road as much as his sore

muscles and shitty vision would allow, but there was no sign of the guy. Not even footsteps fading into the night.

They got ninjas working as strippers in this town or something?

Well. Whatever. He was alone now.

He shifted his gaze back to the phone, gave his eyes a second to focus, and entered a number. It rang several times, before Biaggio, his uncle's consigliere, picked up.

The sleepy, irritated voice muttered, "Hello?"

"It's Dom. I need help."

He could almost hear the old man snapping to attention. "What's going on? Are you all right? Where are you?"

"I'm… down by the marina. Couple of blocks from the gate. Banged up."

"What? My God, what's… Are you all right?"

"I'm… I think so? I just need to get out of here."

"I'm on my way. Do I need to call Rojas?"

Dom knew damn well Biaggio was going to call the family's physician either way—better safe than sorry—but he still croaked, "Yeah. Call him."

Biaggio swore in Italian. "Where *exactly* are you?"

Dom gave him the intersection, and after they hung up, he leaned back against the bench, but that only aggravated the bruises on his back.

As his body ached and throbbed and threatened to just fall apart, his mind reeled. He tried not to think about everything that had happened tonight, tried not to pick apart exactly how the motherfuckers had caught him with his guard down, but that was easier said than done. It was like his brain had split into two pieces, and both sides were pulling him in opposite directions. One wanted to focus solely on staying conscious and watching for his ride. The other wanted to go back to the restaurant where his evening had started and retrace his steps. Figure out exactly when things had gone to shit. When he'd ceased to be meeting with Brigida Passantino, the woman his uncle was pressuring him to marry, and when he'd suddenly been in serious danger. And serious pain. And…here.

He rubbed his forehead, carefully avoiding the goose egg swelling near his hair line. There'd be plenty of time to retrace those steps when he got home. Biaggio had undoubtedly notified Uncle Corrado—no one in the family got roughed up without the boss knowing about it. Corrado was probably already pacing in his office, ready to grill Dom about what had happened. Or more importantly, *who* had happened. Who had dared to fuck with a boss's nephew? Who was Corrado going to order dead before sunrise?

Dom was pretty sure the guys who'd fucked him up were dead already, though. The shouting and struggling in the trunk of the car had ceased after a few small caliber gunshots. Assuming he hadn't hallucinated that part. Had he? No, he was pretty sure that had been real. Along with the red leather clad stripper who'd pulled him out of the car and then vanished. Had *he* been a hallucination?

Except Dom hadn't gotten to his feet, into the car, and out of it again on his own power. Someone had been there beside him—he could still feel every tender spot the kid had touched while helping him up.

No, he'd definitely been real. And dangerous.

The back of Dom's neck prickled. In his mind's eye, he saw the pistol in the stripper's waistband, the way the kid had carried it comfortably and naturally.

The gunshots echoed in Dom's mind. There hadn't been anyone else around. No one else could have pulled the trigger. Which meant…

No way.

But then, who else could have done it? For that matter, it didn't take a big guy like Dom to pull a trigger, though God knew he'd pulled his fair share. A pistol made anyone, however slim and slight, physically capable of killing. If Dom could cope with putting a bullet through someone, he had no reason to believe that stripper couldn't. And those ice cold eyes hadn't held a trace of fear, though Dom had hardly been a threat to anyone by the time he could look at the kid's face. Still, Dom was alive, Floresta and Mandanici were dead, and…

And who the fuck *was* that kid?

IT SEEMED like hours before the sleek black car pulled up and stopped on the curb. Two doors opened. Stan, the driver, hurried around the front as Biaggio, the white-haired consigliere, stepped out of the car.

Biaggio's eyes widened. "Domenico, what happened? Who did this?"

"Couple of Raffaele Cusimano's thugs. I'd know… I'd know Michele Mandanici's fucking face anywhere." Dom held his breath as he tried to stand.

"Easy, easy." Stan took his arm and gently helped him to his feet. "Sir, he's bleeding and that looks like a hell of a bump on his head. Don't you think we should take him to the—"

"No," Biaggio snapped. "Corrado's waiting for him. Dr. Rojas is on his way. He'll there by the time we get back."

Stan pursed his lips, but didn't protest. As the driver helped him into the car, Dom questioned whether Stan and the stripper were right. Maybe he did need a hospital. But that would be for the doc to determine, and Dom wasn't going to the ER unless it was absolutely necessary.

Inside the car, Dom closed his eyes, trying in vain to get comfortable on the luxurious leather seats.

Across from him, Biaggio was silent. Paternal concern radiated off him—he had long been more of an adoptive father to Dom than Corrado, and Dom doubted Biaggio would sleep tonight until Rojas gave Dom a clean bill of health. While Corrado raged and plotted vengeance, Biaggio would be wringing his hands about broken ribs and internal bleeding.

He said nothing, though. He undoubtedly had a million questions, but Corrado would interrogate Dom as soon as the doctor had determined he was all right. Anything Dom told Biaggio, he'd be repeating to Corrado later, so there was no point in asking now.

Thank God for that. Talking hurt. Hell, breathing hurt. Dom really wasn't in the mood to say anything to anyone unless it involved the words "morphine" and "now."

All the way to Corrado's house, Dom swam in and out of darkness. He was exhausted. Completely drained. As if the adrenaline had kept him going until the car arrived, and now he was collapsing. Like both of the other car rides he'd taken tonight, this one was a blur of turns and stops and starts until Biaggio quietly said, "We're here."

Dom opened his eyes as Stan eased to a stop in the portico in front of Corrado's mansion. Beyond the tinted windows, a handful of people were waiting for him. Just four that he could see, and for that, Dom was grateful. This kind of offense—two thugs kidnapping and beating a made man—certainly warranted waking everyone in the family, but Corrado must've known Dom wouldn't be able to handle a crowd of angry Italians. Not until he'd had some pain pills, some sleep, some coffee, and some more pain pills, sleep, and coffee.

Among the tiny cluster of people in the portico were

his uncle, of course, and Dr. Rojas, the physician who'd come any time Corrado demanded it. Like most immigrants in town, the doc was owned by the family, and he was at the beck and call of the Maisanos to show up whenever he was needed, day or night, to treat anything from a child's ear infection to a bullet wound, all the while turning a blind eye to certain things.

Things like exactly why Corrado's nephew-slash-adopted-son was stumbling out of a limousine with blood all over him.

Rojas looked Dom up and down, his tanned face lined with concern. "Rough night?"

"Rough night." Dom swallowed. "You've got something for pain, right?"

The doctor nodded, no humor registering in his expression. "Of course. But first, I need to make sure none of your injuries are serious." The doc inclined his head. "If there's anything internal or broken, there's nothing I can do here."

"Then let's hope there isn't," Dom said.

Rojas nodded. He probably hoped as much as Dom did that this could be handled with a house call—nobody liked broaching the subject of a hospital transfer with Corrado.

With Biaggio and the doctor at each elbow, Dom shuffled up the portico's marble stairs. Aunt Marcella had set up one of the guest rooms on the first floor, and they guided him in there.

Getting his jacket and shirt off was excruciating, but with the doc's help, he was able to strip out of them.

"Sorry they woke you up," Dom whispered.

"It's all right," Rojas ground out. "I got here as soon as I could once I realized it was you."

They exchanged glances, but let the subject drop when

Corrado appeared in the doorway. Wordlessly, Dr. Rojas examined Dom, poking and prodding just right to make his vision turn white, Corrado hovered at the edge of the room, arms folded and lips taut. Biaggio paced outside, occasionally pausing to peer into the room.

Finally, the doctor gave Dom a couple of pills and let him lie down. "I don't see any signs of internal trauma beyond some bruising. Only an X-ray will tell us for sure if any ribs are broken, but if they are, the fractures are mild and there isn't much to be done except wait for them to heal."

"What about his head?" Corrado asked. "That's quite a bruise."

"The concussion appears to be mild. I'll come back in the morning and see how he is." Dr. Rojas paused. "He can sleep, but check on him every couple of hours."

"Thank you, doctor."

They continued talking for a moment, but Dom was already starting to fade out. He had no idea if it was exhaustion or whatever was in those pills, and he really didn't care.

Corrado touched his arm. "Your cousin will come tomorrow and bring you some fresh clothes."

Dom nodded slowly. "Thanks." He didn't need to tell his uncle he'd sworn off clothing forever. There was no way it would be any less painful to dress than it had been to undress, and dressing meant eventually undressing anyway, so he was going to be a nudist for the rest of his life.

"Get some sleep, Domenico." Corrado patted his arm gently. "We'll discuss what happened in the morning."

And that was the last thing Dom heard before everything went dark.

THOUGH THERE'D ONLY BEEN a handful of people waiting when Dom arrived in the middle of the night, the house was crawling with them when he awoke the next day. That was what it sounded like, anyway. From what Biaggio told him, every Maisano within a hundred-mile radius, not to mention every lieutenant and soldier who wanted to stay in the boss's good graces, had flocked to the mansion the minute they'd heard.

Though Dom wanted nothing more than to inhale painkillers and sleep until he was dead, he had no choice but to come out and show his face. He needed to give visual confirmation that last night's "incident" hadn't done any lasting damage, that he was still strong and on his feet. The longer he took to recover, the more word would spread that Floresta and Mandanici had brought him down a peg. A black eye and a cut lip were badges of honor so long as the man wearing them still faced the world like he was ready to take on an army. Image, image, image.

First things first, though—Dr. Rojas came by again to check on him. The doc was bleary-eyed and unshaven, but still looked a hell of a lot better than Dom felt.

"How are you doing?" Rojas asked as he checked Dom's ribs.

"I'll feel a lot better once you stop—" He hissed. "Fuck."

"I'm not the one who beat you up." Rojas pressed his thumb against a particularly tender spot, turning Dom's vision white. "Don't blame me."

Dom tried to mutter about him being a son of a bitch, but he couldn't breathe.

Rojas finally finished and sat back in the chair beside Dom's bed. "You're damn lucky they didn't kill you."

"Am I?"

They locked eyes, and Rojas sighed. Nothing needed to be said. Rojas wasn't much older than Dom, and his involvement with the family had been about as voluntary as Dom's. They'd surreptitiously had conversations like this for years. Rojas was probably the only man on earth who knew Dom would sell his soul to get the fuck out of the Maisano clan. The doc himself felt the same way. He didn't have a drop of Sicilian blood, but his father had essentially sold him to the Maisanos. A desperate Colombian immigrant, the senior Rojas had bargained with Corrado to send his eldest son to medical school, on the condition that the newly minted doctor would, in addition to a legitimate career, be the family's personal physician. Of course, he'd neglected to mention this to his son until the degree had been earned, at which point Dr. Rojas was caught up in someone else's deal with the devil.

In the past, when they were sure no one was around to listen, Dom and Rojas had confessed how much they'd love to run away from all of this. Leave Cape Swan. Change their names. Start over.

But others had tried, and they'd been found. Dom had witnessed what Corrado did to, as he called them, apostates. Those screams were lodged deep enough into his psyche to both remind him why he wanted to leave and why he didn't dare.

Rojas cleared his throat and stood. "I should get going. I'll let your uncle know you're recovering nicely." He glanced at the door, and quietly added, "Unless you want me to tell him you're in no condition to meet with visitors?"

Dom groaned. Right. He had to go out and show his

face, didn't he? And nothing short of being comatose in a body cast would be a severe enough injury to make it acceptable to be bedridden. The message *had* to be clear that Floresta and Mandanici *hadn't* given him more than a schoolyard beating. "No, I'd better do this."

"You sure?" The doctor's brow knitted. "Wouldn't take much to—"

"I know. But…" He shook his head. "I'll be fine. Thanks, though."

"Don't mention it."

Rojas left so Dom could make himself presentable. As promised, one of his cousins had brought him some clothes, and with the help of some more pain pills, Dom was able to shower, shave, and dress himself. Then he came out and followed the steady hum of voices toward the cavernous dining room where Corrado regularly held court.

Outside the room, Biaggio stopped him. "How are you feeling?" His brow creased, and the dark lines under his eyes suggested he hadn't slept at all. Guilt prodded at Dom —at Biaggio's age, he couldn't afford to sacrifice rest.

"I'm fine. They just knocked me around a bit."

Biaggio sighed with relief and smiled, gently squeezing Dom's arm. "Well, you must've had a guardian angel watching over you."

The red-clad stripper flashed through Dom's mind, and he suppressed a shiver. He didn't tip his hand about the stripper. If he did, Corrado would send every Maisano in town looking for him, and either the kid would get roughed up until he told them everything he knew, or he'd coolly take out anyone who hassled him. The thing was, Dom did want answers from the kid, but he also owed him his life. He didn't want to put a bull's eye on his back or get anyone else killed who got too close if the stripper turned out to be a psychopath. He needed to find him and talk to him personally.

Yeah, someone was watching over me last night, but "angel" isn't the word I'd use.

"You'd better go inside." Biaggio gestured at the huge double doors to the dining room. "A lot of people are waiting to see if you're okay."

Dom smiled thinly. They were waiting for Corrado to *see* them waiting. But whatever. Image, image, image.

The second he walked in the door, someone called out, "There he is!"

Every head turned, and instantly, every made Maisano descended on him, shaking his hand and—carefully—clapping his shoulder. Such was the game they all played. The beaten had to show his face and prove he was all right, and anyone who wanted to be on Corrado Maisano's Christmas card list had to show *his* face to make sure the old boss knew he was concerned. Image, image, fucking image.

Aunt Marcella served everyone a massive lunch, and afterward, having played their part as concerned members of the family, the men left. Still in pain, still hazy from the pills, and now drowsy after eating, Dom wanted nothing more than to go back to bed.

But just as duty had called the troops into Corrado's house, it called Dom into his uncle's office.

Only Corrado's innermost circle was invited to this meeting. Biaggio, of course. And Corrado's sons, Luciano and Felice. Like everyone else, they'd all put on a show of strength and solidarity, laughing and carrying on over wine and antipasto, but now they were quiet and serious.

Corrado leaned back in his big leather chair, cradling a brandy glass between his fingers. "We need to discuss what happened last night."

Luciano folded his arms. "If word got out that Dom was meeting with Passantino's daughter, these goons might've been trying to interfere."

Corrado set his glass down. "Biaggio, any word on the girl?"

The consigliere patted the air. "I spoke to Passantino last night. His daughter is at home and is fine. They both give Domenico their best." With a faint laugh, he added, "She was pleased to know she hadn't really been stood up."

Dom didn't dare laugh. He wouldn't be doing much of that anyway until his ribs stopped feeling like they were on fire.

Corrado didn't laugh either. "Well, once Domenico's back on his feet, the two of them can arrange another date. Maybe one with more security."

Can't wait. Dom shifted around, and at least everyone in the room was likely to blame his grimace on the pain. As much as he'd been loath to meet with Brigida, this wasn't exactly how he'd wanted to get out of a blind date. Thank God no one had laid a hand on her and she was all right. Initially irritated that she'd been stood up, no doubt, but all right.

At least no one knew that the date had been the reason the two assholes had gotten the drop on him in the first place. He'd been nervous, almost sick to his stomach, and he hadn't wanted to be there at all. He'd only been there because his uncle insisted it was time for him to get married, and a Passantino-Maisano marriage would be tremendously beneficial to both families. On his way from his car to the restaurant, Dom had been so distracted and queasy, Floresta and Mandanici had been able to get right up on him and—

And here he was.

He had no doubt that his uncle was serious about arranging something in the near future. Corrado and Passantino would undoubtedly have them meeting up again as soon as Dom could move. And as soon as he was presentable in public—nothing like a battered face to charm a lady.

Dom bit back a joke about this being a sign from God that maybe he wasn't ready to get married. Corrado was in no mood for jokes right now. Not even to take the edge off. And as far as he was concerned, there was nothing funny about his nephew pushing thirty-five without a gold band on his finger.

"*Doesn't look good, Domenico,*" he'd lectured him again a few nights ago. "*Doesn't look good at all.*"

"*Maybe I just haven't found the right girl. People aren't getting married so young anymore.*"

Corrado had shaken his head and waved his hand in that dismissive way that meant the discussion was over. "*You're not most people. Image, my son.*"

Image. Fuck image. Just one more thing to resent about this life.

Corrado sat up a little, resting his arms on the desk. "Domenico, I need you to think back to last night."

"I've been thinking about it almost constantly."

"Tell me again, everything you remember."

Dom took a breath and told the story all over again. When he was through, his uncle scowled.

"It doesn't make any sense." Corrado drummed his fingers on the desk. "Either these idiots were too inept to kill you, or they just wanted to shake you up."

Dom gritted his teeth, reminding himself that Corrado wasn't actually angry or disappointed that they hadn't finished the job. He was only trying to sort out what all of this meant. Such was the mind of a boss—a man in his position had to be this businesslike, so wrapped up in the politics and deeper meanings of every move anyone made that everything came down to numbers and messages instead of flesh and blood.

Corrado was quiet for a moment. "The men who attacked you. Are you sure you saw their faces?"

"Yeah. Floresta and Mandanici."

Corrado and Luciano exchanged uneasy glances. Felice shifted his weight, watching his father and elder brother.

Luciano turned to Dom. "Are you *sure* it was Floresta and Mandanici?"

"Absolutely sure. Why?"

"Because their bodies were found last night by Cape Swan PD." Luciano locked eyes with Dom. "Two bullets apiece." He tapped the center of his forehead. "And one of them took one to the knee too. From the gravel in the wound and the amount of blood he lost, it happened before they were put in the back of the car."

Dom shuddered.

"They were killed in the car," his cousin went on. "Somebody put them in the trunk, drove them down to the marina, and shot them both."

"The marina?" Corrado's eyes lost focus, and then his gaze slid toward Dom. "That's not far from where Biaggio picked you up last night."

"I know." Dom shifted, wincing when his ribs protested. "And I remember getting out of a car, but not much else."

Except that stripper. The blond stripper with a gun. The eyes. The accent. The stone-cold demeanor that was intimidating despite the guy's small stature. Red leather wrapped around narrow hips and—

"We need more than that, goddammit." Felice fidgeted impatiently. "Someone's trying to send a message if they're offing people that close to the marina. Or they're trying to get cops down there to sniff around."

"If he'd wanted to get cops sniffing around," Corrado said, waving his hand, "he wouldn't have taken them out in the parking lot. He'd have left them on the marina."

Luciano nodded, folding his arms. "Either way, I think we need to increase security measures down there. We can't take the risk of someone interfering with supply lines or leading cops anywhere near the merchandise."

Corrado grunted. "Agreed."

Dom resisted the urge to roll his eyes. Of course, the concern was about supply lines and merchandise. Beating him up was well and good as long as nobody got too close to the stream of cocaine and immigrants flowing through Cape Swan via Maisano hands.

"But as for this guy who took out Floresta and Mandanici," Luciano said, "he had to have been a pro. He didn't leave a thing at the scene. No weapon. No witnesses. No fingerprints. Guy didn't even leave any footprints— they said the ground around the car had been wiped. Like he'd used his foot to erase his prints until he got to the concrete."

Dom drummed his fingers on his arm. "They're going to find my blood in the backseat of that car. I'm almost sure of it. Probably the trunk, too."

"Well, that's your alibi," Corrado said. "You were in the trunk and backseat, so you weren't the one driving. The only thing you might be questioned about is the identity of the shooter." He narrowed his eyes a bit. "Do you remember anything else, Domenico? Anyone else who might've done this?"

Dom shook his head. "I blacked out. After that… nothing." That wasn't entirely true, of course, and he didn't like lying to his uncle—*never* a wise thing to do—so he added,

"I remember someone else being there, but the details… it's all a blur."

Beside Corrado, Felice glanced back and forth from his father to his brother, but he said nothing. Luciano swore under his breath.

Corrado sighed. "Well, in any case, the men who did this to you are dead. When I find out who sent them, he's dead too."

"But we should also find out who the fuck killed *them*," Felice said. "Are you just going to let that slide? I mean, how do we know this guy's on our side?"

"Because he didn't kill me," Dom said through his teeth. "Trust me, he had ample opportunity."

Felice eyed him. "So you *did* see the guy?"

Dom's blood turned cold. He held his cousin's gaze. "I was on my knees and spitting blood while he was putting those boys in the trunk. And *someone* helped me into and out of the backseat. He even gave me a phone to call Corrado. If he'd wanted me dead, I would be."

Felice scowled, shifting in his chair.

Luciano pursed his lips. "He might not have known who you were."

Dom vaguely remembered telling the guy his name. Which seemed stupid now, but he did recall feeling like he didn't have a choice.

"*What's your name?*"

"*Who wants to know?*"

"*The guy who's going to decide whether you wake up tomorrow in a hospital, a jail cell, or a morgue.*"

"*Domenico Maisano.*"

"*You're shitting me.*"

He shuddered, which hurt like hell. Yeah, that kid knew who he was. Exactly who he was. And yet, Dom was still alive.

And his cousins and uncle were still watching him, waiting for him to say... something?

He shook his head again. "If he knew something, he didn't say anything. And he didn't shoot me."

"You've got to remember something about him," Felice said.

"No." Dom looked him in the eye, and despite the mental images of that leather crop top, the sharp cheekbones, and those icy, unflinching eyes, said, "I don't remember anything."

"Then that's all we have," Corrado said. "The important thing now is finding out who sent those boys after you. Because I want a message sent to whoever sent *them*."

Usually Dom would be the one dispatched to send a message. Most hitmen were just goons or independent contractors—they were more disposable, more easily shot and discarded if the cops got too close—but his uncle kept Dom in plain sight. The boss's well-known nephew, the man who everyone assumed was a turncoat coward just like his father, the one who maintained debt ledgers and efficiently laundered even the bloodiest money, was apparently the last person anyone would suspect of carrying out dirty work like *that*.

But the message that needed to be sent couldn't wait until Dom had recovered enough to send it, so Corrado would handle it. Who he'd send and what they'd do to whom, Dom had no idea, but with his uncle involved, the message would be received loud and clear that the Maisanos were not to be fucked with. And although Dom wasn't thrilled about the condition he was in at the moment, he was secretly relieved because being this fucked up meant he wouldn't be the one pulling the trigger this time.

"What about the guy who took them out?" Felice

fidgeted in his chair. He was more agitated than usual, which said a lot. "We just gonna forget about that?"

Corrado shook his head. "No. I've got cops filling me in on what they know, and plenty of ears to the ground in case somebody talks. Domenico, if you remember anything, I want to know about it. Until then, he's done us a favor and he did it for free." He chuckled. "Perhaps we'll find out who he is when he tries to send us a bill."

Luciano laughed quietly.

Felice didn't. "Dad, we need to find—"

"When your cousin remembers more details, we will." Corrado shot his younger son a pointed look. "Until then, you've all got business to attend to."

Felice swore in Italian, and then got up and stormed out of his father's office. Corrado watched him, but didn't try to stop him—he shook his head, muttering something about God blessing him with a bullheaded son, and then dismissed Luciano and Dom.

On the way out of Corrado's office, Dom didn't say a word to anyone. Nobody here needed to know that, once he'd finished licking his wounds and could breathe without pain, he had every intention of finding out who the stripper was and what he'd seen. That he fully intended to find out what this kid's deal was.

But he wasn't bringing the family into it. This he was doing on his own.

Chapter 3

A week after Domenico Maisano had his ass handed to him in the alley, Sergei still jumped every time someone came strolling into the club. On his way in tonight, going in through the back door since he'd gone in through the front last night, he glanced over his shoulder for the hundredth time, searching the shadows for gun muzzles and suited Italians.

He swore in his native tongue and stepped inside, pausing in the dim hallway to catch his breath for a moment. More and more, he regretted leaving Maisano alive. Killing a made man, taking out someone as high up in the ranks as Domenico, was suicide, but so was letting him live after he saw Sergei's face.

On the other hand, so what if Domenico knew Sergei had killed the goons in the trunk? The gun would never be found, and even if it was, there'd be no connection between that weapon and any other killings. There was no way anyone would conclude this was anything but a random murder. A lifesaving one, for that matter—if nothing else, the Maisanos should've been rewarding him for saving Domenico's life.

But someone else had wanted Domenico Maisano harmed, and they might not be too happy about that night's interventions. Whatever the case, though, Sergei wanted to put the whole thing behind him. And over and over, as he wandered to the backstage dressing room to get ready for his shift, he berated himself for leaving that asshole alive. Dead men told no tales, after all.

As he changed out of his shorts and T-shirt and shimmied into some tight black leather, his stomach fluttered with nerves. In a few minutes, he'd be out there in the lounge, and he was certain one of the Maisanos would come in with questions. Or worse—Domenico himself would show up. Sergei wasn't even sure why that was worse, but the thought of the battered Mafioso walking into his club made his skin crawl, as if that would cross lines and make worlds collide after he'd so carefully kept them separate. Even if Maisano just wanted to say "thanks for saving my ass" or something, Sergei didn't like being in the same room as a Mafioso unless it was to accept a job or put a bullet through his brain.

But he didn't want to see any of his contacts now. None of the Mafiosi. Not here. He was sure with every new arrival, though, that one of them would show up, and he was relieved beyond words every time it was just another lonely dude with a hard-on.

He usually got a little thrill out of seeing one of his contacts come in. Although their very existence—every one of the Mafia-connected Italians in this town—sickened him, there were a handful who came in here specifically to see him. They came promising him money in exchange for doing what he loved most: kicking Mafiosi off this mortal coil and, one body at a time, moving the families closer to their inevitable collapse.

Ever since the night Domenico Maisano had his ass kicked, though, Sergei had been more on edge than the town had been after Barcia's body washed up with a mouthful of testicle. Sergei had covered his tracks well enough, but if anyone connected him to the dead men in the trunk, or to Maisano's busted ribs, there was a good possibility he'd be silenced.

For the past week, Sergei varied his routes to and from work. He made sure Roy or one of the other giant bouncers stayed close for all of his private dances with non-regulars. He socialized more than he probably had in years, just to be around people who knew him so some goon didn't surprise him.

But no one had come looking for him. The only people who asked for him were his regulars. Maybe Maisano didn't remember him. Maybe they'd already taken out whoever had ordered the two goons to rough him up.

In all the years he'd spent planning to bring the families down from the inside out, Sergei had never given much thought to Domenico Maisano. He was high up the food chain, and yet… not. Domenico was the Joker in the deck, and this wasn't a game of Jokers Wild. He was that card that nobody knew what to do with. Or why it was even in the deck. The adopted prince who would never be king, but everyone still had to go through the respectful motions anyway.

Sergei suspected Domenico was little more than a pity case. Though he'd never amounted to much as a Mafioso, he was untouchable. After all, he was the orphaned son of Corrado's disgraced brother, taken in as a boy despite the damage his father had done to the family name. Sergei had heard that if Alessandro Maisano had survived two or three more years, his son would've been killed along with him, but Corrado had taken pity on the boy because he'd been so young.

As if the Maisanos had ever hesitated to execute children for sins of the father.

On his way into the backstage dressing room for his shift, Sergei ground his teeth and shoved those thoughts away—the brutal family and the man who shouldn't have been stuck in his mind—as he tried to concentrate on getting ready for work. Another night, another dozen or so dances for horny men with too much money. There hadn't been any goons in here lately, thank God.

It was over. Maisano was in the past. No one was coming to bother him about it, or they would have already.

Focus, Sergei. And not on him.

Once he'd finished preening in the dressing room mirror, he went out to the lounge to start earning his pay. The left stage had just opened up, so he nodded to the deejay and took his place at the pole. The music started. So did Sergei. Undulating, shaking his hips and ass so there wasn't a soft dick in the room. Business as usual.

And right on cue, someone from Cape Swan's seedy underbelly showed up.

Though Sergei didn't miss a beat, the sight of a slick-haired man in a pin-striped suit made his skin crawl. This one wasn't Italian, though. Baltazar was the smooth-talking Greek who'd drawn Sergei into this world in the first place.

Like Sergei, Baltazar could never be made because he wasn't Sicilian, so he worked as an independent contractor. He was the go-between for a motley crew of thugs and contract killers—some who worked together, some lone wolves like Sergei—who carried out some of the families' dirty work. He handled jobs for both the Maisanos and the

Passantinos. Maybe the Cusimanos too. Sergei had never heard the guy say anything remotely endearing about that clan, but their money was as green as anybody else's.

Baltazar sidled up to the stage and sat down at the last empty seat. While Sergei continued to dance, they locked eyes for a split second, and the subtle nod confirmed what he already knew—this was business.

At the end of his dance, as he always did, Sergei grinned down at the men watching him. "All right. Who wants a private dance?"

Immediately, cash came out. Mostly twenties. A few hundreds. Held in wads, waved in outstretched hands, with "I can get more from the ATM" called out over the thumping music.

Baltazar, of course, casually fanned enough hundreds on the edge of the stage to halt all the others in their tracks. The men lowered their hands. Twenties disappeared. Then hundreds. Baltazar and Sergei exchanged grins, and Sergei collected the cash before stepping down beside him.

The cash he laid down here wasn't a bid for a private lap dance, but it wasn't just for show either. It was a means to outbid the others in order to get Sergei alone without rousing suspicion, and it was also a deposit for the deal they were about to negotiate. There was no question that Sergei would take the money and complete the job. He'd learned at a very, very young age that *nobody* said no to the Mafia.

On the way back to the private booths, he surreptitiously thumbed through the cash. Roughly ten grand, which meant the job was a hundred. Somebody fairly high in the ranks, then. At *least* a lieutenant, maybe, or a captain. Not necessarily a made man, but definitely a valuable target.

He was curious about the hit, especially since it seemed to be coming awfully quickly on the heels of Barcia's contract, but he wasn't terribly surprised. There'd been an uptick in violence among the families over the last few months. From all three sides, men were sending up smoke signals to each other in blood and gun powder. There was a war brewing. A big one.

Sergei had played a role in that. None of the families had yet caught on that for the past few years, he'd been methodically arranging them like chess pieces. He'd long ago learned what could mark a man for death. By strategically setting someone up—framing him for embezzlement, planting conspicuous bugs in homes and vehicles so it appeared someone was in cahoots with the law—Sergei could virtually guarantee that the powers that be would issue a contract on that man's head. Getting that contract himself was a plus, and the money certainly never hurt, but as long as it ended with one more Mafioso in a body bag, Sergei was pleased.

The most important part was that when the right people were killed—either by Sergei directly or because he'd set them up—then other people moved into power. With time and patience, he had, for all intents and purposes, sculpted the leadership of all three families until they were, without even realizing it, moving themselves into checkmate. He'd cleared the way for men with bloody grudges to rise to power opposite each other. Removed the more sensible, diplomatic ones in favor of the hotheads and sociopaths. The ones who could be manipulated into going to war with each other and, ultimately, bring all three organizations down in flames.

Causing the right people to move up in the ranks at the right time was like throwing gas-filled water balloons at a bonfire—explosions were inevitable. For a hundred grand,

Sergei could arrange for one of those explosions to happen sooner than later.

He exchanged nods with Roy and then stepped into a private booth with Baltazar.

Baltazar didn't sit down. They faced each other across the small booth, and the man slipped his hands into his pockets as he said, "I've got an invite to a party, Dmitry." Even Sergei's Mafia contacts didn't know his real name. He carefully kept it that way.

"When and where?" he asked.

Baltazar pulled out a photo and handed it to Sergei. On the back, the mark's name, Nicolá Cannizzaro, was handwritten. He knew the name—a member of the Maisano clan. The brother of Luciano Maisano's wife, if he recalled correctly. Sergei committed the name to memory, then studied the photo for a moment until it, too, was well burned into his mind.

He handed it back. He didn't want that photo anywhere near him when the body was found.

Baltazar tucked the photo in his pocket again. "I'd also like to bring a friend."

Sergei nodded. That was code for killing two birds with one stone. "Who's your friend?"

Baltazar handed over a second photo. That was a face Sergei had seen before. Eugene Cusimano, a soldier who answered to one of the Cusimano lieutenants.

He handed back the photos. "Are they both getting in on it? Or does one want to watch?"

"My friend only wants to watch, but *not* participate."

So Eugenio Cusimano needed to be framed, but left alive. Why they didn't want Eugenio taken out too, or why this needed to be on him, or what would happen to him once Nicolá's people got their hands on him, was none of Sergei's business. What was his business was the fact that

Eugenio would be marked after this, which would probably mean another contract for Sergei, but more importantly, Eugenio would be out of the picture. That would remove a worthless drunk from the chessboard and leave room within the Cusimano ranks for one of the hothead newly made men to move up. Perfect.

"I'm in." It wasn't like he could say no even if he wanted to, but he rarely objected to culling Mafiosi. "When's the party?"

"Sunday."

Sergei raised his eyebrows. "That's a bit tight for a party with this much going on."

Baltazar gave a tight shrug. "It's what's offered. Take it or leave it."

"Logistics are what they are. If I can't do it by Sunday, I guarantee no one else in this town can."

Baltazar scowled. "Get it done in ten days, or it's both our necks in ropes. Got it?"

"Got it."

Baltazar handed him an envelope. "This plus what I gave you earlier is twenty grand upfront. The rest on completion."

Sergei quickly thumbed through the bills, and then closed the envelope. "See you at the party."

Chapter 4

"You look much better than you did last time I saw you." Rojas smiled like he meant it. "How are you feeling?"

Dom eased himself onto his plush leather sofa. "Amazing what a week can do. I finally don't feel like I got hit by a truck, so I think I'll pull through."

"Looks like you will." Rojas sat beside him. He checked Dom's various injuries, most of which had faded to angry but harmless bruises. The concussion had left Dom with the odd headache, and his ribs were still sore, but with each passing day, he felt more human.

"Do you need any more pain pills?" Rojas asked.

Dom shook his head. "No. I haven't even had to take them the last day or so."

"Good. Very good. Well if you—"

Footsteps turned their heads.

Biaggio came into the living room. "Well, well. Look who's up and moving."

"Eh, sort of." Dom shifted gingerly. "Doc says I'll make it, so…"

"I should hope so." The consigliere chuckled, but genuine concern creased his forehead. "We were all worried there for a couple of days."

"Tell me about it," Dom muttered. "But I'm good. Much better."

Biaggio smiled down at him. "Very good."

"Yeah. Nice to be functional without pain pills." Dom looked at Rojas and smirked. "But now that I think about it, if you *do* have a few extras…"

The doc laughed. He patted Dom's forearm, and rose. "When you run out, let me know, and we'll see how you're feeling." He glanced at his watch. "I have to get back to my clinic, though. I'll come by in a few days and check on you again."

Dom nodded. "Thanks. I'll see you soon."

Rojas flashed him a slight smile. Then he shook hands with both men, gathered his things, and left.

Biaggio sat beside Dom. "Your uncle will be pleased."

Dom gritted his teeth. "Yeah. He'll be thrilled to have me back on my feet and not making the Maisanos look like weaklings."

The old man shrugged. "It's part of the game, Domenico. We have enemies, and we can't risk looking weak. If they think a beating is enough to hobble one of us, then it'll be open season on the whole family."

"I know." Dom rubbed his neck, which was a little stiff from trying to sleep comfortably with sore ribs. "I get it. I do. But it does put some pressure on when you're trying to recover *and* look like you already have."

Biaggio smiled and patted his leg. "It does. But you're a tough one." The smile faltered a bit. In a quiet voice, one that absolutely wouldn't carry to anyone except for them, he added, "You're definitely your father's son."

Dom winced, but said nothing. From anyone else, that

would've been a grave insult, if not a threat. His father's name was tarnished within this family, and being compared to him was never good. But Biaggio knew Dom, and he'd known his father, and when he said it, he meant the man they both knew Papa really was. Not a traitor. Not a coward.

"*Your father was a good man,*" Biaggio had once told him. "*He made mistakes. He did things that can never be forgiven. But he had a good heart, and the world is a darker place without him.*"

Biaggio squeezed Dom's arm. "Your uncle will want to see you today. To see that you're really back on your feet."

Dom nodded, and they both got up. "All right. I guess I should go show my face, then."

"Good idea."

After all…

Image, image, image.

AS DOM RECOVERED from his injuries, life more or less returned to normal. After a couple of days, when he could move comfortably, he returned to the offices where he oversaw his pieces of the family business.

At his uncle's urging, he also contacted Passantino to let him know he was all right, and that he'd make arrangements with Brigida again very soon. She didn't need to see him when he was still battered like this, and he was in no mood or condition to try to woo anyone.

Not that it mattered—Passantino had sent all three of his daughters to Italy in the name of vacationing and visiting family. When Brigida was back in California, arrangements could be made.

"In the meantime," Passantino told him, "we're glad you're all right. Give my regards to your uncle."

Fine by me, Dom had thought after he'd hung up.

Felice and Corrado had ears to the ground and were scouring Cape Swan for whoever had put Floresta and Mandanici up to beating him, and everyone was searching for that mysterious man who'd killed the pair and saved Dom. Dom didn't remember him, though. No name, no face—nothing. There'd been someone else, but he'd been too fucked up to pick out any details.

So he told everyone, though.

His memory of that night was hazy, but there were bits and pieces that were crystal clear. Little sharply-focused frames of an otherwise blurry film. And in every one of them, that red-clad stripper featured prominently.

Who the hell *was* that guy?

The more he recovered, the more his curiosity came to life. He wanted to find the stripper, but not just for business reasons.

That bleach-blond, barely dressed kid hadn't just saved his life—he'd awakened thoughts Dom had been trying to keep dormant for a long, long time. Those blue eyes, that lithe, strong body…

Dom pushed the thoughts away and forced himself to concentrate on the ledger in front of him.

Tried to, anyway.

Right or wrong, he desperately wanted to see that stripper again.

Who are you kidding? Get that close to a gorgeous man, you're gonna want to do more than see him.

He shifted in his desk chair, glancing at the door in case someone had come strolling into his office. Even with the desk in front of him, he was sure his hardening cock would be conspicuous to anyone who wandered in. As if anyone in this office would dare.

He shook himself.

Jesus, Dom. What's wrong with you?

It was dangerous to even entertain these thoughts. He'd learned that the hard way back in his younger days when he'd sneak off to San Francisco or LA or Vegas at every opportunity. He'd check in somewhere under a fake name, and get his rocks off with any willing set of cock and balls he could find.

He hadn't gone back since he was twenty-one though. Nearly getting caught by a pair of Cusimanos had scared him right out of that sense of adventure. The Cusimano and Maisano families hated each other, and that had been during a period of violent strife between them. If the two goons had seen him and they hadn't killed him themselves, they could've turned him over to his uncle and let him know they'd found him sucking a guy's dick in the backseat of a cab.

Even today, the thought of his uncle finding out he was gay sent chills through him. He knew all too well what happened to cocksuckers in this family. To this day he was haunted by the night he'd had no choice but to carry out a contract on a cousin who'd been outed.

Dom shuddered and took a deep swallow from his glass. Nearly getting busted had scared all the horniness right out of him for a while, and being tasked with "removing that degenerate pervert from this town" had terrified him. There'd be no coming out. No exploring his remaining curiosity, or scratching the itch that a good-looking man had always aroused in him.

So he'd tamped it all down and ignored it, and he'd resigned himself to eventually marrying a woman just like he'd resigned himself to being his uncle's hitman. He hated both roles, wasn't made for either one, but there was no room in this family for men who couldn't kill or men who wanted men, and there was no leaving this family either.

He'd had no choice but to live and breathe as a straight Maisano.

Maybe that was why he was itching to see the stripper again—a chance, however slim, to revisit that delicious past before he surrendered to respectability.

He couldn't do it, though. It was too risky.

Much, much too risky.

No matter how tempting it was.

Chapter 5

Sergei didn't need as much time as he'd thought to arrange the hit.

Framing Eugenio Cusimano would be easy. He was notorious for drinking himself senseless and taking his expensive cars out speeding on the highways while he was drunk off his ass. Though he spent two or three weeknights at his mistress's condo in Crescent City, every Friday and Saturday, like clockwork, he showed up at Dame Kelly's bar at eight o'clock sharp and stayed there until last call. Then he'd hit the road and, by the grace of God, always managed to make it home alive. Sergei just hoped the booze didn't kill the man—and the man didn't kill anyone else—before he'd had a chance to complete the job.

Nicolá Cannizzaro didn't make it quite so easy. He wisely varied his habits and his routes. He didn't drink to excess—few Mafiosi did, and Corrado Maisano frowned on it especially hard. Nicolá wanted the favor of his sister's father-in-law so badly it was pathetic, to the point he toed the line like nobody else in the family.

Sergei stalked the pristine motherfucker for three days before he found a weakness he could exploit. Every man had one, and Nicolá was no exception. In his case, a god and a girl. One he was devoted to as publicly as possible, no doubt to impress the boss. The other, a closely guarded secret, probably because the boss would be decidedly *un*impressed.

As Sergei parked his stolen sedan in the lot outside St. Leo's during Wednesday Mass, he felt a tiny bit guilty. His father would've been horrified if he'd lived to see Sergei stalking a murder victim at a church. Then again, if Papa had lived this long, Sergei wouldn't have been killing Italians in the first place, so he didn't let the thought linger.

Mass finally came to an end. Sergei watched closely as the parishioners filed out the front door, each pausing to exchange a few words with the priest. It was strange, watching Cusimanos, Passantinos, and Maisanos coming out of the same church without giving each other a second look. There was only one Catholic church in town, and even avoiding enemies wasn't a good enough reason for these wise guys to slum it at the Russian Orthodox church downtown. So they'd agreed upon a holy ground ceasefire some years ago. No one discussed or carried out business here.

Which made this the perfect place to abduct Nicolá. Though he wouldn't be taken right from the church steps, it would be the last place anyone saw him alive, which meant it was entirely possible there'd be a rumor that *someone* had broken the sacred agreement. Just another gust of wind to fan the fire Sergei had been stoking. Then he—

A man emerged from the church, and Sergei did a double take so hard he nearly snapped his neck.

Was that—

On second glance, no. It wasn't Domenico. Fine features, but not fine enough. Broad shoulders, but a little too soft around the midsection. No, no. He was all wrong.

Sergei shook himself. Why the fuck did he care? He had a job to do. Domenico Maisano had nothing to do with it. He had nothing to do with anything.

He rubbed his eyes and focused on watching for his target, not the man who'd inexplicably occupied space in his brain lately.

Nicolá didn't leave until everyone else had cleared out. Hands in his pockets, eyes down, strolling down the steps and across the parking lot without so much as a glance around him. Funny how he was so good at varying his routine, so vigilant about situational awareness, and yet here and here alone, he let his guard down. Sergei wasn't sure if Nicolá's faith was admirable or stupid.

The pious wise guy was alone, which Sergei had expected. The rest of the family was a little more half-assed about attending church, and Nicolá didn't dare show his face with that pretty Mexican girl no one knew about yet. Maybe Sergei was doing him a favor by eliminating the need for that conversation.

The mark walked toward his car. Gaze down, brow furrowed, keys spinning around his finger. Deep in thought, apparently. The priest must've had something profound to say tonight. Good—Nicolá could chew on that while he waited to meet God.

Sergei grabbed a map off the passenger seat, and got out. Effortlessly adopting that perfect American accent he'd honed ages ago, he called out, "Excuse me? Sir?"

Nicolá turned around. "Yes?"

Sergei waved the map. "I'm completely lost and my GPS battery is dead. Could you show me how to get back to the highway?"

"Which highway?" Nicolá dropped his keys into his trouser pocket and started toward him. "The 101 or the 103?"

"103." Sergei spread the map across the trunk lid. "I've been driving around for twenty minutes, and I think I'm going in circles."

The Italian chuckled. "Easy to do in this part of town. All right." He tapped the map. "You're right here, and you want to go—"

He froze. Slowly, his gaze slid downward toward the pistol Sergei had pressed in beneath his ribs. "What the—"

"Get in the car."

The mark's lips tightened. "You're doing this here? In a church parking lot?"

Sergei shrugged. "Not my god."

Nicolá's eyebrows rose, his forehead creasing.

"Get in the car." Sergei nudged him with the pistol. His accent slipped, but at this point, he had the upper hand, and this guy wasn't going to live long enough to describe him to anyone. "You're driving."

The mark exhaled, and then nodded.

Slowly, both eyeing each other, they got into Sergei's car. Sergei kept the weapon trained on Nicolá's midsection as the Italian started the engine.

"What's to stop me from driving into the ocean or crashing into a building?"

"Because you don't know if I'm planning to kill you or not," Sergei said coolly. "Or what might happen to Marguerite if I'm not alive to place a certain call later tonight."

Nicolá sucked in a sharp breath, and Sergei knew damn well he'd won.

At Sergei's instruction, Nicolá drove to the edge of town.

Sergei pointed at a deserted parking lot outside a supermarket that hadn't survived the last recession. "Park here."

The mark slowed down, but didn't turn. "Why should I? You're going to kill me either way, aren't you?"

Sergei exhaled sharply. "Because a bullet to the stomach is one of the more painful ways to die?"

Nicolá's eyes flicked toward the gun.

Impatiently, Sergei growled, "And Marguerite might—"

"All right! All right. Don't hurt her. Please." He cursed in Italian, and then pulled into the parking lot. He stopped, kept both hands on the wheel, and turned to Sergei. "If you're going to do it, just be done with it."

"I'm still waiting for orders. Cooperate, and you might walk away tonight. Irritate me, and, well…" Sergei lifted the gun slightly.

Nicolá regarded him uneasily.

"Listen," Sergei said. "I'm not going to kill you unless you fuck with me. I wasn't sent here to kill you."

"Then why—"

"Because someone needs to hold onto you until a decision is made." Sergei shrugged. "If they decide to kill you, that's up to the Georgian. Not me."

"*The Georgian?*" Nicolá went white. "They're sending *him* after me? I didn't do anything!"

"Not my problem. All I know is that I'm supposed to keep on ice until the final decision is made, and that how well you cooperate with me will determine how much he's supposed to fuck you up before he kills you."

Nicolá swallowed hard, as if pushing back a sudden wave of nausea.

Sergei held out his hand. "Keys."

Expression blank, Nicolá killed the engine and surrendered the keys.

"Get out." Sergei opened his own door without ever shifting his gaze away from Nicolá. Try anything stupid, and I'll make you bleed until the Georgian's ready for you. And remember what I said about your girl. Clear?"

The Italian's nostrils flared and his jaw tightened, but he nodded.

Slowly, they both stepped out of the car. Sergei waved him around to the back of the car and popped the trunk.

Nicolá balked. His eyes darted this way and that, but he didn't move—apparently he wasn't going to challenge Sergei's marksmanship. Good. He needed Nicolá alive for the time being.

Sergei put on a pair of thin leather gloves. Then he pulled a foil sheet out of his pocket. It was dotted with gray-blue lumps of a dried paste, and he popped two off. They were a mix of Ecstasy and God knew what else. His poison guy, Katashi, had been selling it to him for the past couple of years, and it worked wonders for subduing marks who needed to stay alive but compliant for a little while.

"Put these under your tongue."

Nicolá arched an eyebrow. "How about you put them in your—"

The pistol pointed at his forehead shut him up.

"Under your tongue." Sergei held out the tabs. "Now."

Nicolá took them, but eyed them. "What are they?"

"They're not bullets. Put them—"

"How do I know they aren't—"

Sergei lowered the weapon and jammed the muzzle against Nicolá's balls. "Both of those under your tongue, or one of these in each nut. Got it?"

Nicolá slipped the tabs under his tongue. He grimaced, probably at the taste.

"Don't swallow it," Sergei said sharply. "And just to make sure you don't spit it out." He held up a roll of duct tape.

The Italian's grimace turned murderous, his lips blanching and nearly vanishing, but he didn't stop Sergei from taping his mouth. If looks could kill...

But they couldn't.

Sergei nodded toward the car. "Into the trunk."

Nicolá hesitated for a split second. A muzzle tap against his dick got the message across, and he climbed into the back of the car.

Sergei bound his hands and ankles with tape. Then he slammed the trunk and went around to the driver side. He wasn't worried about the mark getting loose back there. There were no sharp edges or anything in the trunk—he'd made sure of that. And even if he'd overlooked a potential escape route or a weapon, the drug would keep Nicolá from noticing anything beyond whatever blissed out hallucinations kept his subconscious occupied for the next few hours.

With Nicolá safely getting high in the trunk, Sergei drove over to the clubs that Eugenio frequented. He wasn't at the first two, but the third time was the charm—the goon's car was parked just outside.

Sergei parked nearby. Then he glanced around, made sure no one was looking, and quickly jimmied the man's car door open. He cut a tiny slit into the leather interior of the driver seat, and tucked a needle and small syringe beneath it, with the needle sticking up so Eugenio wouldn't be able to avoid sitting on it and injecting himself with the poison. Once everything was in place, he wiped the car for prints, locked the doors, and returned to the stolen car, which was parked where he could easily see when Cusimano came out.

And then he waited.

Elbow pressed beneath the window, he rested his head on his hand and drummed the steering wheel with his fingers. This was the boring part. Waiting. There were only so many times he could play out his plans in his mind before he wanted to fucking *go*.

He was impatient with short term plans, but he was pacified by the knowledge that his longer term plans were beginning to come to fruition. These days, the Cusimanos appeared to be solid, but the in-fighting was slowly unraveling their entire power structure. The Passantinos just needed their elderly boss to retire or die, and he'd be succeeded by his second-in-command, a vicious Sicilian-born con artist with the Cusimanos in his back pocket.

And the Maisanos were nearly there too. Corrado was in good health and was well-respected by the Passantino boss, not to mention his own family. If something were to happen to him, he'd be succeeded by his equally well-respected son, Luciano. There'd been rumors that Corrado had other men in line for his position in case Luciano died before him. After all, no one wanted Corrado's psychopath younger son, Felice, in power. But a series of tragic accidents, tips to the cops, and blatant executions had removed nearly everyone fit to fill the senior Maisano's shoes. Everyone except for Luciano.

Lovely son you have there, Maisano. Be a shame if something happened to him.

Sergei wasn't ready to make that move yet, though. As twitchy as he was about carrying out tonight's plan—*c'mon, Eugenio…*—he was a patient man when it came to his larger goals. He had to be absolutely sure that all of the families were in checkmate, not just check, before he took out Luciano and Corrado Maisano. He had to be absolutely certain that Felice would take over and all other potential heirs had been eliminated. Once Felice did take over, Sergei would make sure Old Man Passantino "retired," leaving his son in power. Putting those two opposite each other was like dropping a pair of rabid wolverines into a cage together. Except these two rabid wolverines would have an army of made men and the authority to sic them on each other. Then all that remained for Sergei was to skip town while the families finished each other off.

And once again, as he drummed the steering wheel and watched for Eugenio, Sergei's mind wandered back to a particular Maisano. One who hadn't ever played any role in his plans because he never seemed to play a significant role in anything besides the family's bookkeeping.

And getting his ass beat, apparently.

Sergei didn't know who had decided Domenico Maisano needed a beating, never mind why, but it didn't matter. Mafia royalty or not, Domenico didn't seem like much more than a pawn. On the other hand, Domenico's father had left a shameful enough legacy to taint his son's name as well as his own, and although Domenico was apparently a savvy businessman and a made man, there were plenty of people in all three families convinced that he was a rat waiting to happen. Though it was unusual for someone quite so high up in the ranks to be roughed up by a couple of goons, that night behind the club may very well have been a warning.

Whatever the case, Domenico wasn't Sergei's problem. He wasn't even sure why he kept thinking back to that night, besides the intrusion on his territory by idiots who didn't know how to be discreet. Somehow, though, Domenico kept creeping into the back of Sergei's mind.

He shook himself, focusing on the black Lincoln parked outside the bar. The only piece of the Maisano clan he needed to worry about tonight was currently tied up and tripping balls in the trunk.

And what the hell? When it came to Mafia-connected Italians, Sergei didn't have a sympathetic bone in his body. Yet he *was* curious if Domenico had recovered.

Of course he was. A man like that getting fucked up by goons like those was a sure sign that the war was about to begin. It was entirely possible that he'd been meant to be the Archduke Ferdinand for the Maisanos—the nobleman whose assassination ignited years of bloodshed that had been a long time coming.

Did that mean Sergei had inadvertently doused the fire that he himself had been trying to start for the past few years?

He thumbed the grip of the pistol beside his seat. Maybe he needed to finish the job. It had been a necessity, offing those two assholes and moving the would-be crime away from the place where he did business, but Domenico Maisano's survival had been collateral damage.

Right. Which is the only reason you helped him get his ass to a park bench so he could wait for help.

Sergei tapped his gloved finger on the gun. Every bullet he ever fired was part of the plan. When he spared a life, it wasn't compassion or even mercy. He'd spared Domenico Maisano because that was how this business worked. You didn't just kill a made man because he was there. Fulfilling a sanctioned hit was one thing—the person who called in the hit would be blamed and punished if anyone felt compelled. The hitman was doing his job. But killing a made man without a contract put the blame squarely on Sergei's head. If Domenico's death was ever somehow traced back to Sergei, the punishment would be severe and anything but swift. Corrado Maisano had a well-earned reputation for using butchery as a means of making a point or seeking vengeance. The execution for murdering his nephew would probably not be pleasant.

And yet, Sergei's brain kept circling back to... why? He could have easily gotten away with it. The gun was unregistered. .22 caliber bullets were almost never traced back to the weapon that fired them—they were too common, and half the time, damaged by ping-ponging around inside the body before coming to rest in a bone or something. And anyway, he'd flung the gun off a cliff several miles south of town. Neither the cops nor the Mafia—whoever would've found the body first—would've had any more reason to connect Sergei to Domenico's murder than they would the other two men who'd been bound and shot in the Caddy's trunk.

He shook his head and scrubbed a hand over his face.

Focus, damn it. You've got a job to do.

And maybe once that job was finished, he could waste a bit more time wondering why the fuck Domenico Maisano was still alive.

Around two in the morning, right on schedule, Eugenio Cusimano came stumbling out of the bar and staggered to where he'd parked. He dropped his keys three times, but finally managed to get the door open.

Sergei started his engine. Adrenaline was beginning to drip into his veins, and his heart sped up as he put the car in gear.

Eugenio fidgeted and shifted around in his seat for a moment. Maybe he'd felt the needle. Maybe he was just too drunk to control his limbs anymore. Eventually, though, he finally pulled out of his space, and headed out to the road. Sergei followed him.

Three miles later, Sergei was getting nervous. That car was still staying between the lines, Eugenio driving much too well for a man in his state. Between the booze and the cocktail of tranquilizers inside that syringe, Eugenio should've been groggy as fuck by now. He really shouldn't have even been conscious.

Sergei tapped his thumbs rapidly on the wheel. Maybe it hadn't worked. The poison usually kicked in quickly, but Eugenio had a hell of an alcohol tolerance. What if Sergei hadn't worked out the right dose? Or maybe the needle hadn't gone in. Or he'd felt it before he'd pressed down enough to activate the plunger.

No. Sergei had planned for every contingency and variable. It would work. It had to.

But why wasn't it working? What the fuck was—

Eugenio started to weave lazily. Though the brake lights didn't come on, the car lost speed. After a sluggish mile or so, it nosed off the road onto the soft shoulder and came to a lazy stop.

Sergei stopped behind him, left the engine running, and cautiously approached the vehicle. Just as predicted, when he reached the window, Eugenio was passed out against the steering wheel.

Sergei pushed the fat asshole into the passenger seat. He carefully withdrew the syringe from the seat and tossed it into the bushes. Then he went back to the stolen car, killed the engine, and got out again to open the trunk. From inside, Nicolá stared up at him, mumbling something against the duct tape across his mouth.

"We're going for a walk." Sergei cut the tape that was wrapped around the man's ankles, and took his arm, guiding him up out of the trunk. After he'd closed the lid, he walked him to Eugenio's car and shoved him into that trunk. He taped Nicolá's ankles again, and slammed the lid.

With both of his marks doped up and contained, he

drove out of Cape Swan and out onto Highway 103. Out here, with nothing but trees, mountains, and the occasional podunk town or meth lab between here and Interstate 5, the world was dark and quiet. The only light came from the high beams. When Sergei slowed down and started nosing off onto the shoulder, everything in the rearview lit up bright red from his brake lights.

There wasn't a soul in sight, and he was confident that no one would come by this time of night. He'd been out here enough times to know how deserted this highway was. How much blood could dry on pavement and how hoarse someone could become from screaming before a passerby finally showed up and called the cops.

Sergei suppressed a shudder as he eased the car to a halt. Nightmarish memories flashed through his mind—his brothers and father bleeding out in the headlights' glow, Mama screaming until her voice gave out, the certainty that the car pulling up had come to finish off him and Mama—but he tamped them down. That night couldn't surface now, or it would distract him from the job at hand.

He left the engine idling and got out, pistol in hand. The air was thick and oppressive, tasting of hot asphalt, but he was cold beneath his thin T-shirt. He paused to roll his shoulders, forcing back that memory that always tried to bubble up when he came out here.

Work to be done. No time to dwell on the past.

Slowly, the chill receded and his focus returned. Time to get the job done.

He opened the trunk. "Get out."

Nicolá blinked. Then he saw the muzzle of Sergei's gun pointed at him, and he obeyed, scrambling to get out and on his feet. The drug made him waver a bit, but he managed to get on his feet.

"Go." Sergei lowered the weapon and nodded at the highway. "Get the fuck out of here."

"What?"

"You're a lucky man." Sergei grinned. "Got a message. Turns out they don't want you dead after all."

The Italian's face went slack. "So, the Georgian…" He struggled to form words, and still slurred them. "They're not sending the…"

"He's not coming. But I would suggest you start walking before someone calls me back and tells me they've changed their mind."

"Where am I supposed to—"

Sergei held up the pistol again. "You want me to change my mind?"

"N-no. But…" Nicolá looked around. "Why did you bring me all the way out here? And… where *are* we?"

"Outside." Sergei shrugged. "Fuck if I know. But if I were you, I'd start walking before this phone starts ringing." He held up his cell.

The mark got the message. He spun on his heel, wobbling a little, and started walking down the highway.

Sergei got back into the car beside Eugenio. He pulled out onto the road and followed Nicolá.

Nicolá looked over his shoulder and then started running. Or trying to, anyway—he was still unsteady on his feet, and his gait was uneven and clumsy. He looked to his right, probably trying to make a quick decision about jumping into the deep, rocky ditch or taking his chances on the shoulder.

He didn't think fast enough.

Sergei slammed on the gas. Nicolá hit the hood with a meaty *thud* and rolled up onto the windshield, cracking the glass. Sergei swerved, and the man's body tumbled off hood and into the darkness of the ditch.

Sergei parked, got out, and made his way down to where Nicolá lay. He shined a small flashlight into the shadows and quickly found Nicolá. The impact had contorted his hips and spine, and his head was attached to his neck at an unnatural angle. If he wasn't dead, he was close to it.

Just to be sure, Sergei climbed down, peeled off a glove, and touched the man's neck. Yep—dead.

Now all he had to do was finish with Eugenio.

He put the glove back on, returned to the car, and drove it a short ways down the road. Then he nosed it off the shoulder, put the car in neutral, cranked the wheel toward the ditch, and got out. He went around the back, gave it a push, and let physics do the rest. The car rolled off the road and down into the ditch.

Eugenio was still slumped in the passenger seat, and at this angle, Sergei wasn't going to be able to move him, so he improvised—he pulled the man's feet up hooked one under the pedals, giving the impression that the crash had sent him tumbling into the passenger seat. His forehead had even left a little smear of blood beside the glove box, completing the illusion that he'd been tossed around.

Mission accomplished.

Normally, Sergei would just leave both bodies and let the authorities find them in due time, but he didn't want to risk Eugenio waking up and finding a way to cover his tracks. For that reason, he'd brought along a burner phone.

He dialed 911 and cleared his throat.

A woman answered, "911, what is your emergency?"

"I… oh my God…" Sergei breathed heavily for effect, making sure it sounded ragged and panicked, and devoid of his accent. "I'm up on the 103, out by Mountain Junction and a car just ran off the road!"

"Sir, stay calm, do—"

Sergei hung up. Then he wiped the phone, tossed it into the bushes, walked into the forest, and headed toward Cape Swan.

And in the distance, sirens started wailing.

Chapter 6

E very attempt to find out who'd paid Floresta and Mandanici to rough up Dom had come up empty. It was highly unlikely that they'd done this on their own. Neither was made, and for them to fuck with a made man, especially one as high up in the ranks as Dom, had been asking for a lot worse than the stripper had given them. In a way, he'd done them a favor—had Corrado gotten his hands on them, they'd *still* be screaming now, three weeks later.

But every lead came up empty and every trail went cold. Dom still had questions, though, and there was only one person he could think of who might have answers. Now that his body had healed enough that he could move around comfortably—thank God for ribs that were bruised and not broken—he decided it was time to pay the enigmatic stripper a visit.

Tracking him down would be easy enough. There weren't many clubs in Cape Swan with male strippers. If he wasn't there now—laying low, maybe—someone had to have seen the guy before. And just in case they weren't willing to talk, Dom brought a thick stack of hundreds with him.

He debated going incognito. Civilian clothes that wouldn't get him spotted from a mile away like pinstriped Armani had a tendency to. But he wanted anyone who saw him to know he was there for business. Nothing personal. Showing up in a strip club occupied only by men—the strippers *and* most of the clientele—was dangerous to say the least.

On the way into town, following the directions to a cluster of clubs along either side of a rundown road, Dom tried to conjure as many details as he could remember. Though the face was clearly etched in his mind, he replayed everything over and over anyway, just in case there was something he'd missed.

Blond. Definitely bleached. He wasn't sure why, but he was certain that hadn't been a natural color. And he'd heard a subtle but unmistakable accent. Sharp, both the accent and the voice. Slavic of some kind? Russian? That would match those prominent, hawk-like features he was sure he remembered.

Yeah, he'd recognize him. This guy was committed to memory, and Dom would know exactly who he was the moment he laid eyes on him. Assuming he was here, of course.

Dom parked a block or so away, and walked down the sidewalk that was lined with sex shops, strip clubs, and all the kinds of places his mother had warned him to stay away from. Of the two with male strippers, he picked the closest one.

He paid a cover charge to a stony-faced bouncer, strolled inside, and—

Stopped dead.

He'd been bleeding and half out of his mind the first

time he'd seen him, but looking at him now through clear eyes with a lucid mind… holy shit.

He was indeed a stripper, and he was good at what he did. At least a dozen men were crowded around the table-stage, staring up at him as he writhed against a metal pole. He was wearing—barely—black leather this time, and it left little to the imagination, especially when he lifted himself up off the stage, bent, twisted, showed off his mouthwatering strength and flexibility.

Dom forced himself to look away while he took a few slow breaths. He wasn't here for that. This was business. And not the kind of business that usually went on here.

He collected himself, and then turned toward the stripper again. By this point, the dance was over, but the stripper wasn't done yet. He'd come down from the stage, and he beckoned to a sleazy-looking bald guy with a lecherous grin on his lips. The client rose. As they started toward a hallway guarded by a pair of burly bouncers, Dom pushed himself away from the bar.

A few paces shy of the hallway, Dom stepped in front of him. "Wait. I need to talk to you."

Their eyes met, and the stripper halted, his eyes widening for a split second. An instantaneous *Oh shit.*

Quickly, though, he schooled himself, every trace of surprise—was there some fear in there?—vanished in favor of annoyance. Those piercing blue eyes narrowed. "I'm working."

"Whatever he's paying"—Dom nodded toward the bald guy—"I'll double it."

The stripper's lips tightened. "You want to talk, you wait out here."

"Triple."

The stripper laughed humorlessly. "Offer accepted, but

wait your turn." He didn't wait for a response, and sauntered into the back with the other guy.

After they'd disappeared, Dom swore. Irritated—and yet impressed by the kid's cojones—he went to the bar to wait for him. He ordered a Coke, and while he sipped it, desperate to cool down despite the air conditioning, Dom couldn't shake the image of the stripper in the bald guy's lap. He'd never had a lap dance from a man before. Women, yes, but the idea of a man undulating and writhing on top of him took his breath away. The thought of the stripper in his lap took him back to the frantic fucks he'd had as a teenager and in his early twenties.

He'd put all of that behind him, though. Sworn off his dangerous tendencies.

But something about this place and the sharp-tongued stripper brought those desires right back to the surface.

If he was even remotely smart, if Floresta and Mandanici hadn't knocked every last fragment of common sense out of his skull, he'd get the fuck out of this club right now and forget he ever saw the blond stripper.

But he didn't. He stayed there, nursing his Coke, his heart thumping and his palms sweating, until the bald guy staggered out of the hallway. The man disappeared into one of the restrooms. Probably to jerk one off. Dom supposed he'd have been in the same state if he'd just had an up close and personal dance from—

Oh mio Dio. Him.

The stripper sauntered out from the same direction, a hint of sweat gleaming on his forehead. His platinum blond hair was straight again, as if he'd taken a moment to make himself presentable before coming out here.

He walked right up to Dom and leaned on the bar beside him. "All right. You wanted to talk." He paused to make a sharp gesture at the bartender. "Cough up the cash and talk."

"Not here." Dom swallowed. "Someplace private."

Those slim lips pulled back across straight, gleaming teeth. "That can be arranged, but"—the stripper winked—"I charge extra for that."

Dom suppressed a shiver. He was here for business. For information. Not for a chance at putting his hands all over that slim, powerful, lithe—

He cleared his throat. "I'm here to talk. Nothing more."

The stripper's expression suddenly hardened, all traces of humor gone so quickly Dom wondered if he'd imagined them. The bartender materialized and set a bottle of water in front of him, then disappeared again, but besides picking up the water, the stripper gave no indication he'd even seen him. "Look, I know what you are." He eyed Dom. "My boss doesn't want your kind in here, and I don't want to do business with you unless it involves—"

"I'm not asking you to do business." Dom leaned in closer, lowering his voice. "But we've met before, and I need to know what else happened that night."

He didn't get defensive. He also didn't get nervous. Dom did, though—this guy wasn't stupid. He knew what night Dom was talking about, and if he knew who and what Dom was at a glance, then he knew he was in a dangerous spot. But he held his gaze like Dom couldn't have intimidated him if he'd wanted to. No fear whatsoever. Just icy indifference.

The stripper sighed with theatrical boredom. "What happened that night? I rubbed my ass all over a couple of dicks. Some Italian guy showed up in the alley with blood all over his fancy suit. And I rubbed my ass over some more dicks." Another shrug as he brought his water bottle up to his lips. "Isn't much else to tell."

"I doubt that."

"That's all you'll get from me."

Dom sighed. "Look, I'm not leaving until we talk."

The stripper lowered his water bottle and narrowed his eyes. "First, we are talking. Second, I'll see your cocky attitude and raise you several bouncers who take shit from no one." He gave Dom a derisive down-up. "Especially not your kind."

Dom was probably the mellowest guy in his entire family, and even he was struggling not to strangle this jackass. "I need to know what you saw."

"You know as much as you're going to know."

"You can tell me or you can tell the cops."

The stripper laughed. "A Mafioso talking to the cops. Does your uncle know that you—"

"Enough," Dom growled. "All I'm asking for is a few minutes and some information. And then you can get back to more"—he nodded toward the stages—"lucrative pursuits."

The kid glanced at the stages, and then rolled his eyes and slammed his water bottle down. "All right. But we're making this quick."

He didn't wait for a response and started walking. He led Dom down a dark hallway and out into the back alley. It was another hot, sticky night, the breeze off the ocean doing nothing to counter the lingering heat from the California sun.

Dom peeled off his jacket and draped it over his arm. "You got a name?"

The stripper snorted. "Small talk? Really?"

Dom shrugged. "Seems like introductions are a customary way to start a conversation."

"A polite conversation, sure." He folded his arms tightly across his bare chest. "Those rules don't apply to this one."

Dom blinked. This kid was something else. He didn't show even a hint of that subtle wariness that Dom's kind had cultivated in the population at large.

And damn it, that should have annoyed the shit out of Dom. While he didn't particularly like the way people cowered or moved to the other side of the street when they saw men from the families, sometimes it did make these "I need some information" conversations a hell of a lot shorter.

But this kid intrigued him too. He wasn't afraid of Dom, and he didn't seem naïve about it. This wasn't some idiot who couldn't see far enough past his own bravado to realize he was talking to someone dangerous. He didn't strike him as someone who'd panic if Dom tipped his hitman hand and let him know exactly what he was dealing with. No, he looked Dom straight in the eye, cool and collected, and silently dared him to make him blink.

Dom swallowed. He hadn't hallucinated that night, had he? This stripper really had shot Floresta and Mandanici before taking him to—

"Come on." The stripper released an impatient breath and cocked his hips sharply. "We going to stand out here, or was there something you wanted to talk about?"

Dom cleared his throat. "I just want to ask you about the night we met."

"Fine. But let's get one thing clear right away." He nodded sharply at the door. "Every five minutes I'm out here is a dance I'm not doing, and every fifteen is a private dance. You already owe me three grand, and every five minutes costs you another two hundred. Fifteen costs a grand. Got it?"

Dom had to admit, he admired his fearlessness. He

pulled his billfold from his pocket and withdrew some cash. "How about this." He held up the money as he put his wallet away. "We talk, I give you two grand."

The stripper's eyes darted toward the folded bills.

And in a split second, the money was gone.

Dom blinked, glancing at his empty hand, and then at the stripper as he inspected the money he now held. How the—

"Fine." The stripper tucked the cash into his waistband. "What do you want to know?"

How you moved that fast, for one thing.

Dom pushed his shoulders back. "I want to know what happened."

The kid laughed. "You had your ass kicked by two idiots."

"And you showed up, and the next thing I know, I'm on a bench and you're gone."

"Yeah?" A slender shoulder lifted in a sharp half-shrug. "What did you expect me to do? Hold your hand until the medics showed up?"

"I didn't expect you to do anything. But you did something." Dom tilted his head. "And I want to know what, especially after both men were found in the back of a car with .22 rounds in their foreheads."

No flinch. No surprise.

"Two fewer wise guys to fuck up this town? What a loss." He smirked. "No offense."

"Mmhmm."

He held Dom's gaze without flinching. "I don't understand why you're here. We both know what happened."

"I think you know better than—"

"No, I don't. And it doesn't seem like I'm telling you anything you don't already know." He stepped closer, right into Dom's space, and before he realized he'd done it,

Dom backed up against the railing. The stripper grinned triumphantly. "You really here for answers you've already got?"

Dom folded his arms. "You really want me to pass it along that you're the one who put a couple of bullets into those two? Because that's still an option if you refuse to help me."

The stripper's lips twitched, but so subtly Dom couldn't read if it was more irritation or if he'd struck a nerve. And then the stripper snorted with laughter. "You really want *me* to believe you'd go tell your boys that a queer little dancer like me saved your ass when you couldn't do it yourself?"

Dom clenched his jaw.

"That's what I thought." The stripper's eyes narrowed. "You wops and your obsession with image." Shaking his head, he clicked his tongue. "Guess you don't have any cards left, do you?"

Dom turned his head and cleared his throat, so he wouldn't cough right in the stripper's face. "Look, I'm just trying to figure—"

"I know your type, Maisano." That sharky grin made his knees shake. "All business. All efficiency and numbers. You don't waste your time driving all the way across this shithole town just to ask a stripper a few questions when you already know the answers. Especially not three weeks after the fact." Closer still, his bare abs almost brushing Dom's shirt. "So tell me. Why did you come here?"

"Because I need to… I need to know"—*what your skin tastes like, and*—"what happened that night."

"Yeah?" He bared even more teeth and leaned closer, reaching past Dom to rest his hands on the railing on either side of his waist. "That the only reason?"

"Yeah." Dom swallowed. "It's the only reason."

The stripper studied him, and gradually, the triumphant cockiness faded. His features hardened.

"Look, here's the deal, Maisano." He stepped in close again, this time getting right up in Dom's face, their noses almost touching as he snarled, "I've told you everything I'm going to tell you, and now you're going to get the fuck out of my club."

"For God's sake, I—"

"You stay the fuck off my turf, I'll stay the fuck off yours." There was a menacing, murderous undertone to his Russian-accented voice.

Dom gritted his teeth—this fucker had no idea who he was really tangling with.

The stripper continued, "You and your kind run this town, but you've got no business in this club. Get the fuck out of here, and let my customers enjoy their night without having to worry about Mob guys starting shit. You got it?"

And then he was gone, the club door banging shut behind him.

Dom slouched against the railing, the humidity sticking to the goose bumps on the back of his neck.

Well. That was that, wasn't it?

He swore into the night. There was no point in staying here, then. Maybe he'd come back in a few days. When he knew what to expect and wouldn't be so flustered and caught off guard. He was *not* intimidated by a stripper half his size.

The stripper half his size who'd slammed a door that locked from the inside.

Dom wiggled the knob, then swore and stomped down the porch steps into the alley. As he made his way toward the road, an odd sense of déjà vu rushed over him. He looked around. The shoddy buildings, the boarded up windows, the rusty Dumpsters—they weren't familiar, and yet they were.

He froze. This was where it had happened, wasn't it? Right out here? But he only remembered that night in painful flashes. Bits and pieces of scenery that didn't seem to go together now that he saw the big picture.

He shook his head and kept walking. No sense reliving that night again, especially not here. Instead, he returned to his car and got the hell out of there.

As he drove away, though, there was no getting that kid out of his mind. None.

And not just because he was annoyed by the refusal to tip his hand. The fact was, the stripper had him dead to rights. Dom had convinced himself he'd only come here for answers, but what had he really expected? For this kid to have some kind of insider knowledge about the intricacies of the Mafia?

No. That wasn't why he was there.

It had nothing to do with the night Dom had been roughed up, and everything to do with how he'd felt when the stripper had stepped up into his space.

Everything about him was like catnip to Dom. The smoking hot body was just the start of it. That cold fearlessness? The unabashed sexuality radiating from every move he made? Even the way he spoke drove Dom crazy. His accent was sharp but subtle, and it made Dom hang on his every word. Made him pay attention to the way his mouth moved, hypnotizing him with the way his lips shaped consonants.

Dom thumped the steering wheel. He couldn't go back. He didn't dare. The stripper wanted nothing to do with a man from Dom's world, and Dom would've been wise to accept that and move on because *he* had no business with someone from *that* world. He'd sowed his gay oats as a kid and nearly been killed for it. Even going back for a lap dance was dangerous. Someone might see him there.

Or worse, those desires might come back.

Fuck. Who was he kidding? They'd never gone away.

And now, with that stripper's face and body and voice seared into his mind, there was no ignoring them anymore. There was no silencing them.

There was no ignoring the truth—everything he desired was in that strip club, wrapped in sweat and leather.

I want him. I need him.

Dom turned the car around.

Chapter 7

Sergei downed the rest of his water bottle in three swallows. He was still fired up after his exchange with that fucking Italian, but the guy was gone now, and it was time to make up for lost pay. Not that he was hurting for money after getting paid for last night's job.

And not that the last ten minutes hadn't been profitable. He'd taken a couple grand off Maisano in one motion. But he was annoyed. Rattled in a way he couldn't quite describe.

That night in the alley should've been the end of it. Domenico Maisano had no business occupying as many of Sergei's thoughts as he had recently, and he definitely had no business strolling into this club like he owned the place.

Sergei glanced at the door Maisano had come through, and his stomach twisted. The guy was gone now, and that was the way it needed to be. He especially wanted Maisano out of here because the guy piqued his interest in a way his kind usually didn't. Sure, he was attractive. Domenico Maisano was apparently one of the better-looking Italians in this town. Then again, even the ugly ones could wear a suit well enough.

But there was something about him that had made Sergei look twice. Something that had struck a different chord tonight than the other Mafiosi ever did. Especially now that his face had mostly healed. Without the blood and swelling, with his dark hair flawlessly arranged except for a couple of strands fluttering in the breeze, he was…

Hell, he was hot.

Really… really… hot.

Sergei scrubbed a hand over his face. He was losing his mind, wasn't he? Entertaining any thoughts of a Mafioso that didn't involve bullets? Stupid.

He couldn't help himself, though. As he leaned against the bar, waiting for one of the stages to open up so he could dance again, he indulged in a few replays of that moment when he'd backed Maisano up against the railing. A veil had definitely lifted just then. A little bit of fear, but a lot of something else. Something Maisano didn't want to think about.

Sergei's skin prickled beneath his crop top, but he forbid the shiver from making it up his spine. The only thing he wanted from the wops in this town was blood, no matter how attractive they were. Attractive, and repressed, and—

He shook himself. He did want a piece of Domenico, but for the same reason he wanted pieces of some of the other hot Italians—to literally stick it to the families. An orgasm for him, a death sentence for the other guy if word ever got out. Just the way it needed to be.

On the middle stage, Jesse finished his performance. As he stepped down to escort someone into the back for a private dance, Sergei tossed his water bottle in the recycling bin behind the bar. Then he strode across the floor to the now vacant stage. Time to forget that Italian asshole and dance.

It was a good night. A busy one. Guys were coming in out of the heat for some air conditioning and cold liquor, and sweating right through their expensive suits and silk shirts as Sergei and his boys took turns dancing on poles in the middle of waist-high stages. Booze was flowing, tips were piling up—it was early yet, but looking to be a great night for those in G-strings.

When Sergei went up for yet another dance, there was a crowd around his stage before the deejay had even started the next song. Wide-eyed "gentlemen" sucked on highballs and longnecks as Sergei made that pole his bitch. He leaned against it, legs apart, positioning himself just right to make it look to anyone in front of him that the pole was right up his ass, and judging by the way the combed-over businessman in front of him nearly dropped his drink, the illusion worked.

With a full audience around him, Sergei didn't usually pay any attention to anybody else. These boys were here to scatter Andrew Jackson all over the stage and shove his uncle Benjamin into Sergei's G-string. Everyone else was irrelevant.

But as Sergei leaned against the pole and undulated, using his hips and abs to mesmerize four guys tugging at their sweaty white collars, he glanced to his left. The shimmering bead curtain beside the bar had parted, as it did a million times a night, but this time, he looked.

And missed a beat.

What the fuck was *he* doing here again?

Maybe he'd rethought that whole "I'm just here for information" thing. Sergei knew what he'd seen—there was more in Maisano's eyes than just a need to know what had happened three weeks ago.

Then a memory flickered through his mind of grabbing the cash out of Maisano's hand.

Shit. Had he come back for his money?

Well, that could get... awkward...

Sergei quickly focused on entertaining the men below him. Maisano hadn't tried to interrupt him so far, hadn't made a scene, so maybe he'd wait for Sergei to finish here. He'd waited last time. Of course, last time, he hadn't been there to collect money he'd been unexpectedly relieved of.

Well, whatever had brought him back, he could wait until Sergei had finished his business unless he wanted to be escorted out by grizzly-sized bouncers. And hopefully that would be enough time for Sergei to figure out a strategy for dealing with him.

As he danced, Sergei ground his teeth, hoping his customers were focused on his body and not his expression. He didn't like Maisano coming here, especially for the second time tonight. This was *his* turf. Mafiosi only came here when it was business, and—

Fuck. What if it *was* business? What if he knew who and what Sergei was, and he'd come here for that?

"*You took my money,*" he could hear the bastard snarling, "*so now you're going to earn it.*"

Son of a bitch. How many times had he told himself he'd never, ever give the Mafia an advantage over him in a business dealing? He should've left the money in Maisano's hand. He'd had plenty of control over that conversation, and still, fucking with the nervous wise guy had been irresistible. Stupid, but irresistible. At worst, he'd stolen from him. At best, he'd screwed him—taking far more than offered and giving back much less than demanded.

Shiiit.

The song changed. The regulars knew what that meant —the table dance was about to become a lap dance for whoever ponied up the most money and got Sergei's attention. Three guys waved twenty dollar bills at him, but they lowered them when two others started flashing hundreds.

Ignoring Maisano's looming presence as best he could, Sergei grinned down at each of them, eyebrows up and head tilted. *That all you got, baby?*

More money came out. They eyed each other, digging into their wallets. Each time one brought out a hundred, the other did too. Sergei's favorite kind of night—when he had two men equally willing to pay up, and they happened to be sitting right next to each other.

The first was hot—probably mid forties, with a few lines and some gray around the edges. A wedding ring too. Bet his wife had enough expensive cars and trinkets to turn a blind eye to his extracurricular activities. The other was older. Early sixties, at least. He may have looked like Hugh Hefner, but he also appeared to be loaded like the Hef, so… fine.

Sergei plucked the money out of each of their hands, and leaned back to drop it in the center of the table. The bouncers would make sure nobody tried to grab it.

Then he stood over his two customers. "Turn your chairs. Face each other."

They exchanged wary glances, but did as they were told. As Sergei lowered himself onto the edge of the table, a large shadow moved in his peripheral vision, and he glanced up to see Maisano standing just a few feet away. He had a bottle in his hand—water, maybe?—and stared at him over it.

Sergei tore his gaze away from that unsettling presence. He had work to do.

He sat in Hef's lap, straddling him, and Sergei hoped the man's cardiologist was okay with whatever happened when he started rubbing his groin on his chest. Sergei wrapped his legs around him, then leaned back so his head was in the married guy's lap. With practiced agility, he slid from one man to the other, teasing each in turn and making sure both got their money's worth.

As he moved from Hef to the married man, he glanced up.

Maisano was watching.

Intently.

If he'd come here for money, he was at least distracted for the moment—his lips were apart, and his eyes were round.

Staring right back at Maisano, Sergei ground his ass against the married man's rock hard dick. Over the pulsing music, he heard the guy beneath him whisper, "oh God."

Sergei tilted his head back, making sure his lips brushed his ear, and murmured, "You haven't had any attention in a while, have you?" He wiggled his ass, and the man groaned. "Such a shame." He ground harder, and then turned around and did the same on Hef's lap, squeezing the married man's waist with his ankles as he made Hef whimper and moan.

From the sidelines, someone else breathed, "Holy shit." He had his hand over his own crotch. Fine, let him feel himself, as long as he didn't whip out here in the lounge.

Sergei got them all—the two men paying him and the half dozen watching—riled up and panting, and then he stopped, lifting himself to his feet. "So who wants that private dance?"

Hef dug into his wallet.

The breathless middle-aged husband tugged at his tie. "How much is—"

"Five large." Maisano came out of nowhere and held out a stack of hundreds.

Sergei stared up at him.

"I ain't got that much," Hef muttered, and took his drink and left.

"My wife would kill me." The married guy skulked away too. No one even tried to pony up more.

Sergei gritted his teeth. On the other hand, Domenico was offering five Gs for a fifteen minute private dance. Sergei hardly needed the money, but if this guy was willing to cough up that much, Sergei couldn't help but be intrigued. If Domenico was here to ask Sergei to take somebody out, he'd have even more in his pocket. And if he'd come for the money Sergei had taken earlier…

Keeping his nerves beneath the surface, he asked, "You got the cash?"

Domenico held up the wad of hundreds.

Sergei forced himself not to scowl as he plucked the money from the man's hand. "Looks like you're the lucky winner."

Domenico shivered. That was odd—the Mafiosos were strictly business when they came in here. They'd pay a fortune for a dance that wasn't really a dance, and if anything, curled their lips at the strippers and clientele.

And suddenly Sergei was fighting a grin instead of a scowl. Maybe he'd been right about Domenico after all. Those little glances. The nerves.

He led Domenico to one of the private booths in the back. Roy the bouncer met his eyes, and Sergei gave him a nod. Code for "Don't worry, I've got this." He'd stay close enough to intervene if shit went down, but otherwise he'd keep his back turned and watch the other guys giving their dances. Then he'd get a cut of whatever Sergei made from the against-club-policy activities he'd turned a blind eye to. He got fifty bucks for ignoring a blowjob that never happened, and Sergei got a shitload more than that for taking whatever contract was offered to him in hushed tones behind a curtain.

Or maybe, unlike all his other brethren who came in here with wads of cash, Domenico really wanted a lap dance.

Sergei pulled the curtain across, and didn't quite know why his heart was beating so fast as he turned to face Domenico.

The Italian unbuttoned his jacket and lowered himself into the crimson armchair. Most guys flopped down on the cushion and waited like a drooling dog for the show to get started. Not this guy. Arrogant Mafioso, royalty in name only, he sat like an overlord taking his throne instead of a sleazy asshole panting for dick in a chair where a thousand men before him had blown their loads.

The music came on.

Sergei assumed his usual provocative stance, standing close enough to fuck with his mind and pulse while he ran his hands up and down his own sides. *Here's the goods. You like what you see?*

"So." Sergei gazed down at him. "You want more information, I assume."

"Not this time." Domenico met his eyes, and he grinned, knowingly and dangerously. "This time I want a dance."

That was… unexpected. This was the moment when his contacts usually started speaking in code, and "a dance" wasn't part of that code.

Sergei ran the tip of his tongue across his lip. "Just a dance?"

"Yes." The long, lingering down-up Domenico gave him, his breath hitching here and there, raised goose bumps on Sergei's mostly exposed flesh. When their eyes met again, Domenico spoke just loud enough for Sergei to hear him over the music, "I suspect with you involved, there's no such thing as just a dance."

Apparently he wasn't here in any official capacity. And maybe he'd given up on his pursuit of more details about the night they'd met. Sergei would certainly keep his guard up, but if Domenico wanted a dance...

Sergei stripped down to his G-string, watching Domenico's eyes widen. He swore he could feel the man's pulse rising, especially when Sergei stepped closer and slid a knee between his thighs. Domenico parted them farther, and his fingers curled over the edges of the armrests. Maybe the arrogant overlord...wasn't. Eyes wide and spine stiff, knuckles turning white, he suddenly seemed in over his head.

"You ever had a dance like this?"

He gulped, and a flicker of something—nerves?—broke the rest of the calm and cool façade. Slowly, he shook his head.

"Rules are simple." Sergei climbed onto his lap, sliding his hands over broad shoulders. "I dance. You don't move. Don't touch me. Got it?"

His eyes were fixed on Sergei's abs, and as he nodded, he whispered, "Yeah." He looked Sergei up and down. "My God..."

"Why did you come back?"

"I had to." Domenico's voice was just loud enough to be heard. "I can't..." His gaze drifted up and down Sergei's torso. "Can't stop thinking about you."

Sergei swallowed. Gay wise guys weren't unheard of, but they didn't last long.

"What's your name?" Domenico asked again.

Sergei shook his head. "It's not important."

"Isn't it?"

"No."

"Do I ever get to know what it is?"

"Why do you need to know my name?" Sergei turned around and leaned back against him, pressing his ass against an incredibly hard cock and his shoulders against Domenico's broad chest. "My name isn't relevant. You don't know what it is, but I'm still turning you on, aren't I?"

"Yes. Yes, you are." The man's breath tickled the side of Sergei's neck.

Sergei lifted himself up and faced Domenico again, settling onto his lap as he added, "That's all you need to know, isn't it?"

"I don't need to know anything. I *want* to know." He slowly ran his tongue across his lips. "Just like I want to know what it feels like to…" He trailed off, gazing drifting over Sergei's body, and if Sergei had been able to breathe —*what the fuck is going on?*—he'd have asked him to finish his sentence.

Dance. You're here to dance.

Sergei ground against him, and the firm ridge of Domenico's cock beneath his balls made his pulse soar. And not only that, it made *him* hard. Sergei often got into it when he was dancing, and sometimes if a guy was particularly hot, he even got a little turned on.

But not like this.

Domenico's eyes flicked downward, and he gulped. "That… that G-string isn't quite big enough for you."

Sergei glanced down. "Isn't when I'm like this." And he was rarely like this when he danced. Fuck.

"Maybe you should take it off."

"Can't take everything off," he murmured. "The… the law."

Domenico's eyes flicked up and met his, burning with lust. "You think I'm gonna report you?"

Sergei glanced back at the curtain. Then he stood and shimmied out of the G-string.

There was something deliciously dangerous and irresistibly sexy about this. Though a G-string hardly counted as clothing, losing it left him feeling like he'd just thrown off ten protective layers. Like he'd gone from fully-dressed to naked in just a few beats, and now he was against Domenico, cock and balls rubbing against the soft silk of his shirt and tie.

"You're breaking the rules," Domenico breathed, and Sergei swore he could hear his heartbeat in his voice. "Does that mean I can too?"

For five thousand dollars and that look in your eye? You can do any damned thing you want.

"I don't think you want to break the rules." He wrapped his arms around Domenico's neck, pressing his dick against the man's chest and bringing his abs close enough to Domenico's face to feel his breath. "You like looking without touching." He slowly fucked against him, his own head spinning as the smooth silk turned his nerve endings to pure electricity. "Don't you?"

Domenico exhaled hard, the warm air whispering across Sergei's abs and making him gasp. "I want… I want to touch you."

"I know you do." Sergei leaned forward enough to murmur in his ear, "But this turns you on. Doesn't it?"

Domenico shivered beneath him. "Everything about you turns me on."

Likewise. It shouldn't, but… shit.

Sergei leaned down to let his lips *almost* touch Domenico's neck, teasing him with their proximity, and as goose bumps sprang up on the Italian's skin, they sprang up on his too. He was too turned on to think. More turned on than he should've been. And he didn't stop. Didn't want to stop.

Dizzy and breathless, he let his lips graze Domenico's neck, and he was rewarded with a helpless moan that made his whole body tingle.

And before he could think twice, he whispered, "My name—" He shivered hard, thrusting against him like he was thrusting inside him. "Sergei." His pulse sped up— none of his contacts had his real name, but Domenico did. Why? He didn't know. He didn't care. He just needed… this time… "My name is Sergei."

"Sergei," Domenico breathed, as if it was the sexiest thing he'd ever heard. "Are you close?" He looked up at Sergei, eyes wide and watering. "Please tell me you're close."

"I…" Oh God, he was. Sergei had never gotten off in one of these rooms, never come during a lap dance, but he was right there on the edge, on the brink of blowing his load all over this Italian's expensive shirt, and he should've backed off, but he wasn't interested in coming to his senses. He wanted nothing else in that moment, nothing more in the whole fucking world, than to come.

Sergei sat up, holding onto Domenico's shoulders, and thrust against him, and Domenico groaned and whispered, "Ooh, yeah…"

"Gonna…" Sergei gripped his shoulders tighter. "Oh shit…" His eyes rolled back, his balls tightened, and even over the deafening music, he heard himself whimper.

"God, yeah," Domenico groaned. "That's… shit, that's hot. Come, Sergei."

Everything went white. Sergei arched against him, thrusting against wet silk until a shudder almost knocked his arms out from under him. He slumped over Domenico, trembling from head to toe. This was the first time ever—

since he'd discovered he could make a fortune by grinding against a man in a dark back room—that he'd come during a lap dance. That he'd even come inside this godforsaken building.

And he'd come all over Domenico's shirt and tie. For a split second, he thought Domenico would get upset, but then the breathless Italian whispered, "That was the hottest fucking thing I've ever seen."

"G-good." Sergei licked his lips as he struggled to hold himself up on shaking arms.

"Can I touch you?"

Sergei swallowed. It was strictly against club policy, but so was coming on a guy's shirt during an illegally naked lap dance. Nothing about Domenico pegged his danger radar now—chances were, he had no idea who Sergei really was, and at least the men near the top in his world were usually civilized when it came to those not involved in the Mob.

"Yeah," Sergei panted. "You can—"

Domenico cupped Sergei's face and kissed him.

Every instinct Sergei had honed as both a killer and a stripper screamed at him to shove the man back and get the fuck out of there, but…

But.

Domenico's fingers twitched against the sides of Sergei's face. His lips were softer and gentler than he'd thought they could be. If not for the coarse stubble abrading his chin, Sergei might've forgotten this uncertain tough guy was a Sicilian wise guy. That he was Domenico Maisano, for God's sake.

He couldn't help it—his curiosity got the best of him. He opened to Domenico's kiss, and let himself be pulled in closer as Domenico gently explored his mouth. Against his better judgement, he slid a hand into Domenico's hair, cradling the back of his head as lips and tongues sent

Sergei's pulse into overdrive. Domenico was tentative, and yet bold at the same time, his hands light on Sergei's skin even as his mouth demanded more.

Eventually, Sergei lifted his head. Domenico stared up at him, and goddamn, he looked as surprised as Sergei felt. They were both out of breath, Sergei's hips pressed against Domenico's rock-hard dick, and even though Sergei had already come, that look in Domenico's eyes sent his heart rate surging upward.

The bass in the lounge thumped against Sergei's nerve endings, reminding him where he was, why he was here, what the laws and common sense said he could and couldn't do.

Knees shaking, Sergei got to his feet, thankful for the muscle memory that kept the motion graceful and deliberate when he felt this clumsy.

As Sergei pulled on his G-string, Domenico rose. He didn't say a word, and they both cleaned off and straightened their clothes, Domenico tugging at his tie and his sleeves while Sergei shimmied into the barely-there leather shorts.

Then they faced each other, and before Sergei could make heads or tails of any goddamned thing, Domenico held up a card between two fingers. "I want to see you again."

Sergei took the card. His mind knew of at least a thousand reasons why that was a bad idea, but his body was definitely intrigued. He shouldn't have wanted a damned thing to do with him, and he should've turned tail and gotten the fuck away from him, but he wanted to know what it was like to get him alone.

"See me again?" Sergei thumbed the edge of the card. "When?"

"Soon." Domenico ran the backs of his fingers down

Sergei's arm. "Very soon."

Sergei looked him up and down, sizing him up. Domenico was a few inches taller, and much wider in the shoulders. If Sergei didn't know a fuckton of ways to kill men twice his size without breaking a sweat, he'd have backed away. He told himself that, anyhow. Standing this close to him, smelling his cologne and sweat as Domenico loomed over him with cum all over his shirt, Sergei was half-tempted to suggest they fuck there and then.

He'd probably lost all the good sense he'd had left, but at least he was losing it with someone who had as much reason as he did to keep his trap shut. More reason, actu-ally. All Sergei had to do was leak it to the world—or the media—that he'd had sex with Domenico Maisano, and his family would have him killed. Fags didn't last long in their world.

Sergei wasn't worried about his own safety. Only a handful of Mafiosi knew who he was. They *all* knew him by reputation, but nothing more. His very, *very* select few contacts knew his face and his profession, but they didn't know his real name, and they absolutely knew what would happen if they betrayed his confidence. Outside those contacts, no one—least of all the man in front of him with the cum-stained shirt—knew the killer who handled the lion's share of all three families' hits was a smart-mouthed bleach blond stripper.

"There's…" He hesitated. "There's a motel near the waterfront. The Sandpiper. My shift is over at one thirty."

Domenico glanced at his watch. Then he nodded. "I'll meet you there."

"Get a room. Put it under the name Sullivan."

"Okay."

They held each other's gazes. Then Domenico straight-ened his wet tie, buttoned his jacket, and started to go, but then he paused. He met Sergei's eyes. "By the way, um… thanks. For what you did that night. In the alley."

"Don't mention it." Sergei hadn't done it for any altruistic reasons, but he had to admit, he was glad this guy hadn't been killed. In a weird way, he was starting to like him.

They held eye contact for a few more seconds. Then Dom broke eye contact and brushed past Sergei.

Sergei exhaled. He ran a shaky hand through his hair, wondering what the hell had just happened. Or what was going to happen later tonight. Or why in the world he thought this was anything but a stupid, potentially deadly idea.

Mind reeling, he straightened his hair just for something to do. Then he headed back out to the lounge.

Domenico was nowhere to be seen. Good. He was serious about the whole discretion thing, and wasn't a complete fuckwit about it.

Sergei looked down at the card in his hand. There was a handwritten phone number and nothing else. If he had any sense at all, he'd have set that card on fire and never let Domenico cross his mind again.

But it was too late for that. Sergei was intrigued.

He had to know what it was like to fuck Domenico Maisano.

Chapter 8

Dom left the club and drove a few blocks before he had to pull over and collect his thoughts. He scrubbed his hands over his face, but that didn't help—he could still smell Sergei's cologne, sweat, and semen.

Semen? Had he really...

He looked down at his shirt and the damp spot he hadn't been able to completely wipe away. Holy shit. He'd lost his mind. He shouldn't have even been in that club, never mind letting a stripper come all over him and then making plans to meet that stripper later for sex.

A shiver ran through him. In his mind's eye, he could still see Sergei's face in that unbearably hot moment—eyes screwed shut, lips apart, fair skin flushed as he'd rubbed against Dom and shuddered. And that kiss. Maybe it had just been too long since he'd kissed a man, but Dom couldn't remember a kiss ever turning him inside out like Sergei's had.

He stared out the windshield. What the fuck was he *doing*? For all he knew, this kid was a goddamned sociopath. He was, after all, capable of cold-blooded murder. That hadn't been self-defense. Not when they were bound and gagged in the trunk of a car, and dispatched with two expertly-placed rounds apiece. And the bullet to Mandanici's knee? Even if that had happened by accident—say, during a scuffle—a lot of time had passed between that wound and the lethal one.

But still, something about Sergei drew him in. Dom couldn't deny that the cold detachment was part of it. Sergei was so in control, and all Dom could think was that Sergei was exactly what he needed so he could *lose* control.

And when Sergei's control wavered, as it had tonight in that private booth, he was mesmerizing. Dom wanted more. He wanted to get under his skin. He wanted to see him and hear him and taste him when he let go completely. He needed to know what it felt like to—

His phone buzzed. He jumped, and panic shot through him. Was Sergei canceling?

He dug his phone out of his pocket and looked at the screen.

Shit—that wasn't a call he could ignore.

"Hello, Biaggio. What's—"

"Where have you been?" the consigliere snapped. "I've been trying to reach you for the past half hour."

Dom gulped. "Sorry. I was out on the highway. No signal."

Biaggio huffed sharply. "Well, I hope you're back in town now. Your uncle wants to speak with you."

Dom mouthed a curse. Unless he had a damn good reason—one that involved blood, in most cases—Corrado didn't like excuses. If he wanted to speak with him, that meant *now*. Dom just hoped this meeting was a quick one.

"I'll be there as soon as I can."

"How long?"

"Thirty minutes. Forty-five tops."

"I'll let him know."

Dom hung up and pulled out on the road again. He was only about twenty minutes away, but first, he needed to stop by his own place long enough to change his shirt. Better to walk into his uncle's office a few minutes late than with semen on his shirt. While he was there, he grabbed some condoms and lube from the bedside table. One less stop to make en route to the motel, and thank God, the condoms weren't expired.

Then he headed straight for his uncle's house.

ON THE WAY down the hall toward Corrado's office, Biaggio wrinkled his nose. "My God, Domenico. That cologne is horrible."

Cologne? He wasn't wearing any—

Dom took a breath and caught the lingering scents of leather, sweat, and—though he was probably imagining it, since he'd changed his shirt—other traces of Sergei. He cleared his throat. "Smelled better in the store, I guess."

Biaggio clicked his tongue but let the subject go. In silence, they walked on, and when they reached the massive double doors, one of Corrado's security guys pushed it open and gestured for them to go in.

The office was crowded with several of Corrado's top men. Near the desk, Felice and Luciano hovered, speaking in hushed tones.

The air was tense. Something had happened.

Biaggio stepped around behind Corrado's desk and whispered something to the old man. Corrado lifted his gaze, and looked right at Dom. Then he stood, waving a hand. "Luciano, Felice, Dom—stay. Everyone else—out."

Immediately, everyone headed for the door, and within

seconds, they were alone. Biaggio didn't even stay, which was weird—he knew every bit of the family's inner workings, and Corrado's secrets were Biaggio's secrets.

With only the immediate family remaining, Corrado sat back in his enormous leather chair. "Nicolá's body was found early this morning."

Dom's stomach dropped. Death was a routine part of this life, but it was still hard to lose someone he knew. He turned to Luciano. "Does Serafina know yet?"

Grimacing, he nodded. "I told her this afternoon."

"Is she…"

"She's devastated," he whispered.

Dom exhaled. As much as he disliked Luciano's wife, she'd adored her brother. Hell, they all had. "You'll give her my condolences?"

"I will. Thank you."

Dom nodded, and turned back to his uncle. "What happened?"

"Run down out on the 103." Corrado folded his long fingers, and his voice was nearly a growl as he added, "By a drunk Eugenio Cusimano."

"Eugenio—" Dom inclined his head. "Run down? As in, on foot?"

Corrado scowled, and nodded slowly.

"What the hell was he doing out there?"

"We don't know. It sounds like it happened last night, but it took until today to find the body. A medic stumbled across it, actually, while they were investigating a one-car 'accident' in the vicinity."

Dom shifted his weight. "That doesn't make any sense."

"I know." Corrado took in a long breath. "This was no accident, and someone is going to bleed for it." The vicious undertone of his uncle's voice made Dom's skin crawl; he was only too aware of what Corrado was capable of.

"I've got ears open on the investigation." Luciano spoke up, his voice quiet and calm despite the shock of his brother-in-law's death. "But word is that Eugenio was drunk off his ass and—"

Felice laughed bitterly. "He's *always* drunk. And if the Cusimanos won't keep a leash on him, then we'll have to take care of him before he kills another of our own. He's fucked up enough, Dad. It's long past time to—"

Corrado put up a hand. "We'll take care of him when I say we do, and that won't be until after we're certain of his connection to Nicolá's death."

Felice's expression darkened. "Cusimano was found almost half a mile up the road in a ditch. With blood on the windshield *and* on the bumper. If that blood doesn't match Nicolá, I'll eat my hat."

"Wait." Dom grimaced. "A half mile up the road? So, he hit him and kept driving?"

"Yes," Luciano said. "Don't know if it was an accident or deliberate, but there's no way he didn't notice when he hit Nicolá. My contact says it wasn't just a sideswipe." An angry undercurrent was slowly working its way into Luciano's voice. "He didn't clip him—he hit him dead-on. Took him up on the windshield and tossed him into a ditch."

"Then why are we fucking around and not offing this asshole?" Felice snapped. To his brother, he said, "For God's sake, this is the man who keeps trying to fuck your wife, and—"

"I'm aware of that," Luciano snarled back. "But I'm not shooting anyone until—"

"Until I give the order." Corrado glared at both of his sons. "No one makes a move without my say-so."

Felice clenched his jaw but didn't speak. He'd been closer to Nicolá than Luciano—regardless of Corrado's decision or permission, this would *not* go unanswered.

Corrado met Dom's gaze, and the subtle arch of his eyebrow told Dom everything he needed to know. Indeed, Nicolá's death would not go unanswered, but it wouldn't be Felice who carried out the sentence.

Dom responded with a nod that was just as subtle. Though neither of them said a word, he understood all too well what his task would be. There were plenty of hitmen in this town who worked as contractors, but no one suspected that Dom was Corrado's hired gun. His own royal assassin, as he'd somewhat jokingly called him after his second or third hit.

Beside him, Felice bristled. "Dad, we need to be proactive. Even if that idiot didn't kill Nicolá, the Cusimanos are out of control. They *need* to know we aren't going to tolerate—"

"The Cusimanos know where I stand on their encroachment of our businesses," Corrado snapped. "I will not have blood spilled over trade relations until it's clear we've exhausted all other means for resolving our differences."

Felice cursed in Italian under his breath.

Dom and Luciano exchanged uneasy glances. The Cusimanos had been aggressively elbowing their way into Maisano stakes in both immigrant processing and cocaine distribution, not just eroding their bottom line but taking it in chunks. Several of the more business savvy and diplomatic members of the family's leadership had been killed in the last couple of years, replaced by these psychos who would stop at nothing to claim a monopoly in Cape Swan. Things were going to get violent sooner or later. It was just a matter of who drew first blood. Or if Nicolá had been that first blood. If not him, then someone else, and it was up to Corrado to decide who.

Assuming, of course, that Felice didn't take matters into his own hands.

"We'll wait until the investigation is complete," Corrado said. "With the police involved, every eye is going to be on us, just as they were after Barcia washed up. No one makes a move until I order it. Am I clear?"

Luciano, Felice, and Dom all nodded and muttered, "Yes."

"Good. Out of my office." He paused. "Dom, you stay here."

Dom planted his feet. His cousins shot him looks—a puzzled one from Luciano, an undeniably hostile one from Felice—but quickly vacated.

Alone with his uncle, Dom waited.

"Eugenio Cusimano is becoming a problem," Corrado said at last.

"So you're sure he did this?"

"Of course." Corrado steepled his fingers. "I should have taken him out before he killed Nicolá. He's becoming a thorn in my side." He exhaled. "Felice didn't tell me until tonight, but that bastard Eugenio made an attempt on Luciano a few nights ago."

Dom's gut flipped. "What?"

"Someone fired through the front window of his house, but no one inside was hit."

Wow. Luciano's house, like Corrado's and Dom's own, was walled off and set far back from the road behind a couple of hills, guarded by everything from cameras to Dobermans. Getting a bullet through a window of that house meant firing from a sniper perch *well* within the walls.

"Fortunately," Corrado went on, "the children were out

with their mother." He slid a small envelope across the desk. "Even though Luciano was unharmed, this was clearly meant to either kill him or send a message."

Dom nodded and took the envelope. The families were getting more and more violent lately. Slights were answered with murder, and murder was answered with more murder.

Dom opened the envelope and pulled out the photo. It was grainy surveillance footage of a sniper in a perch near Luciano's house. Dom couldn't see the guy's face very well, but the rifle was obvious, and he recognized the poplar tree beside Luciano's long driveway.

"And you're sure this is Cusimano?"

Corrado nodded. "Felice was there that night. Got a good look."

"But he's just now saying something about it?"

Shaking his head, Corrado sighed. "He thought he'd take care of it himself. God knows what he would've done to Eugenio if last night's... incident hadn't happened."

"Maybe we should let him."

"Absolutely not. If he starts thinking he can take things into his own hands, there'll be no reining him back in."

"Good point." Dom eyed the photo for a moment, then looked across the desk. "I'm surprised Luciano hasn't tried to fuck up Eugenio for trying to sleep with Serafina."

Corrado's lips pulled into a bleached line, and he nodded. "Indeed. And I suspect that's part of why Eugenio took a shot at Luciano. Remove the husband, and the woman becomes available."

"She'd be quite the merry widow too," Dom grumbled.

Corrado glared at him, but didn't argue. Everyone knew Luciano's wife had affairs all over Cape Swan. Leaping into bed with a Cusimano right after her own husband's funeral wouldn't be a tremendous stretch for her, but she knew better—as far as they all knew—than to bed a rival Mafioso while Luciano was still alive. The woman was lucky her father-in-law drew the line at taking out hits on women.

"We'll see what conclusion the medical examiner comes to," Corrado said coldly. "And then… well."

Dom nodded. His insides twisted and knotted. Eugenio Cusimano was a made man, a soldier who was close to both sons of the boss, Raffaele Cusimano. High enough in the ranks to know better, close enough to the upper echelon to matter.

Which meant Corrado wouldn't want him let off easy, and he wouldn't leave the man's punishment in the hands of just anyone. When Corrado played judge and jury, he chose his executioners like some men chose fine wines.

It was only a matter of time, then, before he gave Dom the word.

"That'll be all," Corrado said. "And be vigilant, Domenico. The violence is getting worse, and we might have a war on our hands before all this is over."

"Understood," Dom whispered. There hadn't been a turf war in this town in decades, and the last one had left scores of bodies in its wake. The Frazzano family had been wiped off the map, and the Passantinos had taken years to recover. Strong as the Maisanos were, no one wanted that degree of bloodshed again.

"Before you go," Corrado said, "there's one more thing."

Dom fought the urge to check his watch. Sergei would be leaving the club soon, and he doubted he'd wait around if he showed up to the motel and Dom wasn't there.

Corrado studied him for a few long seconds. "You've been out of sorts lately. Ever since the incident with Floresta and Mandanici."

Dom shrugged, avoiding his uncle's gaze. "Just keep

rethinking that night, trying to figure out how they got the drop on me."

"How *did* they get the drop on you?" The accusation wasn't overt, but it was there.

"I'm still not sure, but I'll figure it out."

"Good." Which, from Corrado, meant, *You'd damn well better figure it out, idiot.* "Have you made arrangements to see Brigida Passantino?"

Dom fought the urge to shift his weight, and lifted his gaze. "She's in Italy. Her father insisted, just in case there was more violence."

Corrado grunted, nodding slightly. "I suppose that's prudent."

"I agree. When she comes back, though, I'll make arrangements."

"Good." *Sooner than later, if you know what's good for you.*

And once he did see Brigida, the pressure would be on for them to get married and cement the civil relations between the two families.

And now he suddenly needed this night with Sergei even more. The hit wasn't official, but he'd have been an idiot to think it wasn't coming, and that it wasn't coming soon. There was no avoiding it. There was no avoiding any murder his uncle ordered him to commit. Whether he liked it or not—and he didn't—Dom was going to have more blood on his hands soon.

Corrado leaned back in his chair. "When I know for certain Eugenio took out Nicolá, I'll let you know. At this point, focus on picking up where you left off with Brigida. Understand?"

"Yes."

His uncle waved him toward the door. "We'll speak soon." Translation: *Get the hell out of my office.*

Dom didn't wait around. He left Corrado's house and

put the pedal to the floor. The motel was on the other side of town, and even a small town like Cape Swan still took time to cross. Thank God there weren't many other cars out this time of night.

On the way, he tried to focus on the job Corrado would be giving him soon, but it was pointless. Tonight, he had other things on his mind. Tomorrow, he'd work out exactly how to remove Eugenio Cusimano when the time came.

On the other side of town, he drove past the agreed-upon motel and parked a few blocks down. Then he walked back, eyeing his surroundings just in case anyone had followed him or suddenly took a nefarious interest in him. No one did. No one was around at all. The whole place was silent except for some crickets in the bushes and the tinny, muffled sound of a TV in someone's room.

A green neon Vacancy sign buzzed halfheartedly above the office. Dom paid cash for the room and gave the receptionist the fake name, and she gave him the key. Upstairs, he let himself into the room. It was small, not particularly nice, but it had a bed and a shower, so it would do.

All he needed now was Sergei.

It was creeping up on one forty-five in the morning, so hopefully Sergei hadn't already been there and gone. On the other hand, he might very well have been there, waiting for Dom to get them a room, and he would materialize from the shadows when he was ready to be seen.

For now, Dom shrugged off his jacket. Set the condoms and lube on the table.

And waited.

Chapter 9

Per their agreement, Sergei picked up the room key from the half-asleep receptionist. She didn't ask for an ID and didn't so much as raise an eyebrow over the false name he gave her. This was the kind of shithole where rooms were rented by the hour and bodies were occasionally found, so she was probably unflappable by this point.

Just as well.

Keep your head down, sweetheart. The less you see around here, the better.

The room was on the second floor with an interior entrance. Good—places like this didn't have cameras, and interior hallways meant fewer witnesses. Not that he and Domenico were doing anything illegal, but for those dancing the dangerous dance of contract work for the Mafia, there was something to be said for not being seen slipping into a motel room with a made man at two thirty in the morning.

He keyed himself into the room. Immediately, he was aware of Domenico, but as he closed the door behind him, he paused to do a quick sweep, taking in every detail of his surroundings.

One bed. A small dresser with an old TV that still had rabbit ear antennas. A table and chairs on the other side of the bed. Domenico sat in one of the chairs. His jacket was draped over the back of the other, and a paperback novel was facedown on the table next to a half empty bottle of some prissy-ass brand of water. Beneath the jacket was a shoulder holster, the edge of a wood grain pistol butt sticking out. Probably a .357—every fucking Maisano loved his .357 revolver for some reason.

Beside the paperback was an unopened bottle of lube and a new pack of condoms. Magnum. Good.

And from beside that table, Domenico watched him. He sat in the crappy little armchair, legs crossed and tie loosened. He sipped his water like he was drinking top of the line brandy from a highball, watching Sergei over the rim with unreadable eyes.

He didn't move, aside from tipping the glass against his lips. Sergei didn't move either.

An odd silence settled between them. Sergei was used to being onstage in front of gawking men, but this was unnerving. Like he was being displayed and was expected to perform a dance he didn't know. "Are we just going to stare at each other all night?"

"Of course not." Domenico set the glass down with a quiet click that echoed up Sergei's spine. "I just..." He slowly gave Sergei a down-up that was weirdly appreciative. Not a leer, nothing creepy. The way he might've looked over a painting or a new car—scrutinizing, and yet somehow admiring.

His eyes met Sergei's, and almost sent him back a step. Sergei barely heard him whisper, "You're fucking beautiful."

"I…" Sergei swallowed. "Thanks?"

"Would you do something for me?"

Sergei held his gaze. "I hope you don't think I'm here as a whore."

"A—no! No. God, no." He put up his hands and shook his head. "I didn't mean it like that. But I… look, you can say no, and no hard feelings. Consider it a favor." His voice was smooth even when he was stumbling over words. Sergei noticed now that Domenico didn't have that affected New York Italian accent a lot of the Mafiosi had in this town. His voice carried a hint of the Old Country, but not a trace of New York, and Sergei liked it more than he probably should have.

"A favor?" Sergei resisted the urge to shift his weight. "What kind of favor?"

"I want to see you strip."

Sergei narrowed his eyes. "If you wanted another dance, we—"

"No, not like that." Domenico fidgeted in the chair, and his prominent erection pressed against the front of his expensive trousers. "Not a dance. It… to be honest, I rarely have the chance to be with a man. I barely had a chance to really see you at the club, so before we get to…" His eyes darted toward the bed, then back at Sergei, as if this Mafioso who'd worn his semen out of a club was suddenly too shy to say he wanted to have sex. "First, I just want to look at you."

Sergei swallowed. "So you…"

"No dancing. Nothing like that." He gestured at Sergei. "I just want to see what you really look like."

Sergei didn't move yet. This still felt weird. Like they'd met up to have some casual sex as two horny guys, and now they were back to a horny guy and a stripper.

"I know it sounds weird." Domenico's voice was gentle

and not in the least bit patronizing. "I know. Believe me. But I…" He swallowed, shifting in his chair. "If you'd rather not, I'll understand."

Sergei hesitated. He moistened his lips. Domenico might've been about to say something else, but Sergei peeled off his T-shirt, and Domenico was suddenly mesmerized. The Italian's breath caught. He sat back, and neither of them said a word as Sergei started unbuckling his belt. The room was so quiet, the sound of his zipper seemed to echo off the walls. He wasn't adding any flourish this time—no circling or thrusting with his hips, no undulating his abs—just methodically taking everything off.

The last to go were his black briefs. When Sergei dropped them on top of his other clothes, Domenico jumped like a bomb had gone off. He stared up at Sergei, eyes wide and lips apart, looking equal parts hypnotized and scared out of his mind.

"Well?" Sergei grinned despite the weirdness of this situation. He gestured at himself. "What do you think?"

"I think…" Domenico just stared. After a moment, he drained his glass and set it aside. Then he stood.

Sergei fought the urge to gulp nervously. He wasn't going to show any uncertainty. Not to this guy. But he was nervous. This was a position he'd never been in before—completely naked, hard, vulnerable, in front of a fully-dressed and well-armed Mafioso.

This was a mistake. I shouldn't have come here. I—

"Can I…" Domenico lifted a hand as if he were about to reach for Sergei, but then pulled it back, hesitating like someone afraid of a potentially dangerous dog. "I'm…"

Sergei took his wrist and guided his hand to him. "You say you've rarely had a chance to be with a man." He brought Domenico's hand down on his waist, letting it rest just above his hip. "Does that mean you're a virgin?"

"No." Domenico stared at him for a moment, as if drinking in the sight of him for the very first time. "Definitely... definitely not a virgin. It's just been a while." He took a breath. "I've seen you naked once already, but it's different this time." He met Sergei's eyes. "I can touch you all I want." He tensed a little. "Right?"

Please do. Sergei licked his lips. "Yes."

Most men would have gone straight for Sergei's cock, or done some clumsy groping. Domenico was apparently not most men—the first thing he did was run the backs of his fingers down the center of Sergei's chest. Creases formed between his eyebrows as he watched his hand drift down Sergei's abs, and when the vaguely ticklish touch made Sergei's muscles contract, Domenico pushed out a ragged breath.

He turned his hand over as he brought it back up, and this time, went all the way to the back of Sergei's neck. For a split second, Sergei's defenses surged up—that strong hand was too close to his throat—but Domenico changed direction and traced the length of his arm instead.

Sergei swallowed. "You said it's been a while."

Domenico nodded.

"How long is a while?"

"Too long." Domenico met his gaze. "We both know what I am. Men like me aren't gay. Not if they want to survive."

Sergei nodded. "So I've heard. But... you are."

Domenico nodded, his gaze drifting to Sergei's erection. "Very."

"That makes two of us." Sergei stepped closer and ran his hand over the very prominent bulge in Domenico's trousers, making the man gasp and squeeze his eyes shut.

Sergei grinned. "But now you've seen me naked twice, and you still haven't shown me anything, Domenico."

Domenico flinched. He opened his eyes. "Just call me Dom."

"Okay. Dom." Sergei swept his tongue across his lips. "You haven't shown me anything." He lifted his hand away, and Domenico—Dom—tensed as if Sergei had smacked him. Speaking softly, Sergei said, "Let me see what you're hiding under your suit."

Dom hesitated. His Adam's apple bobbed above his collar. Then he unbuttoned the collar. The next button. The one below that.

Sergei stepped back. He closed his fingers around his own cock and started stroking.

Dom's lips parted. He fumbled with the next button, gaze fixed on Sergei's dick while his motor skills seemed deteriorate a little more every time Sergei's hand crested the head of his cock. Maybe it was the sight of a naked, aroused man, or maybe the realization that he was going to be able to do more than just look—whatever the case, Dom couldn't have faked that level of distraction if he'd tried.

And that turned Sergei on something fierce. Reducing a client to a blubbering mess was part of his job. He was paid to tease them until they couldn't see straight.

This was a man who knew he was going to have sex with Sergei tonight, and he was so nervous, turned on, excited that he couldn't even work the buttons of a shirt he'd likely worn a million times.

"Am I distracting you?" Sergei asked.

"Just a little." Dom cleared his throat and looked down, focusing on undoing the buttons instead of staring at Sergei's cock. Once the buttons were undone, he took off one cufflink, then the other. Watching that fucked with

Sergei's head almost as much as his strokes had fucked with Dom's—well-dressed men turned him on, and the little details made him dizzy. Cufflinks especially.

Dom took off his shirt and undershirt.

Sergei gulped. Holy fuck. There were men in this town who were just good racks for expensive suits. The suits made them irresistible, but as soon as they were off, Sergei's erection was gone and so was he.

Dom was not one of those guys. He wore his Sicilian genes as well as he wore Armani, and a body like that would've been just as hot in a skintight wife beater. Tan skin. Muscles that didn't quit. Enough dark hair to make sure Sergei hadn't forgotten Dom was every bit a *man*.

And as Dom stripped out of his trousers and slipped off his boxers… yeah, Sergei could see why he'd picked up some Magnum condoms. Apparently small dicks *weren't* mandatory for Maisanos after all.

Dom put the last of his clothes aside, and faced Sergei. With a note of nervous laughter in his voice, he held out his arms. "Well? Like what you see?"

Sergei laughed. He stepped closer and ran his hands up Dom's bare chest, sliding his fingers through the thin hair. "I do like what I see."

"Good." Dom wrapped his arms around Sergei, his warm skin making Sergei's pulse jump. "I hope you're planning on doing more than just seeing it."

"You're damn right I'm—"

Dom cut him off with a kiss so soft it could almost have been mistaken for tenderness.

Sergei froze. That wasn't a kiss that belonged… here. In a room like this. In an encounter like this.

Dom drew back a little. "Something wrong? You—"

Sergei grabbed him and pulled him back into a kiss, and Dom held him closer. Sergei pushed Dom's lips apart with his tongue, and Dom's fingers twitched against Sergei's skin as the kiss deepened.

By now, they should have been in bed, making out and groping until one of them finally came up for air long enough to put on a condom. But they didn't move. They stood in the middle of the room, skin to skin, arms around each other and kissing like… like…

Like this. It was as if no one had ever given Dom the memo about the difference between fucking and making love. About how to kiss a one-night stand versus how to kiss a boyfriend.

Sergei wasn't going to give him that memo, though. If it had been a long time since Dom had been with a man, it had been even longer since anyone had kissed Sergei like this.

He led Dom toward the bed. When they got there, before Sergei could pull away and suggest they move from vertical to horizontal, Dom cradled the back of his head in one hand, wrapped the other arm around his waist, and lowered him onto the mattress. Sergei's pulse went crazy—as much as he liked to get down to business and get rough, he had a weakness for a man with a soft touch. A man who could be in bed with someone he may very well have viewed as a prostitute, and still hold onto him like he would have with someone he actually cared about.

Sergei hated larger men on top—it tripped every survival instinct he had. He didn't like being pinned or cornered, and the laws of physics gave a bigger guy an advantage. But Dom's body felt good on top of his. Being underneath a made man was dangerous, but there was something oddly… safe about him. Non-threatening, anyway, which was weird for a career criminal who was so much bigger and likely stronger than Sergei. The lion getting cuddly with the lamb—he didn't need to know that the lamb was a wolf in sheep's clothing.

This was wrong. All wrong. Dom was one of them. He shouldn't have… he…

He was kissing Sergei's neck, soft lips and coarse stubble skating across flesh, and Sergei couldn't stop himself from tilting his head back to expose more. It didn't make any sense, baring his throat to a man like Dom, but those featherlight kisses were addictive.

Dom kissed him all over—down his throat, his chest, his abs. Every touch seemed genuinely appreciative, too. He'd press a soft kiss to Sergei's skin, wait for a response— a hitch in his breath or a quiver of muscle—and then he'd move down a little and nip gently or flick his tongue, and again wait for a response.

He continued down, down, down, and Sergei couldn't breathe as Dom kissed his way along the ridge of his hipbone. Warm breath. Soft kisses. Rough stubble. All inching toward Sergei's hard-on.

Oh yes. Please. Do it.

Yes.

Like that. Holy shit. Holy…

Sergei stared up at the ceiling with watering eyes. He couldn't remember the last man who'd been *so into* giving head. Dom groaned with pleasure, his breath hot on Sergei's skin and his voice vibrating against sensitive nerve endings.

Sergei combed his fingers through Dom's hair. This was not what he'd expected tonight. Not even a little bit. It was dangerous, too, but it didn't feel dangerous. It was sexy and amazing, and nothing else mattered.

Dom stopped abruptly and pushed himself up. "If I keep doing that," he panted, "I'll come too soon."

"You'll come?" Sergei reached for Dom and pulled

him down on top of him. "You're not the one who was getting his dick sucked."

"I think you underestimate how long it's been since I've done this." Dom kissed him deeply, tenderly, hungrily. "Just being here with you turns me on. I can't... I can't even describe..."

"Then don't." Sergei pulled Dom all the way down, and let himself get completely lost in Dom's kiss. This may have been completely physical sex with no investment whatsoever, and maybe he was just a sex worker to Dom, but God, Sergei liked the way this man felt against him and on top of him. And though Dom wasn't a virgin, he may as well have been, and in an innocent, endearing kind of way that Sergei liked.

Dom broke the kiss and started on Sergei's neck again. "The whole time you were dancing," he whispered against Sergei's skin, "all I could think was how good you were with your hips." He kissed beneath his ear, making Sergei shiver. "Tell me you fuck as good as you dance."

Oh. God.

"Only one way to find out." *Why am I shaking?*

"I'll get a condom."

Sergei let him go, and Dom got up long enough to retrieve the condoms and lube from the table. Dom tore open the box of condoms, but their eyes met, and his hands stopped.

Sergei reached for him, grabbed his neck, pulled him in, kissed him. God, he wanted to fuck Dom, but he had to kiss him again, and Dom didn't protest at all. The gentleness was gone now. They kissed hard, taking sharp breaths through their noses and gripping each other's shoulders, arms, necks—whatever they could get their hands on.

Sergei couldn't take anymore. "Turn around," he breathed.

He fully expected Dom to put up a fight, insisting he'd be on top, but instead, he damn near tore himself out of Sergei's grasp and turned around. Sergei's heart sped up as Dom leaned forward onto his hands.

"You want to be fucked, don't you?"

Dom nodded. "*Yes.*"

Sergei grabbed the partially open box of condoms. He tore one of the strip and tossed the rest on the nightstand. "You've done this before? Bottomed?"

"Not… recently."

"I'll go slow." Slow sounded both torturous and amazing. As much as he wanted to pound Dom into oblivion, the thought of fucking him slowly was enough to make Sergei's hands tremble as he rolled on the condom while Dom got on his hands and knees.

Sergei put some lube on his index and middle fingers. Steadying them both with a hand on Dom's hip, he pressed a slick finger against Dom's tight hole. Carefully, patiently, he worked his fingertip in.

"Fuck," Dom breathed as Sergei teased him open.

"Doesn't hurt, does it?"

"N-no." Dom shook his head. "Just… intense."

"As it should be." Sergei fucked him with a finger for a moment, and then added a second. Jesus—he could have listened to Dom moan like that all damned night. Helplessly, hungrily, as if this—just being fucked by a couple of fingers—was the most amazing thing he'd ever felt.

Sergei's mouth watered. If Dom was this responsive…

He shivered. Gently, he stretched him, pushing his fingers apart as he slid them in and out.

"Just fuck me," Dom slurred. "C'mon. Please."

Sergei chuckled. "Eager?"

"Very."

"Good." Sergei withdrew his fingers. He put some lube

on his cock, and some more on Dom. Then he guided himself to Dom and pushed against him. After just a second of resistance, Dom yielded to him. Sergei eased himself inside—sliding in, withdrawing, sliding in a little deeper.

They were both panting already. Cursing in their native tongues and English and maybe some other languages that they couldn't even identify. Sergei knew as many ways to tease a man as he did to kill him. Tonight, he didn't care about impressing him with any hip-centric sex voodoo. The only thing that mattered was getting as deep inside him as he could, fast and hard. Sex wasn't an art form tonight—Dom had tapped into some primal, animalistic side of Sergei, and there was no reining it back in. Not until he came. And Dom came. And they both came again.

Gritting his teeth, Sergei slammed into him. "This hurt?"

Dom's head fell forward, and his shoulders rippled. "N-no."

Sergei held his hips tighter and fucked him even harder. "How about now?"

Dom cried out, and God knew if it was pain or pleasure, but he didn't try to stop him. He dug the heels of his hands into the bed and rocked against him, and it was even getting painful for Sergei now. Fuck, but he felt good.

Little by little, Dom fell apart, swearing and shaking, hopefully unaware of how difficult it was for Sergei to concentrate on keeping a steady rhythm. Sergei's muscles burned. After a full shift at the club, he should've been completely exhausted, but he kept fucking Dom, kept slamming into him, silently begging him to—

Dom cursed aloud in Italian, and clenched around Sergei. "My God…"

And for the second time tonight, Sergei lost it, this time

deep inside Dom. He thrust as hard as he could, squeezing his eyes shut and cursing in his own mother tongue.

Dom relaxed. Then Sergei did. Together, they sank down to the bed, and Sergei panted against Dom's shoulder.

"Holy fuck," Dom murmured. "That was…" He trailed off, slurring something in Italian.

"That's good, right?"

"Very. Very good."

Sergei kissed the side of his neck. His arms were wet noodles, but when he could trust them to hold him up, he carefully pulled out, and then got up to get rid of the condom.

When he returned to the bed, they shifted around and collapsed on the pillows, side by side. Not cuddling, but not on opposite sides of the mattress either.

For the longest time, neither of them spoke. Sergei couldn't quite believe he was lying beside a Mafioso. A Maisano, of all people. And it had occurred to him that it would be a hell of a "fuck you" to the family, knowing he'd been inside one of their own, but he didn't feel that way now. Dom was one of them, but he was different. He hadn't been selfish like the last man Sergei had been with, or rushed like the one before him.

Dom cleared his throat. "I, um… I noticed your accent earlier. Russian?"

Sergei nodded. Nerves, he guessed. Not sure what to say after a tryst like that, so he was making small talk.

The attempt at conversation didn't get off the ground, though, and the silence set in again.

After a while, Dom turned on his side, propping himself up on his elbow. "Listen, you already know what I am." His eyebrow rose slightly. "I'm sure I don't need to tell you that discretion is… a priority."

The dangerous undercurrent in his voice sent a chill through Sergei—either he trusted the promise to keep things quiet, or he'd already decided Sergei wouldn't have the opportunity to let his secret out. The presence of that .357 tingled on the ends of the hairs standing on the back of Sergei's neck.

Sergei wasn't afraid of him, just... alert. If Dom tried anything, he'd be expecting a terrified stripper to fight back. Surprise, motherfucker...

But he hadn't tried anything yet, so Sergei played it cool and didn't let on that he was mentally calculating a few escape strategies as he said, "I dance all over men who could lose their jobs and wives if anyone caught them. Discretion may as well be my stage name."

Dom laughed softly. "Discretion the Dancer. It's catchy. I like it." The upward curve of the corner of his mouth leveled out, and he watched himself trail the backs of his fingers down Sergei's arm. "To be serious, I need to be sure no one knows about this but us." His eyes flicked up and met Sergei's. "Especially if there's any possibility of continuing this... arrangement." The slightest lift of his eyebrow put the ball in Sergei's court.

"Continuing?"

Dom nodded. "I want to see you again."

Every instinct told him to run like hell, but they'd told him that at the club too. And at the door. Lying here now, body aching from sex with Dom, he was hard-pressed to convince himself this was a bad idea.

"Continue, how?" he asked. "Sleeping together?"

Dom nodded. "That's probably all I can offer or ask for."

"So I'd be... your concubine?" Sergei meant it playfully, but the words came out with slightly more venom than he'd intended. *I'm* not *a hooker*, he wanted to tersely remind him.

"If you think about it," Dom said quietly, "I'd be yours too."

"I hadn't thought of it that way."

"It's only good if we're both getting something out of it." Dom smoothed Sergei's hair. "But it can't go any farther than sex. And it's not forever. There's going to come a time when I have to get married. I'm not the slightest bit interested in women, but marrying one is part of the life I live, and once I do…" He shook his head, and his voice softened a bit as he ran his fingers down Sergei's arm again. "Once I do, there won't be any more of… this."

Sergei studied him. "So what you're telling me is that you want us to fuck on the down-low so you can get gay sex out of your system before you get married?"

Dom hesitated. "I'm not sure I'd put it quite that crudely, but… yeah. I guess."

If it had been any other man, Sergei would've told him where to shove that arrangement, but this time… he didn't. He liked the sex they'd had so far. He liked that this was discreet with no strings attached.

But that wasn't what made the decision for him. Regardless of their arrangement, Dom was the first man in a long time who'd touched him like a lover and not an object. Sergei had to admit, Mafioso or not, that was addictive.

"All right." He sat up. "Total discretion. Just sex."

Dom grinned. "You're in?"

Sergei licked his lips. "I'm in."

Chapter 10

Orgasm still tingling along his spine and curling his toes, Dom collapsed. Sergei dropped to the bed beside him. This was the… fourth night they'd met up? Fifth? He was losing track. The days and nights were starting to blur, especially since the two of them always met at eye-wateringly late hours, but he didn't care. As long as they kept burning up the sheets like this, he didn't care what day it was or how much he paid for it the next day.

Sergei kissed his temple, then got up to get rid of the condom. Eventually, they'd no doubt move to the bathroom for a shower, but for the moment, Dom didn't dare stand up. Not with his head still spinning and his knees still shaking.

His uncle would've had his head if he knew where Dom was spending the wee hours of most nights.

Let him find out. Dom wiped a hand over his sweaty face. *Don't fucking care. Feel too fucking good.*

He knew damn well this couldn't and wouldn't last long. Once Brigida Passantino was back from Italy, the pressure would be on again to think about getting married. As long as she was gone, though…

Sergei returned from the bathroom and climbed into bed again, his movements graceful and catlike even after he'd just finished fucking Dom for the second time tonight. He lay beside Dom and propped himself up on his elbow. "I'm curious about something."

"Hmm?"

Sergei studied him, his blue eyes intense with scrutiny. "You said it's been a long time since you've been with another man."

Dom nodded. "Almost fifteen years, I think."

"Why?"

"Why… has it been so long?"

"Yeah."

Dom moistened his lips. "It's too dangerous. If someone in the organization found out I was gay…"

"They'd shoot you." The comment was matter-of-fact. Not quite flippant, but not spoken with great concern.

Dom swallowed. "Yeah. Which means this can't get out or—"

"Dom. Relax." Sergei smiled, and the intensity in his eyes faded in favor of some actual warmth. Sliding a hand up Dom's chest, he said, "We've talked about this. I know the risks. And besides, it's not really in my best interest to out people." He paused, then gave a quiet laugh. "It would cut into my client base."

Dom raised his eyebrows. "You have one dark sense of humor."

Sergei shrugged unapologetically. "How else do you stay sane in a town like this one?"

"Is it even possible to stay sane in this town?"

Sobering a little, Sergei nodded. "Fair point. Makes you wonder why anyone stays here if they have a choice."

Dom laughed dryly. "No kidding. If I had half a chance…" Well. That wasn't even worth thinking about. No sense raising his own hopes, even with a fantasy that he knew could never happen. He shook himself and met Sergei's eyes. "Cape Swan's a shithole, that's for sure."

"Yes, it is." Sergei's hand drifted lower. "It does have its perks, though."

"Does it?"

"Mmhmm." He trailed a fingertip along Dom's thigh. "Some of the… locals are friendly."

Dom sucked in a sharp his as Sergei's hand neared his dick. They'd just finished fucking for the second time. No way in hell did he have enough for another go-round.

Right?

Maybe. But not yet. He took Sergei's hand and brought it up to his lips. As he kissed the backs of Sergei's long, fine fingers, he looked him in the eye. "You're going to be the death of me, you know that, right?"

Sergei swallowed. He blinked a couple of times, as if, despite his dark sense of humor, he had no idea what to say to that. "I…"

Dom let go of his hand and put his arm over him, drawing him closer. "The way you fuck me, you're definitely going to kill me." Just before their lips met, he whispered, "But what a way to go."

Sergei stiffened a little, but he didn't argue.

And then Dom kissed him, and Sergei slowly relaxed within his embrace. As the kiss went on, they held each other closer. Tighter.

Sergei's hips brushed his, and Dom shivered.

Hell. Maybe he had enough left for a third round tonight after all.

Chapter 11

Sergei glanced at his phone as he stepped into his apartment. He still had time before he needed to go meet Dom, and he'd already showered at the club and changed into more comfortable clothes.

He didn't leave yet, though.

He triple-locked his front door and moved into the bedroom. There, he reached under the bed and up into a hole he'd cut into the box spring. From there, he took down a steel box, which he set on the bed. He quickly dialed in the combination. The lock clicked and the lid came open.

From his back pocket, Sergei took out the stack of money he'd made tonight. The club had netted him about a grand. Slow night, but he didn't care. The money he made there was chump change anyway. On top of that grand, he'd also pocketed twelve large for a job he'd recently done for the Passantinos.

The cash box was getting full. He'd need to make a deposit soon. This money would join the rest in one of several offshore accounts. Once his work was done and the Mafia families were fighting hard enough to tear each other to pieces, he'd flee to his property in Tasmania with the help of a fake passport and the substantial amount of money he'd built up by filling contracts for the very people he intended to destroy.

The stripping gig? He didn't care about the money. That was entirely a cover. No one in the families wanted anything to do with a gay stripper, and the club was the last place they came looking if they had questions. He was, essentially, hiding in plain sight.

After he'd stashed the cash, he locked the box and put it back up under the bed. He reached up into the same compartment where he kept the money, and took out some rolled-up papers, which he spread across the bed. On it, he'd painstakingly mapped out the hierarchies of all three crime families. From the bosses on down to the lowliest of soldiers, he had every name and who they answered to.

And it was all in pencil because it changed constantly, in no small part because of strings Sergei had been quietly pulling.

He'd erased Lorenzo Barcia's name the night he'd tossed the fucker into the harbor. Tonight, thanks to some info that had trickled his way from one of his contacts, he put a new name in that space—Rico Barcia. The asshole's very own brother, and an idiot and a hothead. Not someone who needed to be in a position of power, but there he was.

Rico wouldn't last long. Sergei wouldn't even need to do anything to put a target on that fucker's head. As a soldier, he was a benign, if annoying presence. As a lieutenant, he could cause some actual headache for the Maisanos and Passantinos. It wouldn't be long before he was removed from the hierarchy. Sergei probably wouldn't even be the one to take him out—there were plenty of other hitmen in this town who'd do it for half the price. All he really cared about was watching the idiots and assholes move up into the newly vacated places.

He was especially glad that Lorenzo Barcia had finally gotten what was coming to him, and he'd been thrilled to be the one to give it to him. Every Mafioso was a fucking asshole, but there was a special place in hell for men like Barcia. Like many of his ilk, he made his money through narcotics and human trafficking, but he took it a step further. He saw nothing wrong with helping himself to the family's merchandise, and not just cocaine. The women were terrified to do anything about it—he threatened them and their children if they crossed him—but a well-placed camera and some patience, followed by a damning video being "leaked" to the press, and the man's fate was sealed. The video hadn't shown everything—Sergei couldn't do that to the woman—but there was enough to make it clear what Barcia intended to do once he'd dragged her onto that boat.

Legally, it was circumstantial evidence. As far as the Mafia was concerned, it was more than enough. The families put up with and committed a lot of crimes, but sexual assault was not tolerated.

The day after the video broke, the young woman was paid a small fortune to quietly leave Cape Swan, and that very night, Sergei was contracted to kill the bastard.

With pleasure.

So Barcia was out of the picture, and the idiot who'd taken his place wouldn't be around long. It was all part of Sergei's plan, and it was all happening the way he'd predicted.

Well, aside from the part where he was bedding a Mafioso. That had been… unforeseen.

He shifted his gaze to the top of the hierarchy chart. There, among the Maisano underbosses, was Dom. Below him, a small crew of lieutenants and soldiers who, like him, weren't terribly significant. They all seemed to do Corrado's bitch work. Administrative shit. Paperwork. Sergei understood that Dom handled some money laundering, and worked with the immigrants to get their debts paid and documents processed, but his hands weren't in much of the more nefarious stuff.

Good. You stay over there and do your thing, and you won't get caught in the crossfire.

Sergei's stomach knotted. There were no guarantees that Dom *wouldn't* get caught in the crossfire. He was a made man. He was an underboss. By virtue of being Corrado's adopted son, he was virtually untouchable.

But even untouchable men could be taken down. It meant a death sentence for the man who pulled the trigger, but it could be done.

Sergei tore his gaze away from Dom's name and rolled up the chart. Yes, Dom could get killed. It was part of being in the Mafia.

And if he does get killed, so what? What do I care? He's not the only gay man in this town.

Sergei swallowed as he tucked the chart back up under the bed. No, this wasn't something he needed to think about tonight. He'd deal with it if the circumstances arose.

Tonight, Dom was alive and well.

And waiting for Sergei in a motel across town.

Sergei got up, gave himself a once-over in the mirror, and headed out to meet Dom.

SERGEI HAD BARELY SHUT the motel room door before he and Dom were tangled up in a deep, hungry kiss. Dom had been here first, and he'd already stripped off his shirt and shoes, and Sergei immediately had his hands all over him as they kissed up against the door.

One thing was becoming abundantly clear—Dom *loved* kissing. It didn't matter who was on top, or if they were dressed or naked, or standing in a cramped motel shower —every chance he had, it seemed, Dom was kissing Sergei. Frantically. Gently. Deeply. Softly. So much kissing.

And Sergei couldn't get enough either. He loved the way Dom kissed.

Hell, who was he kidding?

As they tumbled into bed, half-dressed and fully hard, he didn't just love the way Dom kissed. Everything the man did drove him insane. This was supposed to be for Dom's benefit—getting gay sex out of his system before he married—but it was feeling less and less like charity with each passing night.

And this time, like every time, Dom touched and kissed Sergei as if this was the first time. Sometimes he'd watch his hands run over Sergei's skin, as if marveling at the sight of himself touching another man. When they had sex, Dom never rushed, not even when he was trembling with arousal. He kissed him like he really wanted to *taste* him— gently exploring his mouth, cradling the back of his neck as if to say "stay here, just a moment longer."

No wonder Sergei couldn't help coming back for more.

"You want to be on top?" he murmured between kisses.

Dom moaned, shivering against him. "Yes please."

They separated long enough to get a condom on. As Dom put on some lube, Sergei turned around on his hands and knees.

Sergei was usually on top, but more and more, he was enjoying letting Dom top him. The man took his time, tonight as always—easing himself in, giving Sergei time to yield to him and relax. Which was especially good because unlike some of the other men in his family, Dom was definitely not lacking below the belt. His cock was thick, stretching Sergei enough to make his eyes water, and Sergei clawed at the bed and rocked back against him, eager for more, more, *more*.

Dom steadied his hips and moved faster, not quite thrusting, but close. Sergei closed his eyes, gripping handfuls of the sheet and slurring curses as every stroke took his breath away.

"You're so fucking gorgeous," Dom murmured, running his hands all over Sergei's back. "Jesus, you're—" His breath hitched. He picked up a little bit of speed, and whatever he said after that didn't make it to Sergei's brain.

Then Dom leaned forward, urging Sergei down with his body weight, and they sank to the bed. This should have set off every alarm bell in Sergei's mind—being underneath a bigger, stronger Italian was dangerous as fuck—but all he could do was melt beneath Dom's hot skin and slow, rocking strokes. What wasn't to love about this trembling man stretched out over him, balls deep in him, cursing in his ear as he rode him into the mattress?

Sergei felt around and found Dom's hand, and they clasped their fingers together. Weirdly intimate? Affectionate? God, he didn't know. He just needed to hold on to something, to Dom. As much as he could in this position, he rolled his hips, fucking against the mattress as Dom thrust deep and hard. All the while, they gripped each other's hands painfully tight, as if they could somehow get more leverage that way or… or something. Sergei didn't know. He didn't care. He only cared about holding on, and letting go, and the orgasm that Dom was pushing him toward with every deep, breathtaking stroke.

Sergei heard himself curse, and didn't even know what language it was, only that he was falling apart, and Dom just kept right on fucking him that way, and then Sergei was coming, shuddering, moaning into the pillow as Dom kept him coming, and coming, and coming.

Then Dom groaned behind Sergei's ear, and his rhythm became sharp, uneven thrusts, each knocking the breath out of Sergei as Dom tried to drive himself just a little deeper before he shuddered, swore, and relaxed.

For a moment, neither of them moved. Their hands relaxed, but didn't let go. Sergei was panting as hard as Dom, and God bless him, Dom had the presence of mind to keep his weight off Sergei's ribs so he could breathe.

Finally, Dom pressed a soft kiss to the back of Sergei's shoulder. He let go of Sergei's hand, pulled out, and got up. "Be right back."

"'kay." Sergei rolled onto his back, mostly to get away from the wet spot, and stared up at the dingy ceiling. Jesus. He could not get enough of this man.

As Dom came back to the bed, his legs not quite steady beneath him, Sergei grinned up at him.

And to think—I thought you were like all the other Mafiosi.

That thought sobered him. Dom *was* a Mafioso. Though everything ceased to exist while they were in the middle of driving each other to mind-blowing orgasms, it was all still real once the dust settled again. Sergei was still a man who killed men like Dom.

Dom eased himself down beside Sergei and draped his arm over him, dark hair and olive skin contrasting sharply with Sergei's fairer skin. "I'm going to be dead on my feet tomorrow." He kissed Sergei's cheek. "But it's fucking worth it."

"Damn right it is." Sergei lifted his head and kissed Dom on the mouth. They faced each other on their sides. For a long moment, they lay in silence, Dom trailing his fingertips along Sergei's skin, watching himself draw lazy loops and swirls as Sergei watched him.

After a while, Sergei said, "You're not like the other Italians in this town."

Dom's fingers stopped. "Is that a compliment, or…?"

"Yeah." Sergei laughed. "Trust me, it's a compliment."

Dom chuckled, sliding his hand over Sergei's waist. "In that case… thanks."

Sergei ran his fingers down Dom's arm. "I guess you don't… you don't seem like the Mafia type."

"What *is* the Mafia type?"

"Well…" Sergei swept his tongue across his lips. "I don't know. Not you."

Dom released a long breath. "I wish it wasn't me, believe me."

Sergei furrowed his brow. "What do you mean?"

"If I had the choice, I wouldn't be what I am."

"Then why are you?"

"Like I said… if I had a choice."

Sergei held his gaze, wondering how far to push the question. He was curious as hell—a Mafioso who didn't want to be? Since when?—but was it his place to ask? Dom wanted him for sex, not questions about a career he apparently didn't want.

So instead, he slid closer, running his hand over Dom's hip, and glanced past him at the ancient alarm clock on the bedside table. "It's almost three. I probably shouldn't keep you much longer."

"I shouldn't be here in the first place." Dom combed his fingers through Sergei's hair. "Damage is already done, I think."

"Does that mean you want to stay for a while?"

"That depends—how many condoms did you bring?"

Goose bumps sprang up along Sergei's spine and a

shudder nudged him even closer to Dom. "More than enough."

"Good." Dom tipped up Sergei's chin and kissed him. "Think we might need them."

Oh God yes. More of you? Fuck yes.

He didn't speak, though. He nudged Dom onto his back. Straddled him. Kissed him.

And didn't ask any more questions that night.

Chapter 12

After every night he spent with Sergei, Dom felt strange returning the next morning to the only life he'd ever known. He may as well have taken a hundred-year vacation from his own existence, and coming back to it was like materializing in someone else's world.

But he didn't let it show. He didn't dare. This morning, as he did every time after checking out of the seedy motel, Dom had gone home, showered, put on a suit, and driven down to the office where he ran his part of the family's operation. To the untrained eye, this was a temp agency where blue collar workers came in for short term employment, not where deeply indebted immigrants came to pay off the hefty bribes that would eventually earn them their citizenship.

As always, there was already a line outside the door. A dozen or so tired, sun-beaten men waited, watching Dom stroll into the building while they clutched weathered papers and manila folders to their threadbare shirts.

He could guess why most of them were here. Some were making payments on their debts to the family. Some needed more time. Some could barely scratch the surface of what they owed, but their circumstances demanded they come here and put themselves even deeper into debt.

Each man who came through here was different, and each was the same. They hailed from South America, Russia, China, even the occasional escapee from North Korea, but they all had the same story. Desperation had forced them from their homeland, and they'd come to America looking for something better. Immigration wasn't easy, though, and it wasn't cheap.

That was where the Maisanos came in.

For a fee, the immigrant's papers would be expedited. For an even bigger fee, the person would get more than a green card—citizenship and everything that came with it. And for a fuckload of money, the immigrant's family would be safely brought over and naturalized in a fraction of the time it would take through legitimate channels.

Felice's crew oversaw the immigration arrangements. They issued the terms and handled the transportation of family members to the United States. Dom's job was to disburse and receive money. He was the financial wizard— the man who could make dirty money disappear and resurface, clean as the day it was printed. When the debt was paid, he issued the people their paperwork, and sent them on their way as freshly minted American citizens.

As Dom settled in for the day, he caught himself wondering if Sergei was a citizen. He was obviously not American-born. Not with that accent. And sex workers in this town were often doing what they could to get by until they could get legitimate work.

Dom had a few Russian families on his payroll. He perused a few, looking to see if any had sons in their early twenties. With a click of a button, Dom could erase the family's debt and expedite their paperwork.

No one came up, though.

Sergei had obviously been here a while. Long enough to soften his accent slightly.

Dom shook himself. Sergei was the last person he needed to be thinking about. Whatever went on between them, he needed to shut it out right now. He wanted to see Sergei again. He wanted a repeat of the night they'd spend in that godawful motel.

But he couldn't let the lines blur between that life and this one, so he made himself focus. All day long, as he shunted money through channels that no Fed would ever find, and updated ledgers for people indebted to the family, he forced himself not to think of Sergei.

Toward the middle of the morning, a tanned, gray-haired Chinese man named Dingxiang came in and sat across from him in his office.

"I just need some more time, sir," the man pleaded. "My daughter, she had to go to the hospital last week. It was... it cost..." He shook his head.

Dom regarded him silently, keeping his sympathy hidden. He hated this, hated everything about it, but he had to keep his cards close to his vest. As much as he wanted to wipe the man's ledger clean and let him leave without ever worrying again, he was already playing dangerous games with the accounting in the name of relieving people of their debts. He could only do so much without someone catching on.

Tone flat, he quietly said, "I've already given you extensions."

"Yes, yes. And terribly... terribly sorry. But—"

Right then, Dom's receptionist Daisy leaned in through the office door. "Excuse me, Mr. Maisano. Biaggio is on line three."

"Thank you." As she stepped back out, he turned to Dingxiang. "Give me just a moment."

Dingxiang nodded.

Dom picked up the phone. "Yes, sir?"

"You have a meeting with your uncle at one o'clock."

Dom glanced at this watch. That gave him just over an hour. "At the house?"

"Yes."

"I'll be there."

Biaggio hung up without so much as a goodbye. That was normal for him—odds were, he had a hundred tasks to perform in the time a normal man would need to complete three. Pleasantries weren't part of his tightly packed schedule.

Dom folded his hands and faced Dingxiang. "Listen, I'm going to waive your payment for this month, and this month only."

The man exhaled with obvious relief. He undoubtedly knew there'd be conditions, strings that would make all but the most desperate man cringe, but almost anything was better than having a Maisano debt collector at his door.

Guilt tugged at Dom. It wasn't at all below him to cancel an immigrant family's debts and send them on their way with their papers in hand, but he'd already waived a substantial amount of money for another family this month. There was only so much he could do before even his financial wizardry couldn't make the numbers line up, and then people would ask questions he couldn't answer. If the truth ever came out, he wouldn't put it past Corrado to find a family who'd been released from their debt, and use them to make a point.

He exhaled. "If the next payment is a minute late or a penny short, your interest rate will go up three percent."

Dingxiang blinked. Dom swore he could feel the man's

heart drop. The interest rate was already high on the loan, and if it climbed much higher, repayment would be nearly impossible.

Dom hated himself for it, but he said, "If you aren't able to make those payments, then we'll need to talk about employing you down at the marina."

Dingxiang blanched. Every immigrant in Cape Swan knew what marina employment meant, and only the most desperate accepted those jobs. "Next... next month will be on time."

Dom nodded. "Good."

Dingxiang left the office, and Dom let Daisy know that he too was on his way out, and that he'd likely be out for the rest of the day. Even if the meeting was short, which they usually were, he had a feeling he'd be indisposed for a while.

FELICE AND LUCIANO were already there with their father.

Corrado scowled. "Glad you could join us, Domenico."

Dom muttered an apology. He hadn't been late, but Corrado didn't like to be kept waiting, and "be there in one hour" meant "one hour is the absolute latest or there will be hell to pay."

Corrado shifted his attention to his older son. "Luciano?" He nodded toward Dom.

Luciano turned to Dom. "We have the detailed police and medical examiner reports for Nicolá." He handed over a thin folder. "You're going to want to see this."

Dom opened the folder and skimmed over the police report. "It says the ME found evidence he'd been tied. And that he'd had tape over his mouth." He lifted his gaze. "I thought Cusimano wiped him out while he was drunk."

"Well." Corrado slowly released a breath. "Maybe as drunk as he was, this killing wasn't as accidental as it appears."

"Of course it wasn't an accident," Felice said. "Why the hell would Nicolá be wandering around the highway at that hour?"

Luciano muffled a cough. "That's where it gets a little more complicated, though. The ME found traces of Ecstasy and a number of other drugs in his mouth and in his bloodstream. Basically, a cocktail of hallucinogens and downers. It's anyone's guess what else was in there that he'd already gotten out of his system."

Dom tilted his head. "Since when did Nicolá get involved in that shit?"

Corrado sighed, running a hand through his thinning white hair. "It's hard to say, Domenico. Sal Greco overdosed on heroin last year, and none of us ever knew he touched it."

"But if Nicolá was bound and drugged," Dom said, "then it's pretty clearly murder." Bile burned its way up the back of his throat. If one of their own had been murdered, then Corrado wouldn't let that murder go unanswered. And Dom wouldn't be able to say no. It was as inevitable as it was sickening.

"Unless he was into one of those weird sex clubs that have been popping up downtown," Luciano said.

"No way," Felice said. "Nicolá wouldn't go near a place like that."

Luciano eyed him. "You don't know——"

"Nicolá was last seen alive at *church*!" Felice said. "They found his goddamned car there."

"Yes. He was there several hours before the estimated

time of death. He could have gone anywhere with anyone during that time, and the ME thinks he'd been drugged for quite some time before he was killed."

Felice shook his head. "No way in hell he'd go from there to... one of those places. And even if he did, Eugenio Cusimano still ran him down on the highway."

"Question is," Luciano said softly, "was it deliberate?"

Felice slammed his fist down on the desk. "Whether he meant to do it or not, this is *murder*. We have got to send a message to the Cusimanos, and take out—"

"I know what we need to do, Felice," Corrado said coolly.

Gritting his teeth against the nausea, Dom closed the police report. "There's got to be a way to settle this without more violence."

Felice rolled his eyes. "For fuck's sake, Dom. What do you want to do? Ask them to write a heartfelt apology?" He laughed, shaking his head. "We gotta send a message here, not pussyfoot around."

"No," Dom said. "But as volatile as things have been lately, this could snowball into a shootout right in the middle of downtown."

"Felice is right, Domenico." Corrado glanced at his younger son, then shifted his gaze to Dom. "Whether Nicolá was killed deliberately or not, we have conclusive proof he was killed by Eugenio Cusimano. I'm not interested in his intent. I'm interested in the fact that he's taken out one of my men. A member of my *family*."

"I can have him dead before dawn," Felice said through gritted teeth. "Just say the—"

His father's upraised hand stopped him. "You'll do what you're ordered to, and nothing more. Am I clear?"

Felice bristled, rocking from his heels to the balls of his feet, but didn't comment any further. Dom wished like hell

Corrado would send his younger son on one of these hits. The only reason he never actually suggested it was that Felice was the kind of psychopath who'd make his mark suffer. At least taking the job himself, Dom could end it quickly, cleanly, and painlessly. Felice would torture the guy for hours. Like father, like son.

"Eugenio Cusimano killed Nicolá Cannizzaro," Corrado went on, calmly and evenly. "This will not go unanswered. If Nicolá's death goes unpunished, the Cusimanos will think they can take out Maisanos with impunity. Felice is right—we need to send a message. A strong one."

Corrado looked Dom right in the eye and gave him a subtle nod.

And that was that. The contract was issued. Corrado had deliberately groomed Dom to pick up certain cues. Even if they were in the middle of a room packed with cops, bugs, and federal agents, he could order Dom to take out a hit, and no one would know except for them. Law enforcement couldn't overhear conversations that didn't happen.

Corrado issued his orders via subtext and subtle gestures, and Dom carried them out without ever breathing a word to anyone. With equally subtle cues, he'd let Corrado know when the deed was carried out. Nothing spoken. Nothing written.

There'd be no evidence except the body and the ever-increasing amount of blood on Dom's hands.

EUGENIO CUSIMANO WAS A DRUNKEN IDIOT, but the family had him on a tight leash after the accident. He didn't go near bars anymore. Didn't drink. He still had his habits and haunts, but he started varying his routes. When he visited his girlfriend in Crescent City, he never returned via the same road, and that was a challenge considering just how few roads went in and out of Cape Swan.

Dom monitored him, stalked him, memorized his every move. He barely had time to go into the office—as always when he was hunting someone down, most of Dom's waking hours were spoken for.

Not for long, though. It only took ten days to get close to Eugenio. As close as he needed to be, anyway.

Late one night, as he often did, Eugenio parked in an alley a few blocks over from his girlfriend's condo. Dom found the man's car, parked his own on another street, and then strolled down the alley. There was no one around this time of night, and a Dumpster hid the car from view of the road. Probably just in case Elena Cusimano came looking for her husband. Smart thinking—the wrath of a made man's wife was not something a mistress wanted at her front door.

Certain he was alone, Dom hid two devices on Eugenio's car. Beneath the front bumper, a GPS tracker. Beneath the rear passenger side wheel well, a small explosive.

Then he went back to his own car, drove a couple of miles, and waited.

Sitting on the shoulder of a back road, he watched the little green dot on the GPS screen and waited for it to move. He tried not to think about the chain of events that would be set into motion when Eugenio left his girlfriend's place. It was unavoidable. Just like he did every time he was on a job like this, Dom had already run through every possible alternative at least a dozen times.

In the past, Dom had tried to convince his uncle that a situation could be resolved without bloodshed, but

Corrado had made his decision, and Dom had his orders. And when he was seventeen, he'd nearly learned the hard way what happened when he didn't obey a command like this.

"Don't let this happen again, Domenico," Corrado had warned him over the top of a nine millimeter, the muzzle digging painfully into Dom's forehead. "Understood?"

Yeah. He'd understood.

But just for good measure, Corrado had pulled him aside a few months later, and without any explanation, taken him to a concrete-walled garage in the back acres of his property.

There, a middle-aged man had been bound and gagged on his knees on the floor, and across from him, a younger man who couldn't have been more than twenty. The faces, the eyes, even the hair—they were quite obviously father and son.

To Dom, Corrado said, "Stand there." He pointed to a place a few feet away from the terrified men. "And learn."

Both tied men had looked at Dom, eyes wide with palpable fear and unmistakable pleas for help. Dom hadn't helped. He'd stood there, as ordered, and he'd watched.

And God, he'd learned.

He'd learned just how much a man could scream around a gag, and how loud a room could get when a person was trying to scream in pain while the other tried to beg for mercy. How much a punch could reverberate through the air when a fist made contact with the younger man's gut. How sickening it was when the impact of a pistol shattered teeth. How much a man had to struggle to spit out teeth fragments, blood, and vomit with a gag pulled tightly across his mouth.

And how much damage Dom's calm, calculated uncle could do with a knife without killing someone. Blood smeared on Corrado's arms. Splattered on his shirt. Pooled in the lap of the younger man. Spread on the floor around his knees. Every cut of Corrado's knife made the son whimper in pain and the father cry out with an entirely different breed of agony.

Eventually, Corrado cut off the younger man's gag.

"Please," the son moaned through tears. "Kill—" He vomited, nearly hitting Corrado's shoes before croaking, "Kill me. Please."

The father's agonized sobs would stay with Dom until the day he died.

Finally, Corrado killed both of them—first the father, then the son—each with a bullet between the eyes.

Afterward, he'd casually wiped down the gun and his hands like a chef who'd finished preparing a meal.

Dom hadn't been able to breathe. He'd witnessed violence before—some far too close to home—but never torture. Not until that day.

His uncle's hand had been heavy on the back of Dom's neck, and though Dom was still partially deaf from the gunshots, he'd heard Corrado say, "Do you want to know why I brought you here, Domenico?"

Dom had been petrified. Shaking. Ready to puke. But he'd nodded anyway because he was pretty damn sure that was the only right answer.

Corrado had put an arm around Dom's shoulders, the smell of blood coppery on his skin and clothes, and herded him toward the two bodies. "This man had a job to do, and he decided not to do it. He undermined my authority and disobeyed me." He gestured at the son. "So this was his punishment—the last thing he knew in this world was his son screaming and begging for death."

Dom couldn't make himself ask what exactly the job had been that the man's disobedience warranted this punishment, or why the son deserved to suffer for his father's sins. After all, then Corrado might remember that Dom's own father had betrayed the family, and that he'd only punished Papa, not Dom. Traumatized the hell out of Dom, but hadn't *punished* him. Not like that, anyway.

"So." Corrado had looked him right in the eye. "I assume we won't have any repeats of that incident last winter, will we?"

That moment, even more than the gun pressed to his head that past winter, had given Dom the deepest, most profound understanding of what fear was. Knowing his uncle wouldn't hesitate to kill him was one thing. Knowing he would torture him and anyone close to him?

All these years later, he relived that moment in his nightmares more often than he cared to admit; *message received, Uncle Corrado*.

To this day, the memory made him ill. He squirmed in the driver seat and swallowed the bile in his throat.

There *were* situations where he could change the rules and take care of things his own way. When it was a minor offense, usually some idiot who'd crossed the family—a dockworker keeping some of the stolen merchandise for himself, a desperately indebted immigrant trying to skip town without paying the family what he owed—then Dom had other options.

Just last year, Corrado had ordered him to take out a trucker who'd been letting the Cusimanos in on Maisano territory. Turned out the guy was getting it from both sides —threats and promises alike. He couldn't say no to a Cusimano, not even when it meant crossing a Maisano, because that put a target on his back. He'd tried to play both sides, not out of any attempt to screw both families at once, but out of a panicked attempt to placate both sides and keep him out of the crosshairs. What choice did he have?

When Dom couldn't talk his uncle out of having that trucker killed, he'd tracked the guy to a deserted truck stop south of Redding, and cornered him up in the men's room. The man never saw his face, but he hadn't questioned the .357 barrel pressing in beneath his ear while he faced the wall with his hands behind his head.

"You've fucked with the wrong family," Dom growled at him, slowly drawing the hammer back and making damn sure the man heard every click. "You know that, right?"

"I'm sorry." The man was shaking badly, his fingers turning white as he laced them together tighter. "I'm sorry. I didn't… I was scared! Please, it won't—"

"No fucking excuse," Dom snarled. "You agreed to work for the Maisanos. Is it true you've been working for the Cusimanos too?"

"Yes! Yes! I'm sorry." The guy was quickly becoming a blubbering mess. "Please, don't hurt my family. Whatever you have to do to me, do it, but please don't—"

"I'm not going to touch your family." Dom nudged him slightly with the gun, and then pulled it back. "I'm going to let you go too."

"You… you are?"

"I am. And if you show your face in Cape Swan again, I promise you, you're a dead man. Am I clear?"

The trucker nodded profusely. He also didn't need to use the restroom anymore.

Dom had given him some strict instructions, laced with some threats he prayed he wouldn't have to carry out, and left, leaving the man to clean himself up. It was a risk, letting a mark walk, but guys like this, they weren't part of the families. They weren't hardened criminals or made men. To his knowledge, the handful of marks he'd allowed to live had taken him at his word. Within days, their families had left town and were never seen again. A few bribes and threats later, Dom had convincing death certificates and police reports, and the marks were as good as ghosts. If Corrado ever found out, Dom would have a bullet in him for every man he'd ever left alive, but it was a risk he was willing to take in order to sleep at night.

But Eugenio Cusimano wasn't someone he could threaten and send packing. Not after he'd run down Nicolá like that. It was either him or Dom. Just like the gay cousin Dom couldn't let walk away. Corrado had insisted that his body be found, that there be proof of death. Disappearance wouldn't do, and so Dom had taken his cousin by surprise—a stealthy break-in, a bullet to the head, and he'd never known what hit him.

The green dot on the tracker started moving. Dom watched it, and once it was well into the middle of nowhere, out another winding highway where cell phone reception was spotty and few cars just happened by, Dom pushed the button on the detonator.

The dot slowed, then stopped.

Dom didn't have to hurry. The explosive hadn't been a big one, but he'd made damn sure it was enough to fuck up more than the tire. Unless Eugenio had a spare axle and a set of brakes in his trunk, he wasn't going anywhere for a while.

Sure enough, there was his car, its hazard lights blinking above a couple of glowing pink flares.

Dom slowed to a stop behind him. He kept his high beams on, and while the car idled, he got out.

Eugenio had been crouching beside the ruined tire, and rose, shielding his eyes as he cautiously faced Dom.

"You need some help?" Dom asked.

Eugenio lowered his hands, and with them, his guard. "Yeah. Must've hit something. The back tire's all—"

Dom shot him.

No warning. No hesitation. Two to the chest, one to the face.

Eugenio crumpled to the pavement and didn't make another sound. Just to be sure, Dom put another bullet through the man's temple. If by some chance he'd survived the first three, there was no need to make him suffer.

Then Dom got in his car and drove back toward Cape Swan. He begged his stomach to stay where it belonged. Gripped the wheel for dear life. Held his breath until his vision started to sparkle.

He made it two miles before the acid in his throat told him he wasn't going any farther. He pulled over, braked hard, jumped out of the car, and just made it to the grass before he puked. Once. Twice. A third time. When he was sure nothing else would come up—that there was nothing left *to* come up—he spat in the grass and leaned against the car. His mind was reeling, spinning, his knees threatening to shake out from under him.

Fuck this life. Fuck this world. Why God had seen fit for him to be born into a family of Sicilians so he could be made, he'd never understand. And damn every fucking person who knew him for not telling him to blow it when Uncle Corrado had asked him to prove he was the crack shot he'd bragged about being. The kid who'd been desperate for approval had made sure to shoot his very, very best when Corrado had come to watch. If he'd known what he was getting himself into, that his uncle would secretly begin grooming him—at *fourteen*—to be a hitman, he'd have made sure no bullet went near the target. He might've even eaten one.

He glanced at the passenger seat. In the darkness, he couldn't see the gun, but he knew it was there. Only four rounds were missing. All he needed was one.

Yeah. And after he pulled the trigger, Corrado would find someone else to fill death warrants. Someone who probably wouldn't let terrified truckers walk or make sure gay cousins just went to sleep and never woke up.

Dom cursed into the night, his mouth still burning with acid. He could only save so many people. The occasional immigrant who he quietly let out of his debt. The rare and fortunate mark he could justify sparing.

He couldn't save himself, though. Corrado had proven he could and would find apostates, and that punishment would be anything but swift. Even those who'd gone into witness protection would, sooner or later, find themselves back in Cape Swan.

Eyes closed, he exhaled, wincing at the taste of bile still on his tongue. He spat into the grass. There was no point in staying out here. A made man this close to a murder scene? Not good.

Though maybe they'd arrest him. Take him to prison and leave him there until one of Corrado's men—or a Cusimano, or some random felon—shanked him in the recreation yard.

That bullet was sounding better and better.

With shaky hands, he pulled back his sleeve and checked his watch. It was after midnight. He was exhausted and he felt disgusting. Sleep and a shower were the only things marginally more appealing than suicide.

On trembling legs, he went back around to the driver side, got in, and pulled back onto the highway again. He made it home on autopilot, showered on autopilot, dressed on autopilot, and before he knew it, he was back in the car.

Once he realized where he was heading, though, he didn't turn around.

He drove faster.

Chapter 13

Sergei leaned against the bar, sipping some water and waiting for a stage to open up. Some of his regulars were lurking nearby, watching the other dancers, but keeping an eye on him too. He'd memorized that body language a long time ago—fidgeting, rocking from heels to the balls of their feet, twitching as they eyeballed the men already seated at the stages. When the stages cleared, it would be like the running of the bulls—everyone vying for a handful of seats.

He grinned to himself. The men here wouldn't actually go to blows over a seat unless they were really drunk, because none of them wanted the cops getting involved. Even if fists flew, the other men would shut it down, and the bouncers would finish it off.

So he wasn't worried about anything getting out of control. Let them pant and froth at the mouth. The more eager they were, the more money they'd toss at his feet.

The bead curtain at the end of the bar moved. Sergei turned his head.

Dom walked in. And scanned the room. And looked right at him. And Sergei's heart skipped.

It wasn't panic or irritation, or wondering why the fuck he was risking anyone seeing them together in public. The second they locked eyes, his gut clenched.

My God. What's wrong?

Though the flickering strobes made it impossible to tell for sure, he thought Dom was shaking. He was definitely paler than the last time Sergei had seen him in this light.

Sergei was getting used to seeing Dom. In fact, he was starting to get a little excited whenever they were in the same room because it meant sex. It meant *good* sex. Except they'd agreed not to meet here anymore. Dom hadn't been back to the club since the first night they'd slept together. Since then, they'd text, exchange a few seemingly benign messages, and meet at a cheap motel.

But Dom was here now, and something in his eyes hit Sergei from all the way across the room. Sergei wasn't supposed to care about him, but that look on Dom's face definitely had him concerned. Had something happened? Had someone found out about them? What the hell was going on?

He pushed himself off the bar and slipped through the thin crowd to Dom's side.

"What's wrong?"

"I…" He met Sergei's gaze, and swallowed. Shaking his head, he whispered so softly it almost didn't carry over the music: "I don't… I don't want to talk."

"What *do* you want?"

As soon as the words were out, Dom's eyes answered in no uncertain terms.

You. Sex. Now.

Sergei gulped. He glanced around. Two of the other dancers were negotiating private lap dances. Their stages would be clear in a matter of seconds. He could feel the gazes of his eager customers prickling his neck.

Shit. He couldn't just disappear into the back. That was a good way for some vindictive asshole to drop an anonymous tip to someone in Dom's circles, and they'd both be fucked.

He turned to Dom. "Meet me in the back. Ask the bouncer to show you to booth seven. Got it?"

Dom blinked a couple of times, as if he didn't quit understand. Then he nodded. "Right. Booth… booth seven."

"Good. I'll be there in a minute."

Dom disappeared into the back. Sergei watched him go, gnawing the inside of his cheek. He should've sent Dom on his way. Or at least told him to meet at a motel like they always did.

And that was perfect. Two weeks into it, Sergei enjoyed the routine already. He had to admit, he looked forward to the nights he spent with Dom. It wasn't even the little thrill he got from sleeping with the enemy.

The sex was… God, it was amazing. And Dom had a way of not just turning Sergei on, not just making him feel like the only man in the world, but making him feel… *worshipped*. There wasn't a man alive who couldn't learn a thing or two from Dom about how to rock a lover's world.

A lover?

No. Definitely not. Strictly speaking, maybe—they were sleeping together, after all. But it was just sex. Nothing more than a means for Dom to sow his wild gay oats before settling down like a good little Mafioso.

Having him show up here? Risky.

And Sergei still wasn't sure why Dom hadn't just told him to meet at a motel. Dom should've gotten the fuck out of here so Sergei could work, and they could blow off whatever steam they needed to later. Except Dom didn't seem like he needed to blow off steam. Just thinking about the look on his face made Sergei's gut clench.

"Hey." Paco nudged him. "You gonna dance or not?"

Sergei swallowed. "Yeah. Yeah. I…" He shook himself. "On my way."

Paco stopped him with a big, calloused hand on his shoulder. "You okay, kid?"

"Yeah." Sergei shrugged out of his boss's touch. "I'm good."

He didn't wait for Paco to stop him again, and hurried to the center table.

Immediately, half the men around the sidelines were on the move, damn near sprinting across the room to claim one of the seats. Those who weren't fast enough stood behind them, and Sergei guessed they'd be extra aggressive when it came time to bid on a private dance.

The deejay kicked on some techno. Sergei grabbed onto the pole, took a deep breath, and started dancing. He thrust his hips. Undulated his abs. Shook his ass. He was absolutely convinced that one of the men watching him would catch on that he was distracted, so he poured himself into this even more than usual. He bent farther than he usually did, causing more than a few jaws to drop, and leaned closer to the men watching him. The effect was exactly as he'd hoped—the men squirmed as erections strained against zippers, and they threw twenties on the stage as if they were ones. By the end of his dance, Sergei had to be careful so he didn't slip on a pile of bills and break his neck.

The music ended. All the regulars immediately started thrusting hundreds at him. The men who'd been standing behind the chairs leaned over the others, shoving thick stacks of bills at Sergei.

He forced a grin as he egged them on so they'd up the ante and outbid each other, but his mind was already back in the private booths. In one booth in particular. The thought of getting through a private dance made his stomach turn. Not because he couldn't stand being on a horny stranger's lap—he loved what he did and made no apologies for it—but because he needed to be in that room with Dom. What the fuck was going on? Why did Dom suddenly need him badly enough to risk showing his face in this club again?

He shook himself and focused on the men bidding for a dance. Thank God, they all backed off one by one until there was a last man standing. He didn't think he had it in him to dance on two men out here before finally taking the highest bidder into the back. There was a clear winner, so Sergei stepped off the stage, grinned, and beckoned to the tall black man with the stack of hundreds in his hand.

On the way back to the booth, he glanced at booth seven.

The knot in his gut tightened. What was going on? Why—

Didn't matter now. He had work to do.

Resisting the urge to even lean into booth seven to make sure Dom was all right—*why the hell do I care?*—he led his customer into the booth directly across from seven.

He tried to shove every thought of Dom into the back of his mind as he shimmed out of everything but his G-string. As focused as he could be, he climbed onto the customer's lap. The music thumped hard enough along his bones to remind him of the tempo, but his thumping heart drowned out the rest. All he could think of was Dom. In the other booth. In a chair just like this one. Turned on in a way Sergei had never seen him. Not just needy, but *needy*.

Focus. Dance.

Like he had on the stage, he threw himself into this dance as much as he could. Grinding against the customer's thick erection, rubbing all over him until the man's breath was coming in hot, heavy huffs. The client bit his lip, shifting in the chair. A rush of breath rushed across Sergei's abs.

Just like Dom's did when—

Sergei bit down on a curse. Every lap dance customer who could breathe did that. It wasn't just Dom.

Get a grip, idiot.

Mercifully, though, the song eventually wound down. Sergei rubbed a few more times against the prominent hard-on, and then rose.

"OhmyGod," the man slurred, and wiped a hand over his face. "Thank… thank you."

Sergei grinned and held up the cash. "Thank *you*."

Dazed and unsteady, the client left.

Sergei exhaled. Finally. He'd covered himself—no one in the club had any reason to believe anything was going on besides business as usual.

Quickly, he put on his clothes and straightened his hair, but before he moved to the next booth, he paused, holding his own gaze in the dingy mirror on the wall.

This was dangerous. Sergei was in Cape Swan to kill Mafiosi, not fuck them. Doing this at all, especially here, could get them both killed. Except he knew that wasn't likely. Dom's life depended on maintaining the illusion that he was straight. He was about the safest man in town for Sergei to fuck, because he relied even more on discretion than Sergei did.

He pushed his shoulders back and stepped out of the booth.

Before he'd reached number seven, Roy stopped him. "Hey, kid. That Italian guy, he asked for you. Said you—"

"He's waiting in seven, right?" He gestured at the curtain.

Roy glanced at it, and nodded. "Yeah. So, you and he are cool?"

"We're cool." Sergei forced a smile. "Relax."

"All right." Roy backed off and returned to his perch near the end of the row, where he could see and hear if anyone needed his help. He was a bit overprotective, but Sergei appreciated it. Wasn't like the strippers—even Sergei himself—were armed to the teeth when they were dancing in G-strings.

Heart pounding, Sergei stepped into the booth.

Dom rose unsteadily.

"Sorry it took so long," Sergei said. "I—"

"Don't worry about it." Dom wrapped his arms around him and kissed him, sending electricity right down to Sergei's toes.

When they separated, Sergei whispered, "What's going on? You're practically shaking."

"Yeah, I…" Dom avoided his eyes. Though the light was dim, it was enough to reveal the color blooming in his cheeks. "It's not something I can talk about."

Sergei chewed his lip. He was well-versed in *omertà*, the unbreakable code of silence within the Mafia, so it didn't take much to figure out that whatever Dom couldn't discuss was related to what he was. Which meant Sergei didn't want to know.

And he shouldn't have cared, but standing here in front of Dom, seeing how shaken he was by something he couldn't talk about, tugged at something in Sergei's chest.

"We can't do this here," he said. "You know that, right?"

"I know. And I… I should've just texted you. But…" Dom met his eyes. "I needed to see you."

Why? Why me? What can I possibly do to fix whatever you just saw?

It didn't matter. He didn't need to know what had sent Dom here, only that he *was* here.

Sergei glanced at the curtain. Then he faced him and whispered, "You can't make a sound, or I'll lose my job."

Gulping, Dom nodded.

"Sit."

Dom obeyed, and Sergei turned up the music. Then he climbed onto Dom's lap, straddling him, and claimed a deep, hard kiss.

Dom's hands were immediately on him. All over him. They were unsteady, but not like they were the first time they'd fucked. It was as if he was no longer uncertain about touching a man, but uncertain about... everything. Like he needed an anchor. Or reassurance. Or *something*.

Between the two of them, they unzipped Dom's pants, and as soon as Sergei's fingers were around that rock hard cock, Dom broke the kiss and let his head fall back.

"Oh God," he breathed almost soundlessly. "Yes. *Please*."

Sergei stroked him, and leaned down to kiss his neck as he whispered, "Tell me what you want."

"You. That's... that's all."

"But, you're——"

"Don't." Dom shivered, thrusting into Sergei's hand as much as this position allowed. "Just need to... forget."

Forget what?

But Sergei didn't ask questions. He pumped Dom's dick harder. He wanted to turn him around and fuck him, but he was certain the slap of skin on skin would attract one of the bouncers. Or someone would just *know* and they'd get caught and then he'd be out of a job in the place where his contacts came to give him the truly lucrative work.

And besides, no condoms. No lube.

Damn it, no space.

"Can you hear me?" Sergei whispered in Dom's ear.

Another whimper, this one an obvious affirmative and the sound of a man about to come unglued.

"After this," Sergei went on, "you're going to meet me at a motel. You're going to text me with an address and room number, just like always, and then you're going to wait—naked, lubed up and ready for me. And I'm going to fuck you right."

Dom shuddered. "Please…"

Sergei raised his head. Dom's eyes were wide, wet as if he was about to break down in tears, and his lips were apart as he struggled to catch his breath. Tightening his grip on Dom's cock, he said, "When I'm done, I'm going to fuck you again, and I'm going to make it fucking *hurt*."

And just like that, Dom lost it.

His eyes rolled back. He held onto Sergei's shoulders for dear life, and fucked against him, shooting hot semen all over Sergei's hand and arm and stomach as his lips formed soundless, breathless curses.

Still shaking, he looked up at Sergei. "Promise?"

"Yeah. Promise."

Chapter 14

The orgasm he'd had in the club kept Dom semi-sane, but he needed more.

Waiting for Sergei was going to drive him out of his mind. He'd already taken two showers—one before the club, and one after he'd checked into the motel room because maybe this time it would get hot enough to rinse away the gunpowder residue on his hands. By the time he'd finished showering—*nope, not hot enough*—he didn't have much time. Sergei would be here any minute.

Sergei had ordered him to wait naked, so he didn't bother getting dressed after he'd dried off. And that wasn't the only thing Sergei had demanded.

Dom poured some lube on his fingers, and then lay back on the bed with his legs apart. Eyes closed, he reached down and pressed one fingertip against his ass.

As his hole started to relax, and his finger slid inside, his thoughts disintegrated. The rest of the night ceased to exist except for that little preview in the booth at the club. The guilt, the shame—it was gone. Temporarily maybe, but he'd take what he could get, and he pushed a second finger inside just so the stretch and the burn would erase even more of his mind.

Oh, it did. And it felt amazing. It was also deliciously rebellious. Ever since he'd almost gotten caught with a man years ago, he'd been so paranoid, he was sure if he finger-fucked himself or used a toy or anything, someone would catch on. The potential for embarrassment was one thing. Knowing all too well what could happen to him if someone suspected he was gay? That was more than enough to keep him from touching himself this way.

He'd jerk off—what man didn't?—but this? He hadn't dared. And now he was. And as he pushed his fingers inside himself, his toes curled and he was getting unbearably hard.

What if he got caught this time?

Oh hell. He was *going* to get caught. Sergei was going to walk through that door, and he was going to find Dom like this—legs spread, two fingers inside himself, dick hard and breath gone.

God, yes. He wanted Sergei to see him this way. And he wanted him to make good on his promise to fuck him, and then fuck him again until it hurt.

No shame. No holds barred. No consequences because no one would catch them. He hadn't realized just how much he'd truly needed this arrangement until tonight. With Sergei, he could be the man he was forbidden to be —a gay man who wanted to feel another man. Just a night of sex. Raw, primal sex. No lies, no gunfire, no filling a role he'd never wanted to fill.

Footsteps outside raised goose bumps on Dom's arms. The click of the door made his breath catch.

And there he was—Sergei.

He took one look at Dom, and grinned. Closing the

door behind him, he said, "Now that's something I could watch all night."

"D-don't watch." Dom slipped his fingers free. "You said you'd—"

"Oh, I know what I said." Sergei took off his shirt. He shifted to one side, then the other. Probably toeing off his shoes. "Did I say you should stop?"

Dom blinked.

"Well?"

Dom started fucking himself with his fingers again. Jesus—it was the exact same thing he'd been doing before, but somehow, doing it in front of Sergei made it a million times more intense. Maybe because Sergei was stripping off his tight jeans now, revealing the thick cock that Dom had been craving. He was quickly getting hard, and after he'd taken off his briefs, Sergei stroked himself slowly, bringing his cock to full attention.

Dom's mouth watered. "Please…"

Sergei grinned. "You're such a gentleman." He climbed onto the bed. "Always asking so nicely."

Dom bit his lip.

Sergei gently nudged his hand out of the way, and then he came down on top of Dom, his thick cock against Dom's and his narrow waist between Dom's thighs.

And he kissed him.

God.

In.

Heaven.

Dom thought he was going to lose his mind. Sergei was, as always, aggressive, but not overly so, and the taste of his kiss intoxicated Dom. His hair was damp and he didn't smell like the mix of sweat, cologne, and booze that stuck to everything in that club, so he must've showered.

Dom didn't care—as long as he had Sergei in bed with him, he didn't care about anything else.

Sergei pushed himself up on his arms, and then moved to his feet in a motion that was way too graceful and coordinated for a man with a hard-on. He beckoned to Dom. "Stand up."

Stand up? Are you kidding?

But he did what he was told, even if his legs weren't quite sure about it.

"Not sure I can stand very well," he said.

"It's okay. I wasn't planning to keep you on your feet." Sergei shoved Dom down onto his knees. Not that it required much effort—the faintest pressure on his shoulder knocked his knees out from under him.

Dom had barely hit the floor before Sergei forced his dick into his mouth.

Oh yes. Yes, this he could handle. Maybe his legs weren't competent enough to keep him on his feet, but with a hand on Sergei's hip and the other around his cock, he was pretty sure he could stay upright like this.

Stroking his hair, Sergei fucked his mouth. "You're a hell of a distraction, you know."

Dom moaned around Sergei's dick.

"Kind of hard to…" Sergei exhaled. He gripped Dom's hair and thrust *just* enough to push Dom's gag reflex. "Hard to concentrate on dancing when I just… when I just want to come back here and fuck you."

Dom moaned again, since it was the only sound he could make.

"In fact, speaking of fucking you." Sergei pulled his cock free. "Bend over the bed."

Didn't have to tell him twice. Dom scrambled to his feet, legs still wobbly, and turned around and bent over the mattress.

Sergei quickly put on a condom, and then stood behind Dom. Dom held his breath. He gripped the sheets, ready to lose his mind from the sheer anticipation, especially as the head of Sergei's cock teased him.

Dom was already slick and stretched, and Sergei took full advantage—one hard, violent thrust, and he was buried to the hilt. Dom moaned, eyes watering and elbows shaking beneath him.

"You did exactly as you were told," Sergei breathed as he started thrusting. "You're… God, this is perfect."

Dom just moaned again. Words didn't seem important anymore.

Sergei forced him all the way down, until his face was pressed against the sheets, and he held him there with a painful grip on his hair as he fucked him harder.

Everything ceased to exist. Even the rough sheets beneath Dom's face and chest faded into nothing. All that mattered in the entire universe was Sergei forcing his cock deep inside, again and again and again, so hard he made Dom's eyes water. He felt nothing except being fucked. The hand in his hair, the thick cock inside him, the thrusts that didn't quit—*please, please, please, do this all night.*

He wanted his orgasm to stay back so he could lose himself, but he felt so good, and his impending climax was so deliciously intense, he didn't fight it. He let Sergei drive him closer, his breath catching as the sheets beneath him added the most amazing friction. The room spun. The darkness behind his eyelids turned white.

Dom gasped. Every muscle in his body tensed. He was almost there. Almost there. Almost—

Sergei cried out something in his mother tongue, and the world exploded. Dom was coming, and Sergei was driving him down into the mattress with painful, erratic thrusts as he too fell apart.

Dom blinked a few times. They were still now. Had he blacked out? Maybe. Didn't matter. Felt great.

Sergei withdrew slowly, and if Dom hadn't already been facedown on the mattress, he was sure he would've collapsed. Jesus fuck.

Somehow, he figured out how to start breathing again. With oxygen moving once more, his head stopped spinning, and he clumsily pushed himself up. Sergei had stepped into the bathroom and came out with a couple of coarse towels, which they used to clean themselves off.

Then Dom dropped onto his back on the bed. Sergei fell beside him.

After a while, Sergei spoke, his voice unusually soft and gentle. "You all right?"

"Yeah." Dom released a long, ragged breath. "I needed that."

"So I see."

The unspoken question in Sergei's voice turned Dom's head, and their eyes met.

Sergei moistened his lips. "Something's different tonight."

"It's… complicated."

"Mmhmm." Sergei's eyebrow arched.

Dom swallowed. "I, uh, I guess I just got to thinking about things tonight. And the thing is, I'm only going to be able to do this"—he gestured at Sergei, then himself—"until I have to get married." Good enough. And not entirely untrue. "After that…" Dom shook his head. "I don't know. I guess I just… I feel like time is running out. Like I need this, and I need to get as much as I can while I still can."

Sergei pursed his lips. "You need… what exactly?"

"This. What we're doing."

"Yeah. That's the part I'm not sure about. You want to

get gay sex out of your system, but tonight, it seemed like you came looking for something more than that. So I need to know, what *do* you want from me?" He narrowed his eyes slightly, as if trying to read Dom's answers before he gave them. "A secret fuck buddy? Or…?"

"I'm not sure. I want this. The sex, I mean. I don't think I could ask for more than that from you because I couldn't honestly say I could give it back."

"So what was tonight all about?"

Tonight happened because every time I kill someone, a piece of me dies with him, and I needed—I need—to feel alive.

Dom sighed. "It's hard to explain. All I can offer you is sex, so that's all I can ask for too." *I need so much more from you. But I can't ask for what I can't give.* "Is that enough?"

"Of course," Sergei said without hesitation. "It's all I want too. I like the arrangement we have. You text me when you want me. Tell me where to meet you. And we fuck."

It sounded so crude. Little more than hiring a prostitute. Except he didn't see Sergei as a prostitute. He should have—it would've made it a lot easier to walk away when the time came—but he didn't. Far from it.

Dom swallowed. "It goes both ways. If you want me…" He hesitated to finish the sentence. He wasn't sure he wanted to hear him say that wouldn't be an issue. "Look, this doesn't have to be one-sided."

Sergei studied him, and then shrugged. "Well, I can't say it's been one-sided when we've hooked up."

"But the hook-ups don't have to always be at my whim. They can—"

Sergei kissed him. Not just a light kiss, or an attempt to shut him up. He kissed him hard—forcing his lips apart, curving his hand around the back of Dom's neck, pulling the breath right out of him.

Dom didn't protest. Screw talking if this was the alternative. He wrapped his arms around Sergei, and opened to his kiss without any resistance at all.

Sergei drew back enough to murmur, "Didn't I tell you I'd fuck you again and make it hurt?"

Dom moaned against Sergei's lips. "You did."

"Uh-huh." Sergei let him go. "Maybe you'd better get me a condom, then."

Dom didn't argue. They could talk about all this another time. For tonight, he had Sergei, and Sergei wanted to have him.

And Dom was definitely glad he'd brought plenty of condoms.

"YOU WANTED TO SEE ME, Mr. Maisano?" Kirill, a middle-aged Russian widower and father of three, stared warily at Dom from the doorway.

"Yes, Kirill. Come in."

The man took a timid step forward, and shut the door behind him. "Was there a problem with my payment?" Kirill's accent was stronger than Sergei's, but every syllable reminded Dom of the man he'd been with last night. "I made sure it was on time. Early, actually!"

"There's no problem with your payment. Have a seat."

Kirill did as he was told, and gripped the armrests tightly, knuckles blanching as if he were on the verge of a full-on panic attack. He was right to be nervous. After all, he was part of that complex racket Dom's family ran on the backs of immigrants. Not only were they required to work their fingers to the bone to pay down thousands of dollars in debt to the Mafia, but they were sworn to secrecy about their duties, which for an unfortunate few meant playing a dangerous role in smuggling cocaine through Cape Swan's deceptively quiet marina. Once the person had worked off his debt to the family, he and his would be given their documents, all of which had been acquired through the proper, legal channels, but held until the debt was paid. It was something Dom could only think of as indentured servitude with a side of human trafficking.

Dom hated it. He hated his role in the whole thing. He hated being the one who'd send out soldiers to put the squeeze on anyone who wasn't making regular payments, or those suspected of leaking information to the Feds.

But it had become his job when Corrado had made noise about putting Felice in charge of this particular industry. Felice had no qualms about doing more than putting the squeeze on people. Threatening a man's wife and kids was not below him.

So Dom had taken it on, if only to be the humane voice of reason.

Dom gazed at the terrified Russian. "How is the family?"

Kirill eyed him. He clutched the armrests tighter. "Please, don't hurt my children."

"I'm not going to hurt them." Dom leaned forward, ignoring the aches and twinges in his lower body and folding his hands on the blotter. "I need you to listen very closely, Kirill."

The Russian nodded vigorously.

"I have your papers," Dom said quietly. "Full citizenship for you and your family. Social security, passports, driver's licenses for you and your sister."

Kirill gulped, and sat straighter, but he didn't speak. He'd been at the family's beck and call long enough to be wary of the strings that would be attached.

Dom pulled a couple of envelopes from a drawer. He

slid the manila one across the desk. "These are all your documents." Then he held up a sealed white envelope. "And this is three thousand dollars in cash."

Kirill blanched, eyeing the white envelope like it was a venomous snake. It didn't take a psychic to read his mind. You didn't say no when a Mafioso offered you money, even if the terms were cruel or impossible. And if he was like any of the other immigrants currently indebted to the Maisanos, he needed that money no matter what came with it.

Dom set the envelope on top of the larger one. "I'm erasing your balance from the ledger. You owe nothing. This"—he tapped the envelope—"is a gift. From me."

Kirill still didn't take it. "I don't understand."

"I'm letting you out of your contract," Dom said, almost whispering. "I want you to take your kids, and your sister, and all of your papers, and get the fuck out of Cape Swan."

"Get… out…" Kirill shook his head. "Where do we go?"

"Anywhere. The money will keep you going until you can find work."

The Russian gulped. "But why? I… I don't under—"

"It doesn't have to be you." Dom started to withdraw the envelopes, but Kirill suddenly lunged for them.

"No! Please. We… my family, we need this. But…" He raised his eyebrows. "What am I to do in return?"

"Nothing." Dom let go of the envelopes and sat back. "All I ask is that you leave Cape Swan. And if you breathe a word to anyone about where this came from, or the erasure of your debt, and you and your family will answer to me. Am I clear?"

"*Da*. Yes! Yes, sir."

"Good." Dom gestured at the door. "You can go."

Kirill stood. "Thank you, Mr. Maisano." He smiled, clutching the envelopes to his chest as if they might suddenly be yanked away from him. "We're very grateful."

"You're welcome."

The Russian quickly left Dom's office, and Dom leaned back in his chair. Corrado and Felice would both have his head if they knew about his little sub racket, but Dom knew how to cover his tracks. He'd learned to use both of his jobs—handling the debts of the immigrants, and overseeing the laundering of the dirty money—to help the people his family was intent on screwing over.

Once a month or so, he quietly released one of the immigrants and sent them on their way. With a little financial magic, he erased the remaining debt and the money he gave them to start their new life, and no one was ever the wiser. If someone started sniffing around and asking questions about the books, he slipped some of his own money in and wrote it off as laundered money resurfacing after being routed and rerouted to separate it from its dirty origins. Since no one but him could follow where a dollar went before it reappeared, no one could prove he'd massaged the books as long as he didn't do it enough to raise red flags.

He hadn't had any issues with immigrants telling each other what he was doing, and he doubted that would ever become an issue. Most of these people had been threatened twelve ways from Sunday by the Mafia, and wisely believed every word of every threat.

If he could've done it without risk to the people, he'd have canceled the debts and sent every one of the families away from Cape Swan. But he couldn't. In some cases, their papers hadn't been processed yet, and they'd be left in a terrible limbo between him and the family. Mostly, though, he knew he'd be marked for death if anyone knew he'd even considered forgiving that much debt and cutting loose the entire pool of cheap labor upon which the narcotics ring depended.

But one family at a time, he let them go.

At least that helped him sleep at night. It didn't clear his conscience, and it didn't rinse away the blood on his hands.

But it helped.

Chapter 15

Baltazar was back. A little thrill shot through Sergei as he continued dancing for the money-waving men in front of him. He wasn't used to seeing the Greek this often. Once or twice a month at the most, but Baltazar had been in here almost weekly since the beginning of the summer. Things were heating up all over the place, weren't they?

After his performance, he went through the motions of letting the other men bid, and of course, Baltazar won. They moved into the booth at the back of the club, where Sergei turned up the music.

"Dmitry," Baltazar said with a subtle nod.

"Baltazar." He didn't return the gesture—felt a little too much like bowing, and he didn't bow to this guy or anybody else.

The Greek absently tugged at his jacket cuffs. "I've got an invite to a party on Saturday. A dinner cruise."

Sergei bit back a curse. This was a seaside town with a lot of illicit activity happening out on the water, which meant that sometimes he had to fill contracts on boats.

And he fucking hated boats. "Who's hosting?" *Who's the mark?*

"The first mate, if he's there."

Sergei nodded. So the mark wasn't specifically named. He was to take out the second highest ranking man aboard. Just as well he knew his way around the complex hierarchy of the families. Pity he couldn't blow up the whole boat and let the crabs finish them off, but overkill was a good way to accidentally take out an ally. Or an ally of someone whose bad side Sergei couldn't afford to be on. Or, worst of all, one of the innocent immigrants who the Maisanos used as slave labor.

Sergei nodded, and as Baltazar put the photo away, asked, "How many fireworks?"

"Just enough for the party."

So the hit was intended to send a message, probably to the highest ranking man aboard. By taking out the next man down, he'd be telling the top dog *"It could've been you, and next time it just might be."*

"What about security?" he asked. "On the boat and the marina?"

"It'll be handled."

Sure it would. Though Sergei's handlers had always come through when they'd agreed to compromise security —disabling alarms, putting personnel out of commission, setting up diversions—there was a first time for everything. He never, ever took for granted that a job wasn't just a means for putting him in the crosshairs of another hitman. Or, worse—law enforcement.

"All right," he said, making a mental note to go to the marina the night before and do a security check. "What time?"

"Saturday. Party starts at three-nineteen."

The boat is in row three, slip nineteen.

"That only gives me a few days to prepare," he muttered.

"That's when the party is. Be there, or don't count on another invitation."

Invisible scorpions crawled up Sergei's spine. This was one of *those* contracts—kill him when you're told, or it's your head next time. No room for error.

"This is another hundred grand job," Baltazar said. "They want it done right, and they want it done on time. You in?"

As if Sergei had a choice. He knew about the job, so now he either had to accept the contract or wait for a bullet of his own.

"Yeah. I'm in."

"Good. I'll pick you up when it's done. I don't see you by 10:30 am, though, you're on your own."

Sergei nodded. "Where will you be waiting?"

"Red four."

When the navigational buoys had been placed out in Cape Swan's harbor to guide watercraft, he couldn't help wondering if anyone had ever imagined they'd be used as rendezvous points for people like him and Baltazar. But, intentionally or not, the buoys served that purpose well, and Sergei would either be at the fourth red buoy by 10:30 in the morning, or he'd be in for a very long swim back to shore.

He settled up with Baltazar, and the Greek left the club. Not long after, so did Sergei. He'd already made arrangements for a shorter shift tonight because he needed to meet with someone out in a remote spot off Highway 103. It was a hell of a drive—almost two hours through hills, forest, and not much else.

Out in the middle of nowhere was a rest stop, and this time of night, there was no one around except a single silver sedan parked near the restrooms. There weren't even any idling semi trucks out here. Most truckers didn't stop here for long unless they were lost or broken down.

He didn't like this area. This whole road was littered with bad memories. He couldn't remember exactly where his family had been massacred, only that it was out here somewhere.

He shuddered and ignored the echoes of gunfire and screaming that always needled him out here.

As Sergei parked, his contact, Katashi, got out of the sedan.

"What've you got for me?" Sergei asked.

"Special delivery, of course." Katashi set a box on the hood. "Eight hundred."

Sergei opened the box and inspected the vials inside. They were intact, full, and appeared to be legit. Katashi had people on the inside of several pharmaceutical companies along the west coast, and they managed to smuggle out all kinds of shit. In this case, an experimental sedative that the FDA hadn't yet approved but was helpful when he needed to put a mark on ice for a little while like he had with Nicolá Cannizzaro.

"Looks good." Sergei paid him. "Anything else coming down the pipe?"

"Well, I got a lead on that stuff you've been asking for. Guy I know says he's got something that'll do the job."

"Yeah? What's he got?"

"Don't know." He shook his head. "But he said it'll put someone out"—he snapped his fingers—"just like that. No pain, nothing."

Sergei raised his eyebrows. "But you don't know what's in it?"

"There's cyanide, that much I know."

"Cyanide? Seems a little old school."

Katashi shrugged. "Gets the job done. Just gotta spray it right in a guy's face, let him breathe a little in, and good night. Long as you get the dose right, it looks like he's had a heart attack."

"Interesting." That was a method of delivery Sergei hadn't considered. Usually he'd heard of putting cyanide in food, or mixing it into a drink, but it was difficult to make sure someone got enough to kill them. Worse, with the wrong dosage, the symptoms were horrific. Surviving cyanide was a hell of a lot worse than dying from it.

"I need to know what's in it to get the dose right, though."

"I'll make sure I get that for you along with the chemical."

"Good." Sergei nodded. "I need that one ASAP."

"Guy wants two grand an ounce."

"He does?" Sergei lifted his chin slightly. "Or you do?"

"Hey, man. I gotta get my cut too."

"Yeah?" Sergei narrowed his eyes. "How big of a cut are you getting?"

Katashi gulped. "I can do eighteen hundred an ounce. No lower."

"Mmhmm." Sergei held the man's gaze.

Katashi shifted. Squirmed. Cleared his throat.

Sergei didn't move. Didn't speak. Didn't break eye contact.

"All right!" Katashi threw up his hands. "Seventeen fifty. Can't go *any* lower, man."

"Fine. Get me three ounces." He counted out three grand and pressed it into Katashi's hand. "You'll get the rest when I get my merchandise. And I want it *ASAP*."

"Man, I can't—"

"For that price, you're damn right you can." Sergei stepped closer, looking straight into Katashi's eyes. "And let's get one thing straight. If this doesn't work, and it's not quick and painless and undetectable like you and your guy are saying it is—"

"I get it, man! I get it!"

"No, I don't think you do, because you're still trying to fuck me over. So if it doesn't work the way it's supposed to, I promise you that you'll be finishing off my supply. Personally."

Katashi gulped, drawing back. "Okay. Okay. Yeah. Got it."

"Good. When can I get it from you?"

The man shook his head. "Dunno yet. I'll let you know."

"You do that. And make it quick, but I want it done right."

"Will do. Definitely."

"Good." Sergei collected his new poison and got back in his car. Having the cyanide-based one for the yacht job would've been ideal—he could test it on his mark and see how well it really worked. But he wouldn't have it in time, and anyhow, that poison would leave the mark looking like he'd had a heart attack or something. For Saturday's job, the kill had to look deliberate. It was meant to send a message, not just quietly remove a piece from the board.

Still, he wanted that poison, and soon. As he drove away, following Highway 103 back toward Cape Swan, he had high hopes that Katashi had come through for him this time. With the government cracking down on every goddamned substance on the planet, it was getting tougher and tougher to get his hands on poisons with specific effects. Katashi had hooked him up a few times, or tried to. Every fucking time, though, there was some side effect. Some potential reaction that happened one time out of ten, or a hundred, or a thousand, that made the victim seize, or vomit, or something other than immediate death. Too much risk. Too much potential for an ME to figure out the victim had been poisoned.

Sergei was patient, though. He had other means to kill and leave only as much evidence behind as he wanted to. The job that required a fast-working, undetectable poison could wait until precisely the right concoction came his way.

But Sergei hoped like hell it came through soon.

WITH THREE DAYS TO go before he needed to kill someone on a boat, Sergei's focus had been solely on his upcoming job and his late nights with Dom. Today, though, he had other things on his mind.

He stared through the windshield at the all too familiar stucco facility gleaming in the midday sun. After all this time, he'd have thought visiting this place might get easier, but it never did.

Chest tight and stomach in knots, he got out of the car and went inside.

There was a desk in front, chest high and staffed by a couple of college aged women. He didn't recognize either of them today, so they might've been new. No surprise—the turnaround here was astronomical.

Can't imagine why.

He shoved his hands into his pockets and headed down the hall that he'd been down a million times in the last ten years. The route hadn't changed for a long time—second left, last door on the right.

"Morning, Sergei." A familiar male voice turned his head. Jason, one of the nurses, offered a subtle, guarded smile.

Sergei forced an equally faint smile. "Morning."

"How are you doing?" Jason asked.

"I'm all right."

He wondered if Jason's co-workers knew how much he liked his private dances. For that matter, he wondered how someone who worked here could afford a stripper like Sergei. But he wasn't paid to worry about his customers' finances, so he danced when Jason came to his workplace and kept a poker face when he went to Jason's.

Jason cleared his throat. "Anyway. Um." He gestured down the hall. "She'll be..." He hesitated, and Sergei heard the words he didn't say: *She'll be happy to see you.*

Not a day went by that Sergei didn't wish that were true.

They exchanged halfhearted smiles, and Sergei continued down the hall. He was almost to his destination when a familiar redheaded nurse came around the corner.

"Oh, Sergei." Brittany's face lit up. "You're right on time, as always."

Sergei shrugged. "No thanks to an accident on the highway, but I made it."

"Good." She handed him a small paper cup of pills. "You know the routine."

"I do. Thanks, Britt."

No one else stopped him. At the door, just as he always did, he paused, closed his eyes, and took a deep breath. Then he forced a smile and stepped inside.

She was out of bed, sitting in the armchair by the window in her robe and slippers, gazing out at the yard.

He swallowed. She hadn't changed much lately. There wasn't any dark hair left to turn gray—she'd been snow white for years. Time had long ago deepened the wrinkles around her eyes and mouth. Her shoulders were thin, her posture hunching a little farther with each passing year.

She turned her head as Sergei pulled a chair up beside hers.

Sometimes she had little flickers of recognition. She'd look at him, and there'd be that spark, like she'd just figured out who he was. Today, it didn't come.

In their native tongue, which he only spoke with her these days, he whispered, "Hi, Mama."

She stared blankly at him.

He set the cup of pills on the tray beside her chair.

"What are those?" she asked in the same language.

"Medicine," he replied. "You need them."

She looked at him and blinked a few times. "Are you sure?"

"Take them, Mama."

"But why?"

"So you'll feel better." *Do they even make a difference anymore? Fuck, I wish I could do something for her.* He squeezed her hand gently. "Please Mama."

She eyed them uncertainly. It was impossible to guess what was going through her mind. If she had any inkling of why she needed to take them. Sometimes she didn't even seem to know how to take them, or what a pill was, never mind what it might do if she swallowed it.

Sergei pulled her water cup closer. "Take them. I promise, they're good."

She shifted her gaze to him. His heart clenched—*please don't ask who I am.*

Then she nodded. "Okay, Vasya."

Sergei had learned years ago how to wince without her seeing it. No need to alarm her. The mention of his long dead brother's name hurt, but he didn't want to upset her. To Mama, the Sergei sitting in front of her didn't exist. She could only make sense of him as her eldest son because she probably couldn't remember that so many years had gone by. That Vasily was dead and the Sergei she remembered—if she remembered him at all—was no longer a little boy.

One by one, he helped her take her pills. It was very much against policy, letting him administer her pills and vitamins, but everyone turned a blind eye. Whether it was out of sympathy, or because he had better luck convincing her to take them than they did, he didn't know and he didn't ask.

After she'd taken her pills, he sat with her quietly. There wasn't much more he could do. She could still speak, but her mind was too far gone to have a meaningful conversation. He'd learned that the first year she was here, when he'd tried to coax her back to him and succeeded only in confusing her. Even frightening her. Most of the time, she didn't seem aware of how unaware she was. When she caught on, when the confusion was unavoidable, she'd get scared, and he didn't know if those episodes were worse for him or for her, but they were hellish.

So he didn't try. He'd simply be here with her. Let her have some company for a little while. She seemed to like that. She couldn't remember enough to look forward to his visits, and she rarely had any idea who he was—sometimes she didn't even think he was Vasily—but his presence seemed to make her happy.

Her presence hurt like hell, though, especially on days like this. When it was painfully clear that she didn't remember. He was thankful she didn't remember what had happened, or why the two of them were all that were left, but God, what he wouldn't have given for a moment— even a few fleeting seconds—of recognition.

He took her fragile hand and stroked it gently with his thumb.

I wish you could see me, Mama.

The docs couldn't agree on what the fuck was the matter. It wasn't Alzheimer's. Brain damage from one of her almost successful suicide attempts? Extreme PTSD? Hard to say. She'd been nearly catatonic since the last suicide attempt, and now she was… this.

Well, it was a wonder Sergei wasn't as fucked up as she was. Or maybe he was. Mama had gone up inside her own head, disappeared from the whole world and never come back. Him? He'd planned and planned and worked his way into a position to destroy every last one of the mother-fuckers who'd destroyed his family.

Which of them was more fucked up? It didn't matter. She was here, and she was all he had left except vengeance. Some of the men filling contracts in this town were psychopaths. Serial killers. Not Sergei. He wasn't a remorseless murderer. But these families were subhuman, menaces to society, and he owed it to his own family to eradicate them. To erase them from existence like they'd done to his father and his brothers and, to perhaps a crueler extent, his mother.

Eventually, he took a deep breath and sat up. "I'm going to go, Mama."

"Oh." She held his gaze. "Okay, Vasya. It was nice to see you."

Sergei cringed. She was making that mistake more and more often these days. Even with his hair cut short and bleached, he couldn't escape how much he was looking like his eldest brother. On the other hand, if she thought Sergei was Vasily, then she didn't remember what had happened, and in her world, Sergei was still eight years old and Vasily was still alive along with Papa and Mikhail.

So Sergei didn't correct her.

He stood, wrapped his arm around her thin shoulders, and kissed her cheek. "I'll be back next week."

"Good, good." She smiled broadly. "Bring Sergei and Mikhail with you. I'd like to see them."

It was a struggle, but he made himself smile. "I'll try, Mama."

He hugged her once more, and then left. He didn't bother avoiding Jason and Brittany; they'd all learned that he wasn't chatty after his visits with Mama. If he was relaxed and calm on his way out, it was one thing. If he was hurrying toward the door, head down and hands in his pockets, his gait fast and determined, no one stopped him.

The blast of summer wind was suffocating and seemed to make the home's sterile, medicinal air burn even deeper into his mouth and nose. He told himself that was why his eyes stung, too. Just like he always did.

And just like he always did when Mama didn't recognize him, he got into his car and drove from the home to the beach. Never the same beach—couldn't be too careful —but one of those places the tourists never went and the locals barely knew about. There were lots of those in Cape Swan. Little fishing spots and places for teenagers to have midnight bonfires and knock each other up. This time of year, it was hard to find one where he could be alone, but he finally found an empty parking lot next to a deserted piece of sand.

He didn't get out of the car. Never did. He just needed a place where nobody would bother him. Every time he left Mama's room at the home, he came to a place just like this, killed the engine, and stayed in the car.

He didn't like people seeing him cry.

SOME NIGHTS, Sergei could work after visiting Mama. Others, he could barely move. Tonight was one of the hard nights. Before his shift, he'd sat in his car for a good twenty minutes, staring at the dashboard and wondering if he even had the energy to turn the key. Somehow, he made it to the club. And he made it through one dance. And now he just wanted to…

Sleep? Die? Drink himself senseless?

The answer came as he struggled through his second dance of the night. Every time another customer came in, he caught himself hoping it was one man in particular. And whenever the new arrival wasn't Dom, Sergei felt even lower. Even more lethargic.

He struggled through his dance, and his tips reflected it. The winning bidder for a lap dance barely broke fifty bucks, and probably left feeling like he didn't get his money's worth. Fuck. Sergei's head was not in the game tonight.

Leaning against his locker in the back, he tapped his fingers on the edge of his cell phone. On the screen was Dom's number—under a fake name, of course.

Text him? Forget it?

If they met up, it was for one thing and one thing only, and Sergei couldn't decide if that would be a good thing tonight. Just thinking about the mechanics of sex exhausted him. He'd barely been able to move his limbs enough to shower, drive down here, and change into these skintight leather shorts. Anything more than that—especially something as taxing as sex—made him want to curl into a ball and never move again.

But getting into bed with someone was appealing, too. He craved that close contact with another human being while shutting out the rest of the world—the death, the crime, the shell of the woman traumatized out of her own mind.

He closed his eyes and swallowed. Even if it took all

the energy he had and then some, he needed to feel human again, and he could think of no other place to recharge himself than in bed with the only man who'd touched him like a human being in years. It was a long shot, thinking Dom would be available or willing, but he sent the message anyway.

Can I see you tonight?

As soon as it was sent, he started gnawing his lip. This arrangement had been about Dom, not Sergei. Dom could say what he wanted about this thing being two-sided, but they both knew it was about *him* getting his sexuality out of his system before he had to pen it up forever and be a good straight man. There was nothing in their unwritten agreement about Sergei's needs.

His heart sank lower. No matter how emphatic he'd been on that first night that he was not a prostitute, suddenly he was all too aware that that was exactly what he was now. He was servicing another man. Giving him what he needed with no right to expect anything in return. He might as well bite the bullet and start charging Dom, since this was just—

His phone buzzed.

He looked at the screen. The message was simple as they often were: *When/where?*

Sergei's lips parted. Disbelieving he'd even gotten a response, he sent back, *I can get a room. Send you a msg w/address. ASAP?*

And to his surprise, the response came quickly:

Ready when you are.

WHEN THE MOTEL room door opened, Sergei's jaw dropped.

He really came?

Of course he had no reason to believe Dom would lie to him, but Sergei trusted no one, took no one at their word—and he'd learned long ago not to depend on anyone else. When he needed someone the most, that was when promises came up empty.

But Dom… he was here. Just like he said he'd be.

As he stepped into the room, their eyes met. Sergei's heart sped up. Dom closed the door, and the click hit Sergei's nerves like gunfire.

He jumped, pulling in a sharp breath.

"You all right?" Dom came closer. "You seem kind of…" He slid his arms around Sergei. "I don't know. Tense?"

"I'm fine. I'm just…" Sergei ran his fingers through Dom's hair. "You're here."

Dom cocked his head. "Did you think I wouldn't come?"

Actually…

"I didn't… I mean… I guess I thought—"

Dom cut him off with a soft, insistent kiss. "I'm here. I meant it when I said this thing wasn't just about me."

They separated enough to meet each other's gazes.

"Are you sure you're all right?" Dom asked.

"I'm fine. I'm sorry." He cursed the weakness in his voice. "I just don't really want to be alone tonight."

"You won't be." Dom kissed him softly. "I'm here."

Sergei finally managed to smile. "Yeah. You are." He brushed his lips across Dom's. "We're both still dressed, though."

Dom laughed. "We should do something about that."

"Agreed."

It didn't take them long—with what seemed like a few quick motions, their clothes were at their feet. The next thing Sergei knew, Dom was pulling him down onto the bed, his skin hot and bare. When Dom rolled him onto his back, Sergei didn't resist. He let himself be laid gently on the sheets, and shivered as Dom lay over the top of him. Any reservations he might've had about being under a larger man were gone. There was nothing threatening about Dom, and even if there had been, Sergei didn't have it in him to put up his guard tonight.

Dom kissed the side of his neck, and his hips moved slowly, fluidly, almost lazily against Sergei. They weren't groping or winding each other up—just touching. Kissing. Sergei was in no rush, and he hoped to God Dom wasn't either. Orgasms would happen when they happened. Maybe. He wasn't even sure he could come tonight, but he didn't care. This was the part he desperately needed—strong arms around him, hot skin against his, someone's breath cooling and warming the side of his neck.

He'd never been so grateful for another man's company. He'd needed someone to distract him tonight, but he hadn't even imagined…this. That Dom could not only make him feel alive, but make him feel like it was worth staying that way. That despite everything, he was still worthy of a kind hand and a passionate kiss. He didn't try to make Sergei justify why he needed this tonight or make him earn it. He just gave it as if there was no reason not to.

Sergei could barely keep it up tonight, but he didn't want to stop this. Dom obviously didn't have the same problem—his prominent erection pressed into Sergei's hip, grinding against him every time they moved.

"Want… you on top," Sergei panted.

Dom shivered. "Let me get a condom."

Sergei nodded. He very nearly told Dom to forget the condom and just fuck him, but he still had enough rational thought left to keep that to himself. They barely knew each other. They were both dangerous men. Sex was already pushing the bounds of sanity—unprotected was going a little far.

Dom put on the condom, and Sergei turned onto his hands and knees. He had to struggle to keep his breathing steady as Dom put some lube on him. As Dom slid a finger inside him, Sergei swore; he wanted Dom to hurry up and fuck him, because this position meant they were barely touching. Only the one finger—now two fingers—penetrating him, and a hand on his hip to keep him steady. Otherwise, Sergei's skin practically burned with the absence of Dom's against it.

Finally, though, Dom slid his fingers free, and Sergei held his breath as Dom guided himself in. As Dom pressed into him, Sergei's vision blurred. Hell, his mind blurred. He hadn't been fucked in too long, and now that the head of Dom's cock was inside him, he wanted every inch. All of it at once.

Dom took his time, though. He was big enough he could've made this hurt, but he was too careful for that. He eased himself in until Sergei's body yielded to him, and even then, he moved slowly, taking ages to slide all the way inside, then all the way back out, then all the way back in again.

"Fuck…" Sergei's head spun. He couldn't hold himself up, so he sank down to the bed, and Dom followed.

And… there. Skin. Sergei was stretched out beneath Dom now, and they touched everywhere, from their feet to Dom's lips in Sergei's hair. Even when Dom almost pulled out, he didn't break contact—his body still touched Sergei's, and when he slid back in, Sergei sighed with both arousal and relief. He pressed his forehead into the pillow, arching into Dom's chest.

Stubble scraped his shoulder, and then soft lips met his skin.

"You feel so good," Dom breathed. "God, you just…"

I do feel good. I feel fucking amazing. Overwhelmed, Sergei shut his eyes, squeezing a hot tear free. *Holy fuck.*

Dom groaned. He whispered something in Italian, something that may or may not have been meant for Sergei's ears, and a shudder rippled through him. Hot breath rushed across Sergei's shoulder. Dom thrust a few times, then buried himself all the way inside and groaned.

With a heavy sigh, he relaxed, though he didn't put his weight on Sergei. "My God."

Sergei exhaled.

Dom kissed the back of his shoulder. "You didn't come."

"It's okay." Sergei found Dom's hand and laced their fingers together, ignoring the fact that a touch like that should've been out of place between them. Or the fact that it wasn't out of place right then.

He turned his head, and Dom's lips met his.

Yes. This was perfect.

Absolutely perfect.

I don't have to come. I just don't want you to go.

SERGEI KNEW damn well he had no business getting too attached to Dom, and he told himself he wasn't. He had to admit, though, he really, really liked this—lying beside Dom, his arm draped over Dom's broad chest and his head resting on a powerful shoulder, with a strong arm around his own shoulders. The hand laying gently on his upper arm, the slow rise and fall of Dom's chest, the warmth of his skin—it was luxurious. Almost as addictive as the sex. Maybe more than that.

It was no wonder their late night liaisons were inching farther and farther into the mornings after. And the fact that Dom was one of *them...* it barely even registered anymore. Right or wrong, dangerous or not, he was just Dom.

After God only knew how long, Dom broke the silence. "Can I ask you something?"

"Can't promise I'll answer."

"Fair enough." Dom absently ran his hand up and down Sergei's arm, probably oblivious to how much Sergei loved that gentle, affectionate contact. "Why do you work at that club?"

"Hmm?"

Dom's hand stopped. "You've got an amazing body, but... I can't imagine stripping is the only thing you can do."

Oh, it isn't.

He was much too raw to talk about what he did in the club, but it was better than thinking about what *else* he did. Sergei shifted a bit, lifting himself up on his elbow so he could see Dom's face. "I don't think there's anything wrong with stripping. Do you?"

"I—well..." Dom stammered, his cheeks turning pink. "That's not what I meant. I'm sorry. I guess I just..." He touched Sergei's face. "I guess I was just curious. I'm sorry."

"It's all right." Sergei hooked his leg over Dom's, slipping his bare foot under Dom's other calf. "And it isn't like I'm going to strip forever." He laughed quietly. "There's... a point of forced retirement, you know?"

"I suppose there is." Dom combed his hand through Sergei's hair, fingertips grazing Sergei's scalp and sending goose bumps prickling down his spine. "What will you do after that? I mean, ten, fifteen years from now—what do you think you'll be doing?"

Sergei swallowed.

It doesn't matter to you. You'll probably be in prison. Or dead. And I'll be in another hemisphere, moving on from this life.

Sergei cupped Dom's cheek, the stubbled skin warm beneath his palm. "I guess I'll figure it out when I get there."

Dom gave a subtle nod, as if that was enough of an answer. No judgment, no approval or lack thereof—simply an acknowledgment that the question was answered.

"What about you?" Sergei asked.

"What about me?"

"In ten or fifteen years, do you think you'll still be…"

Dom sighed. "If I'm still alive, I'll still be in Cape Swan, still a part of my family's organization." He drew a soft arc along Sergei's cheekbone with the pad of his thumb. "If I saw an alternative that didn't involve a bullet, I wouldn't be part of it in fifteen minutes, never mind fifteen years."

"Have you ever thought about leaving?"

"Every day of my life." Dom's voice sounded hollow. Haunted, even.

"But you can't? Ever?"

Shaking his head, Dom looked in Sergei's eyes. "If I could, I would. But other people have. And Corrado always finds them. Wherever they go, he finds them. And when he does…" The shudder finished the thought.

Sergei chewed the inside of his cheek.

Dom smoothed Sergei's hair. "You do know it's dangerous being with me like this, right?"

Dom, you have no idea…

Sergei just nodded. "Yeah. I do."

"But you keep coming back."

"Yeah." Sergei leaned in and brushed his lips across Dom's. "I do."

For a heartbeat, he thought Dom might question him, ask him why he kept coming back for more when the danger was so clear and present. Instead, Dom wrapped his arms around him and drew him down into a long kiss and a warm, gentle embrace.

Sergei sent up a silent prayer of thanks that Dom hadn't asked. Because this—the way they were holding each other and kissing, bringing every one of Sergei's erogenous nerve endings back to life—was the only answer he had. He needed this for reasons that didn't rationally outweigh the risks. As careful and calculated as he was, as much as he avoided unnecessary risks, Sergei couldn't make himself turn away from Dom now.

So he didn't.

He sank into Dom's embrace, pressed his hardening cock against Dom's hip, and lost himself in the last man on earth he should've touched.

Chapter 16

Dom and Sergei went their separate ways shortly before sunrise. On autopilot, Dom drove home, undressed again, and collapsed in his own bed, but sleep didn't come.

It was weird, Sergei needing him instead of the other way around. He'd started thinking Sergei was doing this because, hey, he knew getting together with Dom meant guaranteed sex, and sometimes an effortless sure thing was exactly what the doctor ordered.

Except last night, it was Sergei who'd asked for it, and Sergei who'd been almost shaking with a need Dom couldn't quite put his finger on. Dom had been serious when he'd told him this shouldn't be a one-sided arrangement, but he hadn't been expecting that.

In the darkness, he sighed and scrubbed his hand over his face. He was glad he'd been able to give Sergei what he needed. Hopefully it had been enough. And he was more than a little thankful that Sergei took care of his needs too.

Dom refused to let that give him any kind of hope that there was—or might eventually be—more to this. Though he would've sawed off a limb to have a real, honest to God relationship with a man, it wasn't happening. Sergei had walls up and Dom had obligations. Sex was as far as this thing could go. It couldn't and wouldn't last forever.

As it was, Sergei drove him to distraction. Dangerously so. When Dom's obligations or his need to preserve his image kept them apart, he thought of nothing except how to make time to see him again. He dodged dates with Brigida Passantino now that she was back in town. Bowed out of social engagements whenever possible. Found any and every opportunity to text Sergei with *busy tonight?* or *I'd like to see you*.

And Sergei nearly always obliged. Sometimes it was three in the morning after he'd worked a shift at the club. Sometimes it was in a shithole motel by a truck stop two hours out of town in broad daylight. Sometimes it was at one of the seedier places as soon as the sun went down. Whenever, wherever—Dom was hooked on Sergei like half of Southern California was hooked on the coke his family processed through Cape Swan.

But there were only so many times Dom could body-swerve his own life. Whether he liked it or not, he was a Maisano, and his uncle wasn't going to accept many more excuses where Dom's bachelorhood was concerned.

So, in between finding every possible chance to get fucked by Sergei, Dom had finally made that date with Brigida. In a few hours, he'd meet her at the restaurant where Floresta and Mandanici had ambushed him, and they'd try this again.

And all the while, as he put on the face of a longtime bachelor who was serious about settling down, he knew damn well he'd be aching for another hit. For one more night that he could lock away in his memory so he'd have fantasies for later. Something to keep him sane while he spent the rest of his life as a committed heterosexual in between committing capital crimes for an organization he despised.

Jesus. I really am in hell.

———————

AT THE URGING of his uncle and her father, there was extra security this time. Dom had adamantly refused a bodyguard for his daily life but relented for this, and as he sat in the restaurant and waited, he tried to ignore the looming shapes hovering behind him.

One bodyguard. I agreed to one bodyguard.

But no. Corrado had to insist on three.

Well, at least he wasn't getting his ass kicked tonight. Which was good, because as exhausted and achy as he was from another night with Sergei, he was in no condition to put up a fight.

At exactly seven o'clock, Brigida Passantino walked into the restaurant, and every head turned. Though Dom didn't feel an ounce of sexual attraction to women, he could definitely see why other men fell all over themselves for her. Her dark hair tumbled over her shoulders, and the black dress was *made* for her tall, slim figure. Knowing what he did about Brigida and her sisters, the dress struck him as a compromise between father and daughter—short enough and low enough for a woman who wasn't afraid to show some skin, but still modest enough for Passantino to let her out of the house. Dom grinned to himself. Though the older generations of men in this town were still stuck in the 1950s, and saw women as currency to be exchanged and objects to be admired, there were women like Brigida who would stand on their own two feet and be who they were regardless of what their fathers thought.

"*I'm a grown woman,*" he could almost hear her snarling in her powerful, dangerous father's face. "*I'm meeting this asshole like you wanted. You're not telling me how to dress too.*"

And then there was the way she moved. Her long strides, her posture—it all screamed not just confidence, but fearlessness. She strode across the restaurant, shoulders back and head high, not giving her security detail a second look as they followed her. He had a feeling she'd be just as bold without a pair of heavily armed men at her back.

As she approached, he stood. Biaggio had taught him young to pull out a lady's chair, but something about the way she held his gaze told him that wouldn't go over well.

Instead, he extended his hand. "Brigida?"

She smiled warmly and shook his hand. "You must be Domenico."

"Just call me Dom."

"All right. Dom." She released his hand and reached for her chair, which didn't surprise him. As she took her seat, he took his, but moved a little slower so that she sat down first but wouldn't think he was making a big show of it. One of her older sisters had berated Luciano for holding a door for her on a date a few years ago. According to her, chivalry and chauvinism were synonymous, so Dom decided to err on the side of simply and subtly being a gentleman.

"Wine?" He gestured at the leather bound wine list.

"Of course." She picked up the list. "Do you have any preference?"

He shrugged. "I could go for something red, but whatever sounds good."

She opened the list, lips quirking as she perused the options. "How about a Domaine Romanée Conti?"

"Sounds great." He was about to flag down the waiter,

but Brigida beat him to it, making eye contact and politely beckoning him over.

When the waiter arrived at the table, Brigida ordered the bottle, handed her the list, and dismissed her. Then she met Dom's gaze, and her confidence faltered slightly.

"You… don't mind…" She waved a hand toward the waiter.

"Oh, no. Of course not." Dom smiled. "You had the list, after all."

"True." She rolled her eyes. "I've been out with some guys who get their noses out of joint if I step all over them trying to impress me."

Dom chuckled. "Well, I'm not going to stop you if it means sparing everyone my horrible French."

Brigida laughed, and… wow, she really had a smile that could light up a room. "Just don't tell my dad we ordered anything French, okay? As far as he's concerned, if it didn't come from Italy, it isn't worth drinking unless it's champagne."

Dom laughed too, bringing his water glass up to his lips. "I don't know if I'd go that far with champagne."

"Same here." She wrinkled her nose. "I think I'd rather drink horse piss."

Dom choked on his water.

Brigida covered her mouth, smothering a laugh. "I'm so sorry. I've been here two minutes and I'm already being crass."

"No, no, it's fine." He cleared his throat. "Just wasn't expecting it."

"So much for behaving on a first date, though." Though she *almost* sounded sheepish, that wink was anything but contrite.

He winked back. "I won't tell if you don't."

She grinned. Then she tapped a long nail on her

menu. "I guess we should settle on something to eat. Do you recommend anything here?"

"Depends." He opened his menu. "You're not a vegan or anything, are you?"

Brigida snorted. "A vegan? I'm *Italian*. I'd starve."

Dom nodded, chuckling again. "That's what I thought. In that case, you really can't go wrong with any of their steaks…"

SHOES LITTERED the floor at their feet. Hands ran under clothes and over hot skin. Soft lips skated across flesh. The bed was still too far away, but they'd get there. Eventually.

Slender fingers ran through his hair, making his scalp tingle, and then gripped it and pulled his head back. Lips and breath on his throat. Jesus. His knees were about to go right out from under him. And if they did, well, the floor wasn't that far down, and the floor was horizontal and sturdy—good a place as any.

"Fuck," he breathed. Corrado and Passantino would have his head if they found out about this, but Dom didn't give a damn.

He slid his hand downward between them and cupped Sergei's thick erection.

Sergei hissed sharply, breaking the kiss. "And I thought… thought I wouldn't hear from you tonight."

Dom grinned, squeezing enough to make Sergei squirm. "I'm just glad you were free."

"As if I'd say no," Sergei murmured, and kissed him again. "Kept thinking about you tonight."

"Did you?"

"Mmhmm. You think about me when I'm not there?"

"All the fucking time." Dom slid his hands down

Sergei's back, pulling him against his hard cock. "You want to know what I think about when I'm not with you?"

"Do tell."

"That first night." Dom shivered. "In the chair."

Sergei licked his lips. "When I came on your shirt?"

"Oh yeah."

"We broke a lot of rules that night."

Dom ran his hands up Sergei's chest. "Pity we couldn't have broken more."

Sergei grinned. "There's no rules tonight. We can do whatever we want."

"Yes, we can."

"Take off your clothes." Sergei freed himself from Don's embrace and nodded toward the armchair beside the table. "Then sit."

"My clothes?"

"That's what I said, isn't it." Sergei still grinned, but in his eyes was the commanding, take-no-shit stripper who'd gotten in his face the same night he'd gotten on his lap. Oh hell yes.

Dom stripped, and then threw a towel on the chair since, well, God knew what else the furniture in here had been used for. As soon as he was seated, Sergei—fully dressed and visibly hard—straddled him, his shirt nearly touching Dom's face and his bulge grazing Dom's chest.

He started to reach for Sergei, but hesitated. "May I?"

"Yeah." Sergei leaned in closer, resting his hands on the back of the chair. "Please do."

Dom slid his hands up Sergei's chest, the fabric of his shirt pulling beneath his touch. This was even hotter than he'd anticipated. The juxtaposition—clothed stripper, naked customer—was a tease to end all teases. Though Dom could put his hands on him, he couldn't *touch* him, and it was Sergei's clothes, not his own, that kept their flesh from meeting. He could touch, but he couldn't feel. Not quite. Muscles moved beneath the surface, but the shirt tempered the heat of Sergei's skin.

Despite the lack of music, Sergei danced. Twisting, undulating, grinding—no wonder men threw wads of money at him at the club. An electric thrill surged through Dom. They could fall all over him, but how many of them could touch him? See him fully naked, in the throes of an orgasm? How many of them knew what his skin tasted like? What his *kiss* tasted like?

Sergei sat back a bit, and peeled off that rumpled shirt.

Jesus. He could look at this body a million times, and never stop marveling at the sculpted perfection. He brought his hands up, and a violent shudder rippled through him as he put them on Sergei's lean, bare torso. Sergei kept on dancing, writhing, undulating, and as he did, he took Dom's wrists and guided them. Suddenly they were part of the dance too, cresting muscles just as they contracted, sliding down them in the same moment they relaxed, palms and fingertips following lines that curved, straightened, curved again.

Dom pulled him closer, so Sergei's clothed cock and balls rubbed against his bare chest. He kissed him, ran his hands all over him. There was no music, but Dom's heart thumped hard enough to make up for it.

"Can I...?" He struggled to catch his breath. "Your clothes..."

"Yes," Sergei murmured, rubbing his groin against Dom. "Definitely too many—oh, fuck..." He tilted his head back as Dom unbuttoned and unzipped his tight pants. Between the two of them, they pushed Sergei's pants and boxers over his hips, revealing his fully erect cock.

Dom was tempted to grab Sergei's ass, pull him up,

and suck his dick until he lost his mind, but instead, he whispered, "Come on me again. Like you did the first—"

Sergei swore in Russian and started fucking against him, the chair protesting beneath them as his hips rocked and his dick slid up and down Dom's abs.

"God," Dom whispered. He ran his hands along Sergei's hips and sides. "I think about that night all the time. You were so…" He looked up, gazing into Sergei's heavy-lidded, watering eyes. "You were so fucking hot." He grabbed the back of Sergei's neck and brought him down, and Sergei whimpered when their lips met, and his thrusts became frantic, the friction so hot it should've been painful.

Sergei broke the kiss with a gasp. His whole body quivered, and then his hips jerked forward, and hot semen jetted across Dom's abs and chest. He exhaled, trembled, and he'd barely finished coming when he murmured, "*Please* fuck me."

"Absolutely." Dom ran his hands all over Sergei's sweaty, trembling torso. "I want you just like this. On my lap."

"I like the sound of that." Sergei reached past him, toward the table where they'd tossed the lube and condoms. The motion stretched his long, lean torso and made Dom's mouth water.

When he came back, though, he had lube in his hand, and a small towel, but no condoms.

"What about—"

"Bareback." Sergei grinned, wiping the semen off Dom's stomach. "I want you bareback."

Dom blinked. "But I—"

"You said yourself you hadn't been with anyone else in ages."

"You sure you should trust me that much?"

Sergei's lips pulled back across straight white teeth. "I think I have a good grasp on who the dangerous one is in this arrangement."

If you only knew.

Sergei covered Dom's cock in lube, and then positioned himself above him. Dom steadied himself and, with a hand on Sergei's hip, guided him down. He watched Sergei's eyes, and goddamn, in the same instant Dom breached him, Sergei screwed his eyes shut and moaned.

"Like that?" Dom asked.

"Uh-huh." Sergei lifted up, then came down a little more. "I fucking love the way you feel."

"Likewise." Especially like this. With no barrier. With Dom immobile, unable to do a thing except sit here and watch Sergei ease himself down. Dom's head fell back. He groaned, overwhelmed as Sergei took him deeper.

And Sergei didn't just ride him—he swiveled and wove like he did during the lap dance. He moved in ways Dom had never felt before. Not while he was this deep in someone.

Dom's hands slid off him, and he gripped the armrests instead, digging in with his fingers as he held on for dear life. "Oh shit, Sergei… that is…" He tried to blink his eyes into focus, but they wouldn't cooperate. Still, he tried—he had to see this, to drink in the way Sergei danced on him and rode his cock at the same time. He could barely see. Could barely breathe. His body didn't know what to do with this much pleasure, this many insane electric sensations, and the climax to end all climaxes was closing in fast, and there was no stopping it even if he wanted to.

"Keep going," Dom slurred. "Jus'… just like…" All the air rushed out of his lungs. He gasped. Tensed. He pulled Sergei all the way down and didn't make a sound as he exploded deep inside him.

Sergei kissed beneath his jaw. "Please tell me we can fuck like this again."

"Yes, *please*."

"Good." He lifted his head and pressed his lips to Dom's. "Because that was hot."

"Oh my God, yes."

When they could finally move, they got up and moved into the bathroom for a shower.

"You really don't mind going bareback?" Dom asked as the lukewarm water ran over both of them.

"No." Sergei hesitated. "But, uh… probably only when you're on top."

Dom cocked his head. "Why's that?"

"Well, it's been fifteen years since you've been with other men." He shrugged, the gesture almost apologetic. "I've… been around a bit more recently."

"Still, I—"

"It's safer." Sergei wrapped his arms around Dom and stood up on his toes to kiss him lightly. "It's better this way, I think."

Dom ran his fingers through Sergei's wet blond hair, a few cool droplets sliding down the back of his hand. "I can still use condoms when I'm on top. If you want."

Sergei shook his head. "No. I…" He shifted his gaze away.

"What?"

Sergei hesitated for a moment. Then he looked up at him with those intense blue eyes. "This, what we're doing, is the only chance you have to be with a man. I want you to feel it. Really feel it."

A condom barely makes a difference in what I feel when I'm with you.

Really feel it? I do. I definitely do. Every fucking time.

But he just drew Sergei in for a soft kiss.

The water was starting to get cold, so they shut it off and dried themselves. Then they turned down the bed that they hadn't even touched so far, and climbed under the covers.

For a while, they just lay there, enjoying the lingering buzz of amazing sex, until Sergei finally broke the silence.

"So." He propped his head up on his hand. "I'm curious about something."

"Hmm?"

"You were out on a date with a woman tonight, and then you texted me and wanted to hook up. And let's face it—you were horny as fuck." His eyebrow arched. "If she turned you on that much, why aren't you in bed with her?"

Dom sighed, scrubbing a hand over his face. "It's… not quite that simple."

"Let me guess—she has to be a virgin when you marry her?"

"No, no. In fact, I'm pretty sure she isn't." He lowered his hand. "For a woman raised in this bullshit environment, she's liberated as hell. I doubt she's been a virgin for a long, long time."

"That doesn't bother you?"

"Of course not. It's fucking refreshing." Dom shrugged. "Just seems like a shame that a woman like her would wind up with a man like me."

"Except she does apparently turn you on?"

"No, she doesn't." Sighing again, Dom stared up at the ceiling. "She's beautiful. She's intelligent. She's everything I would want in a woman if I were straight." He rubbed the bridge of his nose. "But I'm not." He dropped his hand to his side, but still didn't look at Sergei. "When I left the restaurant tonight, yeah, I was horny as hell, but not because I wanted to be with her. It was because being on a date with her, knowing how much pressure there is to marry her, it just made me realize how little time I have left to be who I really am."

"Whoa." Sergei touched his arm. "That's… rough."

"Yeah. And if Brigida and I don't agree to get married soon, my uncle will find me another woman. And there will be even more pressure." He rolled his eyes. "Don't know why he doesn't just throw a goddamned ball and make me find the woman with the glass slipper."

"Well, with as much as he has you meeting potential suitors—" Sergei flashed a toothy grin. "Does kind of sound like you're a Disney princess or something."

Dom laughed, but it took work. "Sometimes it really does feel like it, and not in a good way."

Sobering, Sergei tilted his head. "What do you mean?"

"Because my life is run by people who don't give a damn if I want to be a part of it."

"So why are you part of that life?" Sergei was quiet for a moment. "I mean, you're really going to marry a woman, for the sake of what people think?"

"I was born into this." Dom stared up at the ceiling and exhaled. "I could live a million years and never understand why anyone would want to be involved in this shit. I didn't have a choice, and I've spent my life being reminded of that at every turn, especially after my father fucked over the family. They've all been ready and willing, all this time, to take me out the second I give them a hint that my heart's not in it, and that's all the sign they need that I'm a turncoat like him."

Sergei studied him for a moment. "Why don't you leave? Why stay if—"

"If I could, I would." Dom looked at him. "It's complicated, but… this is the reality I live in. If I leave, my uncle will hunt me down, and he will kill me. In horrific ways you can't begin to imagine."

Sergei shuddered.

Dom swept his tongue across his lips. "The only thing I can do is keep my head down, and hope that when someone finally finds a reason to kill me, they do it quick."

Sergei's Adam's apple jumped. "That's…"

"I don't like it, but it is what it is. And part of that means getting married. Being straight." He sighed, touching Sergei's face. "All I can do for the moment is stall as long as I can, and spend as much time…"

They held each other's gazes.

Without a word, Sergei slid closer, tipped Dom's chin up, and kissed him. As Dom wrapped his arms around him, something settled in his chest. No, this couldn't last forever. No, this wasn't something that fit into his pre-orchestrated world.

But for tonight—for as many nights as he could—this was where he needed to be.

This was the one person on earth he needed to be with.

This was who he needed to be.

DOM STUMBLED in through his front door around eight in the morning. He shuffled upstairs to his bedroom, stripped out of his clothes, and dropped into bed to grab a few hours of sleep before he went into the office. His receptionist already knew he'd be in later.

His head had barely hit the pillow, though, when his cell phone went off.

"You've got to be kidding me," he muttered, and felt around for his phone. Except it wasn't on the nightstand. Fuck, he hadn't even bothered taking it out his pocket.

He jumped out of bed and pulled his trousers from the

hamper, and managed to get the phone into his hand and answer the call before it went to voicemail.

"Yeah?"

"Your uncle wants to see you," Biaggio said sharply. No specific time, which meant *now, Domenico.*

Rubbing his unshaven face, Dom mouthed a curse into the stillness. "I'll be there as soon as I can." After he'd hung up, he eyed his pillow. No, he didn't dare. Even sleeping for fifteen or twenty minutes was liable to backfire on him. He'd oversleep, or it would make him even more tired, or this would be one of those times when Corrado was tapping his watch and demanding to know why Dom hadn't left his house the instant he'd gotten off the phone.

He'd go see Corrado, *then* come home and get some fucking sleep.

But first… coffee.

"YOU LOOK like you had a long night."

From anyone else, it would've been accompanied by some brotherly ribbing, maybe some crude comments about how Brigida was in the sack, but Biaggio's tone was filled with gentle concern. Not surprisingly—the consigliere had been the only man besides Dr. Rojas who Dom could trust as a confidante over the years. Though his loyalty to Corrado was fierce, he seemed to have some sympathy for Dom. Enough that he frequently filled in as the father figure Dom didn't have.

"I'm fine." Dom sighed, rubbing his tired eyes. "Just didn't sleep very well."

"I can see that."

They continued into the house, and Biaggio was silent, walking beside him up Corrado's grand staircase. Dom knew that silence well—the conversation wasn't over, but Biaggio was waiting for him to go on.

"I don't think I can do this," Dom said, barely whispering. "Brigida's great, but it's tough to get to know someone when there's already pressure to get married when you're on your first date."

Biaggio nodded. "I doubt anyone would disagree that you're in a difficult position."

"I'm just not sure what I can do about it."

"Have you made arrangements to see her again?"

"We've been out already."

"Good. Then you're making a good faith effort to see this through, and that should be enough to satisfy her father and your uncle. At least for now."

"One can hope, right?"

Biaggio grunted an affirmative.

As they followed the long hallway toward Corrado's office, Felice came toward them.

"Oh, hey, Dom. I was just about to call you." Felice halted, so Dom and Biaggio did too. "I'm taking the boat out on Saturday morning. One of my new cargo liaisons will be meeting us. Why don't you come out with me and meet him?"

Guarded, Dom held his cousin's gaze. "You really need me out there?"

"Dom, come on." Felice laughed and clapped Dom's shoulder. "It's business. You gotta know all the players, and this boy's a big player. He's going to be bringing you some people soon." He raised his eyebrows, letting that convey the unspoken meaning.

Dom's stomach roiled. Another smuggler who moonlighted as an "immigrant transporter," as Corrado and Felice liked to call them. More like human trafficker.

While he didn't like the idea of being out on the water

L.A. WITT

with his hothead cousin, he couldn't let on. So, he shrugged. "Sure. Yeah. I'll come meet him."

"Great. I'll text you with the time once I talk to the crew."

"Perfect." Felice clapped his shoulder and kept walking.

Dom watched him for a moment. Then he continued down the hall with Biaggio.

"Weird," he muttered. "He's being awfully friendly lately."

"He's probably heeding his father's advice for once," Biaggio said. "Realizing he's a grown man and not a teenager anymore and needs to behave accordingly."

"I don't know." Dom chuckled. "When it comes to Felice maturing, I think I'll believe it when I see it last longer than a week or two."

Biaggio laughed as he reached for the door to Corrado's office. "You and me both, Domenico. You and me both." He pulled open the door but went no farther.

A private meeting, then. Just what Dom needed today.

His uncle was at his desk, perusing the contents of a thin file folder. When the door closed behind Dom, Corrado looked up. Closing the folder, he said, "How did your evening go with Ms. Passantino?"

Dom stopped in front of the desk, hands behind his back. "You called me in here to ask me about my date?"

"I couldn't care less about your date, Domenico." Corrado's features hardened as he and Dom locked eyes over the desk. "But your intentions with her are important. An alliance with the Passantinos would be… timely. Because things are getting hot all over. There is *definitely* a war brewing—I can smell it."

Dom nodded. "Yeah. Me too."

"Which means men are going to start questioning loyalties. Smoking out potential moles."

And killing them to be on the safe side. Dom shuddered. When things got hot in this town, it wasn't at all out of the ordinary for people to shoot first and ask questions later.

"Anything that can be used against you will be used against you." Corrado's eyes bore right into Dom. "And we've discussed this—being unmarried at your age? It doesn't look good. It doesn't look good at all. A man of your stature who hasn't settled down and committed to a woman…" He shook his head. "You've got too many decks stacked against you to—"

"I get it. I do." Dom sighed. "But I've never met a woman who—"

"That's part of the problem." Corrado's voice was low and *almost* threatening. "Even Felice has found a wife. And yet you've barely given any woman a second look. You're barely showing a bit of interest in a lovely, connected woman like Brigida." His gray eyebrows pinched together. "I don't need to tell you what kind of rumors *that* produces."

Dom's heart dropped. "People think I'm—"

"Yes." Corrado shifted, nose wrinkling slightly. "And remember, this organization is more than a business. This is a family. If the men don't think of you as a family man, then you'll never make it."

I don't suppose bowing out gracefully is an option.

"Understood," he said flatly.

"I need you and Brigida to make a decision." Corrado folded his long fingers. "Sooner than later, Domenico."

Dom nodded despite the ball of lead in the pit of his stomach. "I'll see her again soon. And we'll… we'll discuss it."

"Good." The word was made of both approval and dismissal. *We're done here—get out.*

"I'll keep you updated," Dom said, and started for the door. His uncle didn't stop him.

Out in the hallway, he paused, wiping his hand over his face. Just what he needed. More pressure to marry, and more pressure to marry this woman specifically.

Sure, Brigida was a nice woman, but the chemistry was nonexistent. Even if she were attracted to him—and maybe she was; he had no idea—he didn't have even the slightest bisexual tendencies. He was as gay as he was Italian. Any woman unfortunate enough to be his wife would be treated well, and she certainly wouldn't want for anything that money could buy, but the nights might get cold, and he hated that he wouldn't be able to give her what she needed. Enough to have children, he hoped, but passion?

And like Luciano and Felice's wives, she'd be in a certain degree of danger simply by taking the Maisano name. If Brigida Passantino married him, she could be deemed a traitor by the men within her father's fold who loathed the Maisanos. That was to say nothing of the Cusimanos. Very, very few of them would be willing to target a woman or a child, but all it took was one. Or her being in the wrong place at the wrong time when someone shot at him.

He wanted out of this life. Out of his own skin. But short of death, there was no escaping this. He was, and forever would be, a straight Mafioso.

Any wife or lover of his would be in a certain amount of danger.

And that included Sergei.

Guilt twisted beneath his ribs. Though Sergei was fearless—even ruthless—when it came to Mafia men, he was made of the same flesh as anyone else. A bullet would stop him as surely as it would Dom.

And if Sergei took a bullet that was meant for Dom…
Dom shuddered.

He wouldn't allow that to happen. But if he kept seeing Sergei, he was inviting it to happen.

Well, Dom—what are you going to do?

Chapter 17

Three hours before sunrise on Saturday, Sergei parked a mile down the road from the marina. He stepped out of the car and immediately started sweating beneath his wetsuit. Pity the water wouldn't be as warm as the night, especially since he was only wearing a half suit. His arms would be exposed from above the elbow, his legs from above the knee, and even this time of year, the Pacific was fucking cold once you dropped below a meter or two.

The suit wasn't ideal for the conditions, but it was the best thing for the job. A dry suit would have been too unwieldy on land. Even a full wetsuit would limit him too much—the half suit didn't do a damn thing to keep him warm in the water, but it would give him the mobility he needed later on.

He slung his tanks over his shoulder, carried the rest of his gear in a net duffle bag, and made his way toward the marina. Just outside the fence line, he waded into the water and bit down on a string of curses. Despite the warmth of the evening, the water was, as he expected, cold as balls.

Chest deep in water, he attached the bag to the tanks

and secured the tanks to his shoulders but left the regulator out of his mouth. Instead, he put on his mask and used a snorkel. He put on his fins, and then swam toward the marina. The heavy load on his back was cumbersome and annoying, but left his hands free to guide himself through the gently rolling surf.

He was mostly hidden by shadows, and he wasn't worried about the cameras spotting him. He'd already addressed that issue—the men watching the screens in the security shack would be watching an infinite loop of last week's footage and wouldn't see him. As long as he didn't draw the attention of the occasional man patrolling the marina on foot, he'd be in the clear.

Under cover of darkness, he glided along the surface, soundlessly and slowly, following the breakwater that protected the boats and the docks. The duffle bag was cumbersome, the tanks a pain in the ass while he was near the surface, but fortunately he didn't have far to go. When he was within the breakwater, and thus in sight of the goons patrolling the docks this time of night, he took a deep breath and went under, kicking hard and rocketing through the icy water toward the row of gently bobbing hulls. He didn't use the tanks—every second of air needed to be conserved for later, not wasted on a short swim.

A short swim that took plenty of work thanks to the bulky equipment on his back creating drag. Between the exertion and holding his breath, his lungs were burning by the time he broke through beneath the dock. Still, he didn't allow himself to gasp for air. Calling on every ounce of control he possessed, he exhaled slowly, then took in a long, deep breath. And another. And another. Though he'd been here earlier to make sure every electronic security device had been compromised, that wouldn't do him any good if one of the roving guards heard him panting.

Little by little, his heart slowed down and the burn receded. No one wandered down this way.

Now, to find the boat.

As soon as he zeroed in on the slip number, and saw the gigantic profile of the boat, he realized this wasn't just any yacht—this was Felice Maisano's superyacht.

Well, that answered the question about who the *highest* ranking man aboard would be, assuming Felice didn't unwittingly bring Daddy along that day. Good—Felice Maisano was an asshole, and Sergei didn't mind rattling his cage with a "message" by way of a dead second-in-command. Shooting him would be gratifying too, if the opportunity ever presented itself.

What would Dom think if I killed his—

No, no. Don't go there. Business, Sergei. Business.

The craft was hard to miss. This section of the marina was filled with luxury yachts, but Felice's stood out. The ninety-foot, triple deck power catamaran was even more ostentatious than the boss's extravagant boat, or Raffaele Cusimano's monstrosity three slips over. It was huge and flashy with all the bells and whistles imaginable. The boat of a man so rich he couldn't bear anyone not knowing how rich he was. The watercraft equivalent of a diamond-studded Rolex.

As Sergei stealthily cut through the water, he caught a glimpse of the boat's name on the hull, but couldn't read it in the low light. If it wasn't a Sicilian euphemism for "please don't notice how tiny my dick is," it should've been.

Carefully, he swam between the catamaran's dual hulls. Toward the middle—safely away from the props and well out of sight from anyone who might look—he went to work, starting with his escape route. There was no way he could drill into the fiberglass hull without drawing attention, but he'd brought several strong suction cups that, when attached to the hulls just below the surface, weren't coming off for anything. He put them into place, spacing them about two feet apart, and hung off each one for a moment, yanking as hard as he could to make sure they didn't move. They stayed. Perfect.

With some karabiners and a rope, he secured the tanks and all of his gear to the hooks on the suction cups. Finally, he took off his fins, replaced them with a pair of scuba booties. Then he secured the fins to the pack of gear, pushed off gently, and swam to the dock.

He paused for a long moment, holding his breath, and listened. There were footsteps on planks—unhurried men on patrol—but they were far away. In his immediate vicinity, the only sounds were lines and hulls squeaking against wood, and water lapping lazily against pylons.

He released his breath. Took a few more. Then he hoisted himself up onto the dock. He crouched low so the water dripping off him wouldn't make much noise. Once the majority of the water had run off, he rose, glanced around again, and boarded the boat. He didn't worry about leaving wet footprints on the dock or the deck. Any he did leave would be dry by sunrise, any droplets left behind dismissed as a natural consequence of being this close to the water.

Baltazar had taken care of the security and surveillance systems. He'd even had the radar compromised to make sure it didn't show Sergei swimming between the hulls. The crew would have no idea there was anything wrong—the radar would just show some pre-programmed blips. How? Sergei didn't know. Baltazar was the technical wizard.

The Greek had also given Sergei a code to get past the security system and onto the boat. According to Baltazar, the system had been quietly compromised. The alarm would still chirp, and the doors still wouldn't open without the code, but when the cameras and login records were played back, they'd be blank.

Still, Sergei had sneaked onto the marina yesterday and made sure it actually worked—punching it in, then waiting to see if cops or Mafiosi showed up—and it was clean. Good. Couldn't be too careful. He never knew when a job might be the one where Baltazar decided to sell him out.

Sergei looked around again, making sure he was still alone. Then he entered the code and let himself onto the boat. Jesus fuck—this thing was even larger on the inside. Gaudy, ostentatious, and perfect for Sergei's mission. There were ample places for him to lay low and go unnoticed until it was time to make his move. And, for that matter, enough space for him to make that move, get off the boat, and *still* go unnoticed.

The luxury living area had likely been meant for lavish parties, watching movies on the giant HD screen, and lounging on the plush sofas. From what he'd been told, this room, when closed off, was completely soundproof. All the Mafiosi loved their boats with soundproof entertaining areas—ostensibly for movies and parties, but Sergei doubted that was the *only* reason.

And anyway, there'd be no movies or parties today. This was business. The sofas and tables had been covered in plastic and pushed to the sides, opening up the wide floor. He wasn't entirely sure what went on in here during the voyages, but he had a pretty good idea.

He wasn't making his move in this part of the boat, though. There'd be too much activity. Too many people. Instead, he went up to one of the sundecks. There'd be lookouts posted up here once people started arriving, but he'd be able to move below decks and into the bedroom to hide without being detected.

First things first, though, he wanted to make absolutely sure he could move undetected throughout the boat. He went into every room and compartment he foresaw using, and tested the hatches and greased the hinges so nothing made a single squeak.

Once that was done, he headed up to the sundeck. On his way up he pulled his .22 pistol free from the watertight bag and tucked it into his belt. He already had a serrated diving knife strapped to his thigh. When his mark boarded, he'd be ready.

All he had to do now was wait.

AS DAYLIGHT NEARED and he started nodding off, Sergei threw back a couple of pills Katashi had sold him. He couldn't remember exactly what they were, but they worked like Red Bull's steroid-addicted cousin. In minutes, he was wide awake, heart thumping as much from the chemical as anticipation.

Activity down on the pier told him people were heading this way. He wasn't nervous. Everything was in place. Everything was going according to plan.

The only question that remained—who was the mark?

He knew the hierarchies of all three organizations like he knew his own apartment. After all, it was impossible to play chess without knowing what all the pieces were and how they could affect the game. When everyone was onboard, he'd know which piece was going down today.

How he'd make his move depended largely on who the mark turned out to be. Someone who knew how to work on boats? Sergei would fuck up an engine so the man would be sent in to fix it. A day drinker? Sergei would catch him by the immense, fully stocked bar on the second deck. Some poor sap with no sea legs? Sergei'd take him out while he was heaving over the side.

More variables than he liked when he was already on a job, but it couldn't be helped. By the time he disembarked, one of the goons would be dead, and he'd have more money to add to his "get the fuck out of Cape Swan" fund.

Commotion drew his attention to the dock below. He craned his neck. At the end of the pier, near where the fishing boats came in, Felice was right in a fisherman's face, stabbing a finger at him and shouting.

Sergei held his breath.

"How the fuck do you explain this?"

"It was… it was the crabs!" The man's accent made Sergei's skin crawl. He couldn't put his finger on the exact nationality, but the man had clearly come from the same part of the world he was.

"The crabs." Felice laughed humorlessly. "So now I have crabs getting into my merchandise and stealing it from me. Is that what you're saying?"

"I don't… sir, I don't know if—"

"What the fuck happened to my merchandise, Ivan?"

"I don't know! When we pulled up the trap, all the other bricks, they were good. But this one… this one is no good. Cut open. Wet."

"I can *see* that, asshole!" Felice barked. "Do you have any idea how much this is costing me, Ivan? This whole fucking kilo is ruined. That's over a quarter of a million dollars. A quarter. Of a million. *Dollars*, Ivan."

Ivan said something Sergei couldn't hear.

"For that much money," Felice bellowed, "I could sell your family to—"

"Please, please, Mr. Maisano! I'll do anything!"

Their voices dropped, and Sergei couldn't hear them anymore, but he'd heard enough anyway. Cringing, he fought the urge to get sick. It wasn't unusual for the crabs to mess with the bricks, or it could have been sabotage from a competitor. Either way, it wasn't the hapless Ivan's fault.

Felice wouldn't care. And Sergei had heard that the asshole had, on at least one occasion, sold a man's family into a sex trafficking ring in Southeast Asia. No one was quite sure why—maybe to make a point to the man, or make an example of him to others—but it was a very persistent rumor.

This was exactly why Sergei never cut crab pot lines when he was diving. It was tempting, if only to kick the wops in the financial balls, but the hapless middlemen who were responsible for the merchandise left in those crab pots would feel the pain much more severely than their handlers ever would. Just last year, three of them were killed before Corrado Maisano realized it was scuba-diving Cusimanos stealing their coke, not the fishermen.

Which of course, meant that diving out in the harbor was more dangerous than ever. Some of the goons had taken to shooting divers for sport under the guise of protecting their "interests." From what he'd heard, the scuba instructors in town were even starting to warn people not to surface until they were right next to a boat flying the diver down flag. Otherwise, the bubbles had a tendency to attract Mafiosi like blood attracted sharks.

And that meant today's escape route was going to be dangerous as fuck, but there was no other way to off a man on a boat in open water and get away undetected. Once Felice found that body, he'd tear his boat to pieces looking for the killer, and Sergei had no intention of being anywhere near it when he did.

He looked down at the dock again. The commotion had died down, and Felice was on the way to the boat, flanked by his usual posse of assholes. As they boarded along with the boat crew, Sergei immediately zeroed in on one. Agosto Privitera, a lieutenant. Not a big fish, but the other two were no-name soldiers. Not even made men.

Behind the Mafiosi were three workers in dingy, threadbare clothing that contrasted sharply with the expensive tailored suits of the Maisanos. Sergei thought he heard the men speaking in hushed Korean, but he didn't pay them much attention. They weren't part of his agenda.

Privitera, however...

Sergei grinned as he headed down to the bedroom to hide. He had his target.

Cape Swan, California. Population: One less Italian mother-fucker than yesterday.

Question was, he thought as his grin fell, what to do about the Koreans? If Felice blamed them, he wouldn't hesitate to punish them. Sergei couldn't back out, though. He'd just have to make sure the hit happened while there was no possibility of the immigrants taking the fall. That would be easy enough. Just wait for—

"Hey!" Felice called out to someone. "Thought you weren't gonna make it!"

When the response came, the voice turned Sergei's blood to ice:

"I told you I was on my way."

Sergei's throat constricted.

Oh shit. Oh shit. Oh shit.

Dom?

That changed *everything*.

His orders had been clear—kill the second highest ranking man aboard the boat.

Which meant second in line was Dom. No one else on this boat came close to either of their statuses within the family. Being the son of the boss, Felice was the top dog unless Corrado showed up, and there wasn't nearly enough security for that. Felice's cousin-slash-adopted-brother? Easily second in line.

No two ways about it—Dom was the mark.

There was no getting off the boat. No getting out of this contract. He had to finish the job, or it would be his head.

Nausea swept over him. *Oh God…*

As the crew went to work above decks and the boat pulled out of the slip and cruised away from the marina's protected inlet, Sergei didn't dare stay in one place. He moved around as stealthily as he could, staying absolutely silent and out of sight, keeping tabs on everyone he could.

As he passed the living area at one point, he caught a glimpse of the three Koreans lugging empty crab pots in and staging them in neat rows. Felice supervised. Dom hung back in the shadows. Security loomed even further in the background.

And all the while, Sergei prowled around the boat, trying to keep his stomach from coming up his throat. This wasn't seasickness. This wasn't something he'd ever experienced during a hit.

He shook himself. Even if Dom was the mark, he'd come here to fill a contract. Which meant obeying the orders he was given. The fact that he'd been in bed with the man—or that he'd gotten *way* too close to him in other ways—was irrelevant. It was fucking go-time.

The boat headed out of the harbor, and then hauled ass toward the open sea. For the moment, the three Koreans stood outside smoking, and the Italians were out of sight. Likely enjoying some early morning wine in the shade of one of the upper decks.

This much, Sergei had planned for. The boat had its own rendezvous point several miles off shore, and there was nothing for him to do now except use the time to figure out how to get his mark alone after the boat was back in the harbor.

But the game had changed. This wasn't just a nameless, meaningless goon.

This was Dom.

Indisputably the second highest ranking man aboard.

Fuck.

A COUPLE of hours after they left the harbor, the boat was far enough into the open sea that the land was a fuzzy gray-green line on the horizon. Up ahead, a red and black cargo ship bobbed in the waves.

The boat stopped beside the ship. A meeting was going on—Sergei couldn't hear the specifics from his current hidey hole—a small alcove behind the galley—especially not with crew members moving boxes into the living area nearby.

Then everything wrapped up, and the boat was on the move again, but as it neared the harbor, stopped at one of the bobbing orange buoys. A crab pot. Then another. And another. Each time, they came to a halt, and the boat rocked gently in the water while the Koreans switched out a crab pot. Sergei memorized how long it took them to swap out the crab pots, calculating how much time he'd have to get off the boat and grab his gear before the propellers started again.

He was ready.

And as the boat approached another buoy, Dom was in the galley. Alone.

Around a corner, watching Dom in the reflection of a

semi-tinted window, Sergei gnawed his lip. He drew his gun from his belt and rested it against his thigh.

It wouldn't take much. Open the door. Put a bullet through his brain. Climb down off the stern. Grab his gear, dive, and swim like hell so no one saw him beneath the surface and the bubbles off his regulator didn't give him away.

All he had to do was shoot Dom.

Right through the back of his head, so he never knew what hit him.

Shoot him. Let him drop. Watch him die.

Sergei closed his eyes and slowly, silently pushed out a breath.

I'm losing my damned mind. He isn't Dom. *He's a Maisano. He's the mark.*

Except he is Dom.

He's a made man. He's one of them. He's…

Dom.

Shit.

On the other hand, Baltazar hadn't specified the mark's name. The boat was huge, and Sergei could easily lose track of everyone on board.

This kind of job was meant to send a specific message. It was much like when the assassins of old would leave a knife in a sleeping king's pillow, inches from his head, so that when he awoke, he'd know just how easily they could have killed him. This job was meant to tell Felice Maisano how vulnerable he was. For reasons Sergei didn't need to know, someone was putting the squeeze on the man, and they were sending a very loud warning.

One that would, in theory, be received whether the stabbed pillow was Dom or Privitera.

He gulped. It was an enormous risk. He was supposed to

take the shot, not make the call. But they hadn't given him a name. There was no guarantee he'd know Dom was aboard. He hadn't seen the faces and didn't know the names of the crewmen driving the boat, or the men who'd come over from the cargo ship. On a vessel this big, Dom could've slipped past his radar. Especially since he'd arrived late anyway.

Oblivious to Sergei watching him and contemplating his fate, Dom left the galley.

Sergei released a breath. Sweat beaded on his forehead and trickled down his neck.

Privitera it was. He couldn't kill Dom. He just couldn't. If a contract came along, and Dom was explicitly named as the mark, then he'd have no choice. But that wasn't the case here. He didn't think it was all that likely anyway— Dom was high up in the ranks, but not a key player. Men who coughed up money to take out hits wanted more important targets. Someone like Felice, if he didn't listen to the message that Sergei had been sent here to convey.

As long as no one named Dom as a mark, Sergei wouldn't have to cross this bridge again. He hoped.

Now… Privitera.

Sergei's opportunity came when Privitera went past him on the way to the head.

Sergei's stomach clenched.

Do it now, or take out Dom.

Heart thumping, he slipped out of his hiding spot.

He glanced outside. Dom and Felice were on the bow, sipping wine and talking. The workers and security men were in the living area. The boat's crew were… well, they weren't up here. That was all he cared about.

Sergei took a bottle of wine from the rack and sneaked past the door to the head, stepping out onto the exterior deck. He waited there until the latch on the head clicked, and then he crouched, set the wine bottle down, and let it roll along the deck. It was loud enough for Privitera to hear, and when it clinked against the bulkhead, it was less obtrusive than shattering glass.

It worked: Privitera stepped out and leaned down to pick it up.

He had his fingers on the bottle when he froze.

Slowly, he turned his head, and looked right up the barrel of Sergei's pistol.

"Stand up." Sergei drew the hammer back. "And don't make a sound."

Chapter 18

The meeting at the cargo ship had gone well enough. As always, the cargo crew sent a smaller boat out to meet the yacht, and from there, two contacts and two security guards had joined Dom and Felice on board. While the Koreans and a few men from the cargo ship transferred a dozen or so boxes onto the yacht's lower deck, there was wine and food on the uppermost deck. Everyone introduced themselves, discussed business, and negotiated prices. The man on the ship didn't speak much English, but the shipping manifests were clear and appeared to be correct, so Dom could work with that.

Once the meeting was adjourned, the men and workers returned to their boat, and the Koreans got to work on the lower deck. Dom stood in the background while Felice supervised.

Working quickly, the workers tore open boxes and rifled through stacks of counterfeits like children searching through cereal boxes for toys. The counterfeits were mostly designer clothing—not cheap knockoffs, but the real deal, manufactured according to the designer's precise specifications, but in unauthorized factories in Italy and China. They'd be distributed amongst retailers in California, and sold at boutiques for eye-watering mark-ups.

They were just a front, though. Buried within the stacks of dresses, jeans, blouses, and swimwear were bricks of cocaine. One kilo apiece, wrapped in plastic.

Once the bricks were fished out of the boxes, the men quickly wrapped them in additional plastic and taped them. Then the bricks were stacked on a platform that was normally hidden by the coffee table. If the Coast Guard got too close, the platform dropped down and extended into the water between the catamaran's hulls, quickly and quietly jettisoning the cocaine. A potentially costly but effective precaution against one hell of a prison sentence.

Assuming they weren't boarded, though, and things progressed normally, the next step was to load one crab pot with a few kilos, and drop it for one of the fishermen to pick up. By the time the yacht returned to Cape Swan, there wouldn't be a single grain of cocaine onboard. Every boat in the Maisano fleet had been searched a few times, and much to the investigators' frustration, nothing had ever been found except for a few cases of contraband textiles. It was a foolproof system, one carefully developed with a thorough understanding of the laws and regulations they were breaking. A virtual guarantee that none of them would ever do time for narcotics trafficking.

When Felice was apparently satisfied that everything was progressing smoothly with today's shipment, he gestured for Dom to follow him back to the upper deck. There, he poured them each some wine. They clinked their glasses together, and each took a sip.

"So." Felice swirled his. "With business out of the way, I brought you out here for a reason."

Dom's stomach clenched. "Oh really?"

"Everywhere else in town, the walls have ears. And I'm curious…" He paused, gazing into his glass. Then his eyes flicked up and met Dom's. "Has my brother seemed… strange to you lately?"

"Strange?" Dom set his glass down. "How so?"

Felice scowled and shook his head. "It's hard to even put my finger on it, to be honest. But when I've been to his house and his offices recently, I've seen people coming and going who seem… suspicious, I guess."

"In what way?"

"He has a lot more of these people"—Felice gestured flippantly at the two Koreans who were pulling up another crab pot—"working for him than I realized."

Dom scowled. "So he's got some immigrants on his payroll?" *Maybe he's even paying them properly, instead of exploiting them like you do, asshole.*

"Except when I've asked, he doesn't say what they're for. What are they doing?" Felice folded his arms. "Why aren't their pay slips in the books?"

Dom chewed his lip. Undocumented immigrants were hardly unheard of. And it wasn't at all unusual for men to take the immigrants who were under contract, and have them do some work under the table—anything from pulling weeds to transporting drugs. Most of the contractors were desperate to make ends meet and pay off their debts, so they eagerly took the work. Dirt cheap labor for the Italians, extra money for the immigrants—in a perverse way, everybody won. Luciano had never seemed to approve of that practice, but even if he'd changed his tune, it didn't seem *that* out of the ordinary.

Dom shifted his weight. "What do you think his game is?"

"It's hard to tell. He's operating something on the sly, though. I can fucking feel it. And the thing is, well, let's face it. We all know that if something happens to my father, or he retires, Luciano's taking his place." Felice took a deep breath. "I'm just worried he might make a play to get that inheritance sooner than later."

Dom studied him. "That doesn't sound like Luciano."

"Then you haven't been paying attention," Felice muttered into his glass.

"Luciano's the one who tries to talk your father out of calling in hits."

"He is." Felice set the glass down and rested his hands on the railing. "Which means he'd be the last one anybody would suspect of taking out a hit of his own. Especially one on Dad."

Dom pursed his lips. "I suppose that's—"

A panicked shout made them both jump. They turned as one of the workers rushed up onto the deck, screaming something in his own language.

"What?" Felice snapped. "What are you saying? *English*, asshole."

The man stopped, took a few breaths, and in broken English, said, "Downstairs. He's…" He drew a finger across his throat.

Felice and Dom exchanged glances. Then, with Felice's soldiers hot on their heels and their pistols in hand, they rushed down to the lower deck and out onto the stern.

"Oh, my God." Felice covered his mouth and turned around. "Fuck."

Dom stared, swallowing hard to keep his breakfast where it belonged.

On the sun lounge, Privitera lay as if he were sleeping, his hands folded on his stomach, his hair and tie fluttering in the gentle sea breeze. He even had a wine bottle lying across his lap, as if he'd been about to settle in for a drink.

The only problem was that gaping wound across his

throat and the blood trickling between the chair's plastic slats and pooling on the deck like rainwater.

"Get the fucking Koreans out here," Felice snarled. "Now!"

One of the security goons hurried inside.

"They did this," Felice said. "They fucking killed—"

"That's insane," Dom said. "They've been in here working."

"Yeah?" Felice gestured at the body. "Then who the fuck did do it? Because the crew is all upstairs and this doesn't look like a fucking suicide, Dom!"

"I don't know, but it wasn't them. It could have been—"

"Which one of you killed him?" Felice bellowed as the men were shoved out onto the deck.

They all balked, staring at him and gaping.

"No, no!" The one who'd sounded the alarm said. "I saw blood." He pointed a shaking hand at the pool, which had extended far enough across the deck to be visible from inside. "Saw blood! Didn't kill!"

"Uh-huh."

"The hell you—"

"Felice," Dom said in Italian, "you don't know it was one of them!"

"And you don't know it wasn't."

"For God's sake—"

"All right. Fine. Maybe he did. Maybe he didn't. But somebody on this boat did, so *he* can be a fucking example in case they're thinking of trying it again." With that, Felice turned and calmly unloaded a single round into the gut of the man who'd sounded the alarm.

The poor man howled in pain and crumpled to the deck.

The other two surged toward him, but Felice's men stopped them.

"Get back to work," Felice snarled. "Or you can have one too."

Shaking, the men looked at each other.

"Back to work!"

They scattered, hurrying back to their staging area.

Felice scowled at the writhing, moaning man, and stalked back inside. "Security. We've got someone on board, and I want him *alive*."

Dom crouched beside the wounded man and pulled out his pistol. "I'm sorry about this." He tucked the gun up under the man's chin.

The man groaned feebly and grabbed Dom's arm. For a moment, Dom thought he was going to push his hand away, but he guided it upward. To his temple. Their eyes met, and the desperation hit Dom in the gut.

"It'll be over soon," Dom said quietly.

The man released his arm, and his eyes slid closed.

Dom pressed his finger into his own ear, the one closest to the bleeding man, and fired.

The body jerked, and then the man was still, but inside the boat, fresh chaos erupted. Two of Felice's security guards appeared, guns drawn, but Dom put up his hand.

"Relax." He gestured at the body. "Just putting him out of his misery."

The men exchanged glances. They lowered their guns, but didn't holster them.

Felice stormed back out, shoving the men apart so he could get by. "What the fuck?" He threw up his hands. "Dom, what the hell are——"

"We're not animals, Felice." Dom rubbed his ringing ear. "You made your point. There was no need to let him suffer like that."

Felice sighed sharply. To one of his men, he said, "Have the captain take us back out to sea. I don't want a body floating in the harbor." To the other, "Tell them"—he jerked his thumb over his shoulder—"to toss their buddy when we stop."

The men left the deck, and Felice glared at Dom. Gesturing at the body, he growled, "You almost put a fucking bullet through my boat, you know!"

"Put it on my tab," Dom muttered.

Felice's nostrils flared. Under his breath, he muttered, "Piece of shit," and went back inside.

Alone, Dom exhaled. He glanced at Privitera. Then at the dead Korean.

Corrado was going to hit the roof. He loathed Felice's disregard for their immigrant labor. And one of their own being offed right under their noses? On a boat?

Dom's gaze slid toward the interior of the boat. The back of his neck prickled. Someone had done this, and whoever it was, they were still on board. Any other time, he might've suspected Felice, but he and Felice had been all but joined at the hip since they'd pulled away from the cargo ship.

Which meant it could've been anyone else. Literally anyone.

On his way back in, Dom kept his pistol handy. Safety off. Round in the chamber.

Couldn't be too careful…

Chapter 19

Sergei was running out of time. He hadn't anticipated being on the boat this long. It was supposed to be a simple job—kill the mark, jump ship, swim to the rendezvous point to meet Baltazar.

And now they were heading back out to sea. This was going to be a long swim, but he didn't have a choice. Not while Felice's men were tearing the boat apart in search of him. He needed to get to one of the aft sundecks, but there was a security guard between him and his escape route. And the boat was moving now.

He swallowed. If they stopped, and that fuck was still between him and the water, then there'd be two dead Italians on board. No way was Sergei getting caught.

As the boat approached the harbor, the boat slowed, and Felice ordered the shaking Koreans to do their jobs. Sergei winced as they dragged a crab pot outside, but he didn't have time to worry about them now. He had to get off this boat.

Sergei hurried out to the sundeck, past the two bodies, slipped off the rocking boat's stern, and eased himself soundlessly into the water. He swam up between the hulls and grabbed onto the rope securing his equipment.

Teeth clenched to keep them from chattering—he was sure someone would hear him if he made a sound—he clipped the karabiners to his wetsuit. If the boat moved, he'd be dragged along with it, but at least he wouldn't be left behind or caught in the props. As he cut away his tank, a heavy splash startled him. That wasn't a crab pot dropping. Much too big and heavy.

Like a body.

Fuck! Now there was blood in the water. Which meant sharks.

Heart pounding, Sergei worked even faster, cutting away the ties that had secured his tank. Putting it on was a challenge when he was also clipped to the network of ropes, but it was a necessary evil. No way in hell was he getting left out here with no fins, no tanks, and a bleeding corpse nearby.

The tank was the most cumbersome part, especially since he couldn't let it touch the hulls, or else the sound might echo and give him away. Finally, though, he had it secured to his shoulders. Once he had the regulator in his mouth and the air was flowing, he unclipped himself and the rest of his gear and dove beneath the surface.

He was right about the splash—the dead man floated on the surface, a rusty plume swelling beside his torso.

Definitely time to get the fuck out of here.

Safely away from the propellers and hopefully out of sight, Sergei pulled on his fins, cleared his mask, and then started toward the shore. Considering some of the Italians thought it was fun to attract sharks and then shoot them, he dived deep to make sure they didn't see him.

He looked at his watch. Shit. He was running out of

time. Getting off the boat had taken a lot longer than planned, and Baltazar wasn't going to wait for him.

"*I don't see you by 10:30,*" he'd reminded Sergei last night, "*I'm assuming you're shark chum and I'm outta there.*"

Which had seemed more than reasonable right up until Sergei'd found himself unable to make his planned escape from the yacht. He'd lost precious minutes. And not just minutes—the yacht was farther out than he'd anticipated.

It was going to be a long swim anyway, but if he didn't make it to Baltazar in time, that was going to be a *long* swim back to shore.

He checked his compass and started swimming. He had to swim hard—between the current and the time crunch, he had no choice. And damn it, even the exertion wasn't enough to keep him warm this far down. The water was fucking cold. Inside his fins, his toes were already getting numb. His gloves did almost nothing to keep him warm either. Gripping the regulator with his mouth kept his teeth from chattering, but just barely.

Just what he needed—hypothermia. But that wasn't his biggest concern. Between the cold and the exertion, he was asking for the bends, but he'd be okay as long as he could surface gradually.

He passed one of the red navigational buoys, which had been marked underneath with a number six. Only two to go. Thank God.

Motion above his head caught his eye, and he looked up as a catamaran sliced two white gashes into the surface. Another boat—single hull this time—shot past. Moments later, another went by, crisscrossing the wake from the previous one. The closer he swam to buoy five, the more boat traffic cut across the water. It didn't get any better as he neared buoy four.

Damn it. Too many boats out today, and no way to tell

if they were friend or foe. He didn't dare surface out in the open. Even without the goons who liked shooting divers for sport, the harbor was too busy to come up just anywhere. He had to surface beside a boat with a diver down flag flying to warn other boats, or else a hull or a propeller could kill him even before a coked-out Mafioso with a pistol did.

Finally, he saw the buoy he was looking for, and the boat bobbing nearby.

He ascended a few meters at a time, doing decompression stops for as long as he could. Still too far beneath the surface for a fast ascent, he looked at his watch.

10:27.

His heart sped up. He was almost out of time.

All he had to do was let Baltazar know he was here, then go back under and come up again slowly. It would take time—he'd have to go down slowly and carefully since he'd already been down and up once—but the alternative was being left out here in a harbor full of boats, sharks, and trigger happy Italians.

He made a few more decompression stops. Not much farther to go. Maybe he could still—

The props came on.

Sergei cursed into his regulator, and then swam upward for all he was worth, his heart pounding all the way.

The instant he broke the surface, he yanked the regulator out of his mouth. "Baltazar!"

The Greek turned and leaned over the side. "Oh, shit, kid. We almost left without you!" He extended his arm. "Get in! Now!"

"I can't." Sergei shook his head, teeth chattering furiously. "I need to go back down and come back up so I don't get the fucking bends. I need at least—"

"No time." Baltazar pointed past Sergei.

Sergei turned around, and swore. The Coast Guard was out. So were the Cusimanos. With a dead Mafioso dead on a boat out here, Sergei didn't want to be around when fingers—and guns—started pointing.

He faced Baltazar again, and this time clasped his hand around the Greek's forearm. Baltazar grabbed Sergei's tanks with his other hand, and helped him over the side, but as soon as Sergei's center of gravity had shifted enough to keep him from slipping back into the water, Baltazar let him go.

Sergei tumbled unceremoniously onto the deck. "Thanks, asshole."

"Sorry." Baltazar gestured to his nephew, who was at the wheel, and the kid gunned the throttle, knocking Sergei off balance again.

Sergei cursed in his native tongue as he unfastened his tanks and kicked off his fins. "You're gonna get me the bends."

"You should've been here sooner."

"Yeah, well." Sergei spat some salt water on the deck. "Things didn't…" *I got an innocent man killed. I almost had to kill…* Shuddering, he muttered, "They didn't go as planned."

"Occupational hazard, my friend," Baltazar said coolly.

"Just give me a fucking oxygen tank. And a blanket before I fucking freeze."

Baltazar dug into one of the compartments beside the helm, and pulled out a small tank and mask. He also found a thick brown blanket and tossed it to Sergei. "You get it done?"

Sergei shrugged off his scuba tanks. "Yep. Dropped Privitera in the—"

"*Privitera?*" Baltazar froze. "What the hell are you talking about?"

Sergei nearly dropped the tanks on Baltazar's foot, and met his glare unapologetically. "I took out the second man down. What was I supposed to—"

The Greek's hand came out of nowhere and connected with Sergei's face, his ring cracking against bone. "You fucking *idiot!*"

The pain caught him off guard. Sergei touched his cheekbone and narrowed his stinging eyes at Baltazar. "What the fuck was that for?"

"I had a lookout on the marina who said Domenico Maisano was on that boat, Dmitry. How in the *fuck* did you think—"

"What?" Sergei lowered his hand, carefully schooling his expression to hide the shaky panicky feeling in his stomach. At least this violent shivering was good for something. "I didn't see him."

"Holy shit, Dmitry! Did you fucking *look?*" Baltazar shoved his fat fingers through his greasy hair. "How am I going to explain—"

Sergei seized Baltazar by the throat and slammed him up against the bulkhead. "Listen to me, motherfucker."

Baltazar stared at him, eyes huge.

"If you want me to take out a specific person," Sergei snarled, "you give me a goddamned name. From where I was standing, Privitera was the highest man on the roster besides Felice himself." He shoved himself back, using Baltazar's throat as leverage, and let go.

The Greek rubbed his neck.

"You wanted a message sent, and I sent it," Sergei hissed as he snatched the blanket off the bench. "Why the fuck didn't you tell me if you wanted someone specific?"

Baltazar showed his palms. "My orders were to tell you

to take out the second man down. No one said who he was."

"Yeah, you don't say." Sergei jerked the zipper down on his wetsuit and stripped to the waist. As he wrapped the blanket around his shoulders, he growled, "Give me that tank so I don't get fucking bent."

Wordlessly, Baltazar handed it over. Sergei took a seat, put on the mask, and turned the valve. He breathed slowly and deeply through his chattering teeth. The air was cold, which didn't help him warm up, but between the blanket and the brutal sun, his limbs were beginning to thaw.

He leaned over, pressing his elbow into his knees and his stinging fingers into his temples. Muscles ached. His fingers burned. But his biggest worry was that rapid ascent, and he kept on breathing that cold, cold air, no matter how much it made his lungs burn and his teeth hurt.

Baltazar's contact would be pissed, and Baltazar himself was pissed, but at least Sergei had the vague order as an alibi. And thank God no one had been specific, or Dom would've been a dead man.

Just like the poor Korean guy who was probably still floating out there somewhere, assuming the sharks or the Coast Guard hadn't found him yet.

Sergei winced.

He played and replayed the whole incident in his mind, over and over again. It wasn't supposed to happen like that. The Korean's screams echoed in his ears, drawing bile up his throat. Thank God Dom had killed the poor bastard. Sergei was in this to take out Mafia men, for fuck's sake. Not get desperate immigrants murdered. It was his fault. He hadn't been able to kill Dom, so he'd gone for the next best target, and he hadn't been careful enough about when and where he did it, and one of the immigrants had taken the fall. It was *his* fucking fault.

Except it probably would have played out the same if he had offed Dom. Felice would've flipped out, and he'd have blamed one of the men working for him.

It would have happened exactly the same way. The only difference was that Dom would be dead.

Closing his eyes, Sergei tucked his arm against his stomach and gritted his teeth against the wave of nausea. There was no holding it back, though, so he tore off the mask, twisted around, and heaved overboard. God knew if it was the bends, seasickness, or if he was just fucked up in the head after the way things had gone down on the boat. Or a combination of all three.

That *wasn't* how it was supposed to go down. Especially not in that horrific fashion. Wherever the unfortunate man had taken the bullet, his screams had been the stuff of nightmares.

Sergei was convinced the other Koreans were only alive—if shaken—because of Dom. Felice had no doubt had every intention of killing all of them. But Dom had stepped in, and then he'd put the wounded man out of his misery and made no apologies for it.

That was a side of Dom that didn't make sense. Even though he'd known Dom wasn't like the others, that he wanted out of this life more than anything in the world, it was different to see it. To witness his humanity outside the privacy of a shitty motel room, out where the rubber met the road.

He was Mafia. He was one of *them.*

But you've seen him in private. You've heard him say how much he hates what he is. You know what he is and what he isn't.

Sergei cradled his throbbing head in his freezing hands.

He wanted to believe the Dom he met at night was human. He didn't want to believe that a Mafioso was. But Dom was a Mafioso. Dom was human. Dom was…

Fuck. I'm losing my fucking mind.

SERGEI WAS STILL SHIVERING when he made it to shore. Even after he'd changed into some clothes that had been soaking up the morning's warmth in his car, he couldn't get warm. Time to go home and take a shower. A long, hot shower that would take away the cold, the salt, and maybe some of the guilt that—

His phone buzzed in the cup holder. He glared at it for a moment.

Oh Christ. Now what?

Cursing under his breath, he picked it up, and didn't expect to see a text from Dom.

Need to see you tonight. Please.

Sergei swallowed. Fresh guilt clawed at him from the inside. He'd been moments away from putting a bullet into Dom. Now he was going to have sex with him like nothing happened?

Yes. Because nothing did happen. Because for reasons Sergei couldn't quite parse, he *hadn't* put a bullet in Dom, and he *needed* to have sex with him. Just to make sure he was alive. Or to appease his conscience somehow. Or, fuck, he didn't know, but with fingers that were still partially numb, he wrote back:

I'm off tonight. Sooner the better.

Dom's reply came almost immediately:

I can be there any time. Afternoon?

He'd text Dom with an address and room later. For now, he headed home. On the way, he tapped his thumbs on the wheel. He needed to see Dom. Probably more than he had any right to, but after everything that had happened today, he needed to see him, and touch him, and make sure he really was still alive.

I'm not supposed to feel this way for you. I'm not supposed to feel anything for you.

What the hell is going on?

BY THE TIME Sergei checked into the motel, he didn't feel any better. He'd showered. Shaved. Showered again. Scrubbed his skin until it was raw. As he left his apartment, his whole body ached—his fucking *bones* ached—but he ignored it. After a swim like that, and some hypothermia to boot, everything was bound to hurt. Didn't matter. He needed Dom, pain be damned.

After he'd collected the key, he headed up the hall. Not ten feet from his room, the floor suddenly jerked beneath him. He stumbled and smacked his palm against the wall to right himself.

What the hell?

The floor listed again. The walls tilted. He leaned against the wall and took a few breaths. Then a cautious step. The floor was still uneven, but he kept a hand on the wall and guided himself to his door.

The imbalance became dizziness. The dizziness became nausea. That wouldn't bode well for the evening he needed with Dom, so he decided maybe some ginger ale would settle his stomach. The vending machine probably had some. It had likely been in there since the 1980s, but it was better than nothing.

Sergei pulled out his wallet to see if he had any ones. As he did, the simple motion of reaching into his pocket sent a dull ache through his shoulder. Deep inside the joint. In his bones. As he leaned down to get his soda out of the machine, a similar ache radiated from his hip. And his knee.

That's not muscle pain. That's not fatigue.

Sergei gulped.

That's not good.

All the way back to his room, he tried to tell himself it was, in fact, muscle fatigue. After all, he hadn't been diving in a long time, and it was taxing for muscles he didn't use like this very often. Even more so when he'd had to fight the cold.

Except it wasn't a tired muscle. Nor was the ache steadily deepening in his hips.

Oh shit. It was only going to get worse, too.

It was like the flu coming on, only with a fucked up stomach on top of it. The flu would have been welcome if it meant he didn't have the goddamned bends. If that's what this was, then things could get ugly fast.

No. It wasn't that bad. He hadn't been under for that long.

But he'd gone deeper than he should've. And he'd been cold. And he'd swum hard. And then he'd ascended too fast. Way too fast.

Sergei's heart sped up as he sat on the foot of the bed. *Fuck...*

His phone buzzed. Struggling to focus his eyes, he read the message:

Which room?

Sergei chewed his lip. He wouldn't be able to fake his way out of this. Dom was going to see him this way whether he liked it or not. Sex? Well, it wouldn't be rough or acrobatic tonight.

He sent back the room number, and then popped the tab on his soda and took a deep swallow. It didn't help his stomach much. Maybe it just needed more time to settle in. It wasn't an instant remedy. Right?

A sharp knock at the door startled him, as if he hadn't known Dom was coming.

Grimacing, he stood. *Fuck, why do I feel like an old man? You know exactly what it is.*

No. It's not. I do not have the fucking bends.

He shuffled across the floor, keeping his arms out for balance, and opened the door.

Dom met his gaze. His eyes were wide, his face pale, as if he'd seen something horrific. Because he had. God, they both had. And Sergei couldn't tell him.

I can't tell you I was there. I can't tell you I'm shaking over it too.

He stepped aside to let Dom in, but the floor picked just that moment to shift beneath his feet.

Dom caught him before he even knew he was going down. "Holy shit. Are you all right?"

"Yeah, I'm…" *Not. Not at all. This is bad.* "I need to sit."

"I think you need to lie down, actually."

Dom guided him to the bed. That helped. Being flat on his back, without worrying about staying upright—it definitely helped.

But the ache didn't quit. It was getting worse.

"What's wrong?" Dom asked.

Sergei sighed. There was no point in denying it. Not to himself or Dom. He wiped an unsteady hand over his face. "I went in the water today. Scuba diving with some buddies, down by the crescent. I think this might be—"

Dom flew to his feet. "I'm calling a doctor."

"No!" Sergei sat up, and immediately regretted it. The world shifted out from under him again but thank God, strong arms stopped him before he tumbled off the bed.

Dom eased him back down to the mattress. "Sergei, you need to see a doctor."

You have no idea.

"No." Sergei swallowed. "N-not a hospital."

Their eyes locked. Dom's seem filled with a million unspoken questions.

Sergei swept his tongue across his dry lips. "I heard… some shit happened out there today. And the hospital here, they're all in Mafia pockets. If anybody's looking for a diver…"

Dom's eyebrow rose. "Shit…"

"I'll be okay." *I am so fucked. So, so fucked.*

Then Dom cupped Sergei's face and looked him in the eye. "Do you trust me?"

I shouldn't trust you and you shouldn't trust me.

Dom raised his eyebrows.

"Yeah." Sergei swallowed. "Yeah. I do."

"Then let me make this call."

Sergei held his gaze. What else could he do? This wasn't like the night they'd met when Dom had turned down medical attention because he was banged up and could get away with it. This was the kind of fucked-up that could get a lot worse in not a lot of time, and without a trained medical professional…

Swallowing, he nodded slowly. "Okay."

Dom helped him back onto the pillows. Sergei closed his eyes. The world was still rocking and rolling. It was impossible to tell if it was from being out on boats for so long today, or if it was the decompression sickness fucking with his head, but it wasn't helping the nausea either way.

Dom was nearby, but his voice sounded a million miles away: "Hey, it's Dom. I need your help. *Fast.*"

Chapter 20

"You're sure it's the bends?" Rojas grabbed a backpack and a small oxygen tank from his trunk.

"He says he was out diving. I wasn't sure what else it could be."

The doctor slammed his trunk. "Even if it's something else, better safe than sorry." They hurried toward the room, and Rojas asked, "What are his symptoms?"

"He's dizzy as hell. Can't hardly stand."

"Any pain?"

"Says his shoulders hurt. He says everything hurts, but it seems to be his shoulders more than anything."

"Yeah, that's the bends." Rojas walked faster. "Nausea? Any loss of feeling? Paralysis?"

"He's been sick a few times. Don't think he's lost any feeling, though. None that I know of. And he can move, he's just off-balance."

Rojas nodded, but didn't say more.

Dom opened the door to the room. Rojas brushed past him and went right to the bed where Sergei was lying.

"Sergei," Dom said as he closed and locked the door. "This is Dr. Rojas. He's a friend. You can trust him."

Rojas shot Dom a look, as if to ask why there should be any concern, but he'd been around La Cosa Nostra long enough not to actually bring the question to life. Instead, he sat down beside Sergei. "How long have you been out of the water?"

Sergei picked up his phone with a shaky hand and looked at the screen. "A few hours." He swallowed as he set the phone down again. "Did some pure oxygen after I got out, but…"

"Well, that's good. You'd be in worse shape if you hadn't done that."

Sergei muttered something in Russian.

"You an experienced diver?" Rojas asked as he attached a mask and tube to the oxygen tank.

"Yeah. But this time, I—" Sergei paused, glancing at Dom. "I was cold, and I came up too fast."

"Define too fast."

Sergei rubbed his eyes. "Too fast."

Rojas scowled. He and Dom exchanged a look, and the doctor shrugged before facing Sergei again. "I'm going to have you breathe some more O2." He put the tank beside Sergei's chest and started to slip the mask on him, but Sergei winced. "You all right?"

"Yeah. Sorry."

Rojas hesitated, and then put the mask over Sergei's nose and mouth. As he brought the tank closer, said, "Breathe normally, all right?"

Eyes closed, Sergei nodded. The tank hissed as Rojas turned on the valve, and the inside of the mask fogged up, cleared, fogged up again. Dom shifted his weight. He hated this helpless, useless feeling. There was nothing he could do for Sergei now except wait and hope to God Rojas could help.

Rojas set his backpack on the edge of the bed and unzipped it. "I'm going to start an IV and give you some isotonic fluid to keep you hydrated. It should also help dissolve the bubbles in your system." He pulled a plastic, water-filled bag and a long tube from the pack.

"What the fuck is all that?" Sergei asked. "You Mary Poppins' kid or something?"

"Not quite." Rojas uncapped a needle. "Just things you gotta keep handy when you're constantly putting people back together in *this* town."

Sergei's eyes flicked toward Dom.

Rojas pressed the needle into Sergei's arm, and Sergei's lips pulled tight behind the mask. He winced again, but Rojas was quick—he could probably set up an IV in his sleep. In seconds, everything was in place, and he tethered the bag to the top of the bedside lamp.

"How do you feel?" Rojas asked.

Sergei scowled behind the mask. "Like I could use a drink."

"Well, be that as it may"—Rojas shrugged—"alcohol consumption won't help. No booze for the next forty-eight hours."

Sergei muttered something, but the mask muffled it.

The doc checked him over, listening to his chest and taking his blood pressure. Dom stayed out of the way, watching silently as his heart pounded and his stomach tried to flip over. He'd come here needing relief after a traumatic morning, but all of that seemed a distant memory now. Was Sergei all right? Jesus, he looked terrible, and no matter how much Dom tried, he couldn't will any color to bloom in Sergei's sickly pale face.

Rojas draped his stethoscope around his neck and ran

through a battery of questions, mostly asking about Sergei's symptoms, and occasionally throwing in questions about what day it was, where he was, what his name was.

"Have you had any paralysis? Numbness?"

"No," Sergei said. "Balance is fucked, but… no."

"Good. What's your mother's name?"

Sergei's expression darkened.

Rojas stiffened a little. "Where are you right now?"

"In the Salty Air Motel, wondering why some fuck wants to know about my mother."

"Well, you're obviously not confused, then." Rojas checked the gauge on the oxygen tank. "Why don't you just relax for a little while?"

Sergei glared at him, but didn't speak. He let his eyelids slide shut, and breathed slowly, the O2 mask continuing to fog and clear in time with the rise and fall of his chest.

Rojas got up and gestured for Dom to come with him to the other side of the room. Not that there was much space in a room this small, but between the hum of the air conditioner and the hiss of the oxygen, there was a surprising amount of privacy.

Back slightly to Sergei, Dom asked, "How is he?"

"Well, don't ask about his mother…"

Dom pursed his lips. "I mean, his condition."

"Yeah, I know. And it's good you called me when you did." He draped his stethoscope over his neck. "The oxygen should help, along with the IV. As long as his symptoms don't worsen, he should improve."

"And if they do?"

Rojas glanced at Sergei. "Then he *needs* to go to a hospital."

Dom scowled.

The doctor shot him a pointed look. "By all rights, I

should be telling him to go to a hospital now because he's not out of the woods yet."

Dom shifted his weight. "Just tell me honestly—hospital, or no?

Rojas chewed his lip. For a long moment, he watched Sergei.

"Yes or no?" Dom pressed. "I'd just as soon not go to one, but if it's what he needs, then tell me."

"He's…" Rojas swallowed. Finally, he met Dom's gaze. "Look, decompression sickness is unpredictable. Normally, I'd err on the side of caution and get him to a medical facility, just in case things take a bad turn. But, like I said, as long as he doesn't get any worse, he should be okay. Just keep a *close* eye on him, Dom."

"Of course. For how long?"

"Judging by his condition now, I'd say the next four or five hours are critical. To be safe, stay with him for the twelve after that."

Dom nodded. "All right. I'll stay with him as long as I can."

"Good." Rojas glanced around the room. At Sergei. At Dom. When his eyebrows pinched together, the question was unmistakable.

Dom swallowed. "This stays between us, all right?"

"Of course." The doctor touched his arm. "Not a word. I promise."

"Thanks."

Rojas looked back at Sergei for a second. As he faced Dom, he said, "He should be all right in a few hours. If he gets any worse, though, you *need* to take him to the ER."

Dom scowled.

"I know," Rojas said. "But if he doesn't improve on his own, he needs recompression therapy, and that's not something I can do."

Chewing the inside of his cheek, Dom nodded. "Well, there's nothing illegal about scuba diving, so it isn't like it'll raise any red flags."

"Maybe in any other town," the doc muttered. "I've treated four people for decompression sickness in the last year, and they've all turned out to be drug mules." His eyes flicked toward Sergei. "Believe me—it raises questions."

"I don't think he's a…" Dom watched Sergei. *Is he?*

"Listen to me, Dom." Rojas's expression hardened. "Even if he is involved in something like every fucking person in this town seems to be, he still needs treatment if his symptoms don't improve. Promise me you'll take him to the ER if he doesn't get better."

Dom nodded. "Yeah. Definitely."

"Good." Rojas clapped his shoulder gently. "I'll be back in a while. Call me if anything changes."

"You or an ambulance?"

Rojas glanced at Sergei. "Both. Ambulance first."

A chill ran up Dom's spine. "Will do."

The doctor left, and Dom sat beside Sergei. "Feeling any better?"

"Than what?" Sergei turned to him, eyelids fluttering open. "Roadkill?"

Dom chuckled. "Well, you still have a sense of humor. That's promising, right?"

Sergei laughed, fogging up the mask. "If that ever goes, just put a bullet in me because I'm probably done."

That sobered Dom faster than it should have. He slipped his hand into Sergei's—the one without the IV—and laced their fingers together.

This was so weird, sitting beside a sedate Sergei, with no sound in the room except the A/C and the oxygen tank. He tried not to liken it to his mother's final few days when he'd sat with her, when she too had worn a mask to get oxygen into her starving lungs while an IV kept fluid moving into her frail arms. Sergei wasn't dying. He probably wasn't even in that much danger as long as he relaxed and let the oxygen and IV do their jobs. But the quiet room, the near-silence, the fingers laced between his...

Maybe this is a sign that we should be saying goodbye.

Not the same kind of goodbye he'd had to say to his mother, but the kind he needed to be saying unless he wanted Sergei caught in a crossfire he had nothing to do with.

Take a hint, Dom. If you don't want him to get hurt, stay the hell away from him.

But... not now. Not until he's okay.

Dom squeezed Sergei's hand. "That harbor is dangerous, you know. For divers."

"So I've heard."

"I'm serious. The Coast Guard's busted a fuckload of divers who were transporting narcotics."

"They can't bust me if I don't have anything on me."

"They can still harass you." Dom paused. "Hell, Rojas even wondered if you might've been one of the drug mules."

"He thinks I'm a drug mule?"

Dom squeezed Sergei's arm. "It... crossed his mind."

Sergei laughed, his eyelids sliding shut. "A drug mule. That's funny."

"Is it? Why?"

"Dunno." Sergei licked his lips. "Just is."

Dom watched him for a moment. "So, why were you out... today?"

"Why not? Did you see the water out there?" Sergei shrugged, but winced, and rubbed his shoulder gingerly. "It was a perfect day for it."

"Any idea how you got the bends?"

Sergei held his gaze, eyes narrowed just slightly. "It's always a risk when you're diving."

"You said you came up too fast."

"Yeah. Should've done some more decompression stops, but…" He swore softly and shook his head.

"Why, though?"

"I had a malfunctioning valve on my tank. Thought coming up too fast was better than staying down too long."

"Oh."

"Why?" Sergei lifted his eyebrows. "Do you think I was moving drugs—"

"No. No." Dom sighed. "I'm sorry. Just… there *was* some shit out on the water today, and I…" He swallowed. "I'm just glad you weren't tangled up in it."

Sergei was quiet for a moment. He looked down at their hands, and his thumb ran alongside Dom's. "I'm sorry. You came here tonight for something a lot more enjoyable than—"

"I came to see you."

"Not like this."

"I'm not complaining."

"I am." Sergei shifted. "This is bullshit."

"Trust me. I'd rather be here than…" Dom trailed off, not sure how to fill in the rest of that thought without tipping his hand too far. Finally, he shook his head. "Anyway. I'll stay as long as you need me to. God knows you've been there for me lately."

Sergei studied him. "All I've done is sleep with you."

"You'd be amazed how much I need that." Dom gazed at their hands. "Being with another man like this, it's…" He sighed. "I guess I feel like I have to get it as far out of my system as I can."

"It doesn't work that way, you know." Sergei drew slow

arcs along Dom's hand with his thumbnail. "The more you have, the more you want."

"I know. But I'd rather experience it than get married and spend the rest of my life wishing I'd spent more time with a man."

Sergei gently freed his hand and pulled the oxygen mask down.

"You need to keep that on," Dom said. "The doctor—"

"I know what he said." Sergei moistened his lips and took Dom's hand again. "Listen, we both know what happens if the people in your world find out about this. And all you're doing is torturing yourself. Or guaranteeing yourself a lot of torture in the future when you can't have this anymore."

Dom nodded. "Yeah, I know. And maybe I'll regret it later, but I'm not ready to walk away from it yet."

Sergei held his gaze. "Can I ask something kind of personal?"

"If you put that mask back on, yes."

Sergei laughed. He pushed the mask over his mouth and nose again, and as he took Dom's hand, said, "Happy?"

"Yes."

"So, I'm curious…" Sergei paused. "We both know what you are. I've known since the night you got beat up outside my club."

Dom shuddered at the memory.

"Why?" Sergei asked.

"Why what? Why did they kick my—"

"Why do you do it?" Sergei's brow furrowed. "Is it… I mean, I get that you're in it because of your family, but how do you do it? How do you live with…?"

Dom let out a long breath and stared at their loosely entwined fingers. "It's the only life I've ever known."

"That wasn't my question."

Dom wanted to say it was the only answer he could give, but that was bullshit, and he swore Sergei's piercing blue eyes saw right through him anyway. Why lie? Hell, there was probably no one on the planet he could be honest with about this, and with time running out, there was no point in wasting the opportunity.

"Like I've told you before," he said finally, "if I could walk away from this life, I would. And it just kills me that…" Dom swallowed, his throat aching. "Sometimes boys come to us, and they try to get recruited. The Sicilians want to get made so bad they can taste it." Shaking his head, he sighed. "These guys, they have a *choice*. They can do anything. And they want… this life."

"So if you're born into it, you have to…?"

"It's…" Dom sighed. "It's not that cut and dried. Most of us who are born into it stay in it, but for me…" He paused. "Like I said the other night, my father fucked up. He broke omertà and got several people killed. A few more went to prison because of him. The family almost lost everything. My uncle almost lost his power over it because they thought he was unfit to run the organization. Being related to my father and all of that. They thought the genes were defective, and that anyone who was actually a Maisano was a narc waiting to happen."

"But your uncle is still the boss."

"A lot of blood spilled to make sure that still happened," Dom whispered. "Including my father's. My uncle took me under his wing, especially after my mother died, and he told me in no uncertain terms that either I toed the line, or I'd wind up in the same hole my father was in."

Sergei blinked. "Just for bowing out and doing something else with your life?"

Dom nodded. "There's more to it than that, but the punchline is that everything I did was a reflection of my father, and it reflected on Corrado too. Becoming a made man, it was… it was survival."

"Have you ever thought about trying to find a way out?"

"Every day of my life. But there isn't much point."

"If you weren't part of it, what *would* you be doing?"

"I don't know. I really don't."

"You don't?"

Dom shook his head. "Can't let myself think about it, or I'll drive myself insane. I could spend all day fantasizing about things I could do if I weren't a Maisano, but it won't change anything." With a shrug, he added, "So I don't."

"When were you made?"

Dom shifted uncomfortably. "When I was twenty-two."

"Twenty-two?" Sergei's jaw dropped despite the form-fitting mask. "Isn't that, uh—"

"Young?"

"Yeah. That."

"It is." *But he had to get me in while I was still too young and terrified to say no.* He shivered. "My uncle pushed me through because he knew I'd be untouchable after that. No one would fuck with me without serious consequences." Dom pushed out a breath. "What about you?"

Sergei cocked his head. "What about me?"

"What will you do after this?"

His eyes narrowed slightly, and he drew back. "After… after what?"

"I mean, you're not planning to work in that club forever, are you? There's got to be something else out there for you."

He studied Dom, a hint of suspicion in his eyes that Dom wasn't sure how to interpret. But then he relaxed—a little—and offered a taut shrug. "I'll think about that when I have enough money saved to go someplace else. Wherever I go or whatever I do, it won't be in this shit town."

"Good," Dom said with a nod. "I don't want you getting tangled up in all this shit. The farther you are out of the way—"

Sergei laughed dryly, though his amusement didn't last. When he spoke, his accent sharpened the edges of his words, but his voice was soft enough to counter it. "I'll be all right." He squeezed Dom's hand. "But I do appreciate that you give a shit."

"Of course I do." Dom smoothed Sergei's hair. "You're about the only thing I do give a shit about these days. Just you and staying alive."

Sergei swallowed. His eyes were unreadable. Then he pulled his mask down, and before Dom could tell him to put it back on, Sergei drew him down into a soft kiss. Goose bumps prickled Dom's neck, and it wasn't because of the cool air blowing out of the mask. This was the first time they'd kissed when they knew damn well it was as far as things would go, and though he wanted Sergei, this kiss was enough. More than enough. Some tender reassurance that yes, Sergei was okay, and yes, Dom really did care.

When Dom broke the kiss and lifted his head, their eyes met. Sergei's hand slid off his neck, but Dom didn't pull away. Heart thumping and lips tingling, he held Sergei's gaze.

Clearing his throat, Dom gently pushed the mask onto Sergei's mouth and nose again. "You should keep that on," he whispered.

Sergei found his hand again. "I know."

"Are you starting to feel better?"

Behind the mask, Sergei smiled, and squeezed Dom's hand. "Yeah. Feeling a lot better now."

Dom kissed his forehead. "Good."

ANOTHER SUMMONS FROM CORRADO. Fuck.

After worrying over Sergei all night, and then trying to work while simultaneously daydreaming about Sergei and wondering if Sergei was really okay, Dom's morning had come to a screeching halt with a phone call from Biaggio.

A meeting with his uncle. Right now. Of course.

So he'd dropped everything, as always, and driven over to his uncle's place. Biaggio was otherwise indisposed, but Dom knew the way to the office, so he showed himself upstairs.

Before he made it to the office, though, Felice met him in the hall.

"There you are!" His cousin threw up his hands. "Where the *fuck* have you been?"

Dom halted, schooling his expression, though it took work. "Why?"

"Because I've got people breathing down my neck asking what the fuck happened yesterday." Felice narrowed his eyes. "Then you step off the boat and just disappear? Dad's hammering me for answers left and right, and I've got the Coast Guard getting curious after they found that fuck floating out by—"

"Maybe you should've thought of that before you killed him, you fucking idiot," Dom said in a harsh whisper. "Or before you threw him in the water for the Coasties to find."

"Before *I* killed him?" Felice laughed, stepping closer, and stared right into Dom's eyes. "I seem to recall you were the one who killed him."

"Yeah, to put him out of his misery after you decided to put a bullet in his gut."

"And did you really want to sail back into the harbor with a body on the deck?"

Dom gritted his teeth. "*I'm* not the one who decided to shoot the—"

"It's done," Felice snapped. "But that doesn't explain why you dropped off the face of the earth after—"

"Because I wanted to lay low," Dom threw back. "Keeping a low profile seemed like a good fucking idea."

"Yeah? Somebody'd almost think you were hiding. Got a guilty conscience or something?"

Dom held his gaze, and slowly narrowed his eyes. "Are you making an accusation?"

"Depends. Am I hitting a nerve?"

"You think I did Privitera in?" Dom folded his arms. "Because if memory serves, I was with you from the last time you saw him alive until someone else found his body. So pray tell, when exactly did I kill him?"

Felice's jaw tightened. "Okay, it wasn't you. But disappearing doesn't look good."

"I was around. All you had to do was call me."

"You should have been *here*. With everyone *else*."

"Yeah? That why your father told me he'd call me when he needed me?" Dom arched an eyebrow. "Or am I answering to you now?"

Felice scowled. "Listen, I'm just rattled. Yesterday... that was too close. Someone was *on that boat*."

"So you don't think it was one of the Koreans."

Felice shook his head. "I questioned the hell out of the two who survived, told them they'd be joining their buddy if they didn't talk. They didn't know anything."

"Which means we have to consider that it might've been an inside job."

"I know." His cousin exhaled. "But those guys, they've been my crew for years. I trust them."

"Somebody cut Privitera's throat. It wasn't you or me, so…" Proceeding cautiously, Dom added, "We can't rule them out. Not yet."

"Think about it, though. They were all on the deck with us or supervising the Koreans. And the Koreans confirmed the others were there with them the whole time."

"So what do you think happened?" Dom lowered his arms. "I mean, Privitera didn't cut his own throat."

"Someone else had to be on the boat."

"We scoured it from top to bottom." Dom shook his head. "I don't get it. And the security cameras show nothing?"

"That's the weirder thing—all the surveillance equipment was compromised. There's nothing. It's so fucking scrambled, we can't even tell *when* it was compromised."

Dom shuddered. Whoever was behind this was good. They were thorough. They thought of everything. Always one step ahead. "We need to bring in more security, then. Extra bodyguards. Personnel on watercraft, at houses and offices."

Felice nodded. "That's going to get expensive."

Dom gritted his teeth. He could practically hear Felice calculating how many immigrants Dom would have to squeeze to make up the spike in security costs.

"Anyway." Felice shook himself and clapped Dom's shoulder. "I shouldn't keep you. My dad wants to see you, and he won't want to be kept waiting." He flashed an odd smile. "Once we get some more security, you should come out on the boat again soon. Hopefully it'll be a little more boring this time."

Dom's stomach lurched. If he never went back out on

that floating crime scene again, it would be too soon, but… image. "Sure." He returned the smile. "Let me know when you're going out again. I'll bring champagne."

"Perfect. See you later, Dom."

"Yeah. See you."

Dom watched his cousin walk away, then continued toward Corrado's office.

Well. This day was getting better by the minute.

Chapter 21

The conversation with Dom wouldn't leave his mind. They'd left the hotel room before dawn, after Dom's doctor friend had come back one last time and decided Sergei had recovered enough to be on his own. Now Sergei was drinking coffee in the silence of his apartment, his head still throbbing and his bones still aching. At least he had his balance back. He could finally walk without face-planting. He'd even driven home without incident.

And now, he couldn't stop thinking about last night.

It was the first time they'd met up without having sex. Of course Sergei had been in no condition to do anything, but Dom had seemed more concerned than put off. Where other casual lovers would've maybe called a doctor before disappearing to find someone a bit less pathetic, Dom had stayed there, hovering beside him and watching his every move.

As Sergei had recovered, they'd talked. No sex. No touching. Just… talking.

And that felt weird. It felt wrong. Fooling around with

Dom was one thing. Talking to him, listening to him explain how trapped he was in his own life, was a mistake, particularly when Dom was staying attentively by his bedside, making sure Sergei didn't get worse. Somehow, that seemed even more dangerous than when they'd lie in bed naked, talking until one of them finally decided it was time to get dressed and leave. Those conversations had become increasingly intimate. But this… somehow this felt riskier.

After all, hadn't this intimacy nearly earned him a bullet between the eyes? He'd been on Felice Maisano's boat to kill Dom. They hadn't told him exactly who he was meant to kill—probably for some plausible deniability for whoever called in the hit—and when he'd realized his target, he'd made a dangerously different call.

And why? Because Dom could fuck him without making him feel like a sex toy who barely qualified as human?

No. Because they were too close. The sex had given them a reason to be together, and they'd talked, and in the end, they'd softened Sergei out of completing yesterday's hit.

He scrubbed his hands over his unshaven face. This was getting out of control.

Well, they'd only be sleeping together for so long, especially if Dom would be getting married soon. This thing had a finite shelf life. And once Sergei had moved a few more pieces on the Mafia chessboard, Dom would be too preoccupied with a local war to bother hitting up Sergei for sex.

Which was weirdly disappointing. Sergei liked the sex he had with Dom. Much as he was loathe to admit it, he liked Dom. Which he shouldn't. But he did. And what the fuck was—

His phone buzzed, shaking him out of his thoughts. When he picked it up, he had a text from Katashi.

Got what you asked for.

Sergei exhaled. *Finally.*

They made arrangements to meet, and Sergei headed out, getting on the 103 and following the winding highway toward the mile marker where Katashi said he'd be. The persistent soreness in his knees and shoulders made driving more of a chore than usual, particularly as he maneuvered around the twists and curves, but he pushed through. By now, he felt like he did after spending too much time onstage at the club—achy, annoyed, but not nearly as miserable as he'd been last night. And he just tried not to think about how much it was going to suck to get back on the stage this evening.

Sergei neared the designated mile marker, out where Sergei's memories smelled like blood and the backseat of his parents' old station wagon, and slowed down. As always, there was no one around except for Katashi, so he parked behind his supplier's car and killed the engine. When he stepped out of his car in the shade of some evergreens, the whole world was silent.

Katashi got out and grinned, a metal box in his hand. He put the box on the trunk lid, entered the combination, and popped the latches. "Took some doing, but he got it for you." He opened the box and pulled a pair of small bottles free. "It's going to be tough to get more of this, though."

"That won't be a problem." Sergei took one of the bottles and turned it in his hand, watching the fine powder tumble against the inside.

"He said to use these for mixing." Katashi put a tiny measuring spoon on the trunk lid, and beside it, an empty bottle with a spray attachment. "That's what you'll use to deploy it."

"Did he give me a conversion chart?"

Katashi produce a sealed envelope. "Precise instructions based on the mark's body weight."

"Excellent."

"Be careful with this shit." Katashi eyed the assembly warily. "Spray it outside, and the wind's liable to blow it into your face."

"That won't be a problem."

"I'm serious, kid. One whiff of that and—"

"You don't think I know that?" Sergei turned to him. "I wanted it for a reason. I know what I'm dealing with here."

Katashi put up his hands. "Easy, man. Just saying. Be careful."

"Duly noted," Sergei said through his teeth. He held up the vial, and eyed Katashi. "You're sure this shit works?"

His supplier nodded vigorously. "This guy's good, man. If he says it works, it works."

"And you remember our deal if it doesn't work?"

Katashi gulped. "Yeah, man. I remember."

"I fucking hope so." He pocketed the bottle and the other paraphernalia and pulled a wad of hundreds out of his wallet. "It's all there."

Katashi thumbed through it. "Yep. We're good. You need anything else?"

"Not at the moment. But we might be in touch soon."

"You know where to find me."

"GOOD MORNING, SERGEI." Brittany looked up from

pushing a small cart down the hall, and she smiled brightly at him. "It's nice to see you."

"You too." He slid his hands into the pockets of his jeans. "How is she doing?"

The smile didn't quite hold up, though she sure tried to keep it alive. Glancing down the hall, Brittany said, "She's a little less… here today."

Sergei winced. "Thanks for the heads up."

Brittany faced him again. "How are *you* doing?"

"I'm all right." He shrugged. "I should, um…" Clearing his throat, he gestured at Mama's room. "Do you have her pills?"

"Oh! Yes. Sorry." She scanned the tray of meds on the cart, and picked up one of the little paper cups. "Here you go, sweetie."

"Thanks." He took the cup, and they exchanged smiles before continuing down the hall in opposite directions.

Outside the door, as he always did, he took a few seconds to steel himself. Then he put on a smile and went inside.

Mama was by the window as she often was. As he shut the door, she looked up, and she stared blankly at him. "Hello," she said in English.

Well. Good thing Brittany had warned him. The days when there wasn't the slightest flicker of recognition, not even to mistake him for his brother, were the worst.

Also in English, he quietly said, "Hi." He gestured at the chair beside hers. "Do you mind if I sit down?"

Mama looked at the chair. For a moment, she didn't even seem to understand what it was for, or where it had come from. Then she looked up at him. "All right."

He put the pills on the table between them and sat down in the familiar chair while she watched him like she'd never seen him before.

She glanced at the pills. "Are you a nurse?"

"No, I'm..." He swallowed. "No. I'm not."

"Oh. I see." Confusion pulled at her features. Though she didn't say it, the "*Why are you here?*" was unmistakable.

"You seemed lonely." *And I miss you.* "Like you could use some company."

"Oh. Well yes." She smiled a little. "It does get lonely here sometimes."

I'm so sorry, Mama...

Silence descended. He didn't know what to say because he didn't know who she was now, and she didn't know who he was. They were strangers. He could make small talk with strangers, but it was different when that stranger was Mama.

Some days he wished she'd come back, just for a moment, so she could know that the men who'd destroyed their lives weren't getting away with it. The game had taken years, but it was coming to an end. Piece by piece, domino by domino, everything was happening the way he'd hoped, and soon, it would be over. And though he didn't want her to remember what had happened, he wished that on some level she understood that the evil in this town was inching closer to karmic justice.

I'm so close. The whole fucking thing's ready to come down.

"You shouldn't talk that way," she said, calmly making him jump out of his skin. "You seem like such a nice boy."

He hadn't even realized he'd spoken the thought out loud. Quietly, he laughed because at least then he didn't cry. She really didn't know who he was today. Didn't have a clue. Watching some stranger break down in tears would confuse her and terrify her.

"I'm sorry," he said quietly. "I won't talk like that."

"Good. Good boys don't."

He didn't know what to say.

Before he could think of something, she spoke again: "You remind me of my son."

Sergei's head snapped up. "I do?"

She nodded, gaze fixed on something outside. "My Sergei."

Sergei swallowed. "Really?"

"He always swears." Clicking her tongue, she shook her head. "With his language, the boy will be a dock worker someday."

He stared at her in disbelief for a moment but then managed to laugh. His foul mouth may not have been his best feature, but it had started young. Young enough that apparently Mama still remembered.

She laughed softly, and gazed out the window with a smile. "He's a good boy, though, my Seryozha. A good boy."

Sergei pretended to cough just to give himself an excuse to turn away and swipe at the sudden sting in his eyes. When he faced her again, he whispered, "Tell me about him."

She looked at him. "Who?"

No, no, Mama—don't slip away yet.

He moistened his dry lips. "Sergei. Tell me about him."

"Oh, Seryozha." She sighed wistfully. "A boy who wants to be a man too soon." She shifted her attention to the scenery outside. "He's younger than his brothers. They were schoolboys already when he came along."

The memory of his protective older brothers made his chest hurt. They'd kept a close eye on him and never let a neighborhood bully lay a hand on him, but they'd also taught him to be fearless and wild.

"*Climb higher, Seryozha!*" Vasily had taunted from the ground.

Mikhail had egged him on too. "*Mama won't know if you broke your arm from ten feet up or twenty!*"

Sergei had climbed higher. Much higher. And he hadn't broken his arm, but Mama had caught them, and she'd punished them for encouraging him and him for listening to them. The moment their backsides healed from that whipping, they were back out there, climbing higher than ever. They'd been punished for that too, but it was worth it.

Mama laughed softly at something only she understood. "Ever since he could walk, my Sergei's wanted to be just like his brothers. And his brothers, they just love him. They protect him like his father does."

Sergei's throat constricted, nearly cutting off his breath. Memories flooded his mind, but some of the bad ones were creeping in too.

"*Stay here.*" Vasily's voice had trembled as he'd pushed Sergei down between the front and back seats of the station wagon. "*Don't make a sound.*"

"*Promise, Seryozha.*" Mikhail had covered him with a blanket, nearly suffocating him and muffling his last plea: "*Not a sound.*"

"I wish they'd come see me," she said, oblivious to the salt she was pouring in his wounds. "I miss my boys."

Sergei squirmed, pushing back both tears and nausea, and he forced his voice to be calm and even. "I'm sure they miss you too, Mama."

She turned to him, brow furrowed. "Why would you call me that?"

Sergei's heart skipped. "Sorry. Sorry, I…" He cleared his throat. "You remind me of my mother."

"Oh." Her features relaxed and the smile came back. "She's a lucky woman, if you're anything like my boy."

"I'll pass it along," he whispered, almost choking on the words.

"Good. You seem like a good boy." Gazing out the window again, she softly added, "Just like my Sergei."

His chest ached and he turned enough to hopefully hide his grimace. With a few slow, deep breaths, he composed himself, though the lump in his throat probably wasn't going anywhere.

"You should take your pills," he whispered.

"Oh." She looked at him, then the cup, then him again. "Okay."

He helped her take them, and after she'd finished, she gazed out the window.

"I should go," he said.

She turned to him again, and her expression was blank. "Who are you?"

Because he needed one last kick in the balls before he left.

He smiled tightly. "I just came in to help you with your meds." He patted her arm. "The nurse will be in later to take you to physical therapy."

"Oh." She blinked. "All right." Once again, she looked out the window.

He sighed and left the room. As soon as he was out in the hall, he stopped to collect himself. He'd never had any illusions that this would get easier, but he hadn't bargained for how much harder it could get.

"You all right, sweetie?" Brittany's voice turned his head.

He rolled his shoulders. "Yeah, I'm just…" He held her gaze, and realized she'd probably heard it all before. Even if she didn't know precisely what had happened, what Sergei and Mama had seen that horrible night, she worked with dementia patients. As much as anyone in the world could without knowing the specifics, she understood. He didn't need to explain it. For that, he was more grateful than she could imagine.

He exhaled hard. "It's tough."

"I know it is."

They fell into stride together, and walked partway down the hall in silence before she finally spoke again. "It's good that she has you, Sergei. I know it doesn't seem like it, but your visits really do make a difference."

"How can they? She doesn't know who I am." He looked back toward Mama's room, and shook his head. "She doesn't recognize me as an adult. She doesn't even know who I am."

"No, but I think, on some level, she does know. And even if she thinks you're one of your brothers, honestly, it does her good. She gets lonely sometimes, and whenever you're here, she's good for at least a couple of days before she starts getting depressed again."

"She doesn't even know why she's depressed."

"Doesn't matter. She still feels it." Brittany gestured toward the room. "And whenever you've been here, she feels better. She's much calmer."

"That's good, I guess." They walked on, and were nearly to the lobby when he slowed to a stop. She halted beside him too, and after a moment, Sergei said, "I'm curious about something."

"Sure."

"Does she have…" Sergei chewed the inside of his cheek. "Nightmares?"

Brittany's eyes darted away. "Sometimes."

His heart clenched. "Does she ever say what she dreams about?"

Without meeting his gaze, Brittany shook her head.

"She never says what they're about. By the time she's calmed down enough to talk, she's…"

"Forgotten?"

The nurse nodded. "We do everything we can to calm her down, though. I promise."

"I know you do." He forced a smile. "Thank you."

"You're welcome."

"I'll, um, let you get back to work."

"Okay. See you next week."

"Yeah. See you next week." And the week after. And the one after that. How long did something like this go on?

Hands stuffed in his pockets, gaze fixed on the ground, he wondered how the Catholics in town explained situations like Mama's. What exactly their god's "plan" was when it came to a woman traumatized within an inch of her life and left to stare at windows and walls until some ailment finally came along and silenced the nightmares she didn't understand.

He wasn't even out to the car yet before he had to wipe his eyes. He slid into the driver seat but didn't start the engine. Instead, he covered his face with a shaking hand and tried to compose himself. He never fell apart here. Not while he was still out in front of the home. He could always make it somewhere—a beach, an abandoned lot, *somewhere* —before it all came crashing down, but not today.

And he didn't really care. If people saw him, then they saw him. He doubted he was the first person to cry in this parking lot, and he doubted he'd be the last.

He wasn't surprised Mama had nightmares. He'd just hoped for all these years that she didn't. There was a reason it had taken him this long to ask for confirmation, and he wished he'd waited longer.

Mama probably dreamed of the same things he did, though hers would be worse because she'd seen more that night than he had, but she wasn't lucid enough now to know *why*. To know that the dreams were memories. When she woke up, the fear probably lingered, and then it was gone and so were the things she'd seen and felt in her sleep.

For that, Sergei envied her. He knew what the dreams were, what was real and what wasn't, and woke up every day with renewed rage toward the men who'd destroyed his family. Teeth clenched, he balled his fists at his sides. Maybe his encounters with Dom softened him toward Dom himself, but the Maisanos? The families in Cape Swan? The fucking Mafia?

Not a chance.

They were going down.

All of them.

***

IT TOOK A FEW HOURS, but Sergei collected himself enough to go the club. Though he didn't really need the money from this job—it was peanuts compared to what every bullet earned him—this was where his contacts came to find him.

Which one of them did, not two hours into his shift.

It wasn't Baltazar this time. It was Lorenzo, a goon directly connected to some of *the* most powerful men in town, which meant this was a big job.

On the one hand, great—a big job meant a lot of money, and it also meant removing a key player. A huge step toward completing his grand plan.

On the other, he hated this motherfucker, because although their meetings were always quick, they were anything but painless. They didn't even bother going back into the booth because the conversations didn't require much time. That, and Lorenzo could barely handle coming into the club—going back into a private booth was enough to make him break out in homophobic little hives.

When this asshole showed up, it meant Santo Tumino wanted to arrange a meeting with Sergei. Tumino was a Maisano underboss, nearly as powerful as Luciano or Felice Maisano themselves, and he was the only wise guy who Sergei would meet outside this club. It meant he had a contract for him. Usually a lucrative one—Sergei charged him an extra ten large just for making him come to him, and he gladly paid it.

Tumino never came to see Sergei directly. From what Sergei had heard, he never really left his house for more than an hour or two at a stretch. Even bosses and under-bosses came to him instead of the other way around. Rumor had it that it was because he had one of the worst cases of Irritable Bowel Syndrome any doctor in this town had ever seen. Fucker was so vile and miserable, even his own shit couldn't stand to be around him.

Much as Sergei didn't want to face him or his condition tonight, he didn't expect he had a lot of choice.

After he'd wrapped up a stage dance and a private lap dance, he came back out to the bar and found Lorenzo clinging to a bottle of Coke.

"Sorry to keep you waiting," Sergei said.

Lorenzo glared at him.

"I assume you're not here for a dance."

The man gulped like he was trying not to retch. "Of course not." He reached into his pocket and handed Sergei a card. "The boss wants to see you."

Sergei looked at the card, on which someone had handwritten: *$5M.*

Whoa. This was big. Fucking huge.

His pulse shot upward. Things were really about to get

crazy, weren't they? All that patience was about to pay off, wasn't it?

Keeping his excitement and nerves beneath the surface, he met Lorenzo's gaze. "Tonight?"

"Yes. As soon as possible. Don't keep him waiting."

Sergei nodded. "Tell him to give me two hours."

Lorenzo scowled.

"Two hours," Sergei said through gritted teeth.

The man tried to stare him down, but finally grumbled, "I'll let him know."

TUMINO ALWAYS WAITED for him in the guest house behind his massive estate, and Sergei never entered through the front door. It was understood that Sergei would do a perimeter check first, ensuring none of Tumino's goons—especially the security assholes—were anywhere near the place.

"Anyone sees my face," he'd warned Tumino a couple of years ago, "I'll put a bullet in theirs, and in yours for good measure. Are we clear?"

"Clear. Absolutely clear." The fact that Sergei'd been pressing a pistol to his forehead had probably made him reconsider arguing. That was the last time Tumino ever tried to sneak any of his people into the house.

Tonight, Sergei checked through the various windows, making sure the only person in the guest house was Tumino, who was reclining on the sofa with a glass of wine. Sergei had long ago placed tiny motion sensors in the hedge outside the house, and after he'd gone inside the perimeter, he activated them. No one would get near the guest house without him knowing about it.

Once he was sure the coast was clear, Sergei let himself

in through the back door, and moved from the kitchen to the living room where Tumino waited for him.

As Sergei stepped into the room, the beast of a man grinned. "Dmitry! Right on time."

"Of course I am."

He gestured at an armchair. "Have a seat."

Sergei didn't move.

Tumino studied him for a moment, then sat back on the sofa, grimacing as he did. Even from here, Sergei could hear the man's stomach gurgling and groaning.

God, please, don't let him be having one of his "episodes" while I'm in the room again. I may have to shoot him this time.

A few of the Italians in Cape Swan were on the large end, especially the Tumino clan, but this guy always seemed bloated in a sickly way that made Sergei cringe. Not heavy, but distended and swollen, as if everything beneath his skin were battling over which one could kill him first. How he'd lived this long was a mystery.

And Sergei had no desire to be here any longer than he had to be, so he held up the card Lorenzo had given him. "Let's get down to business. You asked me here for a big job, I assume."

"A very big one." Tumino grinned again, despite his brow still pinched with discomfort. "This is the one that'll make you a legend, kid."

"I'd just as soon not be a legend. That means people know who I am."

"They know you by reputation. And that reputation's going to be immortal after this one." He gestured at the chair again. "You really ought to sit down and get comfortable. We've got a lot of details to go over."

Sergei planted his feet. "One question."

"All right?"

"Who's the mark?"

They locked eyes.

Sergei's heart sped up.

Tumino's lips pulled back across his teeth. "I think you know."

Sergei swallowed. He'd had his suspicions. A dollar figure like that could only mean a handful of people. But he hadn't wanted to get his hopes up. "You're serious."

"Completely."

Sergei took a seat, resting his elbows on his thighs and leaning forward. "All right. Let's talk."

He could barely contain the giddiness fluttering his gut. This was the contract he'd been waiting for. Checkmate was no longer close—it was inevitable.

This is it, Mama. They're all going down.

Chapter 22

Whenever Dom met with Sergei, he woke the next morning feeling blissed out and happy, with a side order of depressed as fuck. It was impossible not to be almost giddy after a night like that, but reality was never far behind, always coming in and reminding him how short-lived this arrangement would be.

Last night had been different. He'd spent most of the night beside Sergei, worrying about him, watching for signs that the decompression sickness was getting worse. They'd barely touched.

And yet, a hint of that giddiness was there. Relief that Sergei was all right, no doubt. Nothing else made sense.

Today, Dom's day had been a roller coaster. It started out well enough. Maybe none of that post-coital ache in every muscle of his body, without that stupid grin that always seemed to start before the coffee had even brewed, but like most mornings after, he was pretty damned certain the dark "this isn't gonna last" cloud would catch up with him eventually.

So far so good, though. Maybe things with Sergei

wouldn't last—of course they wouldn't—but just being in the same room with him for a while, sharing the company of someone who wasn't caught up in the same spider web he was, did wonders for what was left of Dom's sanity.

Then Corrado called him in, and the day went downhill fast. Dom had fully expected to be raked over the coals for not being here yesterday, front and center while Corrado tried to work out what had happened to Privitera, but his uncle skipped right over that part.

Instead, he went straight to pushing for a decision about Brigida Passantino.

"In light of the incident on my son's boat," Corrado had said over his immense desk, "I have to accept the possibility that we have traitors on the inside. Which means the Maisanos need all the allies we can get."

"Understood," Dom had responded quietly.

"We need the Passantinos as a friend, and the fastest, most effective means for sealing that friendship is with a marriage between our two families."

The sick feeling had already taken up residence in Dom's gut, and it just kept getting worse.

"Her father's giving his blessing," Corrado went on. "And Brigida herself is willing to go through with it."

Great. Just what Dom always wanted. A marriage to a woman whose enthusiasm came down to being willing to go through with it. Wouldn't they be an apathetically well-matched pair?

But what could he say that hadn't already been said? Especially with Corrado's warning in the back of his mind that bachelors who showed no interest in beautiful, connected women like Brigida raised *questions*.

So he'd released a breath and held his uncle's gaze. "Can I have some more time to think about it?"

"Domenico." Corrado closed his eyes, rubbing his

temples as if this conversation were giving him a migraine. "How much time do you need? You're not getting any younger, you know."

And I'm not exactly ready to be put out to pasture either.

"Give me a week." He felt like a fucking hostage negotiator. "One week from today, I'll have an answer for you."

His uncle lowered his hands and locked eyes with him again. "One week, Domenico."

Dom nodded. "Okay. I'll, um, give Brigida a call. We'll do dinner as soon as she's available. And we'll talk about things."

Corrado studied him for a moment. Finally, he nodded. "All right."

So he had a week. Seven days. Enough time to come to terms with this marriage, maybe. Perhaps the best way to spend that week would be with Brigida so they could both be damn sure they were "willing to go through with it."

But no.

The door to Corrado's office hadn't even closed before he'd texted Sergei.

How are you feeling?

Moments later: *Much better. Meet tonight?*

Yes. Oh God, yes. Dom pounded out his response so fast he thought his phone was going to burst into flames: *Name the time & place.*

They'd made plans. Dom had gone back to work, where he spent the day counting down until Sergei would be off work and checking his watch every time he finished even the tiniest task in the office. At home, he'd showered and shaved, texting Brigida about dinner while he made sure he had condoms for tonight, and—

Then Sergei bailed.

At a quarter past eleven, the message came:

Can't make it—sorry.

Dom stared at the text. Seriously?

Well, shit.

He lounged back on his bed and unbuttoned his collar. Now what?

It was a bit late to see if Brigida wanted to meet sooner than later. On the other hand, maybe Brigida had a spontaneous side. If she was the type who'd drop everything and go out for midnight coffee, then maybe that would give them a little more in common. And maybe they could both compare notes on men they fantasized about.

He groaned, rubbing a hand over his face. This was going to be a fucking nightmare. A great political move, but a marital disaster.

No, he wouldn't bother Brigida tonight.

He did, however, text Biaggio. *Could use some advice—free for lunch tomorrow?*

Biaggio didn't answer immediately. That wasn't surprising. Dom was pretty sure the man never slept, and he was almost always busy with something.

About twenty minutes later, though, the response came: *Come by the house tomorrow. 11am.*

Typical Biaggio. Yes, he was free, and they'd meet up on his terms. At least they were meeting at Biaggio's place instead of Corrado's—Dom needed a little breathing room for once. God help him if Corrado overheard the conversation he planned on having with Biaggio.

Eventually, Dom went downstairs and flicked on the TV. It had been a long time since he'd lounged in front of some mindless television, and that sounded like exactly what he needed tonight.

Halfway through the third or fourth episode of some ridiculous sitcom, Dom's phone vibrated on the end table.

To his surprise, it was a text from Sergei.

Change of plans. Free after all. Still on?

Dom's heart sped up. He quickly texted back, *Definitely*.

Did that smack of desperation? Probably. But he was desperate at this point. In a week's time, he'd most likely be engaged to the woman of his uncle's organization's dreams, so he planned to take advantage of every possible opportunity to get Sergei—*men*—out of his system. Once he and Brigida sealed the deal, that was it. He didn't foresee himself being a particularly passionate husband, but he would be a faithful one. Which meant... no Sergei.

Tonight, though, he was all Sergei's. He went upstairs, grabbed the condoms and lube, and got the hell out of there.

THE DRIVE from his neighborhood to the shady district with all the no-tell motels seemed to get longer every time. Anticipation made every mile drag out until Dom was climbing the walls, gripping the wheel and willing his heart to slow down.

Tonight was no exception. And thank God, Sergei already had a room—Dom was a few blocks away when Sergei texted him with a room number.

No waiting. No check-in. Just park. Walk. Knock.

And there he was.

As soon as the door was closed, they were wrapped up in each other's arms.

"Sorry for bailing," Sergei whispered between kisses. "Something came up, and then—"

"It's okay." Dom cradled his face and kissed him lightly. "You're here now. I don't care about anything else."

Sergei's whole body seemed to relax, and he melted against Dom.

"Are you feeling better tonight?" Dom asked between kisses. "After—"

"I wouldn't be here if I wasn't." Sergei claimed another hard, demanding kiss. "You brought lube, right?"

"Absolutely. Are you in any hurry? To get anywhere?"

"Not anymore, no." Sergei ran the tip of his tongue along the inside of his lip. "Are you?"

"I was. But now that I'm here…"

Sergei grinned.

Dom combed his fingers through Sergei's short hair. "God, this is insane. What we're doing." He paused. "But I think it's the only sane part of my life right now."

Sergei laughed, his devilish eyes sending a shiver through Dom. "I think this is the first time someone's considered me a sane part of anything."

"Their loss," Dom whispered, and pulled him closer.

Sergei lifted his chin, and when their lips met, he wrapped his arms around Dom. As the kiss went on, as it deepened, they gathered handfuls of each other's shirts but made no move to peel off any layers quite yet.

He had no idea who was leading or if their bodies were simply moving, but they inched toward the bed. And then they were on it—lying across the mattress, Sergei strad-dling Dom—and Dom finally managed to push Sergei's shirt up and off. Christ, they were still mostly dressed and he was already lightheaded.

These nights with Sergei were unreal. It went beyond the sex, too. In here, within the walls of whatever cheap motel they'd chosen for the evening, nothing else existed. In here, Dom found a temporary escape from his bloody, violent world.

Sergei had undoubtedly saved his life that first night, but Dom was starting to think he did that every time they were together. He'd become a drug. Not a recreational one, but one that kept everything functioning the way it was supposed to.

I'm going to lose my mind without you.

He pulled Sergei closer, deepened the kiss, and held on. Sergei didn't need to know that their arrangement's days were seriously numbered. They'd both known there'd be an end to this at some point, but Dom had held out hope they'd have more time.

It wasn't to be, though. The pressure was mounting, the end approaching too fast. Whether he liked it or not, this would be over very soon.

So Dom fully intended to do the one thing he could do—enjoy every second he had left with Sergei.

"We still have too many clothes on," he murmured against Sergei's lips.

Sergei pushed himself up and grinned. "We should do something about that."

BIAGGIO SPENT most of his days at Corrado's mansion, and many nights there, too, so he'd never really gone all-out with his own place. It was a modest Spanish-style villa overlooking the water, not far from where Corrado lived. No doubt so he could be at the boss's front door within moments if needed.

Dom arrived a few minutes before eleven, and Biaggio's maid showed him to the shaded terrace where he was waiting.

"Your uncle needs me this afternoon," Biaggio said as Dom took a seat and the maid poured them some wine. "I'm afraid we'll have to make this a somewhat short meal."

"That's fine. I still have some bookkeeping to catch up on."

Biaggio nodded, holding Dom's gaze. They both knew what "catching up on bookkeeping" really meant. Luciano was set to receive almost three million dollars this afternoon for a massive shipment of cocaine and various contraband that had "disappeared" from Naples while a Chinese cargo ship was in port. By the time Dom had finished routing and rerouting that money, no one would ever be able to trace it back to its origin.

The maid offered them each their glasses, and after they'd thanked her, she went inside, presumably to finish preparing lunch. They were alone out here. Biaggio's security presence was minimal, just a handful of men strategically stationed around the property. His bodyguard, Sal, stood back beside the sliding glass door, scanning the yard while Dom and Biaggio relaxed.

"Well, I suppose we should use what time we have, then." Biaggio watched him over the top of his glass. "You said you needed some advice."

"Yeah." Dom absently ran his thumb along the edge of the wrought iron table. "It's about Brigida Passantino."

Biaggio nodded slowly. "I understand you're going to give your uncle a final decision in a week."

"He told you, then."

"Yes." The consigliere folded his hands in his lap. "Your uncle is concerned about you, Domenico."

Dom gritted his teeth. "My uncle is concerned about my *image*."

"But such is the reality of the circles we move in." Biaggio shrugged tightly. "Alliances are necessary for survival. Sometimes the best way to seal those alliances are with marriages."

"Arranged marriages are a little out of date, don't you think?"

Biaggio laughed and reached up to pat Dom's forearm. "Not in our world, Domenico. Not in our world. And besides, you could have married any woman you chose. If Luciano or Felice were still unmarried, their father would be pushing them into this arrangement. It just happens that you've been single long enough to raise eyebrows, and there's an opportunity to use that to the organization's advantage."

Dom pushed out a breath, gazing out at the ocean far beneath the cliffs. "You're probably right. And, I mean, if this is what the family needs, then I'll do it."

"Good. With as much bloodshed as this town has seen recently, a wedding will be good for morale." Biaggio folded his hands in his lap. "And knowing the Maisanos and Passantinos are allied this way might make the Cusimanos think twice about screwing with either family."

"True." Dom tapped his fingers on the table. "So you think it *is* a good move. Marrying Passantino's daughter."

"It makes business sense."

"We barely know each other. What kind of marriage would that be?"

"Well…" Biaggio sat back, idly swirling his glass. "You've gotten along well enough so far, haven't you?"

Dom nodded.

"Give it time, then." Biaggio shrugged. "Don't expect it to happen overnight, but the two of you can continue to get to know each other after you're married."

The 'overnight' part might be an issue…

"I do think this is a wise move, though," Biaggio said. "The two families have been pussy-footing around an alliance for years. The two of you marrying will, in essence, marry the families to each other, so we'll—"

Crack!

Biaggio jerked to the side as blood sprayed the wall behind him.

Dom leaped back, and right when he gasped, a stray droplet landed on his tongue. Before the saltiness had even registered, he turned and vomited.

He spat, and then, staying low in case more bullets came, he turned his head.

No…

Strong arms grabbed Dom, hauled him to his feet, and herded him inside.

"Are you all right?" Sal asked, shielding him with his body and keeping him away from the windows.

"Yeah. Yeah, I'm…" Dom craned his neck enough to look outside. At the table, Biaggio's motionless body was slumped in the chair, blood mingling with scattered pine needles by his feet. "Oh my God. Biaggio…" His throat tightened. What the hell? One second he was settling Dom's mind over this upcoming marriage. The next…

This.

Jesus.

His eyes stung, and he hoped to God Sal blamed it on the puking.

No. Not Biaggio. God, no…

Below them, the yard had exploded with activity. Shouts. Dogs barking. Gunfire. More voices in the distance. He still had his hearing, so the shooter must not have been close by. A fucking sniper.

"Are you sure you're all right?" Sal asked.

"Yeah." Dom coughed and spat. "Didn't hit me. Didn't…" He trailed off as his gaze landed on Biaggio again. "Who the hell would…" He couldn't even say it. Couldn't verbally acknowledge what his eyes wouldn't let him forget.

There wasn't much he could do now. He was powerless. Useless. Biaggio was dead, so no amount of first aid or frantic 911 calls would change anything. It was over in the blink of an eye, and he couldn't make sense of it.

He glanced down at his blood-splattered clothes. "I, uh, think I'm going to grab a shower, though." That seemed pointless. Crass, even. But he desperately needed something mundane, something normal. Some way to get all this blood off his skin.

Sal withdrew his hand. "Good idea. I'll have one of your staff bring over some clothes."

"Perfect. Thank you. And, um…" Dom gestured out at the terrace. "Someone should call a priest. He'd… he'd want that."

"Of course." Sal gestured at the stairs. "I'll take care of the calls."

"Thanks."

The whole place was eerily quiet, the stairs creaking softly beneath Dom's feet as he trudged up to the third floor. By the time he came back down, there'd be activity, but he suspected the quiet would linger. There'd be no sirens. No flashing lights. The police weren't needed and neither was an ambulance. The coroner would, as always, be discreet—his balls were in the same vise as anyone else in this town whose services a family might require.

While calls were made to Corrado, Luciano, Felice and anyone else who needed to know, Dom went upstairs to shower. It felt strange to use Biaggio's shower to clean off his blood, but the consigliere would have insisted.

"*Clean yourself up,*" he could almost hear the old guy grumbling. "*Doesn't do a man any good to be seen like that.*"

He'd have been especially horrified if Dom met the priest like this, so Dom soaped and rinsed until blood no longer swirled in the water at his feet.

And even then, he didn't get out. Not yet.

Eyes closed, he let his head fall forward so the water rushed through his hair and down his neck. He didn't feel anything yet. No grief. No fear. The adrenaline had settled, and now he was just... numb. The rest would be along once the truth settled in, but at the moment, he felt nothing.

Now what?

Death was part of this life, but the body count had been rising at an alarming rate for the last few months. And bullets were coming unnervingly close, hitting not just the family, but *his* family. His uncle and cousins were all he had left, and any of them—hell, Dom himself—could be in the crosshairs at any moment.

Without Biaggio, Corrado was the closest thing Dom still had to a father. He was a brutal man. He'd traumatized Dom, taken people and safety and sanity away from him, but he'd also been the man who'd taken Dom in and raised him, even after he'd been the one to calmly end Papa's life.

"It's business, Domenico," Corrado had told him while they'd watched men dump dirt on Papa's still-warm body. "It's business, and it's family, and families and businesses are only as strong as their weakest members."

"But..." Dom had been too young to make sense of any of that. Much too young to have seen the things he'd seen. "Papa wasn't weak."

"No." Corrado had squeezed his shoulder, grimacing with sympathy. "But he did things that weakened all of us. He had to go, son, because if he stayed, many other men would have died. Do you understand?"

More than anything, Dom had never forgiven Corrado for that. Maybe he could have learned to accept that cold-blooded murder was part of this life, that Papa had done unforgivable things in an unforgiving world. But what man asked a child if his father's death was worth it so others could live?

Even with those lifelong grudges, and with the blood on his hands because of Corrado, Dom struggled with the idea of ever losing his uncle. Some days he wanted to kill the man himself. Other days, he looked around and realized that, for better or worse, in a world that was full of killers and crooks, Corrado and his sons really were the only family Dom had left. What happened if and when they were gone?

He closed his eyes and let the water hit his face.

It was hard to say how life would be without his family, but he suspected it would be short. If someone killed Corrado, or Luciano, or Felice, then it would be open season on Dom anyhow.

What would I be doing if I wasn't part of this life, Sergei? Feeling a little less like I've got crosshairs on my back.

Dom shut off the shower and stepped out. He dried himself, and when he opened the door to the bedroom, a small stack of neatly folded clothing awaited him on the foot of Biaggio's bed. Trying not to overthink where he was, or who wouldn't be sleeping here tonight, or what awaited him when he went back downstairs, he dressed.

He was still a bit queasy and off-balance, but the emotions remained far beneath the surface. He was just... rattled. His bones and muscles felt weirdly disjointed, as if they should have been shaking but weren't. Like after a near-miss in a car, where the danger had passed and now the body didn't quite know what to do with itself.

And God knew he had no idea what to do with himself now. Biaggio was gone. He'd died right in front of Dom, right in the middle of trying to settle his nerves about the future.

Corrado was right. There was a war brewing. Hell, it was *done* brewing. Taking out a boss's consigliere was nothing if not an irrevocable declaration. A shot fired not across the bow, but through the first mate's head.

This was, unmistakably, war.

By the time Dom returned to the ground level, the coroner's van was outside, and two men were closing up the back. Dom was glad for that—he wasn't sure he could stomach watching them wheel Biaggio outside.

Beside him, Corrado materialized, and he placed a hand between Dom's shoulders. "Are you all right, Domenico?"

Dom nodded. "Yeah. Just, uh, shaken up."

His uncle nodded. "We all are." He studied Dom for a moment. "Did you see anything? Anyone?"

"No. I took cover in case any more shots came, but there was just the one."

Corrado gazed out at the yard, saying nothing.

"There's no way it was at close range, or security would've had him," Dom said. "He probably had a perch out that way"—he gestured at a distant hill—"and a high-powered rifle."

Corrado scowled. "Well, when we find him," he growled, "rest assured he will wish he'd never taken that shot."

A chill ran up Dom's spine. Given the sadistic violence his uncle could inflict on someone who'd crossed him, Dom could only imagine what would happen to someone who'd killed his longtime friend and trusted advisor. He hoped like hell that the shooter didn't have children.

Dom cleared his throat. "I, um, hope Brigida understands me canceling on her again."

Corrado's lips tightened. Dom cringed inwardly, fully expecting to be told that now was the time to stand up, be a man, and show his face to let everyone in Cape Swan know that the Maisanos would not be cowed like this.

Instead, Corrado sighed. "Take this evening. Anyone will understand that we need time to grieve. And there's a funeral to plan."

"Yeah. And I… I think I just need to be alone tonight."

Corrado nodded. "If you need anything, don't hesitate to call." His jaw tightened. "Call me directly. Since… Biaggio…"

Dom winced. He really was gone. Biaggio, the closest thing Dom had had to a father since he was twelve years old, was really gone.

Throat aching and stomach turning, Dom took a deep breath. Fuck. He was… he was gone.

"I'll give you a call if there's any developments." Corrado squeezed Dom's shoulder. "But otherwise, you won't be bothered."

"Thank you."

"How is your security? Do you need some—"

"I'm fine."

Corrado eyed him. "I really think a bodyguard is in order after this."

"No. Whoever did this had a chance to shoot me. A bodyguard would just tell him he'd scared me."

His uncle paused, then nodded. "Good point. But be careful, Domenico."

"I will."

Dom bowed out of the conversation and hurried out toward his car. As he did, he pulled out his phone, but hesitated. He couldn't keep turning to Sergei every time this life pushed him to his limits. Corrado was undoubtedly still going to hold Dom to his one-week ultimatum, so the sanity Sergei offered would be gone in a matter of days anyway. And besides, the last thing Dom was in the mood for was sex.

Still, all he could think of was Sergei. Of getting into a room somewhere, getting out of their clothes, and getting into bed. What they did then—if Sergei fucked him, or if either of them came before the sun rose—didn't matter. He just needed to be that close to someone who was alive. It wasn't sex he wanted, per se—though, God, with Sergei involved, there *would* be sex—but a feverish, breathless escape from this life that was spiraling out of control.

More than ever, he needed what Sergei offered, and he was running out of time to lose himself in that passionate distraction.

So, on his way to his car, he texted Sergei.

Chapter 23

Are you busy tonight?

Sergei stared at the message. He definitely hadn't expected that. Really? Dom was in the mood tonight?

And, more to the point, could Sergei even handle seeing Dom tonight?

Yes. Yes, because I need to touch him and know he's okay.

He wrote back, *Tell me when/where.*

After the message had sent, he put the phone aside and shifted his attention back to cleaning the disassembled rifle on the footlocker in front of him. His conscience didn't usually bother him after a job. Today it was gnawing him from the inside out.

He'd had to take the hit. It was a major move toward igniting the war between the families. And besides, if he hadn't taken it, or he'd botched it, then it would be his head.

The phone buzzed again. Sergei wiped gun oil off his hands with a shop towel and picked it up.

Sooner the better.

Sergei chewed his lip. *Text me when you nail down a place. I'll be there ASAP.*

He sent the message and continued cleaning and reassembling the rifle. As he did, he could only imagine how shaken Dom was. Whatever his relationship with Corrado's consigliere, they'd seemed close. Friendly, at least. Their expressions hadn't read like two men having a business discussion.

Three times, Sergei had considered bailing. He couldn't do it with Dom sitting right there.

But he'd already failed to complete a hit on Dom. If he didn't shoot the consigliere this time, there was a small but not insignificant possibility that someone would see the pattern. That when Domenico Maisano was present, Sergei lost his nerve.

So he'd taken the shot.

And now Dom was texting him, eager to see him as soon as possible.

He probably needed an outlet tonight. And isn't that what this arrangement had become? What had begun as Dom getting gay sex out of his system had become an odd lifeline for both of them. The drug of choice when life in this volatile town went haywire. Sometimes Dom needed Sergei. Sometimes Sergei needed Dom. Sometimes they both seemed like they were at the edge of madness, and the ticket back to normal involved skin and lube.

Letting Dom depend on him like this was dangerous. So was letting himself depend on Dom. But on those nights when Dom's touch held the key to making it through until dawn without breaking down, Sergei didn't stand a chance of talking himself out of it. And on the nights when it was Dom who needed him, something in his Italian lover's eyes appealed to a part of Sergei he didn't quite understand. It wasn't the thrill of sleeping with the enemy, or corrupting a Mafioso in a way that would horrify the others. It was something more... human.

Sighing, Sergei screwed the barrel back onto the rifle. This thing he was doing with Dom didn't fit into the world where they lived, but he didn't know why he kept trying to talk himself out of it. He knew as well as Dom that they'd both be there tonight. Whichever crappy motel wound up being their rendezvous, they'd be there, and they'd fuck, and maybe on some plane, it made sense.

Whether it did or not, though, it was still going to happen.

And he couldn't wait.

AFTER THE GUN was cleaned and hidden away and Sergei had showered, he drove across town to the motel where Dom was waiting.

On the way to the designated room, he ignored the weird apprehension tightening behind his ribs. This was the same as any other night they'd spent together, he told himself over and over. Dom needed sex, Sergei would give him sex, and they'd both walk away like they did every time.

At the door, he paused, much like he did whenever he went to visit Mama, and collected himself. Deep breath. Shoulders back. Quiet knock.

Dom let him in, but as soon as Sergei was across the threshold, Dom grabbed him and shoved him up against the door, slamming it with their combined body weight. Panic surged through him. An ambush? Fight or flight kicked in, but just before Sergei could knee him and break free, Dom kissed him. Hard.

Sergei froze. His heart went crazy even as his lips, moving of their own volition, softened beneath Dom's.

Not an attack. Not a threat. Just… hunger.

Exhaling through his nose, Sergei wrapped his arms around him. Dom's erection ground against his hip, and in no time at all, they were both out of breath, panting as they kissed and groped at each other.

When Dom finally came up for air, he touched his forehead to Sergei's, and they both breathed hard for a moment.

"So glad you came," Dom murmured.

Sergei regarded him uncertainly. "You all right tonight?"

"Yeah." Dom swallowed. "Just a… long day."

If that was just a long day, I'd hate to see what qualifies as a bad one.

"The kind of long day that needs to be followed by a long night?"

"Yes. Exactly." Dom took a step back and tugged Sergei with him. "There's too much to explain. I just—"

Sergei cut him off with a kiss. The longer they talked, the more potential there was for truths to come out that would send this night in a very different direction. He'd come here to be what Dom needed, and that was a lover, and he intended to be exactly that.

They made quick work of shedding their clothes, and Sergei dragged Dom down onto the bed with him. Kissing, touching, rubbing—the friction between their skin was almost as intoxicating as Dom's needy but considerate kiss.

And never far from his mind was the awareness that Dom was shaken, grieving, and Sergei had done this to him. He'd fired the bullet that had rocked Dom's world today.

I'm not sorry for killing Mafiosi.

But I'm sorry I hurt you.

You're the last one in the world I want to hurt.

So he held on as tight as he could and did everything he could imagine to alleviate that pain. Dom wanted a diversion? He'd have one.

Dom carefully kept his weight off Sergei, rubbing their dicks together while still holding himself up with his arms and knees. Every bit of friction between them was deliberate but not frantic. It was a weird feeling, like orgasms weren't even close to the most important thing right then, but one of them could—and probably would—come at any moment.

Abruptly, Dom broke the kiss and started down Sergei's neck. Sergei exhaled. He tilted his head back as far as the hard pillow would allow and dragged his nails across Dom's shoulders. As Dom's lips skated over his collarbone, Sergei moaned. Somewhere in his mind, there were words —profane ones, no doubt, and commands and praises and God knew what else—but none of them made it past the tip of his tongue.

Dom kissed his way down the middle of Sergei's chest. Soft lips on his abs were more than Sergei could take, and he bit his own lip, squirming beneath Dom's featherlight kisses. And still, Dom continued lower. Sergei groaned. His head spun. His lungs screamed for air he couldn't remember how to breathe.

Earlier, he'd seen Dom's face through a rifle scope. Now, alive and well, oblivious to the phantom presence of the trigger still against Sergei's finger, Dom trailed kisses along Sergei's trembling abs.

Don't you know what I did to you today?

Before Sergei could find his breath, Dom's lips were around his cock, and even a throbbing conscience was no match for the barrage of sensations. Sergei pushed himself up on his elbow and gazed down at him, mouth watering and breath hitching as Dom teased him with lips and tongue. He loved that about Dom—a man who sucked cock not out of obligation, but as if he could think of nothing else in the world he'd rather do. Sergei ran his fingers through Dom's hair, which prompted a moan that sent dizzying vibrations along Sergei's sensitive flesh.

He swore, and right then Dom's eyes flicked up to meet his, and Sergei's breath caught. From that blissed-out expression, Dom didn't even know where the hell he was anymore. With a dick in his throat that would soon be in his ass, Sergei doubted he *cared* where he was.

Except every now and then, his eyes would meet Sergei's again, and Sergei's pulse went crazy. Dom may not have known or cared where he was, but he knew who the fuck he was looking at. He knew whose cock was in his mouth.

"You're amazing at this," Sergei slurred. "I'm gonna… gonna fuck you so hard after this. Jesus…" He dropped back onto the bed, eyes squeezed shut and spine arching. "Fuck, Dom…"

Lifting his head, Dom grinned. "That sounds like a good idea."

Sergei eyed him, not comprehending for a few seconds, but then the pieces fell into place. As they both sat up, he said, "You'd better get me a condom, then."

Dom grabbed one off the nightstand but paused, eyeing the foil square in his hand as if he were debating going bareback.

"No. Only when you're on top." Sergei took the condom from him. Their eyes met, and if Dom had any thought of arguing, he let it go. Instead, he met Sergei in the middle of the bed, and they kissed hungrily and desperately while Sergei tried his damnedest to get the condom out and on.

Kissing screwed up his coordination, though, so he pulled back. "Gotta... put this..."

"Please do." Dom grabbed the lube and poured some on his hand. Sergei hadn't even rolled the condom all the way on before Dom was stroking the lube onto it.

Sergei sucked in a hiss of breath. "You know I'm not going to last long, right? When you've got me this fucking turned on?"

"I know." Dom grinned. "Then you'll just have to fuck me again."

Sergei blinked. "Yeah. Yeah, I will. Now turn around."

Dom didn't miss a beat. He immediately turned and got on his hands and knees. Sergei positioned himself behind him and guided his cock to Dom's ass. Fingering him was tempting—Dom did just fine bottoming without a lot of prep, but teasing him relentlessly was fun. Sergei wasn't sure he could wait, though. Not after Dom had turned him on like that.

He pressed the head of his cock against Dom, easing himself past the tight ring so he wouldn't hurt him.

Abruptly, though, Dom shoved himself back, and he took Sergei's cock so quickly Sergei damn near blacked out. He grabbed Dom's hips and steadied him.

"Jesus..." Exhaling slowly, he withdrew and then eased himself back in, and Dom squirmed in his grasp.

"Hard," Dom pleaded. "Please..."

"I will." Sergei licked his lips. "Just need to—"

Dom slammed back again and knocked Sergei off balance. In an instant, Sergei was buried all the way inside him, slumped over him, his lips parted for a breath that refused to move.

"Just. *Fuck* me."

Sergei finally exhaled. He righted himself, gripping Dom's hips tighter. "Not gonna argue with that." Rocking his own hips good and fast, he watched himself disappearing into Dom. He kneaded Dom's ass cheeks as he fucked him, mesmerized by this sight even though he'd seen it so many times before. He loved the way Dom felt. The way he looked. The way he moaned and cursed as he took Sergei's dick over and over.

This was definitely going to be quick. Sergei's orgasm was already closing in, so he moved his hands to Dom's hips and fucked him for all he was worth. Deep, hard, violent, until the bed sounded like it was going to fall apart and every slap of skin on skin actually stung.

Dom cried out, and Sergei had no idea if he was speaking Italian or English or some other language, or fucking gibberish. His own mind was too scrambled to make sense of anything, and as his eyes rolled back and his whole body started trembling, he thought he heard himself murmuring in his native tongue, but God, who cared because he felt so good, so good, so fucking—

Everything went white. He forced himself as deep as Dom would take him and then tried to get even deeper, his hips jerking against Dom's ass.

Finally, he exhaled. They both sank back down to the bed, and Sergei had just enough presence of mind to pull out before he'd gone too soft. He pushed himself up and managed to stumble into the bathroom to toss the condom, and somehow he even found his way back across the narrow stretch of floor to tumble back into bed with Dom.

Evidently, Dom wasn't done yet. Sergei hadn't even settled onto the mattress again before Dom pulled him into his arms and kissed him, and it was one of those kisses that said he meant business—they'd both catch their breath and recharge, but they were not done tonight.

Fine by me.

Sergei pulled him closer and lost himself in Dom's needy kiss and warm embrace. They were both sweaty now and shaking, and they made out like they'd just gotten started. Postcoital fatigue tried to close in, but even that didn't last long. Where Dom had found this energy—hell, where Sergei had found it—was anyone's guess. Maybe it was just the need to disappear completely from the rest of the world. And what better place than between the sheets with someone who was willing and eager to provide as much distraction as possible?

Except this was all wrong. Sergei had no business offering a diversion from the very crime he'd committed. Was he assuaging his own conscience? Or truly trying to offer comfort? He didn't even know anymore, and though it was wrong, it was right too, and he couldn't let Dom go.

It was impossible to say how much time passed. They backed off for a little while. Started making out again. Backed off again. And then started kissing like there was no turning back—hungrily, tongues deep in each other's mouths, fingers pressing into flesh and bodies subtly starting to mimic the motions of thrusting and rubbing. Sergei's dick hardened. Then Dom's did.

When Dom broke the kiss this time, he murmured, "Fuck me again."

"You won't be able to move tomorrow."

"Can't move now. Please…"

Sergei was hardly going to tell him no, so he nudged him to turn over, and then he wrapped an arm around him and molded his body to Dom's. He wasn't inside him, but he held him as if they were fucking, as if he were one thrust away from making *sure* Dom couldn't move tomorrow.

"Don't want to stop," Sergei slurred. "Condoms are—"

"Don't care about condoms." Dom rubbed back against him. "I really don't. Just… please. Fuck me."

Sergei kissed the side of his neck. They'd agreed to go bareback when Dom was on top, since he hadn't been nearly as promiscuous as Sergei over the years, but what were the odds either of them had anything that would kill them before this life killed them both?

To hell with it. Dom needed this and Sergei knew damn well why.

You don't want to think anymore tonight, do you?

He pressed into Dom's already slick, stretched hole.

I'll make sure you don't have to.

SERGEI JERKED AWAKE WITH A GASP.

"Sergei?" Dom squeezed his arm, and Sergei realized that was what had woken him up—Dom's touch. "You okay?"

"Yeah, I…" Closing his eyes, Sergei suppressed a shudder. He ran a shaking hand through his sweaty hair. "I'm good."

"You sure?" Dom's fingers trailed down his arm, making Sergei shiver. "You sounded like you were——"

"Just… dreams. It's nothing."

"Does that happen often?"

Not these dreams, no. "Pretty much every night."

"Jesus…"

"Guess I should've warned you."

"I don't think you planned on us falling asleep any more than I did."

Well, that much was true. They'd fucked until there wasn't a snowball's chance in hell of either man getting hard again, and then Sergei must've dozed off. Dom too.

If he had a brain, he'd leave. But this was comfortable. The warmth of another man pressed up against him, arm slung over Sergei's waist, breath cool on his neck—even Sergei's conscience couldn't talk him out of enjoying that for a little while longer.

Especially since he was so damned tired.

His eyes slid closed and he rested his hand on top of Dom's. Before long, Dom was asleep, snoring softly in Sergei's ear. Any other time, Sergei would've been annoyed, but this time, he couldn't help listening, fixating on the slow, steady rhythm of Dom's breathing.

He's alive. The dream wasn't real. Dom is alive.

He shuddered.

They weren't the dreams he was used to. Not that he could ever get used to reliving that night over and over and over, but he knew it was coming. And he'd had those dreams tonight, but there were others. New dreams. They were fragmented now, coming back to him only as emotions—guilt and fear, mostly—rather than actual images. He remembered blood on his hands. Everything else was hazy.

This had never happened before. He did his job, and he felt nothing. No shame, no guilt, no remorse. Did exterminators have dreams about squashed cockroaches and poisoned vermin? Of course not.

So what the fuck is my problem?

He was getting too soft. Too close to Dom.

He should have left. He had no business being here in the first place, and actually sleeping together? What the hell was he thinking?

He needed to get up, get dressed, and get the hell back to his own apartment.

But he didn't.

Sergei was exhausted. Dom was exhausted. Sergei

didn't let him go, and Dom didn't pull away. He let himself be wrapped up in Dom's arms, let the warmth of Dom's body bring his goose bumps and heart rate down.

The fact was, this thing with Dom was only going to last so much longer. Wheels were turning. Things were happening. Soon, Dom would be much too preoccupied to spend nights in the arms of a stripper.

Sergei's heart clenched. There was no way around it—Dom would also be in danger. The more things heated up between the families, the more danger every last Mafioso was in, especially the ones higher up the food chain. Things were going to get bloody, and it was entirely possible that Dom, like his brethren, would wind up dead.

Sergei brought Dom's hand up to his lips and kissed it.

I can't stop what I'm doing. I can't let them go on, not even to save you.

But God, I hope you make it through this alive.

Chapter 24

The next day, as the family was deep in the midst of planning Biaggio's funeral, Dom was called into his uncle's office. It was strange, getting the call from Corrado himself instead of Biaggio, and Dom couldn't help getting a little choked up after he ended the call. Biaggio's death hadn't quite sunk in, but it was beginning to.

Still, there was business to attend to. Grief would be allowed at the funeral. Stoic, straight-faced grief, but grief nonetheless. Until then, the family had to show solidarity. They had to carry on and refuse to show their enemies the faintest hint of weakness.

So he collected himself, drove across town, and showed himself to Corrado's office, ignoring the empty space beside him as he walked down that long hallway without Biaggio.

At the giant double doors, he paused. Took a breath. Tamped down his emotions.

When he was composed, he stepped into the office. To his surprise, only Felice and Corrado were there.

"Where's Luciano?" he asked as he shut the door.

"That's actually why you're here." Corrado leaned against his immense desk, hands folded loosely in front of him. His expression was blank, his tone level. "Felice says he has some information that involves Luciano."

Dom turned to his cousin. Felice was usually ice cold and together, but he looked rattled this time. Unsteady. A little pale. Which might've been grief, but even that didn't seem right—Felice was the type to grieve with fists and weapons.

"Well. We're here." Corrado inclined his head. "What's this about, Felice?"

Felice took a deep breath. "I know who killed Biaggio. And… who ordered it."

Both Corrado and Dom stared at him.

"Luciano had him killed." Felice exhaled hard. "He didn't pull the trigger, but he orchestrated it with—"

Corrado backhanded his younger son across the face, sending him stumbling backward. "*Vaffanculo!* Don't you dare accuse your own brother of—"

"I didn't want to accuse him." Felice righted himself, dabbing at the blood welling up on his lip. "Do you think I would've come to you about this if I thought it could possibly be anyone else?"

"How do you know this?" Corrado asked through clenched teeth. "Speak up, or I will—"

"I tracked down the man who shot him."

Corrado and Dom glanced at each other, then back at Felice.

"Who?" Corrado asked.

Gingerly rubbing his jaw, Felice said, "It was the Georgian."

Corrado tensed. So did Dom. The Georgian was an independent contractor who would take any hit if the price was right, and he never missed his targets. Ever. There were rumors he was actually several people working under one name, that he was a team of crack shots and psychopaths, but only a handful of people knew for sure. And like the Mafia itself, the Georgian demanded his own form of omertà—strict confidence that, if broken, meant death.

Felice dabbed blood away from his lip. "I've hired him before. For other contracts. I don't know anyone else who could get that close to a house that secure and make a shot without anyone ever seeing him. Nobody else could've pulled off that hit and made it out."

Dom resisted the urge to fidget. He couldn't make himself run through the logistics of Biaggio's death and determine if he could've pulled it off as cleanly as the Georgian apparently had.

"So you've spoken to him?" Corrado asked quietly. "Directly?"

"No. He's got a handful of liaisons and won't speak to anyone but them. I'm not even sure there's anyone else in town who's seen his face and is still alive."

"But he killed Biaggio."

"Yes."

"And he did it…" Corrado hesitated. "He did it at the request of Luciano."

Felice nodded slowly.

His father studied him, then straightened and shook his head. "There's no way to be certain. Not unless—"

"I can show you." Felice pulled out his phone. He tapped it a couple of times, and then turned it so Corrado and Dom could see the video.

A man knelt on pavement, blood trickling from the corner of his mouth and a gun pressed against his temple. Someone held a handful of his greasy black hair so tight it stretched his facial features, and though he struggled, he couldn't move.

Felice's voice was tinny through the speaker as he said, "You say you're one of the Georgian's liaisons."

"Y-yes, sir," the man stammered.

"And my father's consigliere, who hired the Georgian to kill him?"

The man grimaced. "Please, I can't——"

"Answer my fucking question, Baltazar," Felice snarled. "Unless you want the Georgian to see this conversation on YouTube."

The man's gaze slid toward the camera, and his eyes widened. He mouthed something, a prayer maybe, and then said, "Luciano Maisano. He… he hired me. Said he'd kill my family if I didn't take the job to the Georgian."

"So you took the job?"

"Of… of course. I had no——"

The gun went off, and the man's skull blew out. Dom winced and looked away, and thankfully, the video stopped a second later.

"You should've kept him alive," Corrado barked. "He had a direct line to the Georgian, you fucking idiot."

Felice scowled. "And you wanted him to stay alive after he took the order to the Georgian to kill Biaggio?"

"If it meant he could help us find the fucking Georgian, yes!" Corrado sighed, rubbing the bridge of his nose. "Your temper is going to get you killed, Felice."

"I think my brother is more likely to get me killed," Felice snapped. "If he's willing to take out Biaggio, then he——"

"I'm aware of that." Corrado lowered his hand. "But why? Why would Luciano do this?"

Felice shook his head. "Who knows?"

Dom chewed the inside of his cheek. This didn't make

sense. Luciano wasn't the hothead in this family. Felice was. Luciano believed in diplomacy and resolving differences over a table, not a pile of bodies.

He cleared his throat. "Luciano loved Biaggio. I don't—"

"You heard the video." Felice gestured so wildly with his phone, Dom almost thought he was going to throw it in his face. "He hired the fucking Georgian to take out Biaggio." He laughed bitterly. "Is that what you call love?"

"Of course not," Dom ground out. "But something isn't adding up. Why would he do this? If we don't know that, then we can't assume—"

"It doesn't matter why," Felice said.

Dom opened his mouth to protest, but Corrado spoke first.

"I'm afraid Felice may be right." He absently rubbed his knuckles along the edge of his jaw. "With this war brewing, we…" Sighing, he dropped his hand and shook his head. "We may not have time to question the motives of every man who fires a bullet."

"So, what?" Dom lifted his eyebrows. "We're going to shoot back and ask questions later?"

"We can't show weakness," Corrado said quietly. "And we can't let our enemies see that there's strife within the family." He wrung his hands gingerly, as if the slow movements hurt his bones. "This is a battlefield now, Domenico. We can't risk a wound becoming gangrenous. Amputate and keep fighting."

Dom swallowed. If not for the faint note of sadness in his uncle's voice, he wouldn't have believed this was a man contemplating giving the order to kill his own son. In the space of a conversation, the family's relationship with Luciano had been reduced to a metaphorical wound, a gaping invitation for gangrene, and the only solution was to slice away the rotted flesh. To cut off the once useful limb, the piece that had once helped make up the whole, and move on.

"Say the word, Dad," Felice said. "After what he did to Biaggio, I'll—"

"You'll continue running your businesses," Corrado snapped. "And if I order it, you'll take on your brother's responsibilities until someone else can—" He closed his eyes for a second. Exhaling, he looked at his younger son. "Until someone else can fill his role."

Felice pressed his lips together, eyes narrow and jaw clenched, but he didn't speak. Then he swore under his breath and turned away, and as he started pacing across the thick carpet, he snarled, "He can't get away with this, Dad."

"That's for me to decide." Corrado glanced at Felice's back.

Then he looked at Dom.

And nodded.

And Dom's heart sank.

He could barely find the strength to return the nod.

But there has *to be another way.*

Enough killing. God, enough…

IF THERE WAS ANOTHER WAY, Dom couldn't find it. All mental roads led to the same conclusion—he had a job to do.

He made sure Luciano's wife and kids weren't home. His cousin's staff and security knew him well enough that they didn't bat an eye when he let himself into the house.

He waited for Luciano upstairs in the bedroom, sitting in the antique chair beside Serafina's white bureau. This was the part he hated most about every job—waiting. So much opportunity to think about why he shouldn't do this, and come up with possible alternatives, and dwell on just how far out of reach those alternatives were. This wasn't a trucker or an indebted immigrant who could be scared into leaving Cape Swan and never coming back.

This was Luciano. A made man. Someone whose death was not ordered lightly and whose execution couldn't be stayed. Corrado wanted this body found.

This was Luciano. For all intents and purposes, the brother he'd never had.

But Luciano had orchestrated the death of the man who'd been Dom's surrogate father. By all rights, Dom should have been pacing the floor and cursing his cousin's name, and he should've been looking forward to making this death slow and painful.

But he wasn't. He couldn't. As he mentally replayed the video Felice had shown him and Corrado, he couldn't make sense of it. The man had been threatened and tortured into confessing that he'd conveyed the death sentence from Luciano to the Georgian. And while Dom fully believed the Georgian had pulled the trigger, he wasn't convinced by the rest of it.

He didn't need to be, though. This wasn't a federal court. The man had confessed. No cross examination was necessary. And the murder had all the hallmarks of a Georgian killing. Why would a man accuse Luciano if he hadn't ordered the killing?

Why *would* Felice indict his own brother like that unless it was true? Felice and Luciano butted heads like any brothers, but they loved each other, and Felice would've burned Cape Swan to the ground if anyone had laid a hand on Luciano. If Felice had no choice but to accept that his brother had arranged Biaggio's death, then neither did Dom. Especially since Corrado had also accepted it and expected Dom to dispense justice accordingly. Whether agreed with it or not, whether he believed in his cousin's guilt, Dom couldn't refuse the hit.

Footsteps in the hallway sent his heart into his throat.

A second later, the door opened. Luciano walked into the room, fiddling with his wallet as he did, but then he froze. Slowly, he turned toward Dom. Even slower, his gaze slid downward to the pistol in Dom's lap. For a long moment, he studied his cousin and the weapon.

Finally, he toed the door shut behind him with a quiet click, sealing them into the master bedroom.

"They're blaming me, aren't they?" His voice was heavy with resignation. "For what happened to Biaggio?"

Dom nodded. "You hired the Georgian to kill him."

Luciano released a long breath. He sounded exhausted as he asked, "Why would I do that?"

Swallowing hard, Dom resisted the urge to shift uncomfortably.

Luciano showed his palms. "Never mind. If you're here with that"—he nodded toward the pistol in Dom's hand—"then the verdict has been read."

Their eyes met. Dom's heart sank a little deeper. Corrado would never rescind the hit. The man would let his own son take a bullet rather than raise questions about his ability to lead, to determine guilt or innocence. A dead son was better than friends or enemies believing he was gullible.

Luciano's lips curled into an odd smile. Sort of amused, maybe even a bit proud. "I always wondered who my father had for his big jobs. Didn't think you had it in you."

Dom glanced at his pistol. "I wish I didn't, to be honest."

"No, it's probably just as well." Luciano's gaze rested on the weapon for a moment, and then met Dom's. "You're not a psychopath. If there's a man alive who could be a hitman without torturing his marks, I'd lay money on that man being you."

Dom didn't know what to say to that.

Luciano pulled in a breath and pushed his shoulders back. "Would it be too much to ask for a favor?"

"That depends."

Luciano eyed the gun, then met Dom's gaze. "Take me somewhere else. Where my wife and kids won't be the ones to find me."

Dom's throat tightened. All the way to the grave, Luciano was going to have faith in that woman, wasn't he? Dom would've preferred Serafina be the one to find him, that she see that image in her mind every time she got on her back for a Cusimano.

But the kids. Not the kids.

"Your car or mine?"

"Yours." Luciano tugged at his sleeve, fussing with the cuff as if something so minor even mattered now. "People might get suspicious if we leave in my car and then I turn up dead."

Dom's tongue stuck to the roof of his mouth.

"Please, Domenico," his cousin whispered. "We both know you have to do this. Let's get it over with."

God, forgive me...

He tucked his gun inside his jacket. "Let's go."

In silence, they left the bedroom, descended the grand staircase into the massive foyer, and stepped outside. Luciano's house didn't have a huge covered portico like his father's, and they both put on sunglasses while they waited in the thick heat for someone to bring Dom's car.

Neither of them spoke as Dom drove. It seemed like

they should've been reminiscing about the good times, or talking about… well, anything. But conversation just felt macabre while Dom drove his cousin to the place where the cops would find him.

He parked at a remote beach a few miles out of town. As they followed a narrow, sandy path toward the shore, Luciano said, "My father's life is going to be in danger now. You know that, right?"

"He's always in danger."

"I know. But things are getting bad. Sooner or later, someone's going for the throat."

Dom's stomach lurched. "I'll tell him to bring in more security. And lay low."

"Good. Good idea. And be careful yourself. You're too high up the food chain to—"

"I'm pretty sure everyone knows I'm your father's pity case," Dom said coldly. "I'm my father's son. I've been watching my back since I was a child."

Luciano sighed. "I know." He turned to Dom as they stopped on the sand, and his eyes were filled with sadness now. "Makes you wonder how many generations will be paying for the sins of the father. None of us asked for this life."

"Some did."

Luciano seemed to mull that over, and then he shrugged. "They're fucking idiots. But those of us who were born into this…" He gazed out at the water, but didn't finish the thought.

They stood in tense silence. Dom's spine tingled and his stomach twisted—there was no turning back, and they both knew it, but he couldn't find the words to put Luciano on his knees, and couldn't bring himself to just raise the gun and be done with it.

Luciano swallowed, his Adam's apple jumping. "May I have a moment?"

"Yeah."

Dom stepped back to give his cousin some room.

For a long time, Luciano just stared out at the ocean. After a while, he knelt in the weedy sand, and Dom nearly started toward him again, but halted when his cousin folded his hands beneath his chin. Eyes closed, he moved his lips, though he didn't make a sound.

Slowly, he lowered his hands. With one, he crossed himself. His eyes slid open, and he fixed his gaze on the ocean again. "I'm ready."

Maybe you are, but I'm not.

Dom withdrew the gun as he came closer. He clicked off the safety, the sound nearly lost in the crash of the waves not fifty feet away.

Wordlessly, he pressed the pistol to his cousin's temple. He wondered if Luciano's life was flashing before his eyes. His certainly was. Their childhood. Their teenage antics. The day Luciano proudly became a made man. The day he congratulated Dom for doing the same. When they'd both congratulated each other on joining a life they couldn't escape, a life he doubted either of them had truly grasped back then.

And now…

Now this.

Dom swallowed. His finger was curled around the trigger, which the gunsmith had specifically set up to be only slightly less sensitive than a hair trigger. One twitch of Dom's finger, and it would all be over. But he couldn't move.

Luciano pulled in a deep breath through his nose. Eyes closed, he released it. "Just do it."

The trigger was suddenly a hundred pounds. He had

visions of the gun jamming. Backfiring. Exploding and taking them both out. Anything but doing what it had, without fail, done thousands of times before.

And still, his finger didn't move.

Dom lowered the gun. "I can't… I can't do this."

"Dom. Look at me."

He lifted his gaze and met his cousin's. Luciano swallowed. "You don't have a choice. Either you kill me now, or my father kills us both." He reached up and took Dom's free hand. "I can't let that happen. You're like a brother. Always have been."

A lump rose in Dom's throat.

"If someone's gotta take me out, then I'd rather it be you than anyone else." He looked up, straight into Dom's eyes. "At least I know you'll make it quick. You know damn well my father wouldn't do the same for either of us."

Dom shuddered.

"I'm at peace with it." Luciano squeezed his hand. "This isn't your fault. We both know it isn't. You're caught in the machinery as much as I am."

"How the fuck do I get out?"

Luciano laughed dryly. "If I knew, do you think we'd be here right now?"

Acid rose in Dom's throat. "Did you ever wish you could—"

"All my life, Domenico. All my life. Now…" Luciano released his hand. He sat straighter, eyes closed and expression fully relaxed. "Please. Just do it."

There was no avoiding it. And the longer Dom tried to talk himself out of it, the longer he tortured his cousin with the inevitable.

He aimed the pistol at Luciano's temple, angling it slightly toward the back to maximize the damage and minimize Luciano's chances of surviving, even for a moment.

"I'm sorry, Luciano."

"I know."

Luciano was perfectly still. So was Dom's hand.

Holding his breath, Dom closed his eyes.

And squeezed the trigger.

Dom had deliberately foregone earplugs, and the gunshot temporarily deafened him. Long enough to almost completely silence his cousin's body hitting the sand at his feet.

Ears ringing and jaw clenched, Dom opened his eyes. His aim had been true—from the hairline back, there was almost nothing left of Luciano's skull. Blood, bone, and brain matter clung to vegetation and soaked up sand for several feet.

Just to be sure, though, Dom leaned down and touched beneath his cousin's jaw. The skin was still warm, of course, but there was no pulse.

A nauseating sense of relief flooded through him. He couldn't stomach the fact that he'd just killed his cousin, but thank God, Luciano had died quickly.

He rose and walked away. In the car, he put the gun under his seat—he'd toss it in the ocean once he was safely away from here—and drove, not completely sure where he was going yet. He didn't get sick this time. He was too numb. Too fucked up in the head. His stomach would catch up once the booze started flowing, of that he was sure.

Tapping his fingers rapidly on the steering wheel, he drove away from the crime scene and didn't look back. He didn't speed. As much as he wanted to, he couldn't risk getting pulled over and having a record of his presence within close proximity to Luciano.

On one hand, he desperately needed the distraction only Sergei could offer. On the other, he couldn't face him. Couldn't touch Sergei with the same hand he'd used to pull the trigger, or the same hand he'd used to confirm Luciano's pulse had stopped.

Not tonight. Tonight, he needed the longest, hottest shower he could stand, and then he was going to get drunk. As drunk as humanly possible. Until he blacked out. Then maybe he'd wake up and drink more.

For now, though, he had to get out of here. Away from Luciano's corpse.

Luciano, I am so sorry.

Tears stung his eyes. He'd filled more contracts than he cared to think about, but this one was his own cousin. He'd killed a son on the order of a father. Tomorrow, he'd stand beside Corrado while the family grieved Biaggio for his longtime service and loyalty to the family.

There wouldn't be much of a funeral for Luciano. He'd have a Catholic funeral—even disgraced members of the family were buried according to Catholic traditions. Corrado believed men could be judged and dispatched here on Earth, but it was up to God to decide where they went afterward.

It hurt to know that Luciano wouldn't be given the lavish funeral of Maisano royalty, that he would be buried somewhere besides the family crypt, but Dom was admittedly grateful that he wouldn't have to stand beside Corrado and pretend he hadn't been the one to pull the trigger at the orders of the "grieving" father beside him.

Would Corrado grieve his son? Dom suspected he would. After all, killing him was just business. It didn't mean Corrado *liked* it. Even if Luciano had betrayed the family enough to sign his own death warrant, the father would still mourn his son. Dom hoped, anyway.

God, grant Luciano that much justice.

HEART THUMPING AND STOMACH SICK, Dom walked into Corrado's office.

His uncle lifted his gaze. Dom stopped in front of the desk. They locked eyes, and neither spoke.

It was done. There was nothing left to say.

Dom fully expected a dismissal, but instead, Corrado cleared his throat as he pushed his chair back. Rising, he said, "We have a meeting, Domenico."

Dom blinked. "A meeting? In the middle of all—"

"There are things that can't wait."

Not even long enough for me to take a fucking shower? I just killed your son!

Hell, why not? Maybe he could kill two birds with one stone. Take a shower and rinse off his guilt and whatever came up during this meeting. With the way things were going these days, he couldn't imagine this would be a benign discussion about crab pots and cargo ships. Especially if it couldn't wait until Luciano was cooled and Biaggio was buried.

They moved into the dining room where Corrado held his larger meetings. The room was filled with familiar faces. Somber and serious, every one of them underbosses—the highest ranking members of Corrado's inner circle. The uppermost echelon occupied most of the chairs around the table. Those lower on the food chain stood behind them.

Conspicuously absent were not only Luciano and Biaggio, but Felice.

Weird…

In front of them, the broad mahogany table was bare. No food had been laid out. No papers.

His uncle indicated an empty seat, which Dom took.

From the head of the table, Corrado cast a sweeping glance at the gathered men. "Now that we're all here…" He squared his shoulders. "My elder son has betrayed the family. As you all know, I have… taken care of the situation."

Leather protested as a few men shifted in their chairs.

"What this means is that my heir is dead. And, whether any of us like it or not, we have a war on our hands."

Dom swallowed. He kept his gaze fixed right on his uncle, but the other men's scrutiny prickled his skin.

"After the unfortunate events that have happened recently," Corrado continued, "we have to consider that the family may find itself needing a new leader."

The other men shifted some more, leather protesting and clothes hissing softly.

Corrado rested his elbows on the table and steepled his fingers as he looked Dom right in the eye. "You've come a long way from your father, Domenico. You're a sane and reasonable leader."

Oh God. Oh God, no…

"Particularly with Luciano…" Corrado paused, and then shook his head. "Given the current circumstances, in the event that something happens to me, I'm leaving the family to you."

Dom's mouth went dry. *No. No, please. Not this. Anything but this.* Ice cold panic surged through his veins. "I'm… I'm honored, but—"

"You are the best hope for the future of the Maisanos." Corrado folded his hands and exhaled slowly. "My father and my grandfather worked their fingers to the bone to make this family what it is. I have to make sure that when my time is up, the family remains in good hands. Particularly with this… unfortunate turn of events with my son."

Dom's gut twisted. He fought the urge to look around the room. Beneath the table, he rubbed at his hand with his thumb, as if he could get rid of the gun residue that he swore he could feel climbing beneath his skin and into his bones.

"Felice, he's…" Corrado shook his head. "I don't know where I went wrong with him, Domenico, but he's… well, he's an idiot. He's impulsive. Can't be trusted to control himself, never mind lead an organization like this."

Several men murmured with cautious agreement.

Eyes narrow, Corrado drummed his fingers on the table. "In a few years, if, God willing, I'm still here, Luciano's son has the makings of an excellent leader. But"—he waved his hand—"Angelo has a lot of years ahead of him before he's even ready to be made."

The thought of his nephew going through that initiation—killing a man, being officially brought into this poisonous fold—made Dom's stomach twist.

Tamping down the sick feeling in his chest, Dom took a breath. "Felice will never stand for this."

"He will," Corrado said coldly. "As will everyone in this room." He gestured at the other men, and when Dom looked around, they all nodded. "My word will be obeyed and respected. I will inform Felice in private after he's had a chance to grieve for Biaggio and for his brother. Not now. And I'd have waited until we'd all had a chance to grieve, but I can't ignore the rise in violence now, or my own mortality."

Dom didn't know what to say.

Corrado straightened. "Well. Will you accept your place as my heir?"

What choice do I have?

There was only one option—to accept this the way Luciano had accepted his fate.

He nodded. "Yes, Uncle Corrado."

"Good." Corrado beamed. "Then it's official."

The other men rose and, one by one, came up to shake Dom's hand. He stayed on guard, though—everyone in this business was adept at putting on a poker face while looking into the eyes of a man he had every intention of killing. These men all claimed they supported Corrado's decision, but would they? Where would their loyalty fall when the rubber met the road? How many would still be convinced he had traitor's blood like his father?

And what happened when Felice found out?

Corrado dismissed everyone but Dom. After everyone had left and they were alone, Dom turned to his uncle. Tone even—he didn't dare speak to his uncle any other way—he said, "You're painting a bull's eye on my back."

Corrado laughed dryly. "You're a Maisano, son. You've had a bull's eye on your back since the day you were born."

"But now you're putting me in charge of men who think I'm—"

"I'm putting you in charge of men who will respect my decision."

"Like the Gambinos respected Paul Castellano?"

Corrado scowled. "They didn't like him, and they didn't like him in power, but they obeyed him."

"Until they killed him."

The old man gestured dismissively and rose. "They would've let him live if he hadn't squandered his power and reputation. Everything that happened to him was his own choice, not a result of Gambino putting him in power. Which is precisely why I'm leaving the family to you. Felice…" He shook his head. "Let me put it to you this way—I've been told more than once that Felice would be the kind of boss that the Mafia Commission would authorize killing."

Dom gulped. The now-defunct Commission had only given their blessing for one boss hit in all of Mafia history. There were plenty of hits, all sanctioned within individual families, but Carmine Galante had pissed off so many people, the Commission had unanimously agreed that the bastard needed to go.

Corrado came around to his chair and put a hand on his shoulder. "I know this is a great deal to take in. Particularly after what's happened to Biaggio and after my son turned on us."

Dom gritted his teeth. He'd quite possibly killed an innocent man today. Did Corrado know? Did it change anything?

"This is all a tremendous responsibility." Corrado patted Dom's shoulder. "One I hope you won't have to take on for many, many years, but these are dark days for us, Domenico. This is war. Anything could happen. And there's no one I trust more with the legacy of the Maisano name." Corrado sighed, and as his expression fell, he looked older than he ever had. Old, tired, even frail. "Perhaps this is a lesson for me. That I should have scrutinized my own boys more than I did. I nearly left the family in the hands of a traitor."

A lump rose in Dom's throat, but he didn't let it show.

"I scrutinized you the way I should have my sons," Corrado continued. "You proved everyone wrong, time and again, and to be frank, even if my son hadn't turned out to be a traitor, I think I'd have eventually named you the way I am today. You're not your father, Domenico. He could never have amounted to half the man you've become."

The words replaced the lump in Dom's throat with bile. Knowing how much blood was on his hands, and what blood in particular was on Corrado's…

He clenched his jaw to keep from getting sick.

Corrado put a hand on Dom's shoulder. "This means we need to think seriously about this arrangement with Brigida." He squeezed firmly. "Your image will be even more important now."

Dom's mouth went dry. "Are you that convinced someone is going to take you out?"

"They can try, Domenico. They can try." He chuckled, but it faded. "It's the reality of our situation. I fully intend to retire from this business an old man, but for the sake of the family, I have to make sure provisions are in place." He smiled broadly. "At least now I will know for certain that the organization is in good hands."

Dom forced himself to smile back, but he was dying on the inside.

Because now, more than ever before, there was no escaping this life.

Chapter 25

The text was benign enough: *Can I see you tonight?*

Sergei had hidden his enthusiasm behind a response of *Sure, see you after my shift*, and then struggled to make it through the night. He half-assed a few dances to save energy. Let Jesse take over his table a couple of times. Counted down the minutes.

And then he'd walked into the motel room, and in an instant, his heart had fallen into the pit of his stomach.

Across the room, as Sergei toed the door shut with a quiet click, Dom watched him from the bed where he sat. If he could've devoured him with those desperate, hungry eyes, he probably would have. He seemed even needier than he had the very first night. Not just excited, not just turned on, but almost vibrating with something that went deeper than the craving for an orgasm.

Slowly, Dom rose. Sergei came closer. They inched toward each other, as if they were skirting the edges of some dangerous chemical reaction that would level the building to their feet.

In the middle of the room, they held each other's

gazes. Any other night, Sergei would be in his arms by now, demanding access to his mouth and rubbing this insistent erection against him. But he was still. And so was Dom.

Finally, Dom reached for his face, and the soft touch sent a shiver through Sergei. They drew each other in, still moving slowly, still being cautious and hesitant for reasons Sergei didn't understand.

"This might be the last time I see you for a while." Dom brushed his lips across Sergei's. "For..." Sighing, he shook his head, and then moved in for a kiss that said he wasn't going to elaborate on what exactly "for a while" meant. And Sergei... God, he didn't want to think about that.

"If tonight's the last time I'll see you for a while," he whispered, "then let's not waste it."

"Agreed."

They drew each other in for another kiss, and this one didn't stop. Though it had taken them an age and a half to get across the floor to each other, now they couldn't get close enough. Belts jingled. Fingers fussed with buttons and zippers. Sergei was glad they'd both worn button-up shirts tonight. It meant fiddly buttons to deal with, but clothes that could be removed without breaking this addictive kiss.

Naked, they sank onto the hard bed. The cheap, rough motel sheets beneath Sergei's back emphasized the warm softness of Dom's skin against his chest and between his thighs. He ran his hands over smooth muscles, pressing his fingers into the grooves and contours as if he needed to memorize every plane of Dom's body.

Dom broke away for a moment. Before Sergei could protest, he was back, and he pushed a bottle of lube into Sergei's hand. Sergei wanted to ask who it was meant for— *who's fucking who tonight?*—but he couldn't form words anymore, and he hoped Dom wanted the same thing he did anyway.

He poured it into his hand, and then reached between them, and when he closed his fingers around Dom's thick erection, they both exhaled. Dom closed his eyes, licking his lips, and rocked his hips a little as Sergei smoothed lube onto every inch of his dick.

Dom offered a pillow, and when Sergei lifted his hips, Dom slid it under him.

Sergei spread his legs wide, heart pounding as Dom guided himself in. God, yes. The burn made his toes curl. Even more, though, the sight of Dom, brow knitted with concentration, lips taut, abs quivering with the exertion of slow, smooth strokes as he worked himself deeper.

Once he was moving easily inside Sergei, Dom leaned down and kissed him. His hips still moved, but he seemed more focused on what they were doing with their mouths. Sergei didn't mind. Not in the least. One hand in Dom's hair, the other on his ribs, he kissed him and rocked his hips beneath him and loved every goddamned second.

He'd never had sex like this before. Usually it was sweat and panting and driving each other insane until they came. And then maybe they'd collapse together if they liked each other well enough, and maybe they'd catch their breath and do it all over again until sleep took over and tomorrow hurt.

This... this was all that and more.

Every touch, every kiss, every frantic, trembling movement, added up to something he'd never imagined. This wasn't the cooperative pursuit of pleasure and orgasms. They held each other, clawed at each other, like they thought they might actually start fusing together. Molecule by molecule, cell by cell, not just getting under each other's skin but becoming part of each other. One thing that could only become two again if it was broken.

Dom's breath caught. He groaned softly, breaking the kiss for a couple of heartbeats, and then claimed Sergei's mouth again as he rode him faster. Sergei gasped, letting his head fall back. Though he missed the touch of Dom's lips to his, he was too overwhelmed, and then Dom was kissing his neck anyway, warm lips skating along his throat, and Sergei swore softly.

Dom pushed himself up onto his arms. Eyes screwed shut, he bit his lip and rode Sergei harder. He muttered something—Italian curses, no doubt—and groaned, thrusting hard enough to slam the headboard against the wall. Sergei's eyes watered—Jesus, he loved Dom's cock.

"Fuck," Dom breathed. "Oh… *fuck*." With a violent shudder, he threw his head back. The only sound that escaped him, though, was a strangled cry, and then he was completely silent as he thrust a few more times.

He slumped over Sergei, trembling and panting. Even after he'd pulled out, he just stayed like that for a moment, as if he wasn't sure his arms could handle anything more complex than simply holding him upright.

Then he lowered himself a little and planted a soft kiss in the middle of Sergei's chest. And another one, lower this time.

Three kisses, and Sergei was ready to come unglued. Squirming beneath him, kneading handfuls of coarse motel sheets, he struggled not to come from anticipation alone.

Yes, Dom. Yes, please. Please…

In the same moment Dom took Sergei's dick into his mouth, he slid two fingers inside him, and the twin sensations almost sent Sergei through the roof.

Fingers moved. Lips and tongue teased. Nerve endings

turned to electricity. Sergei was sure he was levitating off the bed, and he didn't care as long as Dom's mouth kept working that insane magic. When did he learn to deep-throat like that? Hell, it didn't matter. He'd learned, and he was doing it, and then he was focusing on the head of Sergei's cock, swirling his tongue as if he knew that would drive Sergei right out of his fucking mind.

Sergei's vision blurred. He thought he heard himself cry out, but he wasn't sure and didn't care—he was flying, and he was trembling, and Dom didn't stop until Sergei managed to whimper "N-no more."

Sergei collapsed onto the pillows again. "Oh… my God…"

Dom kissed him lightly, his lips slick and salty. "I think you've spoiled me." Another kiss, shorter this time. "Sex with you is amazing."

"L-likewise." Sergei wrapped his arms around him, and they just kissed lazily.

After a while, Dom got up, and he helped Sergei up. They showered together, barely noticing how cramped the stall was since they were still wrapped up in each other.

Clean, more or less dried off, they climbed into bed together. Sergei had little doubt they'd be fooling around again before long, but for now, they just held each other.

Why don't I want to let go?

Dom said he'd be gone for a while, but he'd fucked Sergei like he never wanted to leave this hard bed. And now Sergei didn't want to leave it either.

In the beginning, Sergei hadn't even bothered promising himself that this was sex and nothing more because there'd been no need to promise that. He didn't get attached to gangsters, especially not Maisanos. And there was no room for attachment. He had Mama, and he had his plan. He needed nothing else, and he welcomed nothing else.

But here he was, lying beside Dom, listening to him breathe and memorizing every arc those calloused fingers drew on his shoulder. He didn't want to leave, and yet his chest hurt because this felt like goodbye. Like a real goodbye. The kind people said when they knew they'd never resurface. The kind that happened in this brutal, unforgiving world where a man, upon realizing there was a price on his head and a red dot on his chest, would often just surrender. Perhaps out of honor, perhaps out of the realization that there was no escape, so why run? Perhaps out of relief, as if this were the closest to suicide their god would allow.

Make it quick. Make it count. Ciao.

Why the hell did this feel like that?

But more than that, why did Sergei care?

Chapter 26

This morning, he'd taken his cousin's life.

This afternoon, he'd learned he was his uncle's heir.

And tonight, he'd lost himself in his lover's arms.

Dom was wide awake, but Sergei slept soundly beside him. The faint light coming in from the parking lot illuminated the very edges of him, tracing his profile as he breathed softly with his back to Dom.

Dom envied his ability to sleep tonight. Then again, after the way they'd fucked, and how exhausted and shaky he'd been after the third time, it was a miracle he'd been able to stay awake long enough to join Dom for another shower before he'd collapsed in a heap. If he was going to lose any sleep over this, it would apparently have to wait until *after* his body had recovered.

Dom was exhausted too, but not enough to pass out like that.

Tomorrow the family would bury Biaggio. Then God only knew what would happen. All he knew was that Corrado was right. The family had a war on its hands.

These were, to say the least, dark times. He'd painted a target on Dom's back by declaring him heir to the organization, and he was an idiot if he believed this wouldn't ignite civil war within the family once Felice found out. Infighting would be a disaster on its own, but with shit hitting the fan with the Cusimanos…

In the faint light coming in from the parking lot, Dom watched his fingers run through Sergei's bleached hair. Sadness and affection mingled in his chest. He wanted to stay like this all night. Hell, forever. From the first time he'd slept with Sergei, he'd found himself circling back to him whenever the rest of his world went off the rails. Sergei had become a source of sanity. An escape.

But there was no escaping now. All eyes were on Dom. People would be watching his every move. Some of them, he guessed, through rifle scopes.

Whatever violence came was part of Mafia life. Sergei wasn't a part of that life, though. He was someone Dom never should have touched, and someone he never should have come to need like this.

Most of all, he was someone Dom couldn't put in danger. And whether he liked it or not, every time he went near Sergei, he was lining him up with crosshairs that should've been for Dom and Dom alone. Bullets and car bombs were indiscriminate. There weren't many hitmen who'd lose sleep over a stripper getting caught in the crossfire.

In his mind, he heard the father screaming for mercy as Corrado tortured the son.

"*So this was his punishment,*" Corrado had calmly explained. "*The last thing he ever knew in this world was his son screaming and begging for death.*"

Dom shuddered as much as he could without disturbing Sergei. What if Sergei was there when someone finally closed in on Dom? What if the last thing Dom ever knew was Sergei screaming in pain and begging for the release of death?

No.

That wasn't going to happen.

As much as he wanted and needed Sergei's touch, he refused to put him in danger. And the only way to guarantee his safety was to put as much distance between them as he could. Maybe Dom would go insane without these interludes with Sergei, but insanity was a small price to pay for Sergei's safety.

Closing his eyes, he sighed.

Then he gently eased himself out of Sergei's sleepy embrace and got up. Moving as silently as he could, he separated his clothes from Sergei's and dressed.

In the darkness, he touched Sergei's arm.

I'm sorry, he wanted so badly to say.

But if he started speaking, he'd say something he couldn't take back, and even if Sergei didn't hear him, he'd hear himself. And he couldn't let himself hear the things on the tip of his tongue.

So he squeezed Sergei's arm.

Walked out the door.

And didn't look back.

Chapter 27

E yes still closed, Sergei had followed every near-silent rustle of Dom getting dressed. A few times, he'd thought about asking him where he was going, why he was leaving like this instead of saying something. But he said nothing. It didn't take a rocket scientist. And if Sergei spoke, then Dom might stay, and no matter how much Sergei wanted him to, it was best if he didn't.

Dom had come back and stood beside the bed for a moment, and it had taken all Sergei had not to hold his breath or tense. He didn't want Dom to know he was awake.

Softly, Dom brushed his fingers along Sergei's arm, and without a single word spoken, he'd slipped out of the room. Sergei stayed still and silent until the door clicked and Dom's footsteps had started fading into the night.

Alone, Sergei sat up in the bed where they'd had sex earlier.

The emptiness was weird, vibrating with a strange sense of finality. They weren't going to see each other again, were they? Not up close and personal, anyway.

Sergei exhaled, rolling his tense shoulders. Everything was as it should be. This was right, even if it hurt. After all, being together was dangerous for Dom, and it was a distraction for Sergei.

Besides, he needed to get moving himself. It was still painfully early, but there was work to be done. Today was an important day.

Dom had a funeral to attend.

And Sergei had a job to do.

THROUGH THE SCOPE, Sergei watched the church's double doors. A few people lingered outside on the steps, all looking just as somber as the people who'd filed inside at the beginning of the service. Several were armed. They scanned the parking lot, the street, the hills—any place where danger might be lurking.

A thousand yards away, safely perched on top of an apartment building, Sergei paid them little mind. An earpiece kept him abreast of the service going on inside, so he'd know when to be ready.

Unsurprisingly, there were only Maisanos at this service. Though the three families mingled peacefully at St. Leo's most of the time, there was violence in the air right now. Blame being thrown around like New Year's confetti. Too much potential for a sidelong glance or a misheard whisper to spark a fight, a gun battle right there in the pews. No one could take anything for granted these days. Not even the safety of holy ground.

Which meant that after Sergei was finished, the Maisanos would be out for blood. The Cusimanos and Passantinos would be blamed, and they'd be answering to a sacrilegious hit at a funeral.

The service began to wrap up. The people on the stairs turned toward the doors. Sergei shifted slightly and peered even more intently through the scope.

A pair of suited men pulled the doors open wide. Slowly, mourners emerged.

Six Italians held the casket on their shoulders, and carefully started down the steps, moving out of the crosshairs.

Behind them, several black-clad Italian women dabbing away tears. Family members, he assumed.

And then…

There.

Corrado Maisano.

To his left, Felice. To his right, Dom.

Luciano was MIA. Sergei had heard on the radio that his body had been found by some unfortunate teenager early this morning. One less hit to line Sergei's pocket, but one less piece to remove from the board before shit started going down. Had he and Dom been close? Was Dom grieving for his cousin? The consigliere?

The three Italians slowly descended the steps.

Sergei's eye flicked toward Dom, and for a second, his heart clenched. Dom had been so passionate last night, and now he was somber. All in black. His face pale and his features pinched with grief.

The crosshairs landed on Dom's throat.

Sergei tore his gaze away, covering his mouth as vomit lurched into the back of his mouth. He recovered quickly, swallowed hard, and looked through the scope again. He fixed the crosshairs on Corrado's chest, and refused to let his gaze slide toward Dom.

They were too close together. An unexpected movement, even a change in the wind, and Dom could take the bullet meant for his uncle. Sergei was an expert marksman, but even he couldn't control what happened on the target end. Once the bullet left the barrel, things were out of his hands, and he had to accept that Dom might not survive this.

And it didn't matter, for God's sake. He was one of *them*. No matter how good the sex was, or how much Sergei might've softened for Dom when the lights were low and all the guns and violence were elsewhere, he was a Maisano.

And besides, he'd left. He hadn't said a word, hadn't given any warning, and was just… gone.

His eyes stung, and his vision blurred momentarily.

Get a grip. Take the shot.

Hit him, and he's just another dead goon like the one he's grieving.

And you're almost out of time to take the shot.

Sergei quickly wiped his eyes and swallowed again, making sure the acid was well on its way back down, and then put his eye back up to the scope. The scope reduced his peripheral vision to almost nil, but in the background, he could still make out Dom's shape.

Ignore him. Ignore him and focus. Focus on Corrado.

Sergei slowed his breathing. He stared at the crosshairs. At the man behind it.

And squeezed the trigger twice in rapid succession.

The rifle jerked. Corrado dropped. Felice went with him, throwing himself over his father as if to both catch and shield him. Sergei squeezed the trigger again. Blood exploded onto the stairs behind them, and Felice jerked, grabbing his arm as his mouth opened with a cry that Sergei couldn't hear.

The whole church yard erupted into chaos, but Sergei didn't watch. He slung the rifle over his shoulder and ran like hell. Down the stairs, out the back, into his car. With the rifle covered up in the backseat, he drove away, driving calmly despite his heart pounding as much from the run as adrenaline. He couldn't risk drawing attention.

All the way out of the neighborhood, he watched the rearview as much as he watched the road.

No one followed him. No one stopped him.

He casually cruised right through downtown Cape Swan, then off toward his apartment. A clean getaway, as always.

Normally, he'd be itching to go meet Tumino to get the rest of his money, but all he could think of now was Dom. Had he been hit? Was he okay?

Sergei shook himself and gripped the wheel.

He didn't want to know.

———

HE LAID low for a few hours to let the dust settle, and then called Tumino from a burner phone.

"I'm on my way. It's payday."

"Not so fast." The man muffled a belch, making Sergei wrinkle his nose. "There's… a problem."

"A problem?" Sergei exhaled sharply. "The show went as planned. What more do you want?"

"I need you at your usual place tonight. I've got a contact coming to see you about another show. Finish that one, and we'll talk payment for this one."

"That wasn't our deal," Sergei snapped. "Pay me for—"

"This is a big one, son," Tumino said. "And it needs to happen fast. Wrap that one, and your salary's doubled for today's show."

Sergei resisted the urge to whistle. That was a metric fuckload of money. Still, he didn't want to be played. "Have your contact bring fifty percent of today's pay. He shows up with that, we'll talk about the next show."

Tumino grunted. "No, I don't think so."

"You want to tell your boss we're not doing business?"

Silence for a moment. And then, "I'll send him with cash. But be there. He'll be coming your way at ten o'clock."

"Fine."

Sergei hadn't planned to go to the club tonight, but apparently he was going after all. He finished cleaning and reassembling his rifle, and then showered, dressed, and headed to the club.

And right at ten o'clock, a very uncomfortable looking guy in a suit wandered in. Uncomfortable guys weren't unusual, but this type, they stood out.

Sergei sidled up to him. "Hey, sugar. You want a dance?"

The man scowled, but nodded. "I've got… cash."

"That's what I thought." Sergei gestured toward the back. "Let's go." The man followed him into the hallway. Sergei gave Roy a nod, and he turned his back just before they stepped into the booth. Almost immediately, the music started.

"Cash?" Sergei held out his hand.

The man produced an envelope. "Fifty percent of today's show. As requested."

"Good." As Sergei thumbed through it, he asked, "Where's Baltazar?"

"He's no longer employed by the production company."

Sergei's eyes flicked up. Baltazar was dead? Whoa.

He tucked the money into his waistband and folded his

arms. Stomach roiling, he asked, "So, I understand there's a problem?"

"Yes." The man shifted uncomfortably, eyeing his surroundings. "Mostly a change in the line-up."

"Yeah? So what do you want from me?"

"The full Monty." He lowered his sunglasses and looked Sergei in the eye. "Happy ending and all."

A big hit that needed to *look* like a hit. Of course.

Sergei nodded once. "How much?"

"Five million for the whole production."

Whoa. "Who's the star?"

The guy glanced past Sergei, then pulled his jacket open, revealing the pocket on the inside before he slipped two fingers in and withdrew a folded photo. Smart man—he knew better than to let Sergei think for even a second that he might be pulling a gun.

He held out the photo, and after Sergei took it, the man fidgeted nervously.

Sergei unfolded the photo.

And his stomach dropped straight into his feet.

Dom.

Shit. Oh shit. Cold water flowed through his veins, and he held the photo tighter to keep his hands still.

"Another five million? For *this* guy?" He forced a laugh. "He's not even a star."

The guy shrugged. "He is now. Inherited the production company."

Oh. No. Fuck!

Corrado had left the organization to Dom? *Dom* was the boss now?

No. No, no, no. No, that—

"You got a problem?"

Sergei's stomach lurched. If he declined the contract, he'd be rolling in with the tide before sunrise. If he took it but failed to fill it, he'd be hunted down and given a bloody lesson in what happens to people who cross the Mafia.

"Hey." The goon straightened. "I asked you a question. You got a—"

"There's no problem." Sergei met his gaze, and just as he'd hoped, the guy drew back. Sergei held out the photo. "This will take some planning. It isn't going to happen overnight."

The contact huffed and snatched the photo back. "But you'll make the arrangements?"

Sergei nodded. "It's... it's going to take time."

The goon's expression hardened. "Boss wants this one to go forward as quickly as possible."

"That's fine and good, but a production this big takes work."

He scowled. "You ain't getting paid to take your time."

"No, I'm getting paid to make sure everything is done *right*." Sergei narrowed his eyes. "Unless you'd like to tell me how to do my job."

The man gulped but then set his shoulders back. "Just get it done, kid."

"Will do." Sergei's voice barely made it over the music.

His contact left. Alone in the booth, Sergei raked a hand through his hair. This was bad. Real bad.

He needed to get the fuck out of here. The booth. The club. The town.

But he couldn't. Because getting out of town wouldn't do him any good unless he got out of this contract first. By knowing the hit even existed, he knew too much, and if he didn't join into the solemn pact of silence—committing a capital crime, and thus being disinclined to rat out the others—then he'd be a liability. The Maisanos would hunt him down like they hunted down apostates, and the punishment would be...

He shuddered.

What do I do?

For now, he just needed to get out of this club and… and… *think*.

Sergei left the booth. He found Paco at the bar and pulled him aside. "I, uh… I need to go."

"You okay?" He glanced past him. "That asshole rough you up or something? You need—"

"No. No." Sergei thought quickly. "I got a text from the place that takes care of my mother. They—"

"Jesus, why didn't you say so? *Go!*" Paco damn near shoved him toward the lockers. "Get out of here and make sure she's all right."

"Okay, okay. I'm going." Relieved, Sergei hurried to his locker, took out his wallet and keys, and left.

He probably wasn't in any state to be driving, but he didn't know what else to do. Gripping the wheel tightly, he drove around with no particular destination. He just needed to move. To not be sitting still where a laser dot might find him.

Eventually, he found one of the beaches where he often came to compose himself after visiting Mama. No amount of venting his emotions would fix this, though.

Corrado's hit was the one he'd been waiting for. The big contract, the one he'd use to topple the three families' precarious house of cards. Launch the Maisanos into the chaos that was inevitable with Felice in charge. With a psychopath like him on top, the muzzles would come off, and the Maisanos would shake off that businesslike, diplomatic front Corrado had maintained. When they started killing each other, other carefully-positioned men—the stupid ones with no sense of strategy or reason—would move into place. The Cusimanos would take advantage of the internal strife and chaos and bring the Maisanos to their knees. Before long, the violence would bring the Passantinos into the mix.

Then the coup de grace: a folder full of names, names, and more names—not to mention the locations of bodies —mailed anonymously to the police with a copy sent to the FBI. Then the house of cards wouldn't just topple, it would go down in flames, and Sergei would be smoke in the wind. Gone before anyone knew it was burning at all.

Corrado Maisano's younger son was supposed to become the boss. That was how it worked, and Sergei's plan had hinged on it, and he had no doubt Felice had been banking on it too. If things had worked out that way, the pieces would have gone down as planned.

But Corrado had played a wild card. Now Dom was a target because Felice didn't have the power he needed to unwittingly put Sergei's plan into action.

Secretly, behind closed doors, Dom had been named the heir. Now it was he, not his volatile cousin, who would ascend his uncle's coveted throne.

And now, this contract. The one that would restore the equilibrium he had so carefully orchestrated so his plan could move forward.

The pressure would be on, too. Everything was touchy right now, everyone edgy from the recent violence, even more so than they'd been after bodies had started washing up earlier this summer. No one, least of all the snubbed Maisano heir, had any patience left.

There was no way out. Dom was marked. Sergei was contracted. For all intents and purposes, the bullet had already been fired.

Sergei slumped back against the driver seat, struggling to find his breath. His heart pounded, blood surging through his veins. He'd spent the last several years moving these pieces into place. Setting up the endgame on a bloodstained chessboard. Piling up kindling so he could watch the whole thing topple and burn.

And now he had the torch.

And the torch had been lit.

And there was no blowing it out.

Chapter 28

A police investigation was unavoidable. Gunfire in a public place, murder in broad daylight at a funeral —there was no escaping legal attention.

The cops were undoubtedly left frustrated, since no one in attendance had anything to say to law enforcement. Every last mourner was questioned, and as soon as they could, left the area of the church currently cordoned off by yellow tape.

Now, hours after Corrado's death, every Maisano in town was at Felice's place. Still dressed for grief and visibly rattled by Corrado's death, they spoke in hushed tones while every woman in the family alternated between consoling Dom's aunt and putting out food and wine.

Dom stayed away from everyone. The day had started out hellish. Between grieving Biaggio, killing Luciano, and leaving Sergei, he'd been a reeling mess before he'd even arrived at St. Leo's. The service had been grueling as he forced himself to be stoic and strong for Biaggio's wife.

And then... fuck. It was the second time in a matter of days that a bullet had missed him by a wire-thin margin.

He and Felice could've easily been killed today. Thank God Felice had only been hit but not killed. It was still a hell of wound, but nothing life-threatening. A blessing in the form of a well-placed bullet hole.

Right now, Felice was upstairs with Dr. Rojas, who'd treated the wound earlier and had come back to change the dressings. If he knew what was good for him, he'd brought more painkillers this time.

Dom drained his wine and went upstairs to see how his cousin was doing. Several of Felice's associates were on their way down the hall, and they all looked right at Dom, locking their gazes on him for a few seconds and eyeing him coolly before they passed him by.

He paused and looked back, watching them leave. His stomach churned. Did Felice know yet? Had someone told him that Corrado had left the family in Dom's hands?

He gulped. Hopefully, they'd give the man a chance to grieve his father and recover from his wounds first. Felice didn't need to know the truth. Not today.

As Dom approached Felice's bedroom, Dr. Rojas stepped out and closed the door behind him.

"How's he doing?" Dom asked.

"He'll be all right." Dr. Rojas glanced over his shoulder, then scanned the hallway. He gestured for Dom to come closer. "You need to be careful right now, Dom."

"Tell me something I don't know," Dom muttered.

"How about the fact that there's already a contract with your name on it."

Dom stared at him, and lowered his voice to a whisper. "What are you talking about? How do you know?"

"Because I heard—" Rojas's eyes flicked past Dom. Louder, he said, "The stitches will come out in a few days, and then he should make a full recovery as long as the wound is kept clean and doesn't get infected."

Two of Felice's men walked past them, pausing to give Dom a respectful nod before continuing into the room where Felice recovered.

When they were gone, Rojas led Dom a ways down the hall. "Listen, I know Felice. I've been treating him long enough to know how he works. What he's like when he's upset. And he just lost his father, his brother, and Biaggio, so..."

"So he's bound to be upset." *Hopefully someone's locked up anything fragile or valuable.*

Rojas chewed his lip. "Today, though... he was weird."

"How so?"

The doc glanced around again, and whispered, "I thought at first that he was just numb over what happened to his father. He was quiet but didn't seem all that upset."

That was unusual for Felice—the slightest shift in his emotional status quo made him violent.

Rojas went on, "But then one of your uncle's associates came in. And he told Felice that you'll be inheriting the family, not him."

"Oh shit."

Rojas grimaced. "He hit the roof, Dom. Barely a twitch over his father, but when he found out you were the new boss, he flipped out so bad I had to re-stitch three of his sutures." Even quieter now, he added, "After he calmed down, he told an associate to get in touch with another associate in Atlanta."

"Atlanta? What?"

"*Georgia*, Dom."

Dom's stomach fell into his feet. "You've got to be shitting me."

Rojas put up his hands. "I could be wrong. And I hope to God I am. But if I were you, I'd be watching my back right now.

"Yeah. I was… I was planning on it." Watching his back was one thing. Having the Georgian on his tail was another matter entirely.

"I'm sorry." Rojas put a hand on his shoulder. "If you need anything, call me."

"I can't ask you to help with this. It's family."

"I know. But if there's anyone in this family who's worth helping…"

Their eyes met.

"Thanks," Dom whispered.

Rojas squeezed his shoulder, and then let him go. "I should get out of here."

"Yeah. I should, uh…" He gestured at Felice's door. "See how he's doing."

The doc's lips pulled tight. "Be careful."

"I will."

Rojas left, probably getting the hell away from this place as fast as humanly possible. Lucky bastard.

Dom regarded Felice's door warily. He should've gone in there. Shown his face. And he would.

But first, he needed a moment to himself, so he wandered the hallways of Felice's enormous house, hands in his pockets and eyes down.

He'd expected a hit. He'd known it was coming. But so soon? And from *Felice*? Jesus. Corrado's body wasn't even cool yet, and Felice was already arranging a hit on Dom. And, assuming Dr. Rojas had understood the coded talk correctly, that hit was contracted to none other than the Georgian.

The back of his neck prickled. The Georgian was a relentless hunter and a brutal killer. Legend had it, he aspired to be the west coast's Richard Kuklinski—the prolific hitman all the New York City families had come to in the 70s and 80s to for their most valuable hits that needed to be taken out in the most brutal fashion. Dom didn't know what was true and what was myth, but he knew they didn't call in the Georgian unless they meant business.

He could go in there right now and shoot Felice, but Felice was surrounded by his crew and security. There were too many people here. All it would take was one of them who believed Felice should've inherited his father's place, and they'd shoot him for killing Felice.

Any action he took, he couldn't do it here. Not now. Had to stay calm even when he was shaken and betrayed. Put on the stoic face. Image, image, image.

And really, what action *could* he take? The fact was, there was no escaping it now. Dom's number was up. He knew how this game was played, and certain things were inevitable. The only variables were how they killed him and when. This was one of those moments like when the doctor says to go home and get your affairs in order. Especially because it was the doctor himself who'd delivered the news.

He could either stand and fight...

Or he could quietly take his fate with dignity. It's what Luciano had done. It was what Papa had done. He'd known when they were coming for him. Dom never forgot that day. Papa had come home early, and he'd disappeared with Mama for a little while. When they'd returned, there was saltimbocca alla Romana and his favorite wine. It had almost seemed like the family was celebrating, except the somber air between his parents had told him that something was terribly wrong. So wrong that, to this day, he couldn't eat saltimbocca.

Then Papa had kissed them both and told him he wouldn't be coming back.

"Take care of your mother, Domenico," he'd said.

And then he was gone.

That would've been it. In fact, it should've been. A week later, Dom had knelt beside his mother in St. Leo's, listening to her quietly sobbing. No one else had been there. Just Dom and his mother and the priest, and he'd struggled not to be sick as his mother prayed for Papa's body to be found so he could at least have a proper burial. He'd sinned, he'd betrayed the family, but he was still a good man. Couldn't he at least go to God the way every man good man should?

And Dom had had no choice but to kneel there, wiping tears away and trying not to throw up because he knew what Mama didn't know. He'd been warned to keep quiet, and the gunshots were still ringing too loudly in his ears for him to even think of defying his uncle's orders. So while Mama begged God for guidance, she had no idea her only son knew exactly where Papa was and exactly who had put him in that shallow grave. It was why he'd sobbed that morning when she'd yelled at him for having dirt on his good trousers. He couldn't explain it. Not without telling her what he'd promised not to tell.

She'd gone to her grave not knowing where her husband's body was or that her son had been there. He'd never been able to tell her that, yes, Papa had been given last rites before he died because then he'd have to tell her how he knew.

He shuddered at the memories. It was just as well he had no wife or children now, and he'd already walked away from Sergei. There'd be no one left to ask God where his body was or grieve him the way Mama had grieved for Papa until the day she too had died, or worry if he'd been given a proper send-off to the Lord.

The only question that remained was how long he could elude his fate, and if he should bother. He could either run and keep looking over his shoulder, or accept the inevitable with the dignity instilled in him by his father. He could run, or he could sip a glass of wine and know it was likely his last.

Dom wiped a hand over his face. What he needed to do was think. Disappear somewhere, collect his thoughts, and figure out what to do next.

And as long as he was having that last glass of wine...

He texted Sergei.

I need to see you.

And then he went in to check on Felice.

Chapter 29

Sergei stared at the text.

Dom had no idea, did he? No fucking clue. But then, how could he? Sergei had carefully kept his name and face hidden from all but his select few liaisons. He'd given Dom no reason to suspect him.

Maybe it would be easier this way. Dom could come to him, and Sergei could finish the job quickly. Dom didn't have to know who'd filled the contract. He didn't need to have that moment of terror, that split second of understanding that death was imminent.

He didn't want to do this, but there was no backing out of a contract. Not unless he wanted to be skinned alive. And God knew what would happen to Dom if Sergei failed to complete the hit—some of the other hitmen in this town weren't nearly as humane as he was when he wanted to be.

I can make it quick. So he doesn't know what hit him.

Sergei closed his eyes.

He deserves that much.

Holding his breath, Sergei wrote back with shaking fingers: *Come to my place.*

After that, he sent his address.

They'd never been to either of their places before. It was always motels. But tonight, Sergei wanted absolute control over his environment.

His phone vibrated: *I'll be there shortly.*

While he waited, Sergei pulled a footlocker from his closet and popped the latches. The lid creaked on its hinges, and Sergei scanned his options. A .22 would do the job without making much noise, but a higher caliber stood a better chance of finishing him off with a single shot.

A million emotions tangled in his chest, but he had to force himself to be strictly business about this or else he'd break. He'd crumble. He'd earn them both a much worse fate than a bullet to the head.

Sergei withdrew a .45. It would be loud, but people in Cape Swan didn't ask questions. Even if they did, Sergei's neighbors were all shift workers. The place was almost entirely empty during the day—it was why he'd moved in here, since he too worked late hours most of the time.

He screwed the suppressor onto the pistol. It wouldn't do much—what he wouldn't have given for Hollywood's silencers to actually exist—but if he had to fire indoors, it would take the edge off enough to hopefully not do permanent damage to his hearing. Or attract any neighbors who happened to be awake.

He didn't keep the gun on his person, though. As much as it sickened him to think about it, the bedroom was the place where Dom would most likely let his guard down. All Sergei had to do was get him in here, and he'd be able to get the drop on him. No fuss, no fight—wait till he was good and distracted, and end it with a well-placed round before Dom had a chance to—

Sergei sniffed sharply and wiped his eyes.

Come on. Get it together. You don't have to like it. But you have to do it.

Dom, I am so sorry…

He left the pistol with the suppressor in the bedroom, between the mattress and box spring where it wasn't obvious, but it was accessible. Couldn't be too careful, just in case things got out of his control.

He closed the footlocker and pushed it back into the closet. From the bottom drawer of his dresser, he took out the kit full of poisons. Immediately, his gaze flicked toward the poison he'd just bought from Katashi. It was supposed to work immediately. Little if any pain. Seconds at the most. One spritz in Dom's face, and it was all over.

He turned the vial between his fingers. He'd had other plans for this stuff, but he had plenty. There was no reason he couldn't use it on Dom. Put him out quickly and painlessly. Maybe let him go to sleep first. He'd drift off and never wake up. Peaceful. Painless.

Sergei could count on a bullet to get it done, but just in case, he measured out the dose for Dom's height and weight, and then put the poison into the spray bottle Katashi's supplier had included. He slipped it into the top drawer of his nightstand.

When all was said and done, he had weapons strewn strategically around the house, something within easy reach no matter where he was.

Outside, a car door slammed. Sergei looked out the window, and took a deep breath. Oblivious to what he was walking into, Dom came up the path to Sergei's front door. Sergei's heart was pounding so hard he almost didn't hear Dom knock, but he was on the way to the door anyway.

At the door, he paused to compose himself. There was

no turning back, no pretending this could end any other way.

I am so sorry, Dom.

Heart pounding, he turned the deadbolt, opened the chain, put on an unassuming smile, and opened the door.

One look at Dom, and Sergei's breath was gone. Just… gone.

God, I've missed you.

Sergei moistened his lips. He stepped aside to let Dom come in. Neither of them said a word until after he'd closed the door, and it was Sergei who softly broke the silence: "Didn't think I was going to see you again."

Dom grimaced. He pulled Sergei into his arms. "I'm sorry. For disappearing."

"It's okay. You're here now." Sergei winced. In the back of his mind, he heard himself a lifetime ago, shakily whispering "You're here" that night when he'd needed Dom, and Dom had come.

Tonight, Dom needed him, and what was Sergei going to do?

I can't. I don't want to. I have to.

"I need you to do something for me," Dom said.

Sergei gulped. "Okay."

Dom pulled a thick envelope out of his back pocket. "Take this. Get out of Cape Swan. Get out of California."

"Take—" As soon as the envelope was pressed into his palm, Sergei knew exactly what it was. "Why are you giving me money? What—"

"Things are about to get really bad in this town. There's a contract on my head, and…" He shook himself. "Listen, this should be enough to get you out of here and on your feet somewhere."

"But it's—"

"Please, Sergei." Dom kissed his forehead. "And I... I won't be able to see you again after tonight."

If you only knew how right you are.

"Then let's—" Sergei's voice caught. He dropped the cash on the sofa beside them, and managed a hard-won smile as he said, "Let's make it count."

Dom kissed him, and Sergei, despite his conscience tearing him to pieces, put his arms around Dom and let himself be kissed.

They stumbled into the bedroom. Keeping his guard up was his default setting when he was on a job, but tearing off clothes was his default with Dom, and stripping down won. Hungrily, breathlessly, they kissed and groped in between pushing off shirts and kicking off trousers. Every time Dom broke away—to take off a sock, to slip off his boxers—Sergei's body ached and his skin tingled until those warm broad hands were on him again. As they sank onto the bed, with Sergei on his back and Dom right on top of him, he didn't feel the least bit unsettled beneath Dom's larger frame. He clawed at him, pulled at him, tried to bring him down even closer to him, no matter what that might do to his ability to breathe.

They rolled one way. Then the other. Sergei was on the bottom again, and—

Shit.

The .45 and its suppressor were right beneath him. Though they were separated from his flesh by the thick mattress, the shape was undeniably *there*. Every time he or Dom moved, the pistol dug into the base of his spine. He couldn't get comfortable. Couldn't concentrate on anything but that annoying lump beneath his back, like he was the star of a fucked up version of *The Princess and the Pea*.

The Stripper Hitman and the Piece.

Even that thought couldn't amuse him. He tried to put

himself in that cold, predatory state of mind where nothing existed except the need to finish a job. The drive to put a bullet through a Mafioso's brain should've been enough to banish the need to make love to a man who was scared and stoic at the same time. He hated Mafiosi. He hated the Maisanos. He was supposed to hate Dom. Combing his fingers through Dom's hair, though, arching beneath his body and losing his mind despite the gun beneath him, he couldn't hate anything except the way this thing had to end.

Except it didn't have to end that way now. Not yet. Not until...

Dom pressed his hips against Sergei's, unknowingly pushing Sergei harder against the weapon.

What am I doing? I'm supposed to kill *him.*

He should've been hiding the body already.

But he wanted him alive. And here. And under him.

He pushed Dom onto his back and kissed him, and goddamn, every kiss made the guilt burn hotter. Guilt didn't belong in the same room as a marked Maisano, but Sergei couldn't help feeling like a cat toying with a mouse.

Except he wasn't toying with him. He wasn't torturing him. Tonight, Dom wanted sex, and Sergei would give him that. The rest... didn't matter right now.

Dom pulled Sergei closer. "I need you to fuck me."

The next shiver was Sergei's; if Dom's tone was to be believed, he wasn't joking about the word *need*. He was trembling, holding on to Sergei as if he were holding on for dear life, as if he were on the brink of breaking down.

"Let me get the lube," Sergei breathed. "Then I'm all yours."

"Please." Dom's arms slid off Sergei's shoulders.

Sergei got up off the mattress, ignoring the outline of the gun that still seemed seared into his back, and opened the nightstand drawer. The vial full of cloudy liquid caught his eye but only for a second. That time would come. Not now.

He made quick work of putting some lube on both of them. Then Dom got on his hands and knees, and Sergei was already out of breath before he'd even pressed against him.

I want you. I'm supposed to want you dead, but I just want you.

Dom was tighter than usual, even tighter than the first couple of times they'd fucked.

Sergei leaned down, wrapping an arm around Dom. "Breathe, Dom," he whispered against his neck. He withdrew a little, and pressed in again. "Remember to breathe."

Dom exhaled. Gradually, he relaxed and yielded to Sergei, completely unaware he was letting in the man who was going to kill him. Moaning with unmistakable pleasure, he rocked back and forth, drawing Sergei deeper.

Sergei leaned over him, hissing as his nipples brushed Dom's back. God, he was going to miss this. The way Dom's breath hitched when Sergei moved inside him. The way their bodies just fit together. The faint scent of aftershave that had become *Dom* in his mind.

Still rocking his hips and sliding his cock in and out in a smooth, steady rhythm, Sergei curved his hand around the front of Dom's throat. Dom's pulse beat against his palm.

Sergei's heart sped up. He could do it now. Quick. Painless. Dom would never know what hit him, and he'd die with a hard-on.

Dom swallowed. His Adam's apple pressed against Sergei's palm, and a shiver went down Sergei's spine. He leaned closer, rocking his hips a little faster as he kissed the back of Dom's neck.

Maybe let him come first, let an orgasm be the last

thing he ever felt. Then a snap of the neck, and he'd be gone, still smiling. Sergei wasn't going to risk a sleeper hold or try to strangle him. Dom was stronger than he was—if fight or flight kicked in, he could too easily overpower Sergei before Sergei knocked him out, and the gun was out of reach.

He could...

There was always...

Sergei squeezed his eyes shut as he fucked Dom faster. He couldn't think like this. Not while he was this deep inside him. He'd fuck him now, give him a little more of what he'd been craving so badly, and then he'd end it for him in a blink. Make sure he never knew what hit him. *Who* hit him.

For now...

He sank his teeth into Dom's shoulder and thrust harder.

"Shit," Dom groaned. His whole body jerked beneath Sergei, and he clenched around Sergei's dick. "I'm gonna... come..."

Sergei gritted his teeth and fucked Dom as hard as he could. As Dom groaned, trembling beneath him, Sergei shuddered. His eyes rolled back. His body took over, moving of its own volition and trying to get him as deep inside Dom as possible, and as his orgasm rocked him from his curled toes to the hair standing on the back of his neck, he damn near blacked out.

As he came down, taking in gulps of air while his head spun and his limbs trembled, he held on to Dom's hips for balance.

"Oh my God," Dom murmured. "Shouldn't... shouldn't be surprised anymore."

"By what?"

"How amazing it is when you fuck me."

Sergei laughed softly and kissed the back of his shoulder. Guilt, shame, even some fear… he was too deep inside a man to feel this way, but nothing made sense anymore.

When he was sure his limbs would at least try to hold him up, he pulled out, hissing sharply as the gentle motion overwhelmed his hypersensitive nerve endings. He got rid of the condom, and after they'd cleaned themselves up, they collapsed together in Sergei's bed. They kissed for a little while, and then shifted around until they got comfortable. Eventually, Sergei was on his side with Dom cuddled up against him, and like that, they lay in silence for a while.

Fingers laced between Dom's, Sergei stared at the window, watching the moonlight through the gauzy curtains. Dom's arm was heavy on his waist. Any other guy he'd have shrugged off. Made him sleep on the other side of the bed so his skin wouldn't make Sergei's sweat and his arm wouldn't keep him from breathing right.

But he'd quickly grown to like sleeping this close to Dom. And ever since Dom had left him at the motel, he'd missed it. Maybe this was cruel—as much to himself as to Dom—but he couldn't give it up just yet.

Reality sank in faster than he wanted it to. What he had to do. What Dom thought he was hiding from by lying low in this bed. How many weapons were within reach so Sergei could finish the job.

I'll let him go to sleep. Then I'll make it quick. And he'll never know—

Dom shifted a bit beside Sergei and burrowed his face a little closer to his neck. "You're still awake."

"So are you."

"You think I can sleep right now? Somebody wants me dead."

I knew that before you did.

Sergei shivered.

"Relax." Dom reached up and stroked Sergei's hair. "These guys mess with you, I'll break their necks. I won't let 'em fuck with you."

Sergei closed his eyes. "Dom…"

"I promise." He kissed the side of his neck. "Nobody's gonna—"

"It's not me I'm worried about." Sergei started to roll over, and Dom moved back to make room. When Sergei settled onto his back, Dom stayed on his side, head propped up on his arm. The white light from outside made him look pale and picked out deep shadows in his face.

"Dom, I'm not afraid of these guys."

Dom found Sergei's hand in the darkness and squeezed it. "You probably should be."

Sergei laughed dryly. "I can handle you. Trust me, I can take care of myself."

"I don't think you understand what I'm up against."

Sergei squeezed his eyes shut, and he was surprised at how much they stung. Yeah, he understood what Dom was up against. Dom didn't, or he wouldn't be here. He wouldn't be lying beside Sergei, his skin damp and his touch tender, savoring the afterglow even as he tried to warn Sergei away from danger that was closer than he realized. If Dom knew, he wouldn't have kissed Sergei like that. He wouldn't have come here, and stripped off his clothes and his gun, and made himself vulnerable in every way, giving himself to Sergei with no fear, no distrust, no reason to wonder why the air smelled not only of sex, but of gun oil.

Fuck. Sergei exhaled. He couldn't fucking do this.

He pulled away from Dom and swung his feet over the edge of the bed and got up.

"Where are you going?" Dom asked.

"Just need…" *To get away from you before I do something I*

can't undo. "Need a little air." He pulled on a pair of boxers and left the room. Heart thumping, he stepped out into the tiny backyard and took in a deep breath. It was hot as fuck out here tonight, but Sergei was shivering hard.

Not thirty seconds later, Dom stepped out behind him. Sergei mouthed some profanity in his native tongue.

Just give me a few minutes.

Wordlessly, Dom wrapped his arms around Sergei's waist.

For God's sake, don't you know what I am?

Sergei's throat tightened, and in spite of himself, he put his hands over the top of Dom's.

I don't want to hurt you, but you're killing me.

"You okay?" Dom asked.

"Not really."

"I'm sorry." Dom kissed the side of Sergei's neck. "I brought all this right to your doorstep."

Sergei winced. His conscience was going to eat him alive. He'd had a million opportunities to do it and be done with it tonight, and now he was just stringing Dom along, listening to him apologize as if he had half a clue what was really happening.

Finally, he pulled himself out of Dom's arms and faced him. "Listen, you're in a lot more danger right now than you think."

Dom stiffened. "What do you mean?"

"I mean…" Sergei glanced around them. Then he brushed past Dom. "Let's go back inside. I'm not talking about this out here."

He didn't have to look back to know Dom was hot on his heels, and he led him into the kitchen. There, he flicked on the fluorescent light.

"What's going on?" Dom asked.

Sergei leaned against the counter, his back turned. "It's complicated."

"I've got time."

Not as much as you think, because I have to…

There has to be another way.

But there isn't.

Exhaling sharply, Sergei raked a hand through his hair. "You're right that there's a contract on your head." He didn't look at Dom, but he felt him freeze. Like there was a shockwave coming off him or something.

"Of course I—how do you know?"

Arms folded tight across his chest, Sergei stared out the kitchen window. Or at least, let Dom think that's what he was doing—he stayed focused a hundred percent on Dom's reflection, watching every move in case he lost his shit and came at him or something.

"A hit's been ordered." Sergei swallowed, his heart pounding even faster and the shivering getting out of control. "And it's an inside job."

Dom shifted his weight. He studied Sergei, and Sergei swore he could feel the scrutiny prickling the back of his neck.

"The order came from Felice Maisano." Sergei moistened his lips. "Straight from him."

"Yeah, I know." Dom was quiet for a longest time. Easily a minute or more, which felt like for-fucking-ever. "How the hell do *you* know any of this?"

Sergei closed his eyes. His knees were shaking now, and he prayed Dom couldn't see it. And fuck—he'd left his gun in the other room. If this escalated, he—

"Sergei, how do you know this?" Dom stepped a little closer. "Any of it?"

Sergei took a deep breath. "The night we met, you asked about my accent."

Dom rolled his eyes. "Don't play fucking games. What does that have—"

"I told you my accent is Russian. Right?"

He exhaled sharply. "Yeah. What of it?"

Steeling himself, Sergei turned around. "My family didn't come from Russia, Dom. We're—" His stomach coiled so tight he was ready to puke. "We're from a little former Soviet country called Georgia."

"Georgia? So—" Dom's eyes widened. Sergei could almost hear the pieces falling into place inside his head, and he pulled back against the counter. "Shit, Sergei. Are…" He swallowed. "Are you telling me *you're* the *Georgian?*"

Sergei nodded slowly. "Yes."

Dom stared at him, lips apart and eyes enormous. "You…"

"Yeah. Me." Sergei straightened. "They use me because no one would ever suspect someone like me of having any ties to the Mafia." He gestured at himself. "Look at me. I'm a flaming fucking fag who grinds his ass on men's dicks for a living."

Dom winced.

Sergei went on, "They don't want anything to do with anybody queer, so they send me in to do their dirty work and nobody suspects a thing."

Dom scrubbed a hand over his face. Then he froze. Slowly, he lowered his hand and met Sergei's eyes. "They say the Georgian was the one who killed my uncle. At a fucking *funeral.*"

Sergei swallowed. "It's true."

"And his consigliere? With me sitting right there next to him?"

He nodded, his throat tightening. "I'm sorry, Dom."

"Sorry?" Dom studied him, his eyes icier than Sergei had ever seen them.

Sergei steeled himself again. "Look, I didn't know this would end with a hit on you. I—"

"You killed him. You killed… all of them."

Sergei took in a breath. Then he nodded.

And Dom fucking snapped.

Chapter 30

Overcome with rage, Dom lunged at Sergei.

"*Pezzo di merde!*" They both tumbled against the cabinets, and then to the kitchen floor. "I had to kill my own cousin because of you!" Dom got his hands around Sergei's throat, but a swift kick to his knee distracted him long enough for Sergei to slip out of his grasp.

Sergei scrambled up. Dom grabbed his elbow and pulled him back down. Sergei put a heel right in his ribs. Dom grunted, but didn't lose his grip, but a second kick nailed him in the gut, and Sergei was gone again. The son of a bitch was small, but he was fast. And fucking strong.

Dom started to get up, but Sergei came at him this time. They both toppled onto the kitchen floor. He threw an elbow, but Sergei got out of the way, and Dom only grazed his cheekbone. A fist or a knee—something blunt with a lot of force behind it—hit his solar plexus. Not hard enough to knock the wind out of him, but hard enough to stun him, and in the split second it took for Dom to recover, Sergei got behind him and pinned him facedown on the floor. Sergei twisted Dom's arm between their bodies behind Dom's back, and his arm across material-ized around Dom's throat.

"Fucking stop," Sergei snarled.

"I'm going to fucking kill you. You—"

"Dom, listen to me."

"Why the fuck should I? You're *going* to kill me, you son of a—"

"If I wanted you dead, you *would* be."

Dom froze.

Reality sank in quick. Sergei—the goddamned *Georgian*—had him immobile on the floor. He had the order to kill him. But Dom was still breathing. Not easily, thanks to the pressure on his throat and even Sergei's relatively light weight on his ribs.

"If I wanted to kill you," Sergei said quietly, matter-of-factly, "I would have already. And I wouldn't have fucking told you."

"Okay." Dom swallowed, his Adam's apple pushing against Sergei's arm. "Okay. I..." He forced his whole body to relax. "Will you let me get up?"

Sergei hesitated. Then his arm slid free, releasing Dom's throat. A second later, he let go of Dom's arm.

Dom sat up slowly as Sergei moved away from him. Sergei sat against the cabinets, gaze down. He swallowed, his whole body trembling as he ran a hand through his hair.

Dom sat back against the wall, staring at Sergei, and swept his tongue across his lips, catching a drop of blood off the corner of his mouth. "Why..."

Sergei let his head fall back. "Which part?"

"All of it. I mean..." Dom exhaled. "I can't believe *you're* the Georgian."

Sergei laughed humorlessly, eyes sliding closed. "That's the idea."

"How did you even get involved in this?"

"That's the part you want to know right now?" Eyes still shut, Sergei dabbed some blood on his chin. "You want to know how I got started?"

Dom rubbed his eyes, his hands shaking badly as the adrenaline started to crash. "I don't even know which way is up. Seemed... seemed like as good a place as any to start."

Sergei let out a long breath, and his shoulders didn't seem to slump so much as erode, as if the revelation of his identity were dissolving the shell he'd had around himself all this time. After a moment, he opened his eyes.

"Your family killed mine. When I was a child. All that's left is me and my mother, and she's wasting away in a home because of what that night did to her. And for what they did to us, I will bring the entire family down or die trying."

A chill ran through Dom. He could see the killer in him now, the razor-sharp hatred in his eyes. And yet, at the same time, the terrified child. The broken son. Not just the need to extract blood for revenge, but the anguish behind it.

"I'm sorry," Dom whispered, as if it changed anything.

Sergei pulled his knees up and folded his arms loosely on top of them.

"Is that why you had me come here tonight?" Dom asked. "Instead of a motel?"

Sergei straightened, his eyes losing focus. "I..."

"You'd have attracted the cops right to your own front door," Dom said. "And the crime scene..."

Sergei ran the tip of his tongue along his lips. "I think..." Slowly, his eyes focused, and he looked at Dom. "I think I did that on purpose without even realizing it. I'd never kill someone here. No way. Maybe..." He closed his eyes. "I don't know what I was thinking, except maybe, subconsciously, I brought you here because this is the only place on earth where I wouldn't kill anyone."

Dom shivered. How might this have gone down in one of their usual cheap haunts? "Were you still planning to kill me? When we were…"

"I was… I thought about it. Because, I mean—"

"Because you don't have a choice. I understand."

"How the fuck can you understand?" Sergei snapped, his voice wavering. "Do you have any idea—"

"You're not the only one they pay to take people out."

Sergei jumped like he'd hit him. "What?"

Dom shifted uncomfortably. "I'm… my uncle's been sending me on hits for years."

"You? I didn't…" Sergei shook himself. "I didn't think you were capable of…"

With a soft laugh, Dom shrugged. "Guess that's a compliment?"

"Yeah. I guess it is." Sergei rubbed his temples. "I'm sorry. I… I should've said something before, or—"

"What could you have said?" Dom slumped against the wall. "We both know how this works. Once you've got a contract, it's either his head or yours."

Their eyes met.

It's your head or mine.

We both know there's no getting out of this.

Sergei was the first to break eye contact, and he murmured something in Russian—Georgian?—as he rubbed both hands over his face. "What the fuck do we do now?"

"I wish I knew."

"This isn't how it was supposed to happen. This…" Sergei pushed out a ragged breath. "I started working for the families as a contract killer so I could kill the fuckers who killed the people I love." He let his head fall back, and goddamn if there weren't tears sliding down his face. "I never thought they'd tell me to kill someone I love."

Dom's heart stopped. "Sergei..."

"You're everything I'm supposed to bring down." Sergei wiped his eyes, and his rock steady sniper's hands were shaking now, badly. "You're..." He sniffed sharply, wringing his hands as if he could somehow bring them back under his total control. "You're the last person in the world I was supposed to fall in love with."

Dom moved across the floor and sat beside Sergei. He took Sergei's hands between his, holding them tight to still them. This side of Sergei scared Dom more than the contract on his own head. Sergei had always been so strong, so solid—bordering on cold more often than not. But now he was falling apart, trembling like a terrified child and fighting back tears that wouldn't be stopped.

"You're one of them," Sergei sobbed. "I'm supposed to... you're supposed to..." He wiped his eyes with shaking hands. "You're a Mafioso. You're not supposed to be...*human*."

"Sergei, look at me."

Sergei lifted his chin, blinking a few times, and met Dom's eyes as another tear rolled down his prominent cheekbone.

Dom brushed it away with his thumb, and cupped his face. "I'm human and so are you. And I don't know what to do now. All I know is..." He swallowed hard, his own emotions threatening to get the best of him. "I love you, Sergei."

Sergei's lips parted, and he stared at him in disbelief.

The words were out, and Dom didn't know what else to say. So he tipped up Sergei's chin and kissed him.

Sergei broke the kiss and touched his forehead to Dom's. "I don't want to hurt you, Dom. I can't."

Dom's gut twisted into knots.

You have to. We both know you do. This only ends one way.

He knew all too well how those contracts had to play out. Sergei had no more choice than Dom had had when he'd taken out Luciano.

Sniffing sharply, Sergei wiped his eyes. "I don't know what to do."

"We don't have to figure it out tonight."

"There isn't much time. They're putting pressure on me."

"I know." Dom stood, and held out his hand. "But we have tonight."

They locked eyes, and his heart thumped against his ribs. It didn't need to be said, but he knew damn well Sergei was thinking the same thing he was: Tonight was *all* they had.

Sergei clasped his hand around Dom's forearm, and Dom helped him to his feet.

"Let's go back in the bedroom," Dom whispered. "I don't know what we can do, but for right now, I just... I need you."

Nothing else needed to be said. Dom couldn't even remember moving from the kitchen to the bedroom—they may as well have just materialized there. They stripped off what few clothes they had on, and once again sank into bed together.

Sergei kissed his neck, warm breath raising goose bumps all over Dom's back and shoulders and soft lips gliding along Dom's jugular.

Dom ran his hands over Sergei's lean, powerful torso, marveling at the strength, at the simultaneous softness of flesh and firmness of the toned muscles beneath. Everything about him made sense now. His rigid façade, his catlike stealth, the way he moved like a prowling panther. He was a professional killer. A hunter. His lithe body— flawlessly fit and toned—didn't just make him an attractive lover and a mouthwatering stripper. It made him fast. Strong. Not a single ounce wasted by forming anything that might slow down the efficient predator or give his prey an advantage over him.

And Dom should have been afraid of him. He *was* Sergei's prey this time. Dom had been the hunter himself more times than he cared to remember, and he knew all too well how much danger he was in, but there was no pulling back now. As they kissed and groped and turned each other on, Sergei was every bit the assassin who'd subdued Dom in the kitchen as well as the vulnerable kid who couldn't hold back the tears while he'd told Dom he loved him. Still dangerous. Still scared. A man Dom should have run away from and couldn't help protecting.

Tangling up in bed like this, naked and hard with a predator's mouth against his and a killer's hands all over his skin, was deliciously dangerous—if this was what it was like to dance with the devil, then Dom hoped the music never stopped playing.

He pushed Sergei onto his back and pinned his arms. Sergei arched underneath him, and when Dom rocked against him, rubbing the underside of his dick against Sergei's, Sergei groaned into his kiss.

Sergei wrenched one arm free and slung it over Dom. Dom released his other arm, and Sergei wrapped both around him, pulling him down against him as they moved together, rubbed together.

Dom hadn't even realized how many barriers they'd put up until now. It was as if they'd carefully surrounded themselves with wall after wall, protecting themselves on every level, and now they'd all come down and he and Sergei were tangled up on top of the rubble.

He kept one hand around the back of Dom's neck, as if he thought Dom would even consider breaking this kiss, and with the other he stroked Dom's cock.

He desperately wanted to fuck. And definitely no condom this time. That would've been a layer between them. A thin one, but he couldn't stand the thought of *anything* between them now. He couldn't even imagine separating long enough to change positions or find lube or…

Not a chance. With every kiss and thrust, he was as close to breaking down as he was to getting off, and he wouldn't let go of Sergei. He couldn't. He'd never been this close to someone, this wrapped up in something so needy and honest and *raw*. Death was waiting outside for both of them, but at least they finally got to know what it was like to feel this alive.

Sergei broke the kiss with a gasp. "Oh God…"

Dom shivered and didn't dare fuck up his rhythm, not with Sergei this close to the edge. "Fuck. Fuck, Sergei. D-don't…" Dom squeezed his eyes shut, his ability to speak dissolving as he thrust into Sergei's fist.

Beneath him, Sergei moaned softly, and shuddered, and the first jet of semen on Dom's stomach sent him over the edge. Dom squeezed his eyes shut, jerked against Sergei, and they both gasped and moaned and cursed as their semen mingled between them.

Even as they came down, they didn't let go. As soon as they could breathe, their lips met, and they didn't stop kissing. Dom drew away for a second to grab some tissues, but as soon as they'd cleaned themselves off, they picked up right where they'd left off.

After a while, Sergei broke the kiss. He touched his damp forehead to Dom's. "I love you, Dom."

"I love you too." Dom cradled Sergei's face in both hands. "I don't know if we're going to get through this, but—"

"Doesn't matter." Sergei kissed him softly. "Even if we don't…" He lifted his head, and their eyes met.

Neither of them tried to finish his sentence. They spoke three languages between them, and there weren't enough words to convey what they'd take to the grave, what they'd had a chance to taste before fate inevitably closed in.

Dom turned onto his back, and Sergei molded himself to him. He rested his head on Dom's chest and Dom wrapped an arm around his shoulders.

Sergei took a breath. "After tonight, things will get—"

"I know." Dom kissed the top of his head. "But let's have tonight. We'll deal with tomorrow when we get there."

Sergei met his gaze.

Neither of them said it, but it was there in Sergei's eyes as surely as it was ringing in Dom's ears:

Let's have tonight.

Because this is all we have left.

Chapter 31

As the dust settled, they lay in silence, still tangled up in each other in the warm glow of the bedside lamp. Dom's strong arms were wrapped around Sergei, Sergei's arm draped across Dom's chest. Somehow they always ended up like this, but it felt less like lazy affection tonight and more like something much needier.

"You know what's kind of crazy?" Dom asked after a while.

"Hmm?"

"I was talking to my cousin one night. The psychopath." Dom's fingers ran lazily up and down Sergei's arm. "And we talked about the Georgian."

Sergei's neck prickled. "Oh really?"

"Mmhmm. I don't even remember what we were talking about, but at some point I said, 'well, if the Georgian ever gets that close to me, it'll be to suck my dick.'"

Sergei pushed himself up and locked eyes with Dom, staring down at him in horror.

Dom's lips were twisted slightly as if he were fighting a laugh.

Then Sergei snorted. So did Dom. They both burst out laughing. It was gallows humor of the most morbid kind, and laughing at it probably made them the sickest fucks on the planet, but laughing beat the alternative, so Sergei didn't fight it.

"You aren't serious," he said.

"I am," Dom laughed. "I was being a cocky idiot, and I knew it would horrify Felice, and… apparently it was truer than I thought."

Sergei laughed again, shaking his head. "Well, if I'd known you were into that kind of thing…"

Dom rolled his eyes. Then he drew Sergei down and kissed him again. "If I'd known sex with the—with you, would be that good, I'd have come looking for you a long time ago."

Sergei grinned against his lips. Slowly, though, his humor faded, and reality settled back in. Yeah, they'd found each other. And like it or not, Sergei was still the Georgian, and Dom was still…

He sighed, trailing the backs of his fingers down Dom's chest.

Dom sobered too, and touched Sergei's face. Quietly, they cuddled up together again, Sergei's head on Dom's shoulder and Dom's arms around him.

As they lay in silence, Sergei's mind rattled with all the things they'd learned about each other tonight. All the things they were. All the things they wished they could be. All the things that had put them both on the path to where they both were now.

After a while, he whispered, "Can I ask you a question?"

Dom let his hand drift from Sergei's face to his arm, and rested it there. "Can't promise I'll answer."

Sergei managed a soft laugh. He shifted a bit, since his

elbow and shoulder were starting to ache from holding himself up. "What happened to your father?"

Dom stiffened. "What?"

"Your father." Sergei swept his tongue across his lips. "I... people around town talk, you know? I'd heard of you, and they all said your uncle adopted you after your father died. After he..." He hesitated, not sure how raw this nerve was. "Betrayed the family."

Closing his eyes, Dom clenched his jaw. His fingers twitched on Sergei's arm.

"You don't have to answer," Sergei said. "I'm just curious."

Dom's Adam's apple bobbed. After a moment, he opened his eyes, but looked up at the ceiling instead of at Sergei. "The short version is that my father was turning state's evidence. He'd been arrested a few times, and the last time, he was going to prison for narcotics traveling. Which is a hell of a sentence."

Sergei nodded. "So I've heard."

"That's exactly why the Mafia Commission back in the 1980s didn't want the families involved in the drug trade." Dom scrubbed a hand over his face and sighed. "Because drugs meant huge sentences, and huge sentences meant plea deals." He turned toward Sergei. "The Feds cut my father a deal. If he could get them bulletproof evidence tying my uncle and the rest of the family to the narcotics trade, they'd put him—and my mother and me—into witness protection."

"But he got caught."

Dom winced. "Yeah. I don't know exactly what happened. I was twelve, so..." He lifted one shoulder in a heavy shrug. "I didn't even know about most of this until years later. I just know he made a mistake somewhere, or... something. I don't know. Someone caught on, and it got back to Corrado that he was talking to the Feds. So my uncle…" He swallowed hard. "Took care of the problem."

Sergei cursed in his native tongue. "When you were twelve?"

"Yeah. My uncle took in my mother and me, and then she died when I was fifteen, so he adopted me." Dom again stared up at the ceiling, eyes unfocused and lips taut. A long, silent moment passed before he said, "If my father had lived, there's no way in hell I'd be a made man. He even told me when I was a kid, that if the time came and my uncle wanted me to get made, that I shouldn't." He closed his eyes, letting out a long breath. "When that time did come, my father was dead, and my uncle had put the fear of God in me. He made me watch my father *die*, for fuck's sake, so I was terrified of him, and I was terrified to say no." His eyelids fluttered open again, and when he met Sergei's gaze, Sergei swore he caught a glimpse of that fear, of that young, traumatized kid. "And now this is my life."

Those soft spoken words shook Sergei right to the core. It wasn't the first time Dom had expressed how much he would've given to be away from this world, but Sergei hadn't known his backstory involved the same kind of deep-seated trauma as his. That his fate had been sealed in the blood of a parent murdered before his eyes.

Most of the made men in this town—or those doing everything they could to win enough favor to *be* made— embraced the Mafia life. This side of it, a man who'd been caught up as a child in wheels that were turning without his control, was nothing Sergei had ever seen before.

"I'm sorry." Dom cleared his throat and shifted onto his side. Touching Sergei's face again, he said, "Completely killed the mood, didn't I?"

"Well. To be fair." Sergei moistened his parched lips. "I

asked." He caressed Dom's face. They weren't much different, were they? All the hell they'd been through, the inevitability of getting tangled in all this because of what people before them had done…

Dom swallowed. "I don't know if the guys who roughed me up outside your club would've killed me or not…" He smoothed Sergei's hair. "But I'm glad they didn't. At least I got to find out what it was like to fall in love."

Sergei laughed to keep himself from breaking down, and pressed a soft kiss to Dom's lips. "Now you're just being sappy."

"I don't think most sappiness starts with 'that time those assholes tried to kill me.'"

And it usually doesn't end with one of us having to kill the other.

He banished that thought and leaned in for a longer kiss. "I'm glad it brought us together too. Even if things are…"

He didn't know how to finish that thought.

He didn't have to—Dom drew him down.

Kissed him again.

And held on.

FOR ONCE, the nightmares didn't come. It wasn't a surprise, though—Sergei couldn't dream unless he was asleep.

And sleep wasn't happening. Not with Dom lying next to him, alive and well.

Every breath Dom took was dangerous. If he didn't kill him, Sergei would find himself very high on the family's shit list. Another day or two, and there'd be a contract on his head as well as Dom's. These were orders written in blood and carved in stone—there was no rescinding a contract, and no backing out once accepted.

But the whole point of being a contractor for the Mafia was to take out those who'd killed his family. Killing the only person he loved besides Mama? He couldn't. No way.

Question was, how did he keep Dom alive *and* stay alive?

Dom shifted, and then rolled on his side, facing him. "Still awake?"

Sergei turned toward him, just barely making out his silhouette against the darkness. "Not the only one, apparently."

Dom laughed and kissed Sergei lightly. "Big shock, I guess. Kind of hard to sleep after…"

"Yeah." His conscience clawed at him. Finally, he reached for the bedside light and turned it on. They both winced, covering their eyes for a moment until they adjusted to the brightness. "There's something you need to know."

Dom chewed his lip. "I get the feeling there's a lot I don't know yet."

"Probably a lot you don't want to know, but…" Sergei propped himself up on his elbow. "Remember the night I had the bends?"

Dom shuddered. "How could I forget? Scared the hell out of me." He inclined his head. "Wait. Why?"

Sergei took a breath. "I wasn't just out fucking around in the water that day. I was on a job. On… your cousin's yacht."

Dom's eyebrows rose slowly, as if the pieces were coming together. "You're the one. You killed Privitera."

Sergei nodded. "The thing is, I was under orders to kill the second highest ranking man on the boat."

Dom paled.

"No one specified who that was, so I assumed someone was trying to send a message to Felice. But once I realized you were the mark..." He shivered. "I couldn't do it. Not even then."

Dom put a hand on his shoulder. "You could've been killed."

"So could you. You were supposed to be killed."

"But you didn't."

"I had the opportunity. I... I thought about taking it, but..." He shook his head. "Not a chance. I couldn't do it. *Can't* do it."

Dom was quiet for a moment, as if absorbing it all and trying to make sense of it. "How did you——" He stopped, eyes losing focus. "How did you even get on and off the boat? We would've seen scuba gear just lying around."

"It was under the boat. Against the hulls. I put it there the night before, then hid on the boat until everyone boarded. After I'd made my move, I went off the back, swam up in between, and got my gear."

"That's..." Dom laughed softly. "That's actually pretty impressive."

Sergei chuckled halfheartedly. "There's a reason I stayed alive."

Their eyes met, and they both sobered.

Dom touched his face. "Does it ever bother you?"

"Which part?"

"Killing. Does it ever bother you?"

"No."

"Never?"

"Never. The only people I've ever killed have been directly involved with the Mafia, and after what the fucking Mafia did to my family..." He avoided Dom's gaze. "The only time it's bothered me has been when I knew I'd hurt you."

Dom studied him for a long moment. "What happened to them? Your family?"

Sergei cringed.

"You don't have to—"

"My father got caught between the Maisanos and the Cusimanos," he said. "I was pretty young, so I don't remember much of the details. Only that Papa was worried about it. That both families were making demands. Trying to play him against the other. He tried to make it work, but…" Sergei shuddered.

"You don't have to tell me." Dom kissed him softly. "If it hurts that much."

"*Can* I tell you?"

Dom blinked. "Of course you can. If you want to."

"I haven't told anyone about it since it happened." Sergei swallowed. He sat up a bit, and lounged back on the pillows, lacing his hands together behind his head. "I was eight when it happened, so I didn't really know what was going on at the time, but I've figured it out over the years. I guess my father owned a couple of warehouses down near the south end of the Cape. The Cusimanos ran that part of town back then, but the…" He glanced at Dom. "Your uncle decided he wanted to get in on the south side. Raffaele Cusimano was already bleeding my family dry with protection money, not to mention helping themselves to shipments that came through the warehouses."

"That sounds right, yeah," Dom said quietly. "I… I was a kid back then too. But I remember."

Sergei nodded. "Anyway, my father refused to play nice with either family, so they started harassing us. All of us. And then one night, Giacomo Maisano and some of his buddies attacked my brother and his girlfriend. They…" Sergei shuddered at the memory. He hadn't seen what had happened, or understood at the time exactly what the words meant, but the aftermath had told him it was horrific. "They threatened to rape his girlfriend. Made him beg for her life. And when he did, they…"

Dom pulled him closer.

"They raped *him* instead. And made her watch." Sergei swallowed the nausea trying to rise in his throat. "All of them. One after the other. I guess they figured that would send a message to my father. And in a way, it did. My father was ready to pack up the entire family and get the fuck out of town before anyone else got hurt, but my other brother took matters into his own hands. He hunted down Giacomo, and he shot him."

Dom fidgeted, but said nothing.

"My father was furious with my brother for doing that," Sergei said. "He knew damn well Corrado would kill us all, so he got all of us in the car, and we headed out of town." Sergei hugged himself, shivering away a chill as that night played over and over in his mind in horrific detail. "We got out on the 103 somewhere. A car blocked us. Then another came up behind us. My father told my brothers to cover me with blankets, had me hide down on the floorboards. They all said no matter what happened, I had to stay there, not move or make a sound."

He closed his eyes for a moment, icicles forming along his spine.

Dom took his hand, and he kissed it gently but didn't speak.

"I heard the shouting and the gunshots," Sergei said. "I heard my mother scream. Then there were squealing tires, and the two cars left. I waited a few minutes, until I was sure they were gone, and got out of the car."

In almost twenty years, Sergei hadn't gone a day without thinking about the scene that had awaited him when he'd stepped out of that car. In the milky beams of the station wagon's headlights, his father and both of his brothers were sprawled on the pavement, writhing and whimpering in pain as enormous pools of blood expanded beside their midsections. Mama was on her knees, holding Vasily's limp form against her and screaming. Just… screaming.

One by one, right before Sergei's eyes, his brothers had stilled. Then his father.

And Mama still screamed. Even as she let Vasily down onto the asphalt, her shirt and face and arms covered in blood, she'd *screamed*.

"*Mama?*"

"*Seryozha?*" She'd looked up at him, eyes wide and glittering in the headlights. "*Sergei? Are you…*" She reached up and frantically ran her bloody fingers all over his face and through his hair. "*Are you real, Seryozha?*"

"*I'm real, Mama.*"

She'd thrown her arms around him, and they sat there until almost daylight, both crying, both rocking back and forth in the darkness until another car finally came by. When the driver had gotten out and found them, Mama had screamed and pleaded, "*Please don't hurt my son!*"

Then the cops had come, and there'd been a hospital, and social workers, and relatives suddenly sending him to live with other relatives. He saw Mama once more—briefly — before his aunt took him away. To his knowledge, that was the last time she'd known who he was.

In the present, he cleared his throat. "I went to live with some family in San Diego. I didn't have any contact with my mother, and no one would tell me anything, so I ran away when I was fifteen and came back to Cape Swan to find her." He exhaled hard. "No one's ever been able to tell me exactly what happened, but what I've gathered is that she fell into this horrible depression. She thought I was dead. Overdosed a few times on meds, tried to drink herself to death a few times, and then she just kind of… lost it, I guess. So now she's in a home, and barely even knows who she is half the time." His voice wavered a bit as he added, "She doesn't know who I am."

"My God," Dom whispered.

Sergei exhaled, then took a deep breath and rolled his shoulders. "After that, I got my hands on my uncle's pistol, and I found the men who'd threatened my father to start with. And I shot them."

Dom blinked. "Wait, you killed them when you were *fifteen?*"

Sergei nodded. "My cousins had taught me to shoot, and I decided to put that to use. Once I took those assholes down, I realized I could do it, and I decided I was going to kill everyone who'd been involved in what happened to my family." He met Dom's gaze. "At first, I didn't want to take down the entire Mafia." Sergei laughed dryly. "I mean, I don't think God Himself could bring them all down and keep them down—another family just pops up to take the last one's place. But I did realize I couldn't stop until I'd destroyed the Maisanos and the Cusimanos. And once I saw that the Passantinos were fucked up, I put them on my list too. Whoever comes in to fill the void, well, not much I can do about that. But those three? Done." Sergei exhaled, shaking his head. "I just don't know what to do now. If you're not dead soon, then I will be."

"Then take the money I gave you," Dom said. "And get the hell out of this place."

"I don't need the money. I actually have a bit of an insurance policy. I've got a place out of the country. And money squirreled away in about a dozen offshore accounts."

Dom nodded. "Go, then. Blow town and get the fuck out of here."

"Dom." Sergei exhaled. "I'm in love with you. I want you to stay alive, and I want to stay alive myself, but I didn't come this far to walk away and leave the Maisanos standing."

For a long time, Dom didn't speak. Finally, though, he held Sergei a little tighter and said, "Look, I don't know what our next move should be. I say we sleep on it for now, and in the morning… we'll figure something out."

"Do you think you *can* sleep?"

"It's worth trying."

UNSURPRISINGLY, Sergei didn't sleep much. He dozed off for a little while, long enough for a few nightmares, and woke up feeling like he hadn't slept in weeks.

But then he was suddenly wide awake—the bed was empty.

He looked around. Dom wasn't in the bedroom. His heart sped up. Had Dom slipped out during the night? Run like hell the way any sane man would with a contract on his head?

Sergei quickly grabbed a pair of shorts off his dresser, pulled them on, and went looking through the rest of his apartment.

He found Dom on the back patio, sitting on the edge and gazing out at the morning sky.

You idiot. You shouldn't have stayed.

God, I'm glad you're here.

As Sergei stepped out through the sliding glass door, Dom turned. Then he rose.

"Hey," Dom said. "I didn't want to wake you up. Sounded like you'd finally fallen asleep."

"Yeah." Sergei shrugged. "Sort of. You want some coffee?"

"Sure. Yeah."

They went into the kitchen. Despite the daylight casting an entirely different set of shadows and colors on the plain white cabinets and dingy laminate, there was no ignoring that this was where he and Dom had stood last night. Where Sergei had confessed the truth, and they'd brawled until Dom had calmed down. On the cabinet beside the oven, there was a smear of dried blood. His? Dom's? No way of knowing. Not that it mattered.

His mind going a million directions, Sergei went through the motions of starting some coffee.

"So," Dom said. "I've, uh, been thinking about our situation."

Sergei's hands stopped. In an instant, he couldn't remember how to work the coffee maker, and didn't really need the caffeine anyway. Facing Dom, he said, "Okay?"

Dom stared at the floor for a moment before meeting Sergei's gaze. "I think we need to come to terms with some things that are out of our hands at this point."

"Such as?"

"My cousin wants me dead. He's going to make sure it happens. That's…" He paused. "That's why they called in the best for the job."

Sergei winced, forcing back the bile climbing his throat.

Dom took a deep breath. "The contract is out. One way or another, I'm a dead man, and if you aren't the one to pull the trigger, you will be too."

It took a second to read between the lines, but when Sergei realized what he was getting at, he jerked away from

Dom's grasp and stepped back. "Don't even say it, Dom. I won't. I can't."

"You need to."

"Fuck no. I can't do it, Dom. I don't…" Sergei shoved a hand through his hair and started pacing across the kitchen, which seemed almost too small for pacing now that there was a broad-shouldered Sicilian standing in it. "I don't want to hurt you."

"I don't think you have much choice."

"No. No fucking way. You're—"

"Sergei, listen to me." Dom closed his hands around Sergei's shoulders. "I'm dead no matter what. At least I can—" He winced, then softly added, "At least I can trust you to make it quick." His eyebrows rose slightly, as if to ask, *Right?*

"I'd never make you suffer," Sergei breathed.

"Then you have to—"

"*No.*" Sergei set his jaw. "I'm not—"

"Sergei, for God's sake, just do it. Then you can walk away from this town and never look back. You don't fill this contract, you're going to be wearing a bull's eye for the rest of your very, very short life." Dom swallowed. "Because they *will* find you, and they *will* kill me. And I think we both know that they won't just put a bullet through your head."

Sergei shuddered, his mother's screams echoing through his mind as she stared at the bodies of her slowly dying husband and sons. "Dom…"

"You know how this works. We both do. And I don't want you being tortured for letting me live. They're going to kill me either way, so—"

"No. There's enough money. We can… we—"

Dom gripped Sergei's shoulders tighter. "Look at me."

Sergei met his gaze, though it was a struggle, and the

pain and desperation in Dom's eyes only made his heart sink deeper and deeper.

"These people have taken everything from me too," Dom said. "I got roped into this life, and I've done things I'm not looking forward to answering to in the next one. The bottom line, though, is no matter what we do, someone is going to make sure I'm dead."

"Dom, we—"

"*Listen* to me." The hurt in Dom's eyes intensified as he held Sergei's gaze. "The only variables here are *how* I die and *if* you do. If I can't get away from all this alive, then I would rather go down knowing that you're going to make a clean break and get out of here. If you promise me you'll do it quickly, and then you'll leave Cape Swan forever and go have the life neither of us have ever been able to... I can't think of anything that would give me more peace."

That hit Sergei in the chest. He'd craved peace even more than he'd craved vengeance, and to be able to grant that to Dom would mean he could sleep at night. But not like this.

"What if we fake our deaths?" His mouth had gone dry. "A burned out car in the ocean, it'll—"

"No." Dom shook his head. "We both know no one will believe I'm dead without a body."

Sergei chewed his lip. He couldn't argue with that. "And if we run? We have money. We—"

Dom shook his head.

Sergei squeezed his eyes shut. Dom was right. There was no way around it.

Shoulders sinking beneath Dom's gentle hands, Sergei exhaled and met his gaze. "I don't know what else to do."

Dom pulled in a breath and stood a little straighter. "We shouldn't do it here. The cops... they'll..."

Sergei winced. "Are we really..."

"What else do you suggest?"

He flinched.

"There are places all over this area," Dom said. "The woods. The beach." Dom half-shrugged. "I don't care where they find me as long as they don't find you."

"You're…" Sergei struggled against a wave of nausea. "How the hell can you be so casual about where I'm supposed to *kill you* and leave your body?"

"Because the alternative is letting *you* get killed," Dom shot back.

"Fine," Sergei snapped. "But I'm not—"

"Do you hear yourself? This is out of our hands, Sergei. All we can do is damage control."

"And damage control is me killing you?"

"Yes!" Dom threw up his hands. "It's either that or—"

"I know what the fucking alternatives are!"

"Then what else do you suggest, because I'm out of ideas."

Sergei swallowed, wondering when that lump had started rising in his throat. He didn't have any more ideas either. Because there weren't any. The unwritten laws of this town were evil and cruel, but they bent for no man.

"What if we kill Felice?" he asked. "You're the boss, for God's sake. Put a hit out—"

"And how many of Felice's goons know you're contracted to kill me?" Dom shook his head. "Anyone lays a hand on him while I'm still alive, they'll know damn well you turned."

Sergei's skin crawled. Dom had a point.

What the fuck was he supposed to do now? His plan hadn't included this. Dom wasn't supposed to inherit his uncle's position. Felice wasn't supposed to contract Sergei to kill Dom. Even if Dom had and Felice had, Sergei wasn't supposed to care about Dom. He wasn't supposed to be too in love to pull the fucking trigger.

But they had. And he was. And here they were.

And if Sergei didn't kill Dom, someone else would. Brutally. Mercilessly.

Slumping against the counter, he whispered, "You're right. We can't do this here."

Dom exhaled. "I know a few places."

"Me too." Sergei ran a hand through his hair. Then he brushed past Dom. "I'll get my keys."

THEY DITCHED Dom's car in a lot near the edge of town. Then he joined Sergei, and neither of them spoke as Sergei followed that familiar highway into the thickly forested hills.

As he drove. Sergei tried not to think about whether he regretted that they hadn't taken the time to go to bed once more. Now that the truth was out, and they both knew what had to happen, he just… couldn't.

And the hit… It didn't even have to happen today—his contacts all knew big hits took planning. He had time. But making this go on longer benefitted no one.

So Sergei drove. And didn't look at Dom. And tried not to notice the outline of the pistol pressing into his leg.

A few miles past the mile marker where he'd met Katashi last time, Sergei pulled over. Wordlessly, they got out of the car, and Dom followed Sergei into the woods. As they picked their way through the underbrush, Sergei caught himself hoping this was an ambush. That Dom was waiting for the right opportunity to pull out a gun of his own and drop him.

But he didn't. Damn him.

At a clearing, Sergei stopped. "This… this should be far enough from the road. No one will hear anything."

Dom pulled in a long breath through his nose. "Just don't make me dig my own grave."

"That's not funny."

Dom faced him, his expression completely serious. "I'm not joking."

Sergei raised his eyebrows. "I… wouldn't. No way."

"Thank you."

Though he knew he was only making it worse for both of them, Sergei wrapped his arms around Dom. "I'm sorry. I wish there was another way."

"Me too."

Sergei cupped his face and kissed him, and held him tight. When they separated, they held each other's gazes for a few seconds, and then pulled apart completely.

Here we go. This is it.

Sergei slid the pistol out of the holster.

Dom gulped. "Just promise me you'll leave after this." He eyed the gun, and then met Sergei's gaze. "Get the fuck out of Cape Swan and never look back."

Sergei nodded, nausea rising in his throat. "I promise." He glanced at his pistol. "I… I've never done this with someone who's…"

"Not fighting?"

"Yeah. That."

Dom avoided his eyes. Without a word, he knelt on the ground in front of Sergei. "Just make it quick, all right?"

Sergei flinched. "Shouldn't…" His mind raced, searching for any means to delay the inevitable. "Don't you want to see a priest first?"

Dom lifted his gaze. "After everything I've seen, do you really think I still believe in God?"

So much for that stalling tactic.

"Please, Sergei," Dom breathed. "Don't drag this out."

Heart thumping and stomach twisting, Sergei stepped closer. He was tempted to kiss him, or touch his face one last time, but that just seemed like unnecessary torment for both of them.

Dom tilted his head back. Sergei pressed the muzzle up under his jaw.

He curled his finger around the trigger. One pull. All he had to do was give it one pull, and this would all be over.

But his hand shook. Goddammit.

He forced his emotions back. He could break down afterward. Not while Dom was still alive. While he could see him, hear him, realize how much this hurt. No, he'd wait until he was sure Dom's heart wasn't beating anymore.

Dom put his hand over Sergei's. "Just do it." His finger slid over the top of Sergei's, and when he swallowed, his jaw pushed against the muzzle. "*Please.*"

Just one shot. Once his heart stops, I can lose it.

Just one shot.

One bullet.

One—

He jerked the gun away. With shaking hands, he dropped the magazine and cleared the chamber, and then tossed all the pieces on the ground. "I won't."

"Sergei—"

"No." He met Dom's gaze and clenched his jaw. "They killed people I love. If they want you dead too, I'm not doing that dirty work for them."

"But they'll kill you too."

"I know." He dropped to his knees and touched Dom's face, tears falling freely down his face as he whispered,

"And I'd rather have a bull's eye on my head than your blood on my hands."

"You're insane," Dom said, wiping Sergei's tears. "I don't want—"

Sergei cut him off with a hard kiss. He gripped the back of Dom's neck until he knew it had to hurt, and refused to let go.

Dom's lips softened, and he opened to Sergei. One hand appeared on Sergei's cheek. The other arm snaked around his waist. Sighing in unison, they pulled each other closer.

When Sergei's lips left Dom's, his voice was thick with tears, but he managed, "There *has* to be another way. I'm not doing this."

Dom exhaled, touching his forehead to Sergei's. He didn't argue, though. Instead, he drew Sergei in, and for the longest time, they just leaned on each other. With his head against Dom's chest, Sergei could feel every beat of Dom's heart, and just like each beat pushed blood through Dom's veins, it pushed relief through Sergei's. Dom was still alive. They were both still alive. God knew where they went from here, but the bullet was lying harmlessly on the ground, still unfired in its casing.

After a while, Dom smoothed Sergei's hair and said, "If we can't go through with this, then the only thing we can do is take them down with us."

Sergei lifted his head and blinked. "You're serious."

"As a heart attack. We've got hundreds of people in indentured servitude," he said. "We're running narcotics all over the West Coast. The body count…" He shook his head, grimacing painfully. "I don't want this to go on any more than you do."

Sergei chewed his lip. "I've been working on that for years. But it's not going to happen overnight. My whole plan was to have Felice take his father's place, and then Vincente Cusimano would finish the job. But Vincente isn't in power yet and…" He sighed. "They'll catch up to us before that part works itself out."

"Then maybe we need to speed things up a little."

"What do you suggest?"

Dom shook his head. "I don't know yet. We'll have to come up with a plan. We're only going to get one shot, though."

"Yeah, I know." Sergei paused. "Before we do this, though, there's something I need to do." He swallowed. "Alone."

Dom studied him, and then nodded. "All right." He smoothed Sergei's hair. "Do you need to be alone now?"

"No." Sergei drew him closer, his voice dropping to barely a whisper: "Alone is the last place I want to be right now."

"GOOD MORNING, SERGEI." Brittany smiled over the desk at the nurse's station. "Wasn't expecting you today."

Sergei faked the best smile he could. "Had the day off. Thought I'd come visit."

"Well, she'll be happy to see you."

"I'm sure." He started toward Mama's room, but paused. "Do you want to me to take her pills to her?"

"Oh, now that you mention it…" She looked down at the tray she'd been preparing as she always did at this time of day, and handed one to him over the desk. "Thank you."

"Thank *you*." Sergei held that smile for another second, and continued down the hall with the paper cup. Outside Mama's door, he paused, glancing around to make sure he was out of anyone's sight. Certain he was alone, he slipped a couple of capsules from his pocket into the cup.

Then he took a deep breath, forced a smile, and stepped into Mama's room.

She was in her usual armchair, gazing out the window but not really focusing on anything as far as he could tell.

"Mama?"

She slowly turned her head. He held out hope this would be one of those rare moments when she recognized him, but when she smiled and murmured, "Vasya," his heart sank.

"Yes, Mama," he whispered in their native tongue. "It's me."

"Only you?" She looked around, and he couldn't help wondering if she was even seeing the room they were in, or if she saw their old house, the one they'd all been fleeing before the Italians had caught up with them that night. The dementia had taken her so far away, he couldn't begin to tell where she was now.

"It's only me," he whispered.

"Will the others come soon?"

Sergei hesitated. "Yes, Mama. They'll…" He struggled to keep his voice even. "You'll see them very soon."

"Good. Good. Papa has been gone too long. They're making him work so much."

He struggled to keep his emotions together. Today of all days, he refused to frighten her with a confusing breakdown.

After a while, he took a deep breath. "I came to tell you something, Mama."

She turned to him, smiling a little but looking right through him. "What is it?"

"I wanted you to know that…" He squeezed her hand. "That it's all over now. The men who hurt us, they're going away." He sighed. He'd always imagined being almost giddy when he finally told her. When he could finally say the words and hope they connected to some remote part of her mind that might still be lucid, that might grab onto the information and give her peace.

But this wasn't how he'd expected it all to play out. And even though he'd finally reached the endgame, now that it was nearly as over as it would ever be, he was just... exhausted. Relieved in a way, but he couldn't find any joy or excitement in the amount of blood that had been spilled. Justice had been served. There was still some left, and he'd either serve that too or die trying. But now all he wanted was rest. Rest which would hopefully come soon.

He patted her fragile hand. "They won't hurt anyone anymore."

"Good." Her voice was distant, as was her gaze. There was no telling if she had any idea what he'd said, what it meant. "That's good."

"You should—" His voice cracked, and he quickly cleared my throat. "You should take your meds, Mama."

She turned to him, looking right at him. Sergei's heart clenched—it was one of those rare moments when she looked at him and not through him. When she was here and so was he. Maybe, just this one time...

She smiled. "When will you bring Seryozha to visit me?"

He exhaled. Damn it. He coughed again, and whispered, "I'll bring him soon."

"Good." She smiled, and her eyes were distant now, as if she was looking into an entirely distant time and place. "Are you still seeing that lovely girl?"

His throat tightened, and he forced a smile. "Yeah, Mama."

"Good." Mama nodded and gazed out the window. "Good."

Sergei forced back his emotions, but that was getting harder by the second. The stoic outer shell was only going to last so much longer. "Mama, you need to take your meds." He pushed the cup of pills toward her.

She eyed it warily. "But I feel fine."

"I know you do. You need to take them so you'll still feel fine."

"Oh. Okay."

He helped her take her pills, holding the glass of water steadier than her hands could. After she'd swallowed all of them, he set the glass aside and leaned over her.

"I love you, Mama." He kissed the top of her head. "Tell Papa and the others hello for me."

"I will, Vasya," she slurred. Her eyelids grew heavy, and finally closed. After a moment, her breathing slowed, and soon, her chest rose and fell in the distinctive pattern of someone who was fast asleep.

He held her hand, and with the other, took the tiny spray bottle from his pocket, glancing at the door to make sure they were alone.

Then he held his breath, waited until just before she inhaled, and sprayed the fine mist just in front of her nose and parted lips. Her features twitched a bit, probably just irritated by the moisture.

As promised, the poison took effect quickly and quietly. Before he'd even pocketed the bottle, her breath hitched. Her body tensed slightly, her fingers tightening feebly around his before relaxing again.

And he sat there, and he waited, holding her frail hand until he was sure she was gone. After her chest had fallen for the last time, he stayed like that a moment longer.

Then he carefully placed her hand on the armrest.

With a tissue, he dabbed her face, wiping away the traces. He stuffed the tissue into the wastebasket, and then stood beside her and took her hand again. He wanted to kiss her forehead one last time, but couldn't take the risk coming in contact with any residue, so he pressed a gentle kiss to the back of her hand, gave her one final look, and left the room.

Brittany was on her way in, but Sergei stopped her. "She's asleep. She seemed really tired when I came in— might want to let her rest for a while."

"Oh." She glanced at the door, then back at him, and shrugged. "Well, her physical therapy's not for another hour. No reason she can't rest for a little bit first."

He smiled. "Thank you."

She smiled back, and they continued in separate directions.

All the way out to the parking lot, he thumbed the edge of the spray bottle in his pocket. They wouldn't suspect a thing. Not unless the medical examiner did more than a cursory autopsy, which he probably wouldn't. He was already overrun with work, and thanks to Dom and Sergei, he'd be busy for a while anyway.

When they found her, they wouldn't call the police. They wouldn't try to resuscitate her because it would be obvious by then that she was too far gone. Really, it didn't make a difference for him if they went in now or if they waited.

He wanted them to let her be, though. Just for a little while. Not for his sake—he'd be long gone before it occurred to anyone that it might've been him. He just wanted her to have a little bit of peace.

There'd be a burial. A tasteful plot and a headstone that didn't tell the whole story. The home had promised him time and again that if anything happened to him before she died, they'd make sure that when the time came, she had a service and a respectful burial, and he believed them. He didn't need to attend himself. There was no more peace to be made. Her soul was hopefully resting now, and her body was in the hands of people who'd sworn she'd be properly laid to rest.

His only hope was that he'd given her, in death, the peace she should've had in life.

When he reached the parking lot, he got in the car and drove away, and he didn't look in the rearview as he left the home for the last time.

Chapter 32

The heat of the day weighed down on Dom's neck and shoulders as he walked up the path. He could still see his car from here, and sweat was already beading on his forehead and beneath his hair.

The path was mostly overgrown now, but Dom had memorized it. He wasn't supposed to know the way through here. The first time he'd walked this path, following the narrow, winding strip of barely-trampled dirt, his only thoughts had been to keep up with his uncle's long strides. On the way back down to the car in the darkness, he'd focused intently on memorizing everything. He'd counted his steps, counted the bends and switchbacks, made damn sure he committed those numbers to memory. Although Corrado had forbidden him from coming here again, and had probably convinced himself that a twelve year-old would never find his way back to that spot anyway, Dom had been determined to return. Countless times over the years, he'd done exactly that.

As he stepped into the clearing this time, a chill prickled his sweat-dampened skin.

There was no sign that the dirt had ever been disturbed. Hardy coastal desert plants had taken over, climbing one on top of each other like creeping ivy. Between the wind, the vines, and the occasional rainfall over the last twenty-three years, there was no trace of the indentations Dom's bony knees had made in the dirt that night. The smooth, flat spots where shovels had tamped down on freshly overturned soil—long gone.

It was silent out here, perfectly still. In the distances, seagulls cried and the surf lapped at the shoreline, but here in this tiny, shaded place, everything was quiet. All these years later, Dom couldn't step into this clearing without his ears ringing.

When his uncle had brought him here the first time, Dom had been surprised to see Papa there in the clearing. He wasn't alone. There was a priest lurking in the background. Dom didn't recognize him, but the man had on the distinctive white collar and clutched what must've been a Bible to his chest.

Also in the shadows were two of Uncle Corrado's lieutenants—huge burly men, both from the Old Country—standing behind the priest. The ground had been dug up. A big hole. As Dom and Corrado entered the clearing, Papa had faced them, sweat pouring off his face, dirt on his trousers and blood on his shirt, and his eyes had grown huge.

He'd dropped the shovel in his hand and pointed at Dom. "Why is he here?"

Why are you *here, Papa?* He'd told the whole family goodbye. Why was he upset that Dom had come here? Did he *want* to leave him and Mama?

"This is between you and me, Corrado," Dom's father had growled, but there'd been a note of desperation in his voice. A plea that Dom now understood—*do what you must, but not in front of him.*

"This is a family matter," Corrado had said coldly. "Your son is family. And he needs to understand what happens when family turns on family."

Cringing, Dom had braced himself. He'd seen men beaten for their crimes before. Sometimes a man needed an attitude adjustment, Felice—then fourteen—liked to joke, and Corrado would chuckle and agree. Dom had steeled himself, sick at the thought of watching his father get beaten by the burly goons standing in the shadows, but it was the way things were.

"Corrado," Papa begged. "Please. Don't—"

Corrado went over to him and put an arm around him, and he murmured something in his ear. Something Dom couldn't make out, but something that made Papa's shoulders sag. When Corrado let him go, Papa kept his eyes down and knelt at the edge of the hole in the ground.

Dom's blood had turned to ice. What was happening?

Corrado put a hand on Papa's shoulder. "If you'd like to say anything to your son, now is the time."

Papa closed his eyes. Took a deep breath. Looked at Dom. "Tell Mama I love her. And I love you." He'd swallowed hard, and something in his gaze intensified as he whispered, "And remember *everything* I told you."

"And while you're at it"—Corrado withdrew a pistol from inside his jacket—"remember that family comes first. And if it doesn't…"

The gunshot must've echoed for miles. Instantly, the whole world had fallen silent, but not silent enough. Though Dom's ears had immediately started ringing, and he'd clamped his hands over them in terror, it hadn't been enough to drown out the sick thud of Papa's body hitting the ground. Or the thud of his own knees when he dropped onto them.

His father hadn't fallen completely into the hole, so the lieutenants picked him up and tossed him in, and the thud again reverberated through the ground and into Dom's knees and echoed inside his head.

Corrado crouched beside him and hugged him gently, speaking so softly that Dom could barely hear him over the ringing in his ears. "Loyalty is critical, Domenico. Loyal to the family, sworn to omertà. Or…" He'd gestured at Papa. "Or this."

Dom shook himself. In all the years that had gone by, he'd never forgotten the smell of gunpowder mingling with Corrado's aftershave.

Gazing down at the place where Papa remained undisturbed to this day, Dom took a deep breath. "I never forgot what you said. You were right about this life. It's a fucking viper, and anyone who picks it up is bound to get bitten. But I'm getting out of it. I found a way out." He pushed his shoulders back. "I don't know what's going to happen. For all I know, I might be joining you soon. But I won't be coming back here. I… if this thing works, I'll be leaving Cape Swan and never coming back, which means I can never…" He sighed. "I wanted to say goodbye one last time."

He stood there for a while, just staring at the seemingly benign ground before he finally whispered, "Goodbye, Papa."

And then, for the final time, he turned and walked away.

Chapter 33

Sergei and Dom wanted some answers, and Sergei was pretty sure he knew who had them. Through one of their mutual contacts, he reached out to Tumino.

"I need to discuss the job," was all he let on.

As always, they met in the guesthouse. And as always, Sergei was on guard. Especially after such a high-profile job, there was always the risk of a hitman being taken out rather than risking him bragging to someone about the kill. He checked his perimeter motion sensors, and then led Dom inside.

Tumino was in the living room, as was his custom, and Sergei went in by himself.

The man grimaced, shifting on the couch as his innards bubbled audibly. "So it's done?"

"Not exactly."

Tumino glared up at him. "What's that supposed to mean?"

Behind Sergei, Dom stepped into the room.

Tumino's eyes widened. His puffy cheeks lost some

color. "Oh, Jesus." He reached for the phone on the table, but Sergei grabbed it first.

"Make so much as a peep," Sergei growled, setting the phone out of reach. "And you'll be dead well before security gets here."

Tumino gulped. "What the hell is this?"

"We've got some questions," Dom said. "And it seems you're a man who might have some answers."

"No, no." Tumino scooted to the edge of the couch, groaning as he did. "No, I'm not gonna get involved in this." He started to get up, but froze when Dom pulled out a pistol.

"Sit. The fuck. Down."

Sergei glanced at Dom, eyebrows up. Shit. He had a bigger spine than Sergei'd thought.

Tumino wisely sat back down. He leaned against the back of the sofa. "What do you two want?"

"I want to know how far back Felice is involved in all this shit," Dom said. "Is it true that he called in the hit on me?"

Tumino gulped. "I…"

"Answer the question," Dom said in a low growl that made Sergei shiver. He hadn't seen this side of him before. Dom stepped closer, Tumino's eyes tracking the pistol. "Come on. Fucking answer, or—"

"You know I can't say nothing." Tumino shifted, grimacing painfully. "I can't talk just like you can't talk."

"I couldn't give a fuck less about omertà right now, asshole," Dom said. "As long as I'm alive, I am the boss of the Maisano organization. Which means I can order a bullet into your head if I'm so inclined. I could even ask the Georgian to fire it for me."

Tumino's eyes flicked toward Sergei.

"So." Dom folded his arms. "You ready to talk?"

The man still didn't speak.

"Oh for fuck's sake." Sergei held out his hand. "Give me the gun."

Dom hesitated, but gave it to him, butt first.

Tumino watched the exchange and paled.

Sergei stepped in front of him, dug the gun into a couch cushion beside Tumino, and fired. The couch muffled the shot enough that it wouldn't draw attention from the main house, but it was still enough to leave his ears ringing a bit.

He jammed the pistol against Tumino's forehead.

Tumino pressed his lips together, wisely stifling what was probably a scream.

"Hot, isn't it?" Sergei snarled.

"You son of a—"

"Tell us what we want to know, or your balls are next." He shoved the weapon into the man's crotch, and when Tumino whimpered, he added, "Don't think I won't shoot one of them off if you keep testing my patience."

"You fucking psycho! You're—"

"I'm going to give you a ballistic vasectomy if you don't—"

"All right! All right!" The man gulped. "I'll talk."

Sergei withdrew the gun and stepped back. "You've got five seconds to start talking."

"Okay, okay." Tumino fidgeted on the couch, eyeing the bullet hole. "It's Felice. Everything… it all goes back to him."

Dom's expression hardened. "Tell us more."

Tumino nodded. "Felice's been pulling the strings from the start. The orders never come directly from him. It's always one of his boys. But I know who's in charge. They give me the order, and I pass it on to, well…" He nodded toward Sergei. "A while back, after Barcia was killed, Felice was pissed off that Corrado wouldn't authorize a hit on the boys who did him in. He knew he needed to raise the ante to get Corrado to fire back." He gestured at Dom. "So he had someone rough you up."

Dom blinked. "Felice ordered that?"

Tumino nodded. "He didn't think the men who did it would wind up dead, but they did, and that gave him even more leverage against the Cusimanos."

Sergei and Dom exchanged wide-eyed glances.

"It's the same reason he wanted you offed out on the boat that day—because if his father realized you'd been killed, and he saw how easily it could've been Felice, he'd have had no choice but to retaliate. After Corrado didn't react when Felice had Eugenio Cusimano framed for killing Nicolá Cannizzaro, he—"

"Wait, what?" Dom cocked his head. "So who *did* kill Cannizzaro?"

Sergei thumbed the trigger guard. Heart speeding up, he said, "I did."

Dom's eyes widened. "What?"

"I was specifically paid to make it look like Eugenio killed him."

"So then…" Dom shook his head. To Tumino, he said, "Are you saying Felice arranged for Sergei to kill Cannizzaro and make it look like Cusimano did it, so that Corrado would issue a contract on Cusimano?"

Tumino nodded. "So Corrado had Eugenio taken out, but Raffaele Cusimano didn't retaliate the way Felice wanted him to, so Felice had to stir the pot a little more."

"But *why?*" Dom asked.

"Because he wanted the families at war. The more he could convince his father that the Cusimanos were getting violent, the more he could convince his father to respond with the same." Tumino squirmed, grimacing, though it was hard to say if the discomfort came from his condition or the looming threats. "Once things were going to shit, he could get his brother and father out of the way, and take over the family without anyone thinking twice." He stared up at them. "That's all I know. I don't know what else I can say."

"That's what we needed." Sergei pulled a folded piece of paper from his back pocket. "But before we go, I want to get one thing very, very clear." He unfolded the paper and held it where Tumino could see it, and then pressed the gun to his forehead again. "You see this?"

Tumino shifted his gaze, holding his head perfectly still. "Yeah?"

"You recognize those addresses?"

Tumino squinted, and then the color rushed out of his face. "Those are my children's addresses."

"Uh-huh. They are." Sergei slid the paper back into his pocket. "If I have even the faintest reason to believe you're squealing to anyone about this conversation, or that you haven't kept your mouth shut about any of this, I will—"

"I believe you!" Tumino showed his palms. "Just don't hurt my kids."

"Good. We understand each other." Sergei looked at Dom and jerked his head toward the door. "Let's go."

They made a quick escape, hurrying off the property to where Sergei's car was parked a half mile or so down the road.

As Dom buckled his seatbelt, he cleared his throat. "Would you… would you actually go after his kids?"

"No." Sergei casually put the car in gear. "But as long as he believes I will, he'll keep his trap shut."

"And if he doesn't?"

"He will."

IT TOOK a few days to put their plan in motion.

While Sergei made sure weapons were in place and every aspect of security and escape routes were taken into consideration. Dom had to continue playing the role of newly minted boss. On the surface, it seemed dangerous, letting him go anywhere near the men who wanted him dead, but the truth was, Dom could walk safely amongst the Mafiosi. Not despite the contract on his head—because of it. If Sergei had been contracted to kill him, then only Sergei had been contracted. Otherwise, after the deed was done, the other contracted hitmen could go to the police and point to whoever had paid them to commit the same crime, while walking away scot free.

Odds were, no one knew Dom was a marked man except for those directly involved in assigning the hit, and none of them would make an unsanctioned move on a made man, never mind a boss. Dom was effectively bulletproof.

And his brazenly high profile was driving Felice Maisano insane.

"He's getting antsy," Dom said as he and Sergei sifted through papers in his office late one night. "He isn't saying much, but he's definitely not happy."

"Let him squirm." Sergei pushed a stack of folders across the desk. "He's too much of a fucking coward to meet me face to face even if I'd let him. I'm sure Tumino's keeping him placated, though."

Dom chuckled. "Good." He stuffed some envelopes into a box that would be dropped at the post office tomorrow. In between planning their takedown, not to mention Dom going through the motions as boss, they'd been sneaking in here during the night, burning the midnight oil as they sent legal documents to the hundreds of immigrants on the Maisanos' payroll.

With each sealed envelope, an immigrant family received their legal citizenship, and a letter stating their debt had been wiped clean. They owed the organization nothing. By the end of the last night, the entire payroll was gone and the ledger was blank. Now, even if Sergei and Dom were killed, they'd dealt a crippling blow. Without labor, the whole operation would fall apart. The Maisanos needed desperate immigrants as drug mules to collect the coke bricks from the crab pots and smuggle them through the marina.

Dom wasn't worried about anyone back-tracking and telling the people that, no, their debts were not canceled. They were too worried about their image, and for once, that would work in Dom's favor—no one wanted to give the impression that the Maisanos went back on their word.

When they were finished with the last of the documents, they left the office and went back to Sergei's place to rest, regroup, and make sure everything was in place.

Because tomorrow, the Maisanos were going down.

WHEN FELICE WENT OUT on his boat again the next day, Sergei was waiting. He'd slipped on board in the middle of the night, and after everyone had boarded, he kept his head down. Patiently, he rode all the way out to the cargo ship, to each crab pot, and back toward the marina. Tucked into a closet full of Felice's wife's clothes, Sergei waited, even as he had to endure the moans and cries of Felice fucking his mistress.

Toward the end of the voyage, he and the woman exchanged some flirty comments and a few long kisses before he slapped her on the ass and promised to meet her outside as soon as he'd retrieved a few things from the safe.

The woman left. Oblivious to Sergei watching through the slats, Felice changed the bandages on his stitched wound, and then fixed his shirt and his hair, and exchanged a smug grin with his own reflection. Sergei rolled his eyes.

Get over yourself, asshole. I guarantee she's more into your wallet than your "technique."

Felice opened a panel in the floor beside the bed, revealing the safe beneath it. He entered the combination to the safe, and Sergei slipped soundlessly out of his hiding place.

The deck creaked beneath his foot, and Felice started to turn around, but Sergei was faster—he dug the gun into the back of his skull.

"Make a sound," he said just loudly enough for Felice to hear, "and your brains are all over that safe."

Slowly, Felice lifted his hands. "How much do you want?"

Sergei laughed. "Oh, that's so cute. You think I came here for money."

Felice tried to turn his head, but Sergei flipped the gun around and pistol-whipped him, sending him down onto his arms. As the Italian rubbed the back of his head, a little blood smearing on his fingers, he growled, "What the hell do you want?"

"I want you to sit there and not make a sound." He paused. "You might want to cancel your evening plans." Sergei chuckled. "Tell her you've got a headache."

"Fucker," Felice muttered.

The boat came to a gentle stop. Down below, there were voices and activity as the crew secured the boat to the marina.

"All I have to do is say the word," Felice said. "And you're a dead man."

"Yeah? I'm out of things to lose." Sergei nudged him with the gun's muzzle. "You seem like somebody who wants to live, though." He paused. "And now that I think about it, I don't think I'd shoot you in the head." Sergei stepped in front of him and pointed the pistol at his midsection. "I'm more inclined to aim for non-vital organs. Let you roll around and scream for a while before your own gut poisons you."

Felice's eyes widened.

"I think we understand each other. Do what I tell you, and you won't get a hot lead injection."

The Italian gulped.

Through the open window, voices made it into the bedroom:

"Afternoon, Mr. Maisano."

"Good afternoon," Dom said. "I'm taking the boat back out. Felice and I have a… *meeting*." He spoke in that snarled, pissed-off-boss tone, and from the rapid footsteps on the decks, the men weren't sticking around to watch the sparks fly.

At least one hung back, though. "You need security detail or someone to drive—

"This is a private meeting," Dom snapped. "A family matter. I can drive the boat."

"You got it, boss." One more set of departing footsteps.

Felice closed his eyes and exhaled.

Doors opened and shut. People moved around. Someone told Dom the boat was gassed up, and someone else mentioned that an appliance in the galley wasn't working. Business as usual to anyone who might be listening.

Another door opened, letting out a conversation in progress:

"…make sure he calls you. It's just business, hon. I'm sorry."

Felice's mistress huffed. "He didn't tell me he had a business meeting."

"It was last minute. These things come up."

The woman snarled something, and then high heels *thunked* along the ramp and onto the dock.

Sergei chuckled. "I might be doing you a favor."

"Kiss my ass," Felice hissed.

Eventually, everything on the boat was quiet. Voices and footsteps faded into the distance, and Felice and Sergei seemed to be completely alone.

Then the door opened, and Dom stepped in.

"Really, Domenico?" Felice snorted derisively. "You're working with the Russians now, *cousin*?"

"I'm not from Russia, motherfucker," Sergei said through his teeth. "I'm from Georgia."

Felice lost what little color he had left. "You're shitting me."

"Nope." Dom gestured at the door. "Now let's get up to the helm. We're going for a ride."

"A ride? What are—"

Sergei jerked Felice to his feet, dragging a howl of pain from him.

"It'll make sense as we go," Sergei said. "Now walk."

Felice glared at him, still wincing and gripping his wounded arm, but with Sergei's pistol at his back, he walked.

Above decks, Dom fired up the engines.

"You driven this thing before?" Sergei asked.

"No, but it can't be that hard." Dom chuckled. "Out in open water, anyway. A few scratches won't hurt it, right?"

Felice groaned. "You motherfucker."

Dom sobered, narrowing his eyes at his cousin. "How about you sit down and shut up for a little while?"

"Fuck you."

Sergei kicked his knee out from under him, and Felice's kneecaps hit the deck with a loud *crack*. Then he cuffed Felice's hands and shoved him back against the bulkhead, where he bound him to a pipe. Felice's face contorted with pain—the wound would definitely keep him from fighting while he was tied.

Meanwhile, Dom eased the boat out of its slip, and drove it out of the marina. There were quite a few boats out today, but Sergei wasn't concerned about them seeing anything amiss. Felice was out of sight. This yacht turned a lot of heads in Cape Swan—it stood out like a cruise ship among kayaks—but no one had any reason to be suspicious.

"So how do we know which crab pots are yours and which are the Cusimanos'?" Sergei asked.

Felice swore in Italian.

"The buoys are colored," Dom said. "Orange are Maisano. Blue are Cusimano. Not that it matters—we're clearing out everybody's supply today."

"What the fuck are you doing?" Felice demanded. "Are you insane?"

Sergei huffed sharply. "Shut up, or I'll put a gag in your mouth."

Felice eyed the gun in Sergei's hand and must've decided not to push his luck, because he fell quiet and stayed that way.

Dom drove the boat from crab pot to crab pot. At each one, he stopped, and Sergei pulled up the pots and retrieved the sealed kilos, which Dom stacked in the living area.

"How many more are there?" Sergei rubbed his lower back gingerly.

"Ten, maybe fifteen?" Dom shrugged as he steered toward the next one. "We have to keep them spread out."

"There's got to be a more efficient way to do this."

"You have any ideas?"

Sergei exhaled. "No."

Felice struggled against his handcuffs, hissing as he apparently pulled on his stitches. "You sons of bitches. What the fuck are you doing?"

Dom nodded toward him. "Would you shut him—Oh shit."

Sergei's head snapped up. "What?"

"The Coast Guard."

Sergei craned his neck, and his heart dropped. Sure enough, the Coast Guard boat was pulling up, and it was slowing down. They weren't just going to stroll on by, were they?

"What do you think they want?" he asked.

"Don't know," Dom muttered. "They don't usually harass us unless they're getting suspicious."

"Of course they're getting suspicious," Felice said. "My men have probably already—"

"Your men think we're having a private business meeting," Dom snapped. He glanced at the boat and scowled. "We're not required to let them board and search us, but I'd just as soon not raise suspicions."

Sergei thought quickly, and then turned to Dom. "Go out and stall them." Sergei paused. "Take off your shirt and muss your hair a little first."

"Take—"

"Trust me."

Dom hesitated.

"*Trust me*, Dom."

Dom exhaled, but he pulled off his shirt and hurried outside.

The Coast Guard boat pulled up close, its engines getting louder as it did. Not much time.

Sergei turned to Felice. "I'm leaving you here, and you're going to keep your fucking mouth shut, or I will—"

"Fuck you." Felice spat blood at his feet. "You're not going to—"

Sergei pistol-whipped the fucker, the impact of the gun against Felice's cheekbone reverberating up his arm.

Felice blinked a few times. Blood trickled from his face, and he stared at Sergei, stunned.

"I'm not fucking around," Sergei growled. "Make a goddamned sound, and I'll make sure you live a very long, very hellish life. Wouldn't take much to plant some evidence and get you convicted of something child-related. And all it would take is a rumor around the prison yard that you're a child molester, and you'll learn the meaning of hard time. Am I clear?"

The Italian swallowed. Slowly, he nodded.

"That's what I thought."

He double-checked that Felice's bindings were secure, shoved a gag in his mouth, and then headed down to join Dom, peeling off his shirt as he went.

Chapter 34

Dom trusted Sergei, but this seemed insane. Shirt off? Hair mussed? What the hell did he have up his sleeve?

But he hadn't led him astray so far, so Dom stepped out onto the deck and leaned on the railing. The smaller vessel was manned by two young coasties in uniforms and sunglasses, and one was out on the deck.

"Can I help you, gentlemen?" Dom asked.

"Good morning," the coastie said. "Sorry to bother you, but we've gotten some reports of—"

"*There* you are!" Sergei singsonged.

Dom spun around, and his heart stopped. Sergei wasn't just strutting down the steps from the upper deck, he was completely naked with a wine bottle in his hand and a very prominent erection.

Oh God. What in—

Sergei turned to the guys on the boat. "Oh, hey boys!" He waved at them. "We're on our honeymoon!"

The blushing coastie chuckled, shifting uncomfortably. "Oh. Uh. Congratulations. Um—"

"Oh my God." Sergei flashed Dom a grin, then looked back at the coasties. "You boys should join us!" He held up the bottle. "We've got tons of champagne and *gallons* of lube, so—"

"Seriously?" Dom gaped at him. "What—"

"Relax, baby." Sergei wrapped an arm around him and nuzzled his neck. "Just play along." Then he grabbed Dom's crotch and called out to the man below, "Come on, boys! What do you say?"

The other coastie stepped out of the cabin. "What's going on out—oh, lord." His eyes about bugged out of his head, and his face turned even redder than the first guy.

"Um." The first cleared his throat. "Don't worry about—"

"Hey, honey!" Sergei gestured at the red-faced one. "Do you top? Please tell me you top."

Apparently the poor kid's face could get darker. He blinked a few times, and then disappeared inside.

The first guy watched him go, then looked up at the yacht. Shaking his head, he stepped back from the rail and started toward the cabin. "You gentlemen, um, enjoy your... enjoy your day." As he went back into the cabin with the other guy, he said, "Let's move on. They're good."

The boat pulled away, and as the engines throttled up and they left, Dom stared at the boat and its growing wake.

"Worked like a charm," Sergei said.

"Uh-huh." Dom turned to him. "And what would you have done if they'd taken you up on the offer?"

"What do you think?" Sergei shrugged indifferently. "Turned up the music and had a foursome."

"With *how* many kilos of coke onboard? Along with my bound and gagged cousin?"

Sergei's lips quirked. "Well, now you're just making it sound kinky."

Dom stared at him. Sergei batted his eyes.

Finally, a laugh burst out of Dom, and he wrapped his arms around Sergei's beautiful naked body. "That was a pretty genius plan."

"You sound surprised."

"No." Dom drew him closer. "Not really."

A kiss seemed out of place now, standing on Felice's boat and ready to destroy the family that had broken them both. It was insane to be turned on or even affectionate, but what about this *wasn't* insane? A moment of tenderness, playfulness, a promise of more if—when—they made it out of this alive didn't seem like too much to ask.

So for that moment, Dom just lost himself in Sergei, and enjoyed it.

THE SUN WAS SINKING into the sky when they tossed the last empty crab pot into the water.

"That's all of them?" Sergei asked.

"Pretty sure it is. Even if it isn't, I'd say it's enough."

"Good point. Back to shore?"

"Back to shore."

It was completely dark when they made it back. Guided by the boat's lights, Dom parked the yacht in its wide slip, and with Sergei's help, tied it enough to keep it from leaving. If it banged against the dock, he really didn't give a shit—Felice could take that up with his insurance company tomorrow if he was still breathing.

They made sure Felice was still securely bound and then left the boat. Raffaele Cusimano's yacht was a few slips down. Like St. Leo's, this was one of the few places where the families could cross paths peacefully. It was an unspoken rule—don't fuck with my shit, I won't fuck with yours—and everyone abided by it.

Usually.

Sergei made short work of the lock, and the door opened. He quickly disengaged the security system. They did a quick sweep to make sure the boat was empty, and Dom said, "We're clear. Let's move the cargo."

It took a while, but they moved all the cocaine over to the other boat and neatly stacked it on the coffee table.

"All right." Sergei dusted off his hands, probably shaking off the salt from the packages. "Shall we bring over the guest of honor?"

Dom put a hand on Sergei's waist and kissed him lightly. "Why don't you stay with the presents, and I'll go get him?"

"What?" Sergei batted his eyes. "Don't you trust me not to kill him?"

"I know you, Sergei." He kissed him again. "I'll be back in a minute."

One last kiss, and Dom left the boat. He scanned the marina, double-checking that none of the men patrolling the docks were nearby. Certain he was in the clear, he boarded Felice's yacht.

He unfastened Felice's cuffs from the pipe and hauled him to his feet. "Time to go for a walk."

Felice glared at him and muttered something around the gag.

"You've done enough talking." Dom nudged him toward the steps. "Let's go."

Felice said something that sounded an awful lot like "*Or what?*"

Dom coolly drew his pistol and aimed it at his cousin's groin. That got the message across—Felice started toward the steps. Damn. He really could learn a thing or two from Sergei, apparently.

They disembarked, and Dom directed his cousin down the dock. When they stopped in front of Cusimano's yacht, he gestured for Felice to board.

Felice balked, eyes wide, and shook his head.

"I wasn't asking, asshole." Dom shoved him toward the boat, sending him stumbling over his feet and almost into the water. "Get on the fucking boat."

Felice planted his feet and turned around, eyes narrow.

Dom aimed the pistol below his cousin's belt. "You really want to dance?"

Felice glanced down. Then he said something around the gag—no doubt something profane, though it was hard to tell which language it was—and continued up the ramp.

Inside, Sergei stood in front of the pile of cocaine, idly flipping a long knife between his fingers. He flashed a demonic grin. "Welcome aboard, Felice."

"We're going to do some talking in here," Dom said to Felice. "I'm taking off your gag, and you're going to answer my questions. You call for help, or try anything stupid, and I'll let the Georgian take care of things."

Felice's eyes darted right to that knife, and Dom thought he actually heard his cousin's balls jump into his body.

"And go ahead and call for help," Sergei said quietly. "Cusimano likes his boats with top of the line acoustics, just like you do. No one will hear a thing."

Felice paled.

"I'm taking it off." Dom untied the dirty rag and took off the handcuffs. "Now, the sooner you cooperate, the sooner we get off this boat. Because I don't think Cusimano's going to like seeing you in here with all his merchandise."

"You're on the boat too," Felice said in a low growl, gingerly rubbing his bleeding arm.

"Yeah, and I have two functioning legs."

Felice's eyebrows rose. His Adam's apple jumped, and Dom was satisfied the threat had hit its mark.

Felice shifted. "What the fuck are you two doing? Are you insane?"

"No." Dom looked him in the eye. "But what was your father's philosophy? That a family is only as strong as its weakest member?"

"My father was a pussy," Felice snarled. "He didn't deserve the kind of power he had."

"And your brother?"

Felice snorted. "Luciano was just like him."

Dom's temper tried to surge to the surface, but he slowly released his breath to keep himself calm. "I have some questions."

"Fine. Ask. And then let's get the fuck—"

"The day Privitera died out on your boat," Dom said. "You knew I was the target, didn't you? Because *you* set up the hit?"

Felice's features tightened.

"Oh hey, Dom?" Sergei cleared his throat, and the cousins both turned as he pulled a tightly wrapped kilo of coke off the pile. "I'm no expert, but this looks like some really nice cocaine." He turned his knife emphatically between his fingers. "Would be awfully expensive if someone were to—"

"Jesus fuck!" Felice put up a hand. "Don't. Don't cut into that. We can all just walk away, and Cusimano doesn't need to know we were—"

"What's wrong, Felice?" Dom asked. "I thought you wanted a war with him."

"I want to take them down," Felice said through

clenched teeth. "They're thieves and they have no business in this town. But that"—he gestured at Sergei—"is only going to give them an excuse to kill Maisanos."

"No." Sergei let the knife's edge just tease the plastic. "It's going to give them an excuse to kill *you*."

Felice straightened. His eyes flicked toward Dom, then Sergei. "Just tell me what the fuck you want so we can get out of here."

"Tell me why you ordered him"—Dom nodded toward Sergei—"to kill me on the boat that day."

Felice stared at him. Then, slowly, his eyes narrowed. "Anyone ever tell you it's not wise to ask questions unless you want to know the answer?"

"Don't test my patience, Felice," Dom growled. "I know how this business works. Sometimes calls have to be made. Tell me why you made that call."

Felice didn't answer.

Dom exhaled. "Is it true you wanted me dead so your father would believe you had been the target? So he'd actually retaliate against the Cusimanos like you wanted him to?" He huffed sharply. "Way to look after family, Felice. Really, I'm—"

"Oh get off your high horse." Felice's lips pulled tight across his teeth. "You say you want diplomacy and to settle everything with words and negotiations, but you're just a pussy like that son of a bitch who spawned you."

Dom's own teeth ached from clenching them. "I'm a pussy? Why? Because I haven't murdered my way into power?"

"You don't deserve—"

"One last question." Dom stepped closer, making sure he loomed over Felice. "On the boat that day, why did you shoot the Korean?"

Felice laughed humorlessly. "You always did have a soft spot for the wetbacks, didn't you?"

Dom grabbed his cousin by the wounded arm, and Felice choked on a scream.

Getting right in his face, Dom snarled, "Answer the fucking question, Felice."

His cousin moaned pitifully, and Sergei thought for a moment the man might throw up, especially as blood seeped through his sleeve.

"You know what?" Dom said. "I don't even want to know. And quite frankly, regardless of what my father did or didn't do, I'd rather be like him than be anything like you, you piece of shit." He shoved Felice back and let him tumble into the pile of cocaine. "Even your own father didn't see people as disposable to quite the extent that you do. And you know what? You wanted a war." Dom tossed a cell phone to Sergei. "Looks like you're about to have one."

"What are—" Felice clutched his arm, and his eyes flicked toward the phone. "What are you talking about?"

Dom nodded toward Sergei. He watched Felice, and Felice watched Sergei.

"Mr. Cusimano?" Sergei asked with no trace of his accent. "This is Jimmy from the marina. I think there's a problem with your boat."

Felice's eyes widened.

"Yeah," Sergei went on. "*The Merrietta.* Don't know. Someone was messing with—" He jerked the phone away from his ear, and the shouting on the other end was loud and clear even to Dom. "I don't know. I saw them moving some bags of—" The shouting got even louder.

Felice's shoulders sank lower and lower.

"Okay, I'll keep an eye on 'em," Sergei said. "Should I

call the cops or—okay, okay. I won't. I promise. Right. You bet." Then he hung up. "Sounds like Cusimano's on his way."

"Oh Jesus." Felice looked up at Dom, and spoke quickly. "Look, just get me out of here. I'll call off the hit. We—"

"You'll call off the hit?" Dom laughed. "Well isn't that nice. And then I suppose we'll just go on like family? Fuck you, Felice." He nodded at Sergei.

Sergei tossed the phone to Felice, who caught it in midair with his good hand.

"So you have a choice," Dom said. "You can wait here for him, or you can call 911 and hope they make it here first."

Felice laughed. "You want me to call the cops?"

"If you want to." Dom shrugged. "I was thinking an ambulance would be more appropriate."

"An—" Felice froze. His gaze slid toward Sergei.

Dom seized his cousin's momentary distraction, drew his pistol, and fired.

Felice screamed and dropped to the deck, clutching his knee.

"If you call the paramedics now," Dom said coolly, "they might keep you from bleeding out." He glanced at this watch. "Probably better not wait too long, though."

With that, he nodded sharply to Sergei, and they walked off the boat, leaving Felice to bleed and sob beside his enemy's merchandise.

"Isn't a shot to the kneecap a bit clichéd?" Sergei mused. "That's old school Mob, isn't it?"

"I seem to recall you doing the same thing when we first met."

Sergei shrugged. "I was merely making a point."

"So was I. I was making the point that Felice isn't walking anywhere any time soon."

"Well played."

Chapter 35

A t the end of the ramp, Sergei paused to sprinkle some cocaine on the wood. A little anonymous tip to the cops, and the drug dogs would come right to—

"Uh, Sergei?"

"Hmm?"

"We've got a problem."

Sergei turned, and his chest tightened as several pairs of headlights filed into the marina parking lot. Already, men were hurrying down the steps toward the main walkway.

Oh fuck. Someone else must've heard them and sounded the alarm. This wasn't part of the plan.

Time for plan B.

He grabbed Dom's elbow. "Come on. This—"

"We could just get on a boat." Dom gestured at their surroundings. "They'll never find—"

"You remember the big fire this marina had a few years ago?"

"Uh, yeah?"

"That wasn't a fuel spill. That was your fucking uncle

trying to smoke somebody out. We're getting out of here." Sergei gestured toward the sea-end of the dock. "This way."

"What?" Dom hesitated. "That just goes back out to the water!"

"Trust me!" Sergei broke into a run and didn't bother looking back. If Dom knew what was good for him, he'd follow.

At the end of the pier, Sergei stopped. A few seconds later, Dom stopped beside him.

"Help me down," Sergei said.

"Down where? Into the water?"

"No." Sergei pointed at the shadowy outline of a small dinghy. "Into that."

"What the hell are we doing? Paddling out to sea and hoping no one sees us?"

"Just shut up and get in."

Dom sighed, but got in. "How did you even know this was here?"

"Because I put it here as a backup plan. Give me that oar."

Dom handed it to him.

Using the oar, Sergei carefully guided the dinghy under the dock. Using the pylons as guides, he let the tiny boat glide almost soundlessly across the water beneath the walkway.

Feet clomped across the aging wood, echoing above their heads. Sergei glanced up but couldn't see much anyway, aside from a few shadows moving past. There were shouts and commotion, and he doubted anyone would hear, but to be safe, he whispered, "It's going to get shallow down here. As soon as we bottom out, stay low and follow me. There's a path that goes down by restrooms, and it'll take us back up to the parking lot without being seen."

"I get the feeling you've done this before."

"A time or two, yes." He nudged one of the pylons with the oar to keep the boat going straight. "And it'll be tempting to move quickly, but go slow in the water."

"Slow and quiet," Dom said.

"Exactly."

Seconds later, the dinghy's hull ground against the sand and came to a gentle stop. Balancing carefully, Sergei stepped out into the icy water. Then he held the boat still so Dom could get out. Dom didn't make a sound, not even a hiss when he hit the cold water, and he followed Sergei stealthily toward the shore.

Sergei's heart was going crazy. When he saw Dom's car, he was almost giddy with relief—they'd made it.

Squealing tires stopped them in their tracks. They ducked into the trees. Sergei's throat constricted, but then he realized one of the cars was familiar.

"Cusimanos," he said under his breath. "Perfect timing."

"Good. Let them fuck things up."

Using the trees for cover, they jogged along the road to where Dom had parked. There, they got into the car, and Dom fired up the engine and pulled out onto the road.

Sergei kept his pistol in his lap. They weren't in the clear yet.

Not half a mile from the marina, Dom growled, "Shit. So much for a clean getaway."

Sergei looked over his shoulder. Those headlights were coming up way too fast to be a random driver. And there were two cars hot on that one's heels.

"You know these roads, right?" he asked.

"Uh-huh. Hang on." Dom didn't even give him a

chance to brace before he jerked the wheel and gunned the engine. The car swerved, the tires shrieked, and Sergei was sure they were going to slam into the sign in front of the bank before Dom regained control, straightened out, and took off.

He looked back. The other cars were still on their tail. "Faster."

"Any faster is going to attract cops."

Sergei thought quickly. "How well does this thing handle?"

"Depends—how fast?"

They glanced at each other.

"Get out on the 103," Sergei said. "The cops almost never go up there, and we can lose these assholes in the hills."

Dom gunned the engine again.

The three cars stayed hot on their heels.

"Keep an eye on the side streets," Dom said. "There could be more, and they could come from anywhere."

Through the streets of Cape Swan, Dom zigged and zagged, taking turns unexpectedly, doubling back, even screaming down an alley between a couple of apartment buildings, and still, the motherfuckers stayed on them.

Sergei's pulse was out of control. At every turn, he expected flashing blues.

But finally—an on-ramp.

Dom floored it. The engine whined. The speedometer needle drew a rapid arc, and the darkened scenery blurred past them.

And in the side mirrors—headlights.

"Who are these fucks?" Sergei shouted over the road noise. "Cusimanos or Maisanos?"

"You want to stop and introduce ourselves?"

"Good point. Hurry up and get out of town." He

clicked the safety off his pistol. "Then I can start shooting at them."

"Working on it."

Sergei took off his seatbelt and climbed between the seats into the back.

"What are you doing?"

"Putting myself where I can shoot them. Obviously."

"You might want a seatbelt."

"Can't shoot with one."

"And if I wreck?"

"Don't wreck."

"Sergei, for fuck's sake. Are—"

"Simple solution." Sergei wrapped his arm around one of the backseat headrests, and used it to steady himself. "This is gonna get loud."

"Great."

"Sorry."

If Dom responded, Sergei didn't hear him—he squeezed the trigger, shattering the back window and deafening him. Sparks flew off the fender of one car. The driver swerved a little, but recovered quickly.

Sergei glanced around, orienting himself. As his hearing returned—sort of—he shouted to Dom, "There's a sharp curve up ahead. Take it as fast as you can without spinning out."

"Got it."

Sergei held the headrest for support, aimed for the front passenger side tire, and curled his finger around the trigger.

Just before he knew Dom was going to hit the curve, he fired.

The tire blew out. The car swerved, colliding with the one next to it, and as Dom's car swept around the curve, all Sergei could see was glass and metal going in all directions.

"You get 'em?"

"Two won't be going anywhere for a while, but there's still—yeah, there he is."

One car lurched forward, and Dom accelerated down a straightaway before whipping around a switchback. The other car didn't lose them, and he didn't go off the road, but he lost some ground. Even more when he had to slow down for an S-curve that Dom took at full speed.

The road straightened out again.

A bullet pinged off the frame. Another off the trunk, a little closer to Sergei's head than he liked.

The headlights were blinding him, so he adjusted his position. He slid forward, resting his forearms on the rear dash and leaning out through the broken window.

Sergei fired.

From the other car, a bright flash.

Something thumped against his chest. Heat drilled its way into his ribs.

The gun tumbled from his hand. Headlights went everywhere. Sergei dropped onto the backseat. Tires shrieked. His hand went to his chest.

And came away wet.

Cursing in his native tongue, he kept one hand against the wound—*fuck, that's way too much blood*—and with the other, tried to search the darkness for his weapon, but pain turned his vision red.

"Sergei? Sergei, are you—"

"Just drive," he ground out. He braced himself for more nauseating pain, and searched for the weapon, but then Dom swore, and the world lurched.

Sergei clutched his chest and distantly heard himself crying out in pain.

Everything shifted to one side. Then the other.

More gunfire. An engine roaring too close.
Another blast, and Sergei's ears rang again.
Impact. Wobbling.
Tires squealed and the world listed.
Weightless. *Bang.*
Nothing.

Chapter 36

The airbag hit Dom hard enough to stun him.
Everything was still.

His ears were filled with cotton, and his head throbbed. He wiped blood from his lip, and he murmured, "Sergei?"

No answer.

"Sergei?" He craned his neck gingerly. The backseat was empty.

Oh God. Tell me he wasn't thrown out.

Then a shadow caught his eye. He felt around for the dome light, turned it on, and swore.

Sergei hadn't been thrown, but he was between the front and backseats, motionless, with a lot of blood on his clothes and smeared across the upholstery.

"Oh shit." Despite the pain, Dom scrambled out of the car. He scanned the area—the other car was wheels up. The night was silent except the idling engine and the whine of one tire still spinning uselessly in the air. He kept his gun close just in case, but his highest priority was Sergei.

He pulled out his phone and speed-dialed Rojas. As it

rang, he pulled open the door, climbed back into the car, and touched Sergei's neck. Still a pulse, thank God. "Sergei? Can you hear me?"

Sergei stirred, mumbling something.

"Stay with me, Sergei, I'm—"

The phone clicked. "Dom? What's wrong?"

"I need help."

There was movement on the other end, as if Rojas were walking quickly. "Where are you?"

"Highway 103. There's two wrecks out here. I'm the second one."

"That's not good." Rojas paused. A million questions on his mind, no doubt. Then, "I'll be there as soon as I can. What kind of injuries?"

"Sergei's bleeding. There's a shitload of blood."

A car door slammed, and an engine turned over. "Where's the blood coming from? Head? Neck? Anything vital?"

"Hard to see. I don't want to move him or—"

"Paralysis might be the least of his worries if he's sprung a big enough leak."

"Hang on." Phone in hand, he tugged Sergei's shoulder as gently as he could and shined the cell phone's light into the shadows.

Immediately, his heart sank.

Oh, no...

He tucked the phone into his shoulder and pressed his hand against the wound. "Doc, it looks like a gunshot."

"A gun—oh fuck. Where?"

"Chest. Near the middle."

"He's going to need a hospital." On the other end, an engine whined. "I'll be there as soon as I can, but we're going to need to put him in my car and get him out of there fast."

"Should I wait until you're here to move him?"

Rojas didn't answer immediately, and if not for the sound of the engine, Dom would've though they'd disconnected. Finally, he said, "No. I want to put a C-collar on him. That'll take a few seconds, and then we can move him to the car. Just keep pressure on that wound until I get there."

The line went dead.

Dom pulled off his shirt, wadded it up, and pressed it against Sergei's chest. "Hang in there. The doc's on his way."

Sergei groaned.

"Can you hear me?"

Another groan, this time more of an affirmative.

"Doc's on his way. Just hold as still as you can and stay with me, all right?"

"Y-yeah."

Dom pushed the shirt against the wound, and Sergei whimpered.

"Fuck," he ground out. "Should've... shot you when I had the chance."

Dom laughed, more from relief than the comment. Maybe Sergei was more coherent than he thought. "Sense of humor's still intact. That's a good sign."

Sergei groaned. He tried to push Dom's hand away.

"Leave it," Dom said. "You're bleeding."

"Can't... breathe."

"You can talk." Dom took Sergei's wrist with his free hand, and gently moved it out of the way. "Help's coming. Just hang in there. Okay?"

Sergei moaned but didn't speak.

Dom's stomach twisted. The truth was becoming less deniable by the second—if Sergei didn't get help, he was going to die. But 911 would mean paramedics, and paramedics would mean cops. Dom would happily go to jail to save Sergei, but the cops in this town had been known to take people to jail before taking them to a hospital, and he was getting Sergei help or he'd die trying.

"Stay with me," he whispered, and kissed Sergei's temple. "You've come way too far to lose."

Dom had no idea how much time passed, but headlights in the shattered rear window made his heart clench.

Please, let it be Rojas...

"Dom?" The doctor's voice. Thank God.

"In here," Dom called out. To Sergei, he said, "The doc's here."

Sergei moaned again.

Rojas opened the other car door. He had a cervical collar in his hand and quickly put it into place. "This will stabilize his neck. Not much we can do about his back if we want to get him to a hospital in time."

Dom's heart flipped. In time? How much time did he have?"

"All right." Rojas looked at Dom. "Let's get him into the car. You're driving."

"Got it." Dom carefully slid his arms under Sergei, prompting more moans—more like whimpers—from him. He grimaced. It occurred to him that he had no idea how many other injuries Sergei had. Broken bones? Internal bleeding? More cuts?

"I'm sorry," he whispered in Sergei's ear, and carefully lifted him.

Sergei groaned, and Dom's heart sank when he realized it probably meant to be a cry of pain. But the man in his arms was limp and lethargic, his breathing much too shallow.

"Hang in there, damn it. We're taking you to get help." Dom carried Sergei out of the ditch where they'd crashed and laid him across the backseat of Rojas's car. He'd barely let him go before Rojas yanked him out of the way and shoved him toward the driver seat. "Drive! Now!"

Dom didn't hesitate. The engine was idling, so he got in and put it in gear and didn't even bother putting on his seatbelt before he peeled out.

"Gonna get rough," he said.

"Fine, just go! *Go!*"

Dom drove across the median. The car bounced and nearly got stuck in a grassy spot, but it found its traction and made it onto the pavement.

In the backseat, Rojas said, "This is Dr. Rojas. I'm on my way in with a critical emergency. I need an OR team prepped and ready for—yes, I'm aware you're busy. This guy's gonna code if he doesn't get into surgery soon."

Shit. Oh, shit.

Dom gripped the wheel with sweaty, blood-smeared hands.

"Won't know for sure until we crack his chest," Rojas continued, speaking quickly. "But suspect a cardiac temp. Yes, I'm serious. The jugular's distended and his vitals are —thank you. We'll be there…" He looked up. "Where are we?"

Dom gulped. "Less than ten minutes out."

"Dom, I don't know if we have ten minutes."

Cold water rushed through Dom's veins, and he stomped the gas pedal. "Make it seven minutes."

They whipped past the accident scene on the other side. A cop had shown up, and it looked like someone had stopped to help. Thank God they hadn't happened by while he and Rojas were pulling Sergei out, or they might've stalled them.

"Sergei, can you hear me?" Rojas asked, his voice

calm, but with a frantic undercurrent. No response. "Sergei?"

Dom's heart was ready to come right through his chest.

"We're almost to the hospital. Just stay with me, okay?"

The faintest of moans both reassured and terrified Dom.

Please, please, Sergei…

The sign for the hospital came into view. Dom followed the red EMERGENCY signs, and pulled up in front of the ER.

Rojas flew out of the car. Before Dom had even gotten out himself, a team was rushing outside with a stretcher. They descended on the car like a special ops team, shouting in code and breaking out equipment left and right.

"Come on." Rojas grabbed his arm and tried to drag him away. "We have to go."

"I'm not leaving him! Are you—"

"The hospital is crawling with cops and your people," Rojas hissed. "I'm taking you into a colleague's office. When Sergei's out of surgery, I'll come give you an update."

Dom couldn't even process all of that, but he trusted Rojas, so he gave the car one last look—he couldn't see Sergei, damn it—and followed the doc. They loped in through another entrance and down a hall of benign-looking office doors. Rojas keyed him into one and closed the door behind him.

And for the first time, the world was quiet. Both men stood and caught their breath for a moment.

Finally, Dom swallowed. "Is he gonna make it?"

"I don't know." Rojas's features pinched with palpable sympathy. "I know this team. He's in good hands. But…"

"How bad is it?"

"He's lost a lot of blood. My biggest concern is that I think he's got blood pooling somewhere. Likely around his heart. If they can get his chest open fast enough, and get a transfusion going in time…"

If. If. God, *if.*

Dom was about to run a hand through his hair but realized it was covered in blood. He was covered in blood, still missing a shirt, and bloody all over. Some of it was probably his, too—he thought there was a steady trickle down the side of his face.

Rojas scowled. "Let me go get my kit. I'll check you out in here and get you some scrubs to wear for the moment."

Dom nodded. "Yeah. Thanks."

Rojas clapped his shoulder. "He's in good hands, Dom. I promise."

Dom just nodded again. What could he possibly say right then?

The doc guided him to a chair, and Dom's legs buckled. He sank onto the seat, and Rojas kept a hand on him until he was fairly steady.

"Just hang tight." Rojas squeezed his arm. "I'll be right back."

He hurried out of the office, and Dom was alone.

Completely alone.

Nothing but the beat of his heart and the buzz of fluorescents.

And nothing—*nothing*—he could do for Sergei.

He leaned on his elbows and, blood be damned, raked both hands through his hair. He'd never liked having authority over life and death. Not when it meant being able to decide whether to kill someone. Right now, though, he'd have given anything to be able to keep Sergei alive. For the power that came with the pull of a trigger, only in reverse. Why the fuck was it so easy to break bones and tear flesh, but mending it all was like bringing ashes back to life?

He was powerless now. All he could do was pray.

And hope someone was up there listening.

And wait.

Chapter 37

The light hurt. His eyes weren't even open yet, and the light already hurt like a motherfucker.

He slowly pulled in a breath through his nose. The smell—solvents, alcohol, latex—brought to mind the place where Mama had died, but before that memory could settle in, pain tore through his chest, starting dead center and ripping toward his sides. He held his breath, eyes stinging. His right eye didn't quite want to focus. It *could* focus, but the strain made his head hurt more, so he closed both eyes.

Breathing was a pain in the ass. An annoying tube rested on his upper lip and blew cold air up his nose. Something was wrapped tightly around his midsection, which kept him from inhaling deeply. Had they put a fucking corset on him or something? And even without the damned thing, the pain kept his chest from moving much. His ribs hurt. His neck hurt. Some places throbbed. Others were sharp and stabby.

An IV was attached to his right arm. Every time he moved or even thought about moving, the damned thing hurt. Fuck that shit. He had every intention of reaching over and tearing it out, but his body had other plans. The simple act of lifting his other arm was far too much work, and it sent fresh pain tearing down his side and across his chest.

A tall doctor in glasses came strolling in. "Ah, you're awake."

"You don't say." Sergei's voice was raspy, barely more than a whisper. "Where's Dom?"

The doctor arched an eyebrow.

Sergei's heart sank. "Is he—"

"Visiting hours are this afternoon." The doctor glanced over Sergei's chart. "In the meantime, I'm Dr. Walters. How are you feeling?"

Sergei eyed him, but relaxed when he realized that glaring was painful. "Do you really need to ask?"

"I do, actually." The doctor lowered his clipboard. "Any numbness or tingling?"

"Not nearly enough."

The doctor scowled.

Sergei sighed. "No. Everything hurts like hell. Happy?"

That earned him a subtle but obviously annoyed sigh. As Dr. Walters scrawled something into what was must've been Sergei's chart, he said, "You're a lucky man, Mr. Sullivan."

Sergei nearly corrected him, but bit his tongue. It was entirely possible someone had fed him a fake name, so he'd go with it until he had a reason not to. And distantly, he remembered giving that name as an alias once. To Dom. For a motel. Maybe that meant…

He shifted a bit, wincing. "So I'm lucky? Did I win the lottery while I was out, or what?"

The doctor actually laughed. "Well, if I were you, I'd go buy a lottery ticket. The emergency team *barely* had time to crack your chest before the sack around your heart filled up with blood. If you hadn't gone into surgery when you did, we wouldn't be having this conversation."

Sergei suppressed a shudder. "So when do I get the fuck out of here?"

The doctor scowled again. "You feel like going for a jog?"

The very thought of moving nearly made Sergei choke.

"That's what I thought." Dr. Walters put the chart beneath the foot rail. "You're going to be staying with us a bit longer, Mr. Sullivan. At least until I'm confident you're on the mend."

"What about that lottery ticket I'm supposed to buy?"

"You may need to send someone to buy it on your behalf." He looked at his watch. "Visiting hours start soon, so maybe you'll have a visitor."

Maybe?

"Get some rest," the doctor said. "I'll be by this afternoon to see how you're doing."

He left. Nurses came and went. One brought him food. Another came to fuck around with his IV. The first returned, and he had to give her credit—she didn't bat an eye at the cursing he growled out in multiple languages while she fussed with his catheter. It was a good ten minutes before he stopped sweating after that, though it was hard to tell if it was the fact that his dick hurt or how much squirming and fidgeting had reignited the pain in his chest.

The door opened again. Jesus fuck. Now who wanted to—

"Well, well." Dom's voice sent a rush of warmth through him. "Somebody's finally awake."

Sergei's lips parted. In his mind, he was sitting up, maybe even sucking in a startled breath, but a few hours in this reality had trained his body to keep those reactions to himself.

"How are you feeling?" Dom asked.

"Like shit."

"Makes sense." Dom smirked. "You look the part."

"Fuck you."

Dom chuckled, but then he leaned down and pressed a tender kiss to his lips and another to his forehead. "You scared the hell out of me," he whispered against Sergei's hairline. "I thought I'd lost you."

Sergei closed his eyes. "What the hell happened?"

"What's the last thing you remember?"

Sergei thought for a moment, his throbbing brain struggling to make sense of anything prior to the last few minutes. "Don't know. Ask me again when I'm not on so many drugs."

"Fair enough." Dom pulled up a chair and sat beside him, resting his hand on Sergei's forearm. "We wrecked, and I guess right before that, one of the fuckers got a shot in." He squeezed Sergei's arm. "As soon as I saw that bullet hole…" He swallowed hard.

"What about Felice?" Sergei moistened his lips. "What happened to him?"

"He's dead. Apparently we missed a hell of a shootout down at the marina. The Cusimanos showed up, and I guess Felice got a call out to some of his crew."

"That must've been a mess."

Dom nodded. "Six Cusimanos and five Maisanos dead. The cops came in and collected everyone who was left."

Sergei exhaled slowly, letting the truth sink in. It was over. Really *over*. "What about you? Are you okay?"

Dom smiled. "I was wearing a seatbelt."

"Didn't want to fuck up my aim."

"Well, it must've paid off—you hit the driver, and that

was that. They held the road for a few seconds, but then wiped out. All three guys in the car were dead."

"Good." Sergei winced as he tried in vain to get comfortable. "How the hell did *we* wreck, then?"

"When the driver lost control, he hit my back end." Dom shrugged apologetically. "At that speed, on a winding road…"

Sergei looked him up and down. "So you didn't get hurt? You're obviously okay now, but were—"

"The airbag punched me in the face, and I was walking pretty slowly for a few days."

"A few—" Sergei blinked. "How long has it been?"

"A week."

"I've been out cold for a *week*?"

"Not quite. Heavily sedated and hopped up on painkillers." Dom smiled, running his thumb along Sergei's hand. "You've actually been awake more than you think."

"I don't remember anything."

Dom shook his head. "You're not supposed to. They kept you drugged so you wouldn't be in as much pain, and so you wouldn't tear out your IV again."

"Again?" Sergei looked at his hand, and realized there were a number of bruises along the veins. Ditto with his other hand.

"Let's just say you're not the most compliant patient in the world." Dom patted his arm gently. "But you made it."

"And you were here? The whole time?"

"As much as they'd let me." Dom frowned. "Dr. Rojas pulled some strings so I could stay with you in the ICU, but once they moved you down here, that asshole doc in charge didn't want me underfoot all the time." He gestured over his shoulder. "I've been staying down the road at one of the motels we used to use."

Sergei blinked. "You... even with the investigation going on? You should be as far from here as possible."

"Yeah, maybe." Dom squeezed his shoulder. "But I wasn't leaving you behind. I couldn't leave you here any more than I could've left you out there on the road." He leaned down again and kissed him softly. "As soon as you're back on your feet, though, we're out of here."

"The doctor said it might take a while."

"I know." Dom pressed another soft kiss to Sergei's cheek. "But I'm not going anywhere until you do."

Sergei reached up and touched Dom's face. "Thank you."

Dom smiled. He smoothed Sergei's hair and whispered, "I love you."

"I love you too."

It was over. Once Sergei's body recovered, they'd leave, and it would be well and truly over.

And for the first time since he was eight years old, Sergei could know peace.

Epilogue

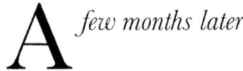A *few months later*

"I DON'T NEED A FUCKING PAINKILLER," Sergei muttered.

"Just take one." Dom took his hand on the wide armrest between them. "It wouldn't hurt you to sleep."

"It's a long flight. I'm sure I'll pass out sooner or later."

"Suit yourself. They're in my bag if you need them."

Sergei nodded.

The plane pulled away from the gate, and as it taxied, Dom's heart sped up, but he took a few slow, easy breaths to calm himself down. He'd never been a fan of flying. As the plane's front end lifted up, though, and the noise of tires on asphalt gave way to the whine of the engines, he exhaled.

"Maybe you should be taking something," Sergei teased.

Dom eyed him.

Sergei snickered, squeezing his hand. "Just take one." He batted his eyes. "It wouldn't hurt you to sleep."

"Very funny. At what point are you healed enough that I can elbow you when you're being a pain in the ass?"

"Don't know." Sergei winked. "I'll let you know when I get there."

"Yeah, right…"

Sergei chuckled.

Dom shifted around to get comfortable in his seat. It was first class, after all. Might as well enjoy it, even if he loathed the idea of hurtling across the sky in a metal tube.

As much as he wasn't thrilled with air travel, he did find a hell of a lot of relief in the idea of the ground getting farther and farther away. Soon, they'd be out over the ocean, and after more hours than he cared to think about, they'd touch down in a new world to start their new life together.

They'd left Cape Swan nine days after Sergei was wounded. He hadn't recovered yet, but they couldn't risk staying in town while the cops and Feds descended on La Cosa Nostra.

So, with the help of Dr. Rojas, they'd slipped out of town in an unmarked vehicle, and though the trip was miserable for Sergei, they made it to Portland, where one of the doctor's colleagues accepted the transfer. It hadn't been cheap—Dom had paid the new doctor an enormous sum to make sure he didn't question or report a patient recovering from an unexplained bullet hole and massive surgery.

From there, Sergei's recovery had been up and down. What began as a minor fever quickly escalated into a massive infection that sent him to the ICU for three days.

As a nurse put it, he almost met God a few times before that was over. By the time he was finally released from the hospital over a month later, he'd lost twenty pounds he couldn't afford to lose and could barely stand. A week after that, he was back in the hospital with pneumonia.

But finally, he started improving, and the setbacks were fewer and farther between, not to mention less severe. He'd put weight back on. He didn't get winded walking up the stairs to the second floor one-bedroom apartment they were renting in Hawthorne, a cruddy little neighborhood in Portland.

And a couple of months ago, after they'd spent the evening talking about flights and fake visas, Sergei had kissed him like he hadn't kissed him in months. The kind of kiss that meant it was going to be one hell of a night. And it was.

Now, they were on their way out of Portland, leaving North America behind for a fresh start in another hemisphere. There was nothing left for them here, and Dom was fine with that. The Maisano name was no longer his. Using some of his connections with the state department, he'd bribed their way into new identities. Passports, driver's licenses, the whole nine yards.

Beside him, Sergei stirred a little. Dom turned his head and couldn't help smiling. Maybe Sergei hadn't needed that painkiller after all—the plane had barely leveled out at its cruising altitude, and he was already snoring softly.

Dom slipped his fingers between Sergei's and leaned across the armrest to kiss the top of his head, his spiky hair tickling his nose.

Though Sergei was out of the woods now, his recovery was far from over. He still had problems with his pectoral muscles on one side, and the concussion and whiplash had conspired to plague him with occasional blinding headaches. But he was okay. He was alive. Not a day went by that something didn't remind Dom of how close he'd come to losing Sergei, and each time, he sent up a whisper of gratitude that he hadn't.

Sergei hated what his wounds had done to his chest. The scars weren't quite such an angry red anymore, but they were hardly inconspicuous. Thick scar tissue knotted around the place where the bullet had gone in, and a long, ropy line down his breastbone marked where the surgeons had opened his chest.

"Guess my stripping days are over," he'd whispered the first time he'd looked at himself in the mirror.

Dom had put his hands on Sergei's shoulders and kissed his cheek. Meeting each other's gazes in the reflection beneath the hospital bathroom's fluorescent light, he'd said, "They'll fade. Give them time."

Sergei had scowled and lowered his eyes. "They'll always be there, though."

"Maybe." Dom had wrapped his arms around him. "But so will I."

They'd locked eyes in the mirror again, and Sergei smirked. "You really are a sap, you know that?"

They both burst out laughing, but a grimace from Sergei brought the moment to a halt.

"Shit…"

"You okay?"

"Yeah." Sergei rubbed his chest gingerly. "Sense of humor's still intact, but I may have to keep it on ice for a while."

"Duly noted."

Over time, though, the wounds had healed, and the bones and muscles mended enough that Sergei could laugh comfortably. Outside of physical therapy, anyway. He wasn't in nearly as much pain these days, thank God. Still plenty of healing to do, still plenty of days that were worse than others, but he was going to be all right.

It seemed like a lifetime ago that Floresta and Mandanici had dragged Dom into a back alley, where Sergei had intervened and saved him. At the time, Dom had had no idea then that they'd become lovers, that they'd fall for each other, or that Sergei would put his life on the line to save him a second time.

And in the end, Sergei had not only saved Dom's life but freed him from a world he'd never imagined escaping. A world that had managed to break them both but hadn't broken them far enough to keep them from bringing the whole thing down before they got the hell out.

The men who'd survived the marina shootout and the wrecks on the highway were all in jail, awaiting trial. The families' lawyers had attempted to work their magic, but that anonymously submitted package of damning evidence to the FBI put a stop to that. The Maisanos, Cusimanos, and Passantinos were all in shambles now.

Last Dom had heard, the Feds were still hunting for him, as well as the mysterious "Georgian."

Good luck with that.

Dom grinned to himself, squeezing Sergei's hand.

He didn't know what to expect from this new life. Sergei had property on the coast of Tasmania, and even without new identities, Dom couldn't imagine anyone finding them there.

It had been a rough road, but they were going to be all right. Between them, they had enough money to keep them going for years, but more importantly, they were free now. He had a new identity that wasn't tied to the Mafia. He had the man he loved.

And against all odds, they'd made it out.
Together.

The End

About the Author

L.A. Witt is a romance and suspense author who has at last given up the exciting nomadic lifestyle of the military spouse (read: her husband finally retired). She now resides in Pittsburgh, where the potholes are determined to eat her car and her cats are endlessly taunted by a disrespectful squirrel named Moose. In her spare time, she can be found painting in her art room or destroying her voice at a Pittsburgh Penguins game.

Website: www.gallagherwitt.com
    Email: gallagherwitt@gmail.com
    Twitter: @GallagherWitt

For more books by L.A. Witt, please visit

http://www.gallagherwitt.com

Romance * Suspense

Contemporary * Historical * Sports * Military

Titles Include

Rookie Mistake (written with Anna Zabo)

Scoreless Game (written with Anna Zabo)

The Hitman vs. Hitman Series (written with Cari Z)

The Bad Behavior Series (written with Cari Z)

The Gentlemen of the Emerald City Series

The Anchor Point Series

The Husband Gambit

Name From a Hat Trick

After December

Brick Walls

The Venetian and the Rum Runner

…and many, many more!

Printed in Great Britain
by Amazon

61921718R10272